Also by Kelly Braffet

THE UNWILLING

KELLY BRAFFET

THE BROKEN TOWER

mira

ISBN-13: 978-0-7783-3365-4

The Broken Tower

First published in 2022. This edition published in 2023.

Copyright © 2022 by Kelly Braffet

For questions and comments about the quality of this book, please contact us
at CustomerService@Harlequin.com.

Mira
22 Adelaide St. West, 41st Floor
Toronto, Ontario M5H 4E3, Canada
BookClubbish.com

Printed in U.S.A.

For my mom, who has been waiting very patiently to read this book, and for Owen and Zelda, who waited very patiently while I wrote it.

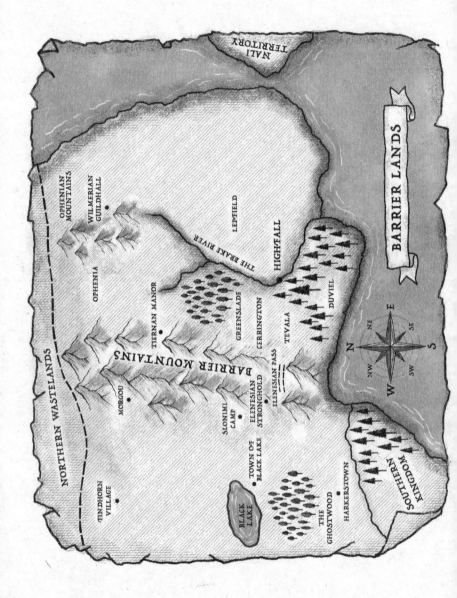

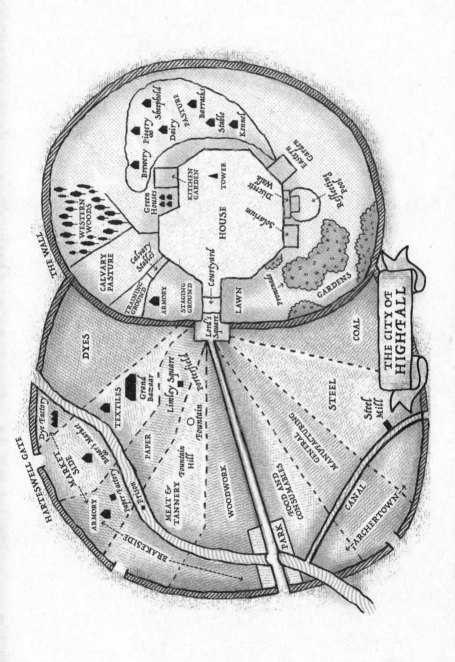

THE CITY OF
HIGHFALL

PREFACE

Once there was a wealthy lord whose family ruled a land flowing with natural power. Each person who lived in the lord's kingdom could access the power, which made their lives easier in a thousand small ways. One day, it occurred to the powerful man, who was called Lord Martin, that a thousand people with a little power each might well be a match for one man with a lot of power, and this idea terrified him. So he called the smartest men he knew to his great House in the city of Highfall, set them to work in a tower, and ordered them to find a way to bind the power so it couldn't be used against him. In this, they were successful: they bound the power, but they destroyed themselves (and part of their workroom) along with it. After that, the land became a sad, grim place. Lord Martin was soon called Mad Martin, because he could never rest easily, but he and his heirs ruled for many generations.

And then, one cold bleak night, across the mountains and on the other side of the continent, a traveling magician named John Slonim stood on a makeshift stage and reached into a hat. But instead of the paper flowers he'd stashed there, the hat burst forth with real flowers: lush, brilliant flowers that spread in ropy vines across the stage, even though it was the middle of winter. Like an overfilled water skin, the binding had sprung a leak. The bound power flowed through the magician and through dozens of others throughout the land. For the rest of his life, he traveled the continent, collecting those others together so they could learn to use the power. Because there were so few of them, the power was stronger in each of them than it had been in anybody before the binding, and over time, with careful management, it grew even stronger. Those who wielded it came to call themselves the Slonimi and the power, the Work. In the Work, each of them was born with a unique identifying symbol, called a sigil, that could be used to join their minds together and access each other's memories. They figured out, all over again, that many people who each had a small bit of power could accomplish great things, and the great thing they wanted to accomplish was to unbind the power and bring down the empire Mad Martin's heirs ruled.

So they chose their own heirs carefully. After many more generations, a child was due to be born among them in whom they hoped all of their power was gathered. Before the child was born, her parents traveled to the great House in Highfall, where Mad Martin's heir, Lord Elban, still lived. Through enormous hardship, they made it beyond the high Wall of the great House, where they both died—but not before the child was born. By absolutely no coincidence whatsoever, the wife of Elban, the current Lord of the City, gave birth the same night to the newest of Mad Martin's heirs. By absolutely no further coincidence, the midwife brought in to assist her was Slonimi. When both children were born, the Slonimi midwife bound them together, so that what one suffered, the other did.

The midwife disappeared from history, but the Slonimi child, a girl named Judah, remained. To protect Elban's heir, Gavin, she was raised alongside him; two years later, they were joined by Gavin's younger brother, Theron. When Gavin and Judah were eight years old, a girl from a family of minor aristocrats—Eleanor of Tiernan—was brought in to serve as Gavin's betrothed. Judah and Gavin developed a way of using their bond to communicate, a code scratched into their skin to send messages to each other. To-gether, the four young people grew to a weird, halting version of adulthood.

Tradition and politics dictated that Gavin would rule the empire, Elly would marry him and bear his children, and Theron would command his army. Judah's only job, though, was to survive, so that Gavin would. Nei-ther Gavin's father nor the Seneschal who managed his household under-stood their strange connection, but they understood that Judah must be kept close and tightly controlled. When she showed an interest in reading, the library was banned. When she fell in love with the stableman, Darid, the Seneschal sentenced him to death, and had her caned. The more time passed, the more she resented her fate; as the completely unwarlike Theron resented his, and the smart, ambitious Elly resented hers. Only Gavin—liv-ing in a world created for his amusement—was happy, and that didn't last.

Gavin's father was determined to break the bond between Judah and his son. To that end, he waged war on the Nali, a nation of people known for the uncanny mental connection between their fighters. While capturing a Nali leader, he was injured in a coup perpetrated by his own men, and died soon after returning to the city. With him died the lavish world of court-iers and luxury inside the House, and into the old man's place stepped the Seneschal, whose vision for the House and the city surrounding it was very different than the one Mad Martin and his heirs had built. The Seneschal didn't want to break the bond between Gavin and Judah; he wanted to understand it, to control it, and—most important—to replicate it, so their scratch code could be put to use over a broader network. The Seneschal thought the Nali leader was the only one who might know how the bond worked, and so he kept the prisoner alive.

In the empty, looted House, the four young people worked to eke out something like survival. When she discovered that Darid hadn't been mur-dered, after all, and that Gavin had known and pointedly not told her, Judah fled to an abandoned tower in the oldest part of the House. The House Magus, Nathaniel Clare—who lived in the city with his young apprentice,

Belinda Dovetail—told the Seneschal he could convince her to come down, so that the Seneschal could experiment with the bond, so the Seneschal agreed to let Nate into the House.

But Nate had no intention of bringing Judah down from the tower, which was—of course—the same tower where Mad Martin's scholars had bound the power so many years before. Nate was Slonimi, and he had come to the city for the sole purpose of teaching Judah about Work so she could complete the Unbinding. He taught her to access the energy leaking from the knot Mad Martin's scholars had tied, all those years ago. The tower wouldn't let her die, he promised—but the Unbinding would require the death of all of Mad Martin's heirs, and the only two remaining were Theron and Gavin. As Elly, unknowing, held off the Seneschal at the House gate, Nate killed Theron himself and urged Judah, in the tower, to slit her foster brother's throat.

Instead, she jumped. Because Nate had said the tower wouldn't let her die, and she didn't. Nate was sent to prison and Gavin and Elly were spirited out of the city by the Seneschal's men, but Judah knew only a timeless white. When the world finally began to form around her again, months had passed. She was a long way from home, and everything she knew was different.

PROLOGUE

THE MAGUS TRAPPED JUDAH AND GAVIN IN THE tower. He wanted her to kill Gavin, to accomplish something he called the Unbinding. And obviously she refused to do that, but the only other way out of the tower had been to jump. So she'd jumped: away from Gavin and the magus and their hands that tried to grab her, through the empty space where the tower wall had been sheared away long before she'd been born, and into the clear emptiness of midair.

Where she'd had time to look down to the brush at the bottom of the light well, contemplate what she'd done, and think, Oh, no.

Then she'd seen—felt?—an enormous flash of purple, and a bizarre sense of being emptied and filled at the same time. Faces flashed through her mind: the magus's mother and an unfamiliar old woman with flinty eyes. Then everything was white and silent and nothing and peace.

Only gradually did she become aware once more of her own

existence, of the actuality of a person named Judah. Eventually she remembered her body, and at some point later, that bodies usually wore clothes; and then she was wearing her gown from Elly and Gavin's betrothal. The gown was the pale green of new grass, the loveliest thing she had ever owned. Experimentally, she thought *feet* and felt the dry crunch of leaves beneath her toes. Then she thought *trees*, and tall smooth trunks melted into view out of the mist. She decided she'd died in the jump after all, and death was a featureless span of white from which a person could form whatever they wanted. Which was an infinitely more pleasant afterlife than any she'd ever been promised or threatened with; who could complain?

She'd kept walking through the forest where she found herself, where a great many ferns grew no higher than her ankles, and round silver-white boulders broke through the soil like fish through water. When she'd first thought *trees* she'd been thinking of the orchard, where the trees were short and neatly pruned and the air smelled like cider. Here, it smelled like loam and something brackish that she could taste in the back of her throat but not quite identify, something that crept over her like winter fog. The leaves on the straight, white-barked trees had a bluish cast to them, as if chilled.

Barefoot, with her shoulders exposed in the elegant dress, she realized that she was cold, too. She tried thinking *coat*, envisioning Gavin's quilted riding jacket, and then *boots*, picturing the ones she'd adopted from Theron and then lost in the pasture with Darid. Nothing happened. Whatever power she'd had to create in the white was gone. After a while, she realized that the taste in the back of her throat and the creeping chill meant snow. Further, she realized that regardless of what had happened to her when she'd leapt from the tower, regardless of where she'd landed, regardless of whether she was alive or not, and regardless of a dozen other factors that presented themselves in fairly short order—lack of fire, lack of food, lack of shelter—regardless of all of that, she was coatless and barefoot in a strange forest, which appeared, despite all theories to the contrary, to be real. And she was wearing a ball gown. And the snow was beginning to fall.

All of which led to one final realization: she was in trouble.

ONE

DEEP IN THE BOWELS OF NEW HIGHFALL PRISON, on a half-flooded island in the middle of the sludgy, polluted Brake, the Nali chieftain—whose name was Korsa—had more or less decided to kill himself. The beatings of his first few months in the prison had mostly stopped, but he had not seen sunlight or sky in six months. The spindly purple flame of the gaslight outside his cell flickered day and night, making his eyes burn and his head ache. He'd come from a warm country and here he was constantly cold; the food was bad and there wasn't enough of it. All of these were conditions typical of mainland prisons, from the stories he'd heard, and all of them were bearable.

But the loneliness—the empty places in his mind and heart where his *kagirh* should have been—the loneliness wasn't bearable at all. Raghri and Giorsa, Faolaru and Meita. He might as well name his left hand, his right eye, his leg bones, his ears. The five of them had been in *kagirh* together since they were young, for almost a quarter of a century. They had lived together and fought together, walked in each other's dreams at night and seen through each other's eyes during the day, until the ghastly afternoon when he'd been unlucky enough to be captured by evil old Elban's army. When Elban's own men had attacked their leader Korsa had felt his last true flare of hope, but he wasn't set free. The old lord, dying, was borne back to Highfall on a litter, and Korsa was borne there in a cage, and all the while Korsa felt his connection to his *kagirh* dwindling as sure as the smell of the sea in the air. The moment when the bond fractured was the most profound despair he had ever felt.

His every breath, since, was infused with that despair. Sleeping he dreamed that his four *kagirhi* walked away from him, and would not hear his cries for them to wait. When he woke, he couldn't help reaching out for them in his mind, to touch the empty places where they should have been. But they weren't there. Nothing was there. This city was dead. He wanted to be dead, too. He had borne the pain for as long as he could, but now he was done with that, and it was time to die.

The only question was how. He had tried not eating or drinking, but his body always betrayed him. The thin, tattered fabric of his clothes wouldn't hold his weight long enough for him to hang. He had no spoon to sharpen, no fragment of rock to hone to an edge. They'd even taken his earrings. Still, the search for death gave him something to live for. He was determined to find a way.

Then, one day—he had only the guard sounds in the corridor to judge time by, in this place of eternal flickering purple light—his cell door opened and the guard who belched too much said, "You, Nali." None of the guards knew his name. Nobody in Highfall had asked. "Stand up."

"Am I going to be killed?" he said, with the dull glimmer of anticipation that passed for hope with him, these days.

"Not today," the guard answered, and put Korsa's wrists in a pair of iron cuffs.

More torture, then. He hadn't been tortured in a long time, and wasn't sure why he would be, now. But the dead people in this dead place didn't seem to need a reason. The aproned man who dealt most of the pain made no secret of enjoying it for its own sake. But his chamber was to the right, and on this day the guard turned left. Down the dank hall they went, and up some dank stairs, until they came to a room where a fire crackled, and oh *kagirh*, there was dry air and warmth, there was sun, there were windows. A man stood in front of one of them. The bright light hurt Korsa's eyes and at first he could see nothing but the man's silhouette. Then his eyes adjusted and he recognized the heavy body, the gray clothes.

"Seneschal," he said.

The Seneschal turned around. A wide scar rippled down the side of his neck. It hadn't been there the last time Korsa had seen him. "Chieftain. Good morning," he said, pleasantly.

"Is it?" Although it undeniably was, with the sun and sky and warmth and dryness.

"I hope so. Come in," the Seneschal said, because somebody was tapping on the room's closed door. A young girl entered, eyes on the floor and red-gold hair neatly braided against her head. She carried a tray almost as big as she was. The Seneschal waved a hand toward the low table in the center of the room. "Over there is fine, thank you." The girl put the tray down, bowed her head, and left as quietly as she'd come. The tray held a steaming pot of something and a metal dome and it all smelled amazing. Korsa's mouth started to water. How long had it been since he'd eaten hot food?

"Sit," the Sensechal said, and indicated the settee next to the table. "Eat."

The settee was too high off the ground. Its thick cushions threw off Korsa's sense of balance. The Seneschal lifted the metal dome, revealing cheese yellow as daffodils and bread and a pot of stewed greens and a bowl of olives. "I ordered a bit of everything," the gray man said, but Korsa was already eating. The cheese was firm and pungent, the bread soft. Food was bliss, flavor divine. The thin sour gruel and rotten bread he ate in the cells made his guts ache.

"There's tea, as well," the Seneschal said. "I'm afraid we're still having a little trouble getting coffee, since the Change-over."

"Changeover?" Korsa said, through a mouth full of cheese.

"That's what the factory managers call it. Lord Elban died. I took over. I never wanted power, but the city could not continue the way it was going." The Highfaller spoke as if Korsa hadn't been on the battlefield and seen Elban stricken down by his own men. Not that it mattered now. The food in front of him was all that mattered. And maybe the cheese knife. The Seneschal continued. "Do you remember our discussions about Elban's son Gavin, and his foster sister?"

Korsa's appetite vanished. He put down the bread he was eating. Yes, he remembered those *discussions*; he would bear the scars of them for the rest of his life. He remembered the two young people as well: the tall, handsome young man, so like and unlike his father, and the woman—no product of pale dead Highfall, that one. Not with that blood-colored hair and the power blazing out of her. The thing that bound the two of them together had been akin to a *kagirh*, but a sick, unwholesome *kagirh*. That was no product of Highfall, either. He didn't know how the woman had ended up where

19

she was, holding hands with Elban's son like a scared child. But he had felt for her.

"I don't remember any discussions," Korsa said. "I remember being tortured."

The Seneschal only nodded. "Yes. I don't like issuing those kinds of orders, but I needed you to help us and I didn't have time to wait. However, the situation has changed. If you're willing to help me now, your situation might change, as well. You seemed ready to help, before."

"Your Interrogator described in great detail how long I could live without each of my organs and exactly what that life would be like," Korsa said. "It was persuasive."

"As I said," the Seneschal said, with half a smile, "the situation has changed."

Korsa had changed, too. At first, he had been weak and afraid, and he'd had hopes of going home to his *kagirh*. Now, he was still weak, but he had no hope, and so was no longer afraid. "But you still want my help with Elban's son and the blood-haired girl."

The half smile vanished. The Seneschal's lips compressed. "That has changed, too."

Something had not gone the way the Seneschal wanted, and Korsa was surprised to find that he was still capable of enjoying that. His appetite returned, he stuffed a piece of bread into his mouth. "How so? Are they dead?"

"No. I've sent Gavin out of the city, where he'll be safe. Judah's situation is—complicated. As it's always been." The Seneschal leaned forward. "Tell me about your Nali fighting groups."

"The Nali do not have fighting groups," Korsa said, pronouncing the last two words with distaste. "We have *kagirh*."

"Then tell me about your *kagirh*."

"Not a fighting group." Korsa searched for the closest High-faller word. "Family."

"You're related? Siblings?"

"No." This hurt to talk about. Raghri and Giorsa, Faolaru and Meita. When he was first imprisoned, he had said their names aloud, to remind himself that they existed.

"Are you born with the bond? Or is it made later?" Korsa didn't answer. This was nothing to talk to an outsider about. But the Seneschal's hunger to know burned in the man like the blood-haired woman's power had burned in her, and just as unwholesomely. "Could you do it here? Could you make a *kagirh*?"

Korsa recoiled. "No," he said, horrified. "No, never."

"Would never, or could never?" Korsa opened his mouth to respond, but the Seneschal held up a hand. "Not even if you had somewhere clean and well equipped to work? Good food, good light, the freedom to move around?"

The gray man looked pointedly at the window, and Korsa couldn't help but follow his gaze. Sun, warmth, air. All at once the food he'd eaten was looping birdwise in his stomach. "One person cannot make a *kagirh*."

The Seneschal nodded. "Of course not. Chieftain—is there another name I can call you?"

"Korsa."

"Korsa." The Seneschal rubbed at the scar on his neck, as if it were stiff. "I don't think I'm deluding myself when I say that New Highfall is a vast improvement over the old, but there is one problem I haven't been able to solve satisfactorily, and that's the orphan houses. You see, one of the founding principles of my new city is that everyone—man, woman, and child, no matter their age—is obligated to work. Most of our orphans are taken in by employers, but unfortunately, some are seen as unemployable, and those are kept in the orphan houses. They're unpleasant places. We do our best, but there are simply too many orphans and never enough money or staff to tend them adequately. My hope is that, among these children, you would find a few suitable for a *kagirh*."

"Wait," Korsa said. "Orphans are children?"

For the first time, the gray man seemed discomfited, as if Korsa had asked him what the sky was, or the rain. "Yes. An orphan is a child with no family to take care of them."

Korsa frowned. "But how would such a child come to be?"

The Seneschal's discomfiture spilled into bafflement. "Death. Illness. Poverty. Lack of caring. Dozens of reasons."

Korsa tried to parse the Seneschal's words, to figure out how anyone could know that a child needed to be taken care of and not...take care of them. That seemed like knowing that you were thirsty and not drinking, or knowing that you needed to breathe and not inhaling. Korsa felt his eyes drawn again to the window, to that tiny square of smoke-ridden sky. Did the children have windows and sky, in these orphan houses? Or did they have dank cells like his, with one flickering purple gaslight that burned through the night? How could any child survive in such a place? How could any Highfaller rest, knowing there were children there?

But you know, beloved, Meita would say, if she were there. Meita, beautiful of eye, kind of heart.

And speaking of cells, you will not survive much longer in yours. Take the foul man's offer, pragmatic Raghri would urge.

"What would you do with this *kagirh*," Korsa said, reluctantly, "if I am able to form one for you?"

"We wouldn't use it to hurt your people, if that's what you're worried about." The Seneschal's expression was bright and eager. "If you succeed, New Highfall will sign a treaty declaring all Nali territory inviolable. No more raids or invasions."

No more killing, said Giorsa, the pacifist, but Raghri said, *Be wary*. "My people know what your people think of treaties."

"No. You know what Lord Elban thought of treaties. I am not Lord Elban."

Korsa thought of the orphan houses, and of those Elban left behind after his raids: not only the dead, but the dying, the maimed, the wounded. To do such things to an enemy was bad enough, but to let misery visit your own people was unthinkable, monstrous. Then again, Elban had been a monster. The Seneschal was no doubt a monster, too, or he couldn't rule this city. "It might not be possible to make a true *kagirh* in this place," Korsa finally said. "It might require something your people simply don't have."

"I understand that," the Seneschal said, "but will you try?"

The tap at the door came again. It was the girl with the braided hair, come to take the tray away. As she shifted the things Korsa had moved, arranging dishes on the huge tray so she could carry it, Korsa saw her pallor and thin arms, the dark circles under her eyes. Too dark, for one so young. He wondered if she had come from one of the orphan houses.

"I make no promises," he said, "but I'll try."

The Seneschal smiled and clapped his hands together with satisfaction. The sound was discordant and jarring. "That's all I ask," he said, and turned to the girl. "Please call the boatman. We need to take the chieftain to his new quarters." He turned his satisfied smile onto Korsa. "You'll find your new housing infinitely preferable to your old, I think. Yes, I think you'll be very pleased, indeed."

A few hours after the Seneschal left the prison, the girl with the braided hair did, too. As the skiff that brought her across the Brake bumped against the dock, she could already hear music and conversation spilling out of the eel shops and taverns scattered among the Brakeside warehouses. She said goodbye to the boatman and stepped out onto the slick embankment, and the boat disappeared into the evening fog. A man stepped out of the darkness. He was older than she was, with broad shoulders that spoke of a life of backbreaking work. His face had little ease in it, but he smiled when he saw her.

"Hello, Bin," he said.

"Hello, Darid. You don't have to meet me, you know," Bindy told her brother. "I managed to go thirteen years walking around Brakeside and Marketside without you, and nothing bad happened."

"I like walking with you."

And the truth was that Bindy didn't really want Darid to stop meeting her. He was one of the Returned, the former staff of the great walled palace that loomed over the city of New Highfall; like all the others, he'd gone behind the Wall at ten years old, before Bindy was even born. Only when Elban died, and the old lord's Highfall became the Seneschal's New Highfall, had all of the staff emerged. If Darid had gone to the Seneschal's office and registered as one of the Returned, he would have been guaranteed employment at any factory in the city. But Darid, who refused to talk about his life inside, refused to do that, too. He hated the Seneschal like poison for reasons he wouldn't explain, except to say that the Seneschal had hurt somebody he cared about, once.

So Darid was left a criminal, with no work papers and no official existence. Rina—the sister between Bindy and Darid—was on the Work Enforcement Committee at the paper factory. Rina was hard-nosed, and the committee was her life. She was honor bound to turn Darid in, but for Ma's sake, Rina and Darid had made a silent agreement that he would stay away from her, and she would forget he existed. Each only came to visit Ma and other children at the cottage when the other was gone. Bindy found it all ridiculously complicated. It would have been simpler to be easy with each other, but that was apparently not an option.

And in the end, the best way to see Darid was for him to meet her and walk her home. "How was work?" he said, now, as they walked through Brakeside.

"Cook the food, serve the food, wash the dishes, repeat."

"That's how it goes. Did you see the magus today?"

Bindy had spent all day hauling pots of water and pots of gruel and firewood and trays and she wouldn't have thought her aching shoulders could feel any heavier, but now they did exactly that. Because she *had* seen the magus: her strange, beloved magus, who'd given her a job and a safe place to stay during the coup and had taught her about herbs, besides. Seeing the magus was the whole reason she'd taken the job at the prison, and she couldn't manage it every day but she did it often enough. "Yes," she said.

"How is he?"

The same, she was going to say—silent, filthy, locked into himself. But it was a lie, wasn't it? "Worse." Against all her best efforts, the word came out hoarse and her eyes filled with tears. "He's getting worse all the time. I don't think he eats unless I'm there to feed him. You can almost see through him. He—"

He's dying, was the end of that sentence. But Darid put a hand on her arm and cut her off. "Hush. Keep walking. We're being followed."

Darid didn't merely hate the Seneschal; he actively worked against him. In small, petty ways, mostly, down on the docks where barges moved goods in and out of the city. Drilling holes in barrels so the contents would leak out, or strategically cutting the individual strands of a rope so it would break with the slightest pressure. He wouldn't talk about this, either, but she'd been to the warehouse where he lived, and met others who lived there, and heard snippets of their conversations. She could draw her own conclusions. She was no fan of the Seneschal's, either—he'd been the one to put her magus in prison—and she was proud of her brother. Still, it was dangerous work. More than one Warehouser had simply disappeared. "Followed?" she said.

"You go ahead," he said, curtly. "I'll circle around."

She nodded. He lifted a hand, as if saying goodbye, and turned down a narrow alley. Bindy kept walking, but she moved out into the middle of the street, away from the taverns and out of the shadows of the attaches that had been built out over the cobblestones. She heard a thud and a grunt behind her, then, the quick, looping whistle of Darid's all-clear signal. Then she turned and ducked back into the nearest alley.

The purplish light from the new gaslamps didn't reach far, but there was enough light for her to see Darid pinning a tall, thin man to the wall. The man didn't seem to be struggling, but Darid had a hand clamped over his mouth, anyway. He glanced over his shoulder at Bindy. "You know this guy, Bin?"

Bindy came closer. The man had light hair and blue eyes, like most Highfallers, but something about his clothes seemed wrong. Odd. Foreign. "No."

The man mumbled something behind Darid's hand, and lifted his eyebrows. Carefully, Darid switched his grip from the man's mouth to his throat, and squeezed. "I know you," the man said, in a voice that was remarkably calm, given the circumstances. "You're Bindy. You were apprentice to the old House Magus, Nathaniel Clare, and now you work at the prison. That's where Nathaniel is, isn't it? That's why you got the job there?"

Darid and Bindy exchanged a quick, uncertain glance. "How do you know all that?" Darid said.

"I ask questions," the man said. "I answer them, too. It's easier to do when I can breathe." Darid's grip on the stranger's throat tightened. The man's eyes widened with panic. "I'm a friend of Nate's!" he croaked. "From when we were children! Let me go! I'm here to help!"

Bindy stepped up and put a hand on her brother's shoulder. "Let him go."

Scowling, Darid did as she said. The man's hand went to his throat, rubbing the places Darid had squeezed. Bindy expected the man to bolt as soon as he caught his breath—it was what she would have done—but she knew Darid wouldn't let him get away. The night had taken an ugly turn, and she felt weary and depressed.

But the man only said, "Much better. I can't blame you for being suspicious. Is there somewhere we can talk?"

"We can talk here," Darid said.

"Yes, but we can't sit, and we can't eat." The stranger adjusted his tunic and smoothed his rumpled hair. He seemed to have recovered his composure very quickly. "And I would like to do both."

Darid looked at Bindy. "If he's the magus's friend," Bindy said, and Darid frowned. He thought this was a bad idea, she could tell. But bad here paled in comparison to the bad that was the dank cell where her magus lived, the way his wrist bones stood out, the way he wouldn't look at or talk to her. Bad was watching him wither away, with the memory always in her head of the warm, kind man her friend had once been.

Darid's lips pressed together in a tight, thin line, the same way their ma's did when she wanted something she wasn't getting. "Alva's," he said.

"Perfectly good," the stranger said.

In the nicer parts of the city, taverns had lovely names like The White Bird or The River's Edge. Lovely names were wasted in Marketside, where most people couldn't read. The sign at Alva's tavern merely said Food and Ale, with a crude painting of a tankard and a loaf of bread. People called the place Alva's because Alva owned it and ran it, and Alva had been a friend of Bindy's ma's since before Darid was born. When Bindy was little, Alva had shaved her beard close and switched trousers for gowns. Eventually, instead of saying, "He has the best pies in Marketside," people began to say, "She has the best pies in Marketside." Bindy and Darid's mother, Nora, had been one of the first to adopt the new phrasing, and Alva had always been particularly kind to the Dovetail children. Bindy wasn't surprised when she came out from behind the bar to greet them.

"Somewhere quiet? And food for three, please," the stranger said. Bindy saw the gleam of silver pass from his hand to Alva's. Alva slipped the coin into her pocket and nodded toward the private room in the back, which was indeed private, but far from luxurious. The table was slightly less scarred than the ones in the main room, maybe. There were no windows, but a second door swung into the kitchen. They weren't trapped.

"Please, sit," the stranger said, as if they were visitors in his home. The way he said his words wasn't quite an accent, but it wasn't native Highfaller, either. "I'm sorry I startled you. As I said, I'm a friend of Nathaniel Clare's from years back, and I've been worried about him. We've all been very worried about him."

Bindy had met one of the magus's friends before, a sad man who dressed like a courtier but wasn't one. He'd definitely been a drop addict, though, and he'd killed himself at the magus's kitchen table. His name had been Charles. That was when things had gone wrong for the magus, when Charles had come to stay. If this friend was like him— "What friend?" she said. "How many years?"

The stranger spread out his hands. "All the years. I've known Nate our whole lives. I'm Saba Petrie. I've come all the way across the Barrier Mountains looking for him."

"The magus is from the other side of the Barriers?" Darid said.

Alva entered, carrying a large tray piled heavy with three of her special chicken pies, along with a cruet of vinegar and a pot of mustard. Bindy's lunch had been a single slice of bread, and that many hours ago. Her mouth started watering instantly. "Lovely, thank you," the stranger said, and when Alva was gone, continued. "Anyway, Nate. Yes, we were friends as children. Not family, officially, but our community is small enough that everybody is like family. We haven't heard from him or any of those who came here with him in many months. What a tale he must have to tell! Arriving here with nothing, then becoming House Magus, and the coup, and now he's in prison—please, what can you tell me? Everyone in Marketside says you were at his right hand, all these months. I care very deeply for Nate." He blinked in an odd, exaggerated way. Was he fighting back tears? "I want to help him, if I can."

Bindy's heart hurt, remembering the way the magus's head lolled on his weak neck, the dull look in his eyes. His right hand? She was both of his hands. "I don't know if you can. I think the Seneschal means for him to die in that cell."

Saba shook his head. "Why? What could Nate possibly have done?"

"I don't know." Bindy felt on the verge of tears, herself. "He was old Arkady's apprentice when Arkady died, and the Seneschal liked him enough then to make him House Magus. Even after the coup. He took care of the Children when they were under house arrest, you know."

"You mean Lord Elban's children? Gavin and Theron?"

"And Lady Eleanor, and the Foundling," Bindy said, nodding. Darid's brows were hooded and dark. "But—I don't know, he began to get sick."

"Sick? Isn't there an Elenesian Refuge here?"

Bindy shook her head. "I don't know what that is, but it wasn't the kind of sick a healer could help, or he would have treated himself. He was weak. Out of his head, sometimes. It got worse when his friend Charles died."

"Charles Whelan?" Saba said, sharply.

"Maybe. Charles, was all I knew him by. He killed himself. Cut his wrists right at the magus's kitchen table." Bindy's urge to cry had dried. "He was a dropper, but he managed to stop at the end. Anyway, one day the magus went inside the Wall, like he always did, only he never came back. After a week or so, the Seneschal's guards came to the manor house and kicked me out. It took ages for me to find out he was in prison."

"Does Nate have any other friends in the city?"

Bindy considered. "There was a man named Firo. He walked like a courtier but he couldn't have been—this was ages after the coup. And there was an old woman who was sometimes around, but she always seemed to be leaving when I got there. I think he bought herbs from her, or something."

Saba pursed his lips. "Are the Children still inside the Wall?"

"They aren't actual children, you know." Darid's voice was harsh.

"The Seneschal read a statement from Lord Gavin at the winter solstice," Bindy said. "But that doesn't mean anything."

"What does Nate say happened?" Saba said.

"He says nothing." Bindy's tears were back. Her throat hurt from swallowing them, and the words fell out of her whether she wanted to say them or not. "He hasn't said a single word, not the whole time since I found him. I try to take care of him. I make him eat. I clean him up. I bring him medicine, when I can. The prison's damp, dug in the middle of the river the way it is. I thought if I gave him time, he'd get better, but he's not getting better. I'm—" she swallowed a hitch in her throat "—I'm afraid he's going to die, and there's nothing I can do. I don't know enough to help him. He taught me how to treat little things, headaches and rashes, but this—"

The tears fell now. Her cheeks burned with rage and grief, and she bent her head. Darid put a hand on her shoulder but it didn't help. Nothing helped.

Saba poured a cup of small beer and pushed it into her hands. Gently, he said, "Here, Bindy. Drink this. I'm here to help, now."

Bindy didn't like small beer but she took a sip anyway, to wash the sob out of her throat. Darid said, "And how are you going to help? Are you going to get yourself hired on as a prison maid, too?"

Saba gave him a cool look. "Do you not approve of your sister's efforts?"

"The magus helped me out, once," Darid said. "I don't wish him any ill. If Bindy could help him, I'd be glad for her to. But it's starting to look like she can't, and there's nothing for her in that prison." He looked up at Bindy, his eyes sad. "I'm sorry, Bin."

"It's okay," Bindy said, softly.

"Darid Dovetail." Saba poured himself another glass of ale. "You're one of the Returned, aren't you?"

Darid stiffened. "No."

"Well, you don't wear the armband. You're not on the official list. You didn't march in the Parade of the Returned. But that's a matter of words, isn't it? Because you did go inside the Wall when you were ten years old, and you did come out after the coup. And I've heard some say they'd heard you died, although they were all quick to say they must have heard wrong."

Bindy was shaking her head. "They told us he died. But it was a mistake."

"Rather large mistake. Does the Seneschal know he made it? If not, that would explain your reluctance to reap the not inconsiderable benefits of being one of Lord Elban's former staff. Why, you could get hired anywhere you wanted, with an allowance on top of your wage, for all those years of un-paid labor."

"My family was paid," Darid said.

"Still. It must have been terrible, as a child, to go into that place, and know you were never going to leave it or see your mother again." Saba gave Darid a sympathetic look and poured himself more ale. "What did you do inside, anyway?"

"Horses," Darid muttered. "I took care of the horses."

"Did you ever meet any of the Children? One of Elban's sons, or Lady Eleanor? The Foundling, perhaps?"

Darid said nothing.

"Only, I'm wondering how it was that a man who took care of the horses found himself owing a favor to the House Magus. I'm not attacking you, Darid," he added, mildly. "I'm just trying to make sense of what happened to my friend."

Darid frowned down at the tankard in front of him. Finally: "I knew Judah the Foundling."

"You never told me that!" Bindy looked at Saba. "The magus knew her, too. Will that help?"

"I don't know. The only person who knows is poor Nate, and from what you said, he's not talking." Saba pulled one of the chicken pies in front of him. Instead of making regu-lar round pies with lids, Alva rolled the filling up in knots of dough. Made them easier to eat, she said. Saba pulled a long strip of dough away, and a cloud of chickeny, oniony steam rose into the air. A glob of filling fell to the table. "I think our next step is fairly clear, regardless. We can't have Nate dying in that filthy prison, can we? So we'll have to get him out."

Bindy and Darid stared, stunned. "You're insane," Darid said.

"But he's barely conscious," Bindy said.

Saba smiled. "We can fix that," he said, and deep in Bindy's heart, a spark of hope flared.

TWO

JUDAH KNEW WARMTH. THE SMELL OF FIRE. A WOODEN spoon in her mouth, sometimes full of water, sometimes gruel, sometimes something that tasted like mint and sour milk. Milk gone bad, milk that should be spat out, so she did.

"It's medicine, lady," a voice said. Warm and kind, the accent entirely unfamiliar. "We wouldn't hurt you."

She laughed.

She wept.

She became aware of the forest around her: the chirps and screes of creatures in the trees, wan sunlight filtering through the bluish leaves, the thick carpet of organic detritus on the floor. Her own body, weak and sore, wrapped in tatters of green fabric and a rough blanket that must have belonged to the men. The men: there were two of them. One was tall and pale, with knife-edged features and an ugly burn scar on the back of his hand. His hair hung around his face, stringy and dark. This was the one who called her *lady* and made her drink the medicine, which he called *godswill*; the one who palpated her skull and moved fingers for her eyes to track. He was the one with the warm, kind voice, but he didn't always use it.

The other man was not as tall, but twice as broad. He wore his long hair in thick ropes that he bound behind his neck in a tail as thick as Judah's neck, and his skin was a rich dark brown. Nobody in Highfall had skin that color. He rarely spoke and never looked directly at her, but he was the one who brought her clothes the second day, dropping the bundle down before her on the dead blue-gray leaves. "Warmer than what's left of that dress," he said.

The moment she touched the clothes, she knew that the last body to wear them had been dead. Still better than the tatters, so she put them on.

They said they'd found her under a bush, starving and half-dead from exposure. At first they had to tell her this several times a day. Her brain didn't seem to want to hang on to information. They asked questions: what was her name, where did she live, where was her family. She found the questions hilarious.

The pale man told her the medicine, the godswill, was what kept her on her feet, walking, alive. It was very important to both of them that she walk. They told her where they were going but the place name fell through her brain like water through cupped fingers. The boots she wore came from the dead person, too. He was as real to her as the two men were: younger than she was, but not quite a boy. Soft hands. The last thing he'd felt was a strong arm around his throat, the last thing he'd heard the snap of his own neck. His boots were too big for her in some places and too small in others. She wrapped her feet in some of the tatters of her green dress to make them fit better. The soles of her feet were bruised and scratched, the nail on her left little toe missing entirely. The pale man gave her ointment for the scratches, said it would minimize scarring. He was annoyed when this made her laugh.

She didn't try to explain, because the reason she laughed wouldn't make sense to him. It was this: all of her scars were gone. Every one of them, over her entire body. Her memory was addled, but she remembered the nights of knives and coals and acid in Elban's study in Highfall, and the mess of scar tissue those nights had left on her feet. She remembered her arms, covered with the curlicue scars from Elban's pokers, the faint marks from years of scratching messages to Gavin, the tidy cuts the magus had made in the tower while he was teaching her the Work. Now, the soles of her feet were perfect. There wasn't a mark on them other than the scratches and bruises left by her barefoot stumbling before the men found her. Her arms were the same. Even the tooth she'd knocked out falling from a tree was back. Her body, from all appearances, was entirely unscathed, entirely new.

Her mind felt like the same old mind, though. The godswill made her dull and easily distracted by things like a falling leaf or the splash of a stream over rocks, and she had trouble remembering what happened an hour ago, but she remembered her life before the white. Gavin and Elly and Theron, Elban and the Seneschal and Darid and the sad, delusional magus, Nathaniel. It was all a bit hazy, as if she'd spent all of her life very very drunk, but she was definitely Judah, definitely herself. The two men had cut off her hair while she was unconscious (because it was filthy, they told her, over and over, and stank) but what was left was the same dried-blood red, and more fiercely curly than ever. The reflection that she saw in streams and pools looked different, but it was still her own self. New body. Same Judah the Foundling.

Her right hand drifted to the inside of her left wrist so often that the pale man checked her for injury there, but she wasn't hurt. It was habit, that was all. She had felt nothing from Gavin since awakening, no friendly scratches *hello* or *where are you*. She hadn't reached out to him, either. The last time they'd been in the same room together, it had almost meant death for both of them. She didn't trust herself to know whether or not she wanted Gavin to find her.

Not that she knew where she was. The trees looked like nothing she'd ever seen before, with their white bark and blue leaves, and the furry white things that ran up and down their trunks were squirrel-like without being squirrels, exactly. The pale man caught these in traps overnight and roasted them. The dark man caught fish from streams they passed, if there were any to catch. Once, the pale man found a stand of mushrooms, which he boiled into a paste, and the three of them ate that, too. It tasted like semisolid nothing but he said they could survive on it.

"For how long?" Judah said, somewhat incredulously, and the pale man said, "Until it makes us so depressed we kill ourselves."

She didn't know why she found that so funny, but her laughter was unreliable these days. The two men exchanged a look. They did that often. It seemed as if they could hold entire conversations without saying a word. Which Judah also found hilarious, because she and Gavin had been able to do the same, once. She wondered if the two men had an invisible rope of purple power connecting them, too, the way she and Gavin did.

"Sorry," she said, when she could speak. "Sorry."

"Lost her mind," the dark man said, and the pale man said, "No. It's the godswill."

The pale man kept a wooden box in his satchel that unfolded into dozens of tiny compartments that held herbs or powders or tools. His burned hand was rippled and discolored but he seemed to have full use of it. The dark man had eyes the color of copper and a long silver knife that he kept strapped to his leg. The pale man's long leather coat was so patched that it was nearly more patch than coat. The dark man wore leather, too, but his had been fashioned into armor.

Sometimes she caught a calculating glint in the pale man's eyes when he looked at her. The dark one rarely looked at her at all. His name was Lukash. The pale man called himself Cleric.

"That's not a name," she said.

"And yet," he said, tersely. "I don't suppose you remember your name yet."

Cleric hadn't always been so curt with her. In the beginning, his voice had been so warm that she'd thought she must know him. Now she understood that the warmth was like his leather coat, and he could take it off or put it on as he needed it. "Nope," she lied. She didn't know where she was, and she didn't know how far the Seneschal's reach extended. Until she knew those things, it was probably better to remain anonymous. "Sorry."

Cleric peeled one of the white squirrel-things out of its fur. "I've started weaning you off the godswill. It might clear up some of the cobwebs in your brain. It might also leave you a gibbering idiot, but let's hope for the former."

"I've never once gibbered," she said. "Since I might actually be able to remember it for more than five minutes, tell me where we're going, again?"

Cleric eviscerated the squirrel-thing with two fingers and tossed the guts into the brush. "A town called Black Lake," Lukash said. "If you were waylaid traveling, it's likely you were either going to or coming from Black Lake. The only other town within easy travel distance is Harkerstown, and we've just come from Harkerstown. We'd know if anyone from there was missing."

Yes. She dimly remembered this theory of theirs, that she was a waylaid traveler who'd been hit on the head and left to die. "That's right. You think somebody is looking for me. You think there'll be a reward."

Cleric drove a tapered stick through the squirrel-thing and looked at his friend. Partner. Whatever they were to each other. "If I stop giving her the godswill entirely, she'll be quiet."

"You said I'd die if you stopped giving me the godswill entirely," she said, and he said, "Yes, and then you'll be quiet."

It didn't sound like a threat. "You came from somewhere," Lukash said. His accent was like a stream falling over rocks. "You have people. If we return you to them, they'll be happy to see you."

"Unless they were the ones who left me in the forest," Judah said.

Cleric reached over and grabbed her arm. His hand was sticky from the squirrel-thing's blood. "Look at your hand," he said, turning her arm so her palm faced upward. "Not a single callus. No wash-water burns, no lye burns. This hand has never worked a day in its life, and neither have you. There's not a scar on you anywhere, and that dress you were wearing when we found you—" He let go of her arm. "Somebody saw to it that you and your perfect teeth were taken care of. Presumably that person will pay us to have their investment returned to them, and you can go back to your servants."

Her arm was smeared with the squirrel-thing's blood where he'd held it. She wiped it on the dead boy's trousers. "Staff," she said, without thinking. "They're called staff."

"Are they, now," Cleric said, with immense satisfaction.

Lukash said nothing, but she saw the hint of a frown around his copper-colored eyes.

The next morning—the cobwebs were indeed clearing, she could trace events back one before the other like footsteps—Cleric mixed a smaller dose of godswill for her. The medicine was a dark blue-green powder that he stirred into water, and the smell was vile.

"I won't miss this stuff," she said. "It tastes awful."

"That it does. Supposed to be the *god's will*, you know—" he left a very deliberate space between the two words "—but most people think *godswill* is a better name for it. I'll give you this much for three days, then half again as much for three more. After that, we'll see."

"I feel healthy enough now," she said.

"Trust me," he said. "The godswill is the only thing keeping you on your feet."

And honestly, by the time they stopped that afternoon to rest and eat the last of the previous night's squirrel-thing, she was exhausted and covered in a thin sheen of sweat despite the chill in the air. Her hands felt filthy and tender where she'd been gripping the hiking stick all day. Lukash, as usual, walked a perimeter around their stopping place, came back and said, "There's a spring and a pool up ahead. Might as well camp here tonight."

Cleric disappeared into the woods to set his traps. Judah and Lukash went to the pool: him to fish, her so she could wash her blistered palms. The canopy of blue leaves spread over the pool so the sun was as wan there as it was everywhere else in the forest, but the water was clean and clear. She took off the dead boy's jacket, pushed up the too-long sleeves of his shirt, and plunged her hands into the water. It was so icy she gasped. Her hand disappeared below the surface and it was all familiar, the wet rock, the feel of the water around her fingers, the smell. Lukash tied his tiny silver fishing lure onto the end of his line. She wondered how many fish that lure had pulled to their deaths. "What if nobody in Black Lake knows me?" she said.

He dropped his line into the water and tugged it gently, to make the lure flash and twitch. "You could stay there. Get work of some kind. Always work to be had in cartel cities."

"Cartel?"

"Like a guild, without all the religious pretense. Black Lake's run by the gloryseed cartel. A drug," he added, when her face made clear that she still didn't know what he was talking about. He made the lure twitch again. His copper eyes flicked to her, and then back to the surface of the water, where the only movements were the faint ripples left from his line. "I wish your memory would come back. There might have been a reason you were in the woods."

She considered. "You mean, what if I was running away from something?"

Lukash shrugged. "It would have to be something serious, to drive you into the Ghostwood."

"Ghostwood?"

He moved his head in a compact fashion that somehow managed to indicate the entire forest, in a general sort of way. "All around us. Supposed to be haunted."

She thought of the dead boy's soft hands and the sweet herbal smell in his dying nose, and said, "Maybe I'm a ghost."

He smiled. "You seem very solid. Also, if you wanted to haunt me, I'm fairly certain you'd have to get in line."

"Killed a lot of people, have you?" she said. It was a joke, but the moment the words left her lips she regretted them. The dead boy. The knife.

But he only said, "Yes, there was a war," and turned back to his line. Embarrassed, she said nothing. The forest was quiet.

She realized for the first time that there were no birds here in the Ghostwood, as Lukash had called it. The only wildlife she'd seen were the white squirrel-things, darting among the blue leaves and occasionally letting forth high, rattling *screes* of indignation. She supposed if you didn't know about the squirrel-things, the noise might sound unearthly enough to give rise to rumors of haunting. Then again, the Work—and the tower?—had spit her out of the white in this forest. Maybe other strange things had happened here, too.

Another moment passed. A squirrel-thing screeched. On the other side of the pool, something splashed. Judah watched the ripples move and fade.

Finally, Lukash said, "We're thieves, not murderers. Usually."

Usually. "Not much to steal in the middle of the forest."

"Sometimes things go wrong."

"Was it me? Was I the thing that went wrong?"

"No," he said. "Whatever went wrong for you happened long before we found you."

Back at the camp, she tore the final remnants of her green dress into strips and wove them into rope with her fingers, so she could carry the bedroll they'd given her over her shoulder. The two men watched, clearly impressed. "Where did you learn that?" Lukash said.

"From somebody who kept horses," she said.

He looked at Cleric, who had picked up the last scrap of her dress and was rubbing it between his fingers. They had another one of those silent conversations that didn't include her. "What?" she said, annoyed.

"The rich ladies where I come from can't weave rope," Lukash said.

"The rich ladies where I come from can barely cut their

own food," Cleric said, but he still seemed more interested in the cloth. "What is this dress made of?"

"Rich ladies where I come from don't concern themselves with the manufacturing of cloth," she said, and went back to her rope.

The next day, the ground took a decided turn upward, and the hiking was difficult. The squirrel-things grew scarce. Now, their meals were sparingly supplemented with strips of pemmican and dried berries from the men's packs. They hadn't planned for a long hike, and were low on supplies, they told her. Having to split food three ways was as wearisome as the hiking, and the third time Cleric brought the tasteless mushrooms out of his pack, Judah said, "All right, I'm ready to kill myself now."

"Not when we're so close to Black Lake," Cleric said.

"Are we close?" she said, and Lukash said, "Be able to see it in a day or two."

And sure enough, a day and a half later, they threaded their way between two boulders and emerged at the edge of a ridge. Far below them, Black Lake—not the town, but the body of water—reached, as black as its name, into the distance. Crouched on its near end, the town looked like a toy city. Toy walls surrounded the toy buildings, except lakeside, where half a dozen stubby two-masted toy ships docked at two toy piers. The land around the town was planted with crops in neat squares of tidy rows, a dusty brown road winding through them into the city.

But Lukash's gaze was set lower, to the blue-green forest canopy between them and the road. "Look," he said, and pointed out at the leafy sea to a place where the slope began to flatten and a single, thin spire of smoke rose into the air.

"Look like home?" Cleric said to Judah, who shook her

head mutely. The thin man shrugged. "Oh, well. Might be interesting, anyway."

The three of them began hiking down the mountain.

They came across a creek first, and then a path. The path was wide enough to push a small cart over. The silence in the woods hadn't changed but it felt different, more watchful. Lukash found a heel print by a fallen log, a perfect semicircle pressed into the mud after a rainstorm and left undisturbed to dry. Not long after that they found a grapevine growing around the trunk of an old tree, thick with clusters of dark red fruit. Cleric tasted one, and spat out a wad of seeds and membrane. "Wine grapes," he said.

The path left the creek and wound through the trees. At every turn they found another grapevine. The vines grew thicker, less hidden, until finally they grew near the ground without any camouflage at all. Then the trees opened up to a clearing where a small house had been built of rough-hewn logs, the thin line of smoke they'd seen streaming from a stone chimney. The breeze smelled of burning wood, earth, and something else, something musty and fermented.

They heard singing. A man appeared around the corner of the house. For a moment, the four of them stared at each other. The man held a basket full of dirty potatoes and onions, and his tunic was stained with muck, but the gray-streaked hair that fell to his shoulders was clean. At first he looked surprised. Then he smiled, broadly. "Well!" he said. "Well! Welcome! Travelers, are you?"

Judah wondered if the first two syllables were speech or stutter. Cleric held his hands up, palms toward the man, in the age-old gesture of harmlessness. "Slightly lost ones," he said, smiling his most charming smile. "We mean you no harm."

"Of course you don't," the man said. "Of course you don't.

Is that Northern speech I hear? Bright gods, what are you doing so deep in the woods so early in the year?"

The words were friendly, but Judah saw something crafty in the old man's eyes. "Like I said," Cleric said, "slightly lost. Are those your grapes we've been seeing?"

"Mine as much as anybody's, although if they could talk, I suspect they'd tell you they belong only to themselves. Grapes are like children. You do the best you can, but they'll be what they'll be." He bowed. "My name is Sevedra, good travelers. At your service."

"Good god," Cleric said, all polish and craft vanished. "Really?"

Sevedra smiled patiently. As if this were something one must go through when one met new people, like handshakes. "I'm afraid so."

Lukash looked from the old man to Cleric, and back again. "You two know each other?"

"Sevedran wine is—simply—the best—" Cleric stopped. Or rather, was stopped, as if not even his nimble tongue could find the words.

Sevedra laughed. "You flatter me, I'm afraid. I do enjoy my work, but—again, like children—the wine turns out how it will. I merely provide water when the rain doesn't come." He smiled merrily. "Today, though, I'm working in the garden, not the vineyard. If you put your packs down and help me harvest dinner, you can help me eat it."

They'd eaten nothing but squirrel, fish, and tasteless mushrooms for so long that none of them hesitated to agree. Sevedra led them behind the house to a small farm: a vegetable garden, a field of wheat, a few goats and chickens. Off to the side a green patch that looked like an herb garden drew Cleric immediately; as Judah and Lukash dug carrots, leeks, and round purplish things that were probably some kind of turnip, Cleric wandered among the plants, sometimes strok- ing one or rubbing a leaf between his fingers. Occasionally, one of his eyebrows lifted.

Finally he joined them. "Quite a collection," he said.

"Most of them grow here naturally." Sevedra gave the herb garden a careless look. "Honestly, I rarely use them."

"No," Cleric said, and Judah couldn't read the tone of his voice. "I wouldn't think you would."

When they were done, Sevedra drew water from the well so they could wash. The inside of the cottage was cluttered and friendly and very ordinary, and the winemaker kept up a steady stream of chatter as he rinsed the vegetables, cut them into small chunks, and added them to a pot bubbling over the fire. Then he added a few pinches from the odd collection of jars and crocks lining a shelf above the fireplace. Whatever was cooking in the pot smelled amazing.

"While that finishes, I'll show you the vineyard," he said, and lit a lantern. He led them through a door and down a staircase that seemed to have been carved out of solid rock. At the bottom was a room lined with wooden casks and more doors, all of them closed. Past this room and another full of wood-fired stoves with pipes snaking up into the earthen ceil- ing, Sevedra stopped at a set of wide double doors and put aside the lantern. Then, opening the door with a flourish, he said, "My vineyard."

The room on the other side smelled like earth and water but was flooded with natural light. It was disconcerting, to be in a room that was so obviously underground, but also so bright. In the middle of the room, under the skylights where the light was brightest, dozens of grapevines grew on tidy rows of trellises.

"How is it so bright?" Judah said.

Sevedra nodded at Lukash. "Your Morgeni friend can tell you."

Lukash shifted, as if uncomfortable, and said, "Prisms set into the earth. The light is refracted through them and spread around the rooms. My people use a similar system in their mines."

Sevedra was nodding. "Exactly. I had to adapt it somewhat, not having those wonderful crystals you dig out of your mountains."

Lukash did not move, but Judah felt him go very still and tense. "I am not a miner. I have dug nothing out of any mountains."

"I meant the collective you, of course," Sevedra said, as if it didn't particularly matter, but Judah sensed that somehow it did. "The pump system was my own devising. The temperature controls, too."

And, indeed, it was very warm in the vineyard room. Sevedra showed them the different varieties of grapes he grew, the fruit pink and green and red and white. The ones needing the most light were directly under the skylight, he said, but the conical skylights enabled the sunlight to reach the ground no matter where it was in the sky. All of the plants looked healthy. Nothing looked like it had been grown in a basement. "This is amazing," Cleric said.

"The product of many years' work." Sevedra's pride was clear.

"But why?" Judah said.

"Control," the winemaker said. "If it needs to be warmer, I light the stoves. If I need more humidity, I turn on the misters. Most of all, I can control the soil content. Wine is only as good as the soil where the grapes are grown, you know. The vines in the forest are fine for table wine, but I never know from one year to the next what they'll be." He gazed lovingly at the nearest vine, running a leaf between his fingers like a lock of hair. "These, I can take care of. Give them whatever they need. Some of them come from very far away, you know, strains that don't exist anymore, except here. I take care of them. I give them the best of everything."

"That must be why your wines are so famous," Cleric said.

Sevedra bowed his head. "I don't know about that. I know that twice a year, the man comes with the cart, buys my full bottles and brings me empty ones. I love my vines. I have a good life." He looked at Lukash. "What's that Morgeni saying? Some birds stay where they are hatched? Well, I was not hatched here. But it is where I prefer to stay."

"Where you have control," Judah said. She saw something flash over Sevedra's face. Before he could speak, she touched a plant growing between two vines and said, "This is pepper, isn't it?"

Whatever the flash had been, it was gone now. His expression was neutral and pleasant. "Yes. It grows well down here, as it happens." He gave Judah a curious look. "I know your Northern friend by the way he talks and your Morgeni friend by the way he wears his hair, but you—you, I cannot place. Where were you born?"

She shrugged. Cleric said, "I'm afraid her memory is damaged."

"Oh, dear. How did that happen?" Sevedra said.

Cleric shook his head with a reasonable facsimile of sadness. "We don't know. We found her in the Ghostwood."

"We're taking her to Black Lake for assistance," Lukash said. "Is that where your wine buyer comes from?"

"It is," Sevedra said, and was it Judah's imagination or did his eyes keep coming back to her? "The stew's probably ready by now. Shall we eat?"

On the way back upstairs, Judah noticed a box of small

stone medals near the stairs, each carved with an *S*. She had seen these before, on bottles of wine at Elban's table and once, after the coup, on a bottle she and Gavin had shared, deep in the catacombs. She was wondering how far away Highfall was when Sevedra—yes, he was definitely watching her—noticed where she was looking. "They hang around the necks of the bottles." He pulled a medal out to show her. "Like little necklaces, eh? An affectation, but I enjoy it. Carving them gives me something to do while the wine ages. Would you like one?"

Judah remembered Elban's fingers tapping the medal and suppressed a shudder. "Thank you. No."

In the kitchen, Sevedra moved baskets of vegetables and gardening equipment off the table. Then he dished out the stew and poured four glasses of a wine so dark it was nearly black. "You'll taste the pepper in that," he said, with satisfaction. "The slightest bite, there behind the richness of the grapes."

Cleric declared it sublime. Lukash said nothing, but poured himself a second glass. Judah took one sip of hers. She could taste the pepper. But while the Sevedran she had shared with Gavin had been velvety and rich, the heavy alcoholic taste of this made her throat tighten, and she didn't take a second sip.

The stew was good, and the wine flowed freely among the other three. When Sevedra noticed that Judah wasn't drinking, he brought out a special bottle for her. Restorative, he said, and in truth it was far easier to drink than the pepper wine. She found herself finishing the glass. At first, Cleric kept his burned hand under the table, but after enough wine, he forgot himself and used it to reach for a piece of bread.

Sevedra nodded toward the scar. "That must have been painful. How did it happen?"

The hand disappeared. "Fell into a fire," Cleric said. "I was quite drunk at the time."

"I'm surprised you can still use your fingers. You had a good healer."

Cleric lifted his eyebrows and grinned. "I *am* a good healer."

"Why did you do nothing about the scarring, then?"

"Everybody has scars," Cleric said.

Not me, Judah thought, and almost laughed aloud.

Another bottle was opened. Cleric, his speech beginning to slur, waxed poetic. The wine tasted of cherries and smoke, he said; of fine tobacco and sweet cream. Lukash said little but drank willingly of everything put in front of him. Judah herself found that the more she drank, the farther away the room seemed. It was easy to let it slip away, and vanish entirely.

"Stand up," the winemaker said, his friendliness replaced by inexorable command. Judah opened her eyes and found Cleric and Lukash slumped over on the table. Lukash was drooling. Cleric's face was obscured behind his hair.

She discovered that she was standing.

"Downstairs, now," the winemaker said, and before the sentence had even left his mouth, her traitorous feet were moving toward the stairs, and down them. No, she told her feet, as sternly as she could. Stop. Do not do this. But her feet refused to listen. They carried her down the stairs and across the basement rooms, through the double doors. It was night, now, and the vineyard was dark. Sevedra carried the lantern all the way inside. "Come," he said, and she had no choice. Perplexed and furious at her inability to do anything to stop what was happening, she followed him between the vines to a dark corner. Then he said, "Kneel," and she found her knees sunk into the soft earth, so that he towered over her.

"Now," he said. "Where did you come from?"

She opened her mouth to say that she didn't remember, but

what came out was a laugh. A high, nervous laugh, as if she were on the edge of panic.

Sevedra smiled. "You can't lie. The drug I put in your wine won't last as long as the sedative I gave your bandit friends, but while it does, you'll tell me the truth. I can feel things, you know. In people. In the soil, the grapes. It's how I make my wine special." He scowled. "Northerners are common as dirt. The Morgeni is a bit of a prize, but he's probably just an ex-soldier. The truly brilliant ones never leave their mountain. But you, I can't place at all." He touched over her cheek, almost a caress. Her skin crawled. She couldn't move away. "What are you? Are you Slonimi? You almost feel Slonimi, but—not quite. Did the Slonimi make you? Breed you like a horse, the way they do?"

The edges of Judah's vision began to go white. That word. *Slonimi.* The magus had said he was Slonimi. He'd said she was, too. She could remember him as clearly as if he stood in front of her, a gaunt man with blond hair falling out of his queue. Weeping. Holding a knife out to her. *His blood. Your blood. Break what his ancestors did.* He and his great Unbinding, the thing that he was convinced she had to kill Gavin to accomplish. But he was also convinced that the purple web of Work in the tower wouldn't let her die and so she'd chosen to take her chances with jumping, instead. The white band around her vision was growing wider. She felt sick.

"No," Sevedra said. "The Slonimi keep tight rein on their people. They would never have let you fall in with the Morgeni or that talks-too-much Northerner." He moved his hand to the back of her head, gripping her by the short curls there. "Tell me where you're from."

Unbidden, the city spread out before her mind's eye, spires and smokestacks and banners and drums. The word forced its way out of her. "Highfall," she said.

"Nonsense. Highfall is in the east, all the way on the other side of the Barriers. And you're no Highfaller. Not with this hair." His grip on her hair tightened, and he shook her head slightly. "How did you get here?"

"Fell," she said. Because fallen, she had. When she jumped from the tower. She was west of the Barriers, now? Really? Everything she knew was to the east. The tower hadn't let her die, but why had it sent her so far away?

"Yes, Highfall. I heard you the first time," he said, a bit impatiently. "Give me your hand." Of its own accord, her hand floated up to his waiting one. He let go of her hair to take it, but she still couldn't move. He took a knife out of his belt. It looked like the same one he'd used to cut the bread earlier. "Now, be quiet. Let's see what you've brought me."

He cut a line down the length of her forearm with the knife, right across her perfect, unscarred arm. She wanted to scream but he'd said *quiet*. It was a shallow cut, he hadn't hit anything important, but the white began to creep back into her vision. The blood welled up from the cut and dripped down onto the earth; he squeezed her arm to make it flow faster and she felt as if somebody kicked the inside of her brain and then the white was everywhere. *She* was everywhere. She was standing in the broken tower with the magus and she was drinking Sevedran wine in the catacombs with Gavin and she was helping Darid mend tack and she was in the Ghostwood and she was in the underground vineyard, all at once. She was herself. She was the dead boy whose clothes she wore, grappling with somebody as a strong arm slid around her throat and a sweet herbal smell filled her nose. She was a dozen other people, voices and minds she didn't know. She was dying, not dying, dead, not dead. She *was*.

Then the white flared to purple, the same sickly, familiar purple of the Work that flowed through the tower. All of her selves collided with a jolt. Now she stood in a room, at a window, staring out onto a bleak, yellowed moor pocked with jagged rust-red rocks. The glass of the window was warped, hazy. Her hands felt strange and when she looked down she realized they were wrapped in thick bandages and then she realized they were not hers. She was in Gavin's body, the thick purple rope that bound them still protruding from his chest. It looked sickly. Not quite there.

Behind her, a woman said, *Gavin, I brought food*, and Judah's heart leapt because the woman was Elly. They were alive. They were alive.

They were *alive*.

But everything was alive. The purple was alive. She could feel it turning its attention toward her, seeking, pulling—a multitude—

She yanked herself away, back to the vineyard. She'd fallen forward, her hands sinking into the soft soil, and the soil was filled with multitudes, too. All the people the winemaker had killed, right here, so their blood could flow into his special, special vines. She could feel their lives in the vines, in the grapes themselves. She looked up at the winemaker. His hands were covered in blood.

"Bright gods," he said, the words hollow with shock. "Bright gods, what are you? You're like—you're like what the Slonimi wish they were, you're—" He seemed to lose the words. Then he grabbed her cut arm again. The blood was clotting but he shook it over the soil. "Give it to the grapes. Give it all to the grapes," he said, panting, almost moaning. The moan turned into a laugh that was half sob. "My precious darling, I'll keep you forever, what a vintage—what a vintage this will be—"

Suddenly, out of nowhere, a figure slammed into him from the side, a tangle of limbs and long ropes of hair. Down the winemaker went, landing with a grunt in the soft ground next to Judah. Lukash grabbed the old man's long hair in one hand, and grabbed for the bloody bread knife with the other. The old man howled and held it out of reach. "No!" he cried. "She's mine! She's mine!"

No. She wasn't.

Judah pivoted on one knee, spun around, and grabbed the old man's knife-holding fist. The drug he'd given her was screaming and protesting in her head but it couldn't hold her anymore. He wailed protest and insult as the three of them grappled in the near dark and the rich damp loam and the musty smell of ripening wine and the metallic smell of blood. Then the old man went down under her, and he still held the knife in his fist but Judah held the fist. She pushed the knife into his throat. His blood pulsed out, disappearing into the soil with hers, and the last clinging tendrils of the drug disintegrated.

Everything was quiet. Her chest heaved, her breath burning. Slowly, she stood up.

Lukash stared at the corpse on the ground, the knife protruding from its throat. "He drugged us. Are you all right?"

She nodded.

"You're from Highfall. I heard you say it."

She nodded again.

"I don't know where that is," he said, and she said, "Neither do I."

Upstairs, they shook Cleric awake. The healer managed to collect enough of his wits to boil them a batch of some foul stuff that cleared the last of the mist from their brains. He sniffed at the bottle of special restorative wine, and visibly shuddered.

"What is it?" Judah said, and he said, "It's evil, is what it is. Almost as bad as the godswill."

"And if you can find any more of it, you'll be bringing it with you," Lukash said.

"Oh, very much yes," Cleric said with a grin. Then the grin faded. "I should have known when I saw the herb garden. Some of those plants—" He shook his head. "People don't just *grow* those."

In one of the rooms in the basement, they found clothes and packs and staffs, knives and boots and bedrolls. All, they assumed, had belonged to the travelers the winemaker had killed. Lukash took gems and small coins—easy to carry, easy to spend. Cleric found the old man's apothecary chest and ransacked it, transferring everything he wanted into sacks and vials from the winemaker's own supply. Judah—who was distracted by a sore lip; she must have taken a blow from the winemaker without realizing it—found a satchel very like the one Cleric carried, a better bedroll, a few coins. She considered switching the dead boy's clothes for others, but something felt wrong about leaving him alone here.

When they had combed the house from top to bottom, and taken everything they could carry that could possibly be of use, they made a pile of old cloth and kindling from the woodpile and doused the whole thing with tallow. Lukash set the fire with his tinderbox, and they left. The smell of smoke followed them into the trees.

"That wine," Cleric mourned. "That sublime, sublime wine."

Judah said nothing. In her head, she remembered standing at the strange window, in that awkward comfortable place where Gavin had always been, all her life; standing at the window, and looking out over a bleak, dead moor. Hearing Elly's voice. *Gavin, I brought food.* Over and over she heard her, and her heart hurt, and there was nothing to do about it. The Slonimi wanted her, and they wanted Gavin dead. She had felt them, in the purple. Watching. Waiting. Looking for her, looking for both of them. If she reached out to Gavin again, they would find her.

Gavin and Elly were alive. Judah was alone.

THREE

ELEANOR—FORMERLY ELEANOR OF TIERNAN, ONCE
the almost-Lady of Highfall, and now merely herself—had
been brought to the guildhall from Highfall with Gavin in a
closed carriage. The trip had taken three days. She had no idea
where they were; she knew it was a bleak place, with great
red boulders jutting from a sea of tall winter-faded grass, and
she suspected there had been murders there before she and
Gavin had arrived. A long pile of soil outside had the look of
a poorly dug mass grave and there were pools of dried blood
in some of the empty rooms. Whatever vocation the guild
members had followed, their hall was thoroughly ransacked.
Like the House had been, after the Seneschal's coup—but
the House had been home, especially after the coup, and the
guildhall was a prison.

After the long, hardscrabble months alone in the House,
they now had a staff of six, which should have seemed luxurious. But four of those six were the same members of the

Seneschal's guard who had spirited them out of Highfall in the dead of night. The other two were a kitchen boy who stole food from their very plates, and a skittering, hooting old woman, her tongue long since cut out, who watched them constantly with glittering eyes to make sure Gavin's perfect, uninjured hands stayed bandaged.

All of Gavin was perfect and uninjured. The Seneschal had ordered Gavin's hands bound before they left Highfall so that he couldn't scratch Judah a message in his own flesh, knowing that wherever she was, she would feel the pain and see the marks of it. For the same reason, he was allowed to experience no discomfort whatsoever. The room where they slept was kept neither warm nor cold but exactly comfortable. They were fed often and copiously, if not luxuriously. Gavin was permitted to walk in the halls, the tongueless old woman like a shadow behind them, but not to train, or run. All of these conditions were enforced by the guards. Early on, Gavin had refused food and the nearest guard had immediately turned and punched Elly in the jaw. She'd lost a few seconds and been bruised for two weeks. Gavin had never defied the guards again.

Wake up each day and figure out how to survive. That was her grandmother's maxim, and Elly felt like she'd been living by it her entire life. She had been sent to Highfall and betrothed to Gavin when she was only eight years old; Elban and the Seneschal had wanted a biddable girl with few political ties, Elly's father had wanted her bride price, and her mother had wanted to see her safe away from her brothers. He'd never touched her but old Elban was as bad in his way as her brothers Angen or Eduard had been, and still she had survived. She had agreed to marry Elban instead of Gavin when it meant saving Theron's life. She had arranged for Darid, the head stableman, to flee the House when it meant saving Judah's heart. She had kept them all alive after the coup, digging through the midden heap for squash sprouted from discarded seeds and convincing the Seneschal to give them oats. She had set the Safe Passage on fire when the Seneschal and his men were coming through it, knowing full well they would burn alive. (One of the burned guards was at the guildhall now, his scars pink and new. She'd expected him to be nasty to her, but he acknowledged her existence little more than he would have a chicken he'd been charged with keeping.)

All of these things, she had done. All of these things, she would do again. But she hated the guildhall. She hated the life they lived. She hated the bandages on Gavin's hands and she hated the way the old woman cackled when the bandages were removed so Gavin could wash. She hated cutting his food for him and she hated buttoning his shirts and she hated the way he let her. Proud Gavin, vain Gavin. Who didn't care, anymore, if tea spilled on his sleeve because his bandaged grip was unsteady, if his hair fell in his eyes because he couldn't push it back. She had tried braiding it in a queue once but had taken it out almost immediately. Better for it to fall than for her to look at him and be reminded of the House Magus, Nathaniel, the lying traitor who'd been their friend until he hadn't been. The last time she'd seen him, he was being dragged out of the House ahead of them. She wondered, sometimes, where he was now. She hoped it was somewhere unpleasant.

More often, she wondered where Judah was. Gavin said Theron was dead, that the magus claimed to have killed him, but if that was true then how had Theron found her at the Safe Passage to give her the fire-making device, and how had he helped her up the tower stairs afterward? No, the lying traitor had lied again. Theron wasn't dead. Theron was extremely clever, knew the abandoned halls of the old wing better than anyone living, and had managed to secret himself away where the Seneschal couldn't find him. Judah, though—Gavin said Judah had jumped from the broken place in the room on top of the tower. The Seneschal's men had searched the overgrown light well beneath the tower, but they hadn't found her body. So perhaps the magus had drugged Gavin, to make him think Judah had jumped. Perhaps she had friends Elly didn't know about who'd helped her. Elly hadn't known about the stableman, after all, and everything she thought she'd known about Judah's relationship with the courtier Firo had turned out to be wrong. All she knew for sure was Judah could never have survived that fall. And therefore she could never have jumped.

(*Tell Elly I'm sorry.* That was what Gavin told her Judah had said, before she'd jumped. Elly didn't know what Judah was sorry for, and the idea that Judah had sent her, specifically, a message, and she hadn't understood it, haunted her.)

On top of everything else, Gavin was still alive, wasn't he? He wouldn't be, if Judah was dead. Any injury Judah suffered, Gavin suffered, and vice versa. Nobody could explain it, but it had been that way all their lives. They shared hunger, cold, thirst, pain—even pleasure, when they got older. (Which had made Elly uncomfortable, during the weeks when she and Gavin had shared a bed in the more traditional sense than they did currently, and was that what Judah had been sorry for?) The bond was why cruel Elban allowed Judah to live with them, all these years—why he'd let Judah live at all, if Elly was honest with herself—and now it was the reason behind their infuriatingly comfortable living circumstances. Because the Seneschal didn't think Judah was dead, either. He thought that if Judah stopped feeling anything from Gavin she would be driven out into the open to find him. Elly didn't think the plan would work; Judah was pretty damned determined when she wanted to be.

But it was certainly having an effect on Gavin. There was

a dead look in Gavin's eyes, now, as if part of him had been severed. Elly could sympathize with that. She felt as if the most interesting parts of herself had been snatched away, too. She didn't have Theron's quiet genius and she didn't have Judah's acerbic perception and she didn't have Gavin's charm (neither did he, at this point). She missed them. She missed everything about them. Was that what Judah was sorry for, for leaving Elly on her own? Was it for fleeing to the tower in the first place? Or was it a general *I'm sorry*, an acknowledgment that nothing was currently good, and nothing had been good for a long time, and probably nothing would ever be good again?

It didn't matter. But Elly still wondered.

All of the windows in the guildhall were glass, and none of them opened. Elly wasn't allowed outside—she hadn't felt fresh air in months—but she was allowed to go down to the empty, dirty kitchen to fetch their food. She didn't know who cooked the food but sometimes it was better than others. Today it was soup, with the bones of the fowl they'd had a few days before floating in it. Tomorrow the soup would be gone and they would probably have nothing but bread and waxy, tasteless cheese. When they'd been under house arrest in Highfall, they'd lived on boiled oats and midden heap squashes, so almost anything else was an improvement. One of the guards had left with a cart for supplies two days before; there would be new meat when he returned. Elly found a wooden tray and filled it with rough-milled dry bread, a pitcher of water, and two bowls of soup. She eyed the door to the kitchen garden, as she always did, but didn't try it. Not yet.

Back in their room, Gavin was staring out the window where she'd left him. There was little else for him to do. There were no books in the guildhall, and with his bandaged hands, he couldn't hold a pen to draw or write. Not that Gavin had been much interested in books, or drawing, or writing. Elly was the one who'd drawn, and Judah the one who'd read, and Theron the one who'd written: pages and pages of notes in his tidy, precise hand, documenting all of his devices and experiments and notions. Gavin had trained with the army. Gavin had caroused with the courtiers. Now Gavin did nothing. "Gavin," Elly said. "I brought food."

As always, the old woman glared at them from her seat in the corner, flint-eyed and sour, as Elly carefully unwrapped the bandage that held Gavin's thumb to the rest of his hand. This one concession they had negotiated, as long as the old woman was there to watch. The thumb was still bandaged, the hand was still bandaged, there was no way for him to scratch a symbol into his skin with a thumbnail the way he and Judah had used to do, to send messages to each other. But he could at least hold a spoon and feed himself. "Thanks, El," he said, sliding a clumsy spoonful into his mouth. "Tasteless as usual, Betsy."

He'd named the tongueless old woman Betsy after the last nursemaid they'd had back in Highfall, who had also been tongueless and scowled at them from corners. Gavin had grown tired of her and put her outside in the corridor when they were sixteen. He couldn't do that with this one. Elly wondered, again, why the old woman had lost her tongue. When Elban had ordered somebody muted, it had usually been more for security reasons than punitive ones. She was sure he'd had the original Betsy's tongue removed so that she couldn't tell anybody of the bond between Gavin and Judah. But who had ordered this Betsy's tongue destroyed, and why, and what would become of her when there were no more secrets to keep?

"Aren't you going to eat, Elly?" Gavin said. Elly picked up her spoon.

Something crashed, downstairs.

Gavin's hand froze. The Betsy was frowning, lips pressed tight and uncertain. Another crash came, then shouts. "What is it?" Elly whispered.

A spark of life lit Gavin's eyes for the first time in months. "A raid, maybe," he said, under his breath. The Betsy glared at him. Then she stood and, with considerable briskness for such an old woman, crossed to the door and locked it with a long key. The new-looking lock had keyholes on both sides. They were all locked in.

"Who would be raiding us?" Elly said, even though she knew it could be anybody. A rival guild. A courtier who wanted the guildhall. Common thieves.

"Not the Seneschal's people. That's all that matters," Gavin said.

Rape hadn't occurred to him, because why would it? He wasn't a woman. Elly looked out the window but saw nothing. Meanwhile, the crashes and shouts grew closer. "Elly," Gavin said, abruptly—but it was too late. The Betsy's arm twisted around Elly from behind. She felt something sharp against her throat. A knife. The Betsy made a tuneless hissing noise that they had learned meant *quiet*, so close to Elly's ear that it hurt. Then she leaned over, pulling Elly with her, and blew out the lamp.

By the light of the full moon, Elly saw Gavin raise his bandaged hands. "Put the knife down, Betsy. You don't need to hurt Elly."

Unmoved, the Betsy pressed the blade more firmly against Elly's throat. Elly's eye fell on the steaming soup on the wooden tray, just out of reach.

There was the sound of fumbling at the lock and one of the guards burst through the door. "What do we do?" he cried, as if Elly or Gavin would know. His helmet was off, there was blood spattered on his cheek, and his eye was swelling. He looked incredibly young. No older than Theron. "It's a raid, what do we do? Do we kill them?"

Yes, idiot, kill the raiders, Elly thought, but then she realized that the boy wasn't talking about the raiders. The Betsy hissed again but the pressure of the knife at Elly's throat eased. Enough for her to grab the bowl of soup and slam it, hot liquid and all, into the Betsy's face. The terrified-looking guard shouted as Gavin, who had spent years training with his father's army in Highfall, leapt on him. Elly heard a strangled cry.

But she didn't watch, because she had her own problems. She and the old woman were scrabbling in the soup on the floor for the knife. Their wet, oily hands reached it at the same time. Elly could feel the old woman's fingers under hers, slick as a fish. They grappled for the weapon and it was almost funny, except it wasn't. "Quit fighting me," Elly said, desperate. "I don't want to hurt you."

The Betsy only hissed, her hard old fingers prying away at Elly's. Elly had been strong once, back in the house arrest days. She wasn't so strong anymore and the wiry fingers wrested hers away from the knife. The pressure of release sent it wild. Elly felt an icy heat against her left cheek, and then pain came, and she knew she'd been cut. The Betsy crowed and came for her, bloody knife held aloft, but by then Elly had the tray, and was shielding her body with it. She could hear thumps and thuds behind her right shoulder as Gavin fought the guard. The Betsy pushed against the tray with all her might. Elly pulled it away and stepped to the side. As the Betsy stumbled past Elly she slammed the tray into the back of the woman's head, where the sparse hair was lank and gray. Elly hated the noise of the tray impacting the too-visible skull but the old woman wouldn't stay down, so Elly hit her again, and this time the woman's thin skin split open, and it was awful.

Then Gavin was there, holding the guard's knife in his thumb-freed hand. His bandages were soaked with blood, but Elly didn't think it was his. "Grab her hair," he said, and Elly wanted to say *wait no* but this was not a time for *wait no*, so she grabbed the Betsy's thin hair and pulled her head up. Quickly, efficiently, Gavin slit her throat. Elly recoiled and leapt away from the spreading puddle of blood, letting go of the old woman's head. It made a wet, hollow sound on the stone floor and Elly hated that noise, too.

But there was no time. Quickly she turned to Gavin, who had already stuffed the knife in his belt and was holding out his hands. As fast as she could, she unwrapped the sodden bandages. "Your cheek," he said.

"It's fine," she said, as the wrappings fell to the bloody, soupy floor. Gavin flexed his fingers. "Now what?"

"Now," he said, "we leave."

They ran through the halls, Elly in the lead. She knew the guildhall better than he did. The sounds of fighting drifted up the main stairs, grunts and clangs and cries of pain. "Another way," Gavin gasped, and she led him to the back stairs instead. At the bottom, the kitchen was deserted, soup still steaming away on the stove. Gavin pushed ahead of her, which would have been annoying if he hadn't had the knife. She wished she'd grabbed the one the Betsy had cut her with. Gavin kicked at the locked back door, the old hinges gave way, and Elly's cheeks were hit with a blast of cold air, fresh and clean as new snow. As they plunged through the open door, the lonely, deserted moor seemed so wide and limitless that Elly almost wept at the freedom of it. Even as the muck sucked at her feet, and even as she wondered desperately where they would go, how they would survive.

Find a way, her grandmother said, in her head.

Then some huge dark thing knocked Gavin to the ground,

and some other huge dark thing picked Elly up bodily and held her in the air. Kicking and fighting, she was carried back into the hateful guildhall, through the kitchen and into the dining room. She could hear a clamor behind her, Gavin swearing and grunting. Elly glimpsed the body of one of the Seneschal's men, who'd been nearly decapitated, and also that of the kitchen boy. That was unpleasant. He'd been a sly little weasel of a child, but he'd still been a child.

Then they were in the front hall, where the guildmaster would have met visitors. The man holding her let her feet touch the ground but didn't release his grip. She was pleased to see that it took two men to hold Gavin back, even after all the months of inactivity. His lip was bleeding, but he was alive, he was conscious. The hall was brightly lit, hot with torch-light and black-clad bodies. The better to disappear into the moor, Elly thought, bitterly. Together Elly and Gavin were pushed forward, toward the center of the knot of men, where a tall hooded figure stood.

"Lord!" the man holding Elly said, and the tall figure glanced up. Elly saw his face and her heart fell through a hole in the center of her.

No. No, no, no.

"Norrie," the hooded man said. "You're hurt." He lifted a gloved hand toward Elly, as if to touch her.

"Who are you?" Gavin said, in an imperious, cutting tone Elly hadn't heard from him in a long time.

The man pushed back his hood, revealing thinning hair and a face Elly knew all too well. "My name is Eduard," he said. "Second Lord of Tiernan. It's good to finally meet you, Lord Gavin. Thank you for taking care of my sister."

FOUR

THE DINNER SHIFT AT NEW HIGHFALL PRISON WAS over. The glutton of a warden had eaten nearly everything on his tray when Bindy picked it up. Normally that was bad news, because Bindy divided his leftovers with Clem the cook to take home, but today she was glad of it. She didn't want to carry food around, not with what she had to do after cleanup was done. Her stomach felt queasy and a tiny muscle at the corner of her eye wouldn't stop twitching, no matter how many times she pressed against it with the heel of her hand.

Still, as she entered the kitchen and put the tray down on the big worktable, she managed to hum a little, the way she usually did. "Left the apple, at least," Clem said, when she saw the empty plates. "You want it, Bin?"

"All yours," Bindy said, and Clem slid the apple into her apron pocket. Then she went back to mixing chalk into the dough for the prisoners' bread. Bindy washed and dried the things from the tray. Her fingers trembled in the suds. When the last plate was dried and put away, she wiped her hands on her own apron and drew a bucket of water from the tap. "Going down to the cells," she said, pleased to hear that the words sounded normal. "Have a good night, Clem."

"You, too," Clem said, without looking up from her dough.

Bindy was careful on her way down the stairs. The steps were slick and today of all days, she couldn't afford to fall. Her fingers coiled around the tiny vial in her pocket. At the bottom of the stairs, she said hello to Bruno, the day guard, who liked her because she kept him in headache poultices. He poked through her bag but didn't think to check her pockets. "Did he eat?" she asked him, as he walked her down to the magus's cell. She always asked if he ate.

"Not much," Bruno said. "That boy's lucky he's got you."

"He's a good man. And so are you, Bruno."

Bruno smiled. "Bring me another poultice tomorrow, will you?" She nodded. Then they were at the magus's cell. The guard told her to call when she was done. Bindy swallowed the bile that rose in her throat.

The only light in the cell came from a single spike of purplish Wilmerian gas, and it took a moment before her eyes adjusted enough to see the huddled shape in the corner. "Hello, magus," she said. "It's Bindy."

The shape didn't move. He never did, at first. She put down the bucket, knelt next to him on the clammy floor, and lit a small lantern she'd brought in her bag. By its warmer, brighter light, she could see him more clearly. A well-defined line between golden and dark marked the point in his long hair when he'd been imprisoned and stopped bleaching his hair. His face was thin and smudged with dirt, his eyes vacant.

He bore little resemblance to the man she'd met for the first time in the alley behind his manor. Her baby brother Canty's head felt strange, and Alva had suggested she try the magus everyone was talking about who took care of poor people in a Porterfield alley. That was Nate. He'd been apprenticed to the old House Magus, then, and she'd liked him instantly: his soft voice, his kind intelligence, the gentle way he'd felt Canty's skull. Sun-starvation, he'd said, and told her how to cure it. A few weeks later he'd offered her a job.

When the old House Magus died, and Nate was made the new House Magus, he'd asked Bindy to be his apprentice even though women in Highfall weren't healers. One day he went to the House and never came back. Weeks, it had taken her to find him, and weeks more to get the job in the kitchen and get in to see him. He'd been in awful shape: dirty, lice-ridden, and starving, with a cough that scared her and that vacant look in his eyes. He wasn't aware enough to eat, most of the time. She didn't know why he'd been imprisoned, or what had happened to him during those lost weeks, but she knew that he was her friend, and she could not leave him to rot away in that cell.

So she'd combed out the lice and made a thick syrup for the cough like he'd taught her, back when he was himself. She'd brought him clean clothes, a warm blanket, decent food. He looked slightly better now, but his eyes were still distant and his face slack. Every time she visited, she hoped against hope that this was the time he'd look at her with his used-to-be eyes, bright and aware and so very kind. Even today, when there was little point, she hoped that, but he was still dirty and distant with a thread of drool dangling from his chin. His cough was worse, which only stiffened her resolve. If he spent much longer in this prison, he would die.

Normally, she would have wiped his face, combed his hair, and switched his filthy shirt for a clean one. Today, none of that mattered. She took the vial from her pocket. "I met a friend of yours, magus," she said, putting an arm around him to pull him upright. "His name is Saba. He says he knew you from home—

your home. He gave me this for you. It's going to help you. We're going to get you out of here." Carefully, she uncorked the tiny vial and tilted the magus's head back on his limp neck. His mouth fell open and oh, how she hated to see him like this. Her magus, her friend. She didn't know if she trusted Saba—there was something like the magus about him, but there was also something entirely unlike him—but his plan represented the first thread of hope she'd had in ages. So she tipped the liquid into the magus's mouth, gently pressed his chin up so his lips closed, and held him that way until she saw him swallow.

She didn't know what she expected. Something dramatic. A gasp, or a shudder. But the magus simply closed his eyes and went limp against her side, like his flame had been snuffed out. His head lolled on her shoulder. She turned, slightly, to touch his throat, right where the vein should have been pulsing, and the shift in position was enough to overbalance him. He toppled over onto the floor. Like there were no muscles in him at all. Like he was dead.

He would look dead, Saba had warned her. That was the point. But she hadn't expected him to look this dead. His mouth was slack, his back buckled at an uncomfortable angle. She had expected him to look sick-dead, or unconscious-dead. But he looked *dead*-dead.

"Bruno!" she cried, and she didn't have to fake her horror. "Bruno, come quick!"

Ten minutes later, Bruno and the captain on duty, whose name Bindy didn't know, stood over the magus, who lay exactly where he'd crumpled on the floor. Bruno shook his head. "I'm sorry, Bin."

"It's a hard place," the captain said, not unkindly. "Bruno, fetch us a shroud, will you? If you were his friend, girl, maybe you want to sew him into it."

Bindy, weeping, nodded. She stayed with the magus while Bruno brought the shroud, which turned out to be nothing but a long, coarse-woven piece of cloth. The guard helped her lay the magus out on it. He was so light, it took barely any effort.

"Not much to him, is there?" Bruno said, and Bindy said, "He was always slender."

Bruno had brought waxed twine and a needle. Bindy sewed the shroud closed down the whole length of the magus's body with big, clumsy stitches, and everything that made the magus himself disappeared behind the rough, anonymous cloth. Bruno told her to leave the top open, for the weights, and she did. When she was done, he said, "I'll take him to the chute. You don't want to see that."

But Bindy thrust out her chin and said that she most certainly did want to see that, so Bruno sighed, slung the long white package over one shoulder, and set off down the hall. The magus's cell had been below the river's waterline so they had to go up more than one narrow flight of stairs to get to the chute. When they finally reached it—a mere hole in the wall, with an oiled leather flap to keep out the rain—Bruno dropped the magus's body to the floor as gently as he could. Then he knelt next to a pile of broken bricks beneath the chute, and picked one up.

"I'll do that," Bindy said, quickly. "You get the latch." She picked up a brick and pulled open the gap she'd left in the magus's shroud. But when Bruno turned to the latch, she quickly dropped the stone into her satchel. By the time he looked back, she was adjusting the shroud around the magus's body, as if replacing it where it had been disturbed. The open hatch let in a breath of Brake-fetid air. The light outside was gray. The sun was going down.

"Ready?" Bruno said.

She nodded.

He hefted the body up off the floor. "Still barely weighs anything, even with the stones," he said, and slid the magus, feet first, through the hatch. The rough fabric of the shroud made a rushing sound on the brick sill of the chute. Then there was a silence, and a splash, and it was over. Bruno put a hand on Bindy's shoulder. "I'm sorry, Bindy. You took good care of him, you did."

Bindy put her hands over her face and wept.

Bruno told Clem what had happened, and Clem told the boatman, and so he was terribly quiet and kind as he rowed Bindy across the Brake. She kept her eyes down, watching the puddle of dirty water in the bottom of the rowboat wash back and forth with every stroke. She didn't trust herself to look anywhere else. As the boatman helped her up onto the dock, he said, "Your brother here?"

He'd better not be, or she'd hit him with the brick in her bag. "Not today," she said. Then—trudging, mournful—she headed down the embankment, walking as slowly as she possibly could, until she heard the soft slap of the oars on the water as the boatman rowed back to the prison. Then she dared a glance over her shoulder, and ran. As fast as she could, her full focus on the uneven surface of the embankment so that she wouldn't trip over any of the random pieces of debris and broken stonework that appeared in the mist. The sun was nearly set now but she caught the thin notes of a mandolin and coarse singing from the eel hall, and knew where she was. When she came to a place where the embankment had crumbled away and an abandoned wooden crane emerged from the mist like a giant spider, she finally stopped. She could still hear the music behind her, faintly, as well as the even fainter street noises from the main avenue and the soft slosh of water against the embankment. Her chest heaved and her heart pounded. She could run no farther. All she could do was wait.

Wait she did, for five minutes or fifty. For an eternity. When she heard once more the unmistakable sound of oar in oarlock, the gentle plash of wooden blades in the water, she tried to hold back, but she couldn't. "Darid?" she called, in a loud whisper. If one could whisper loudly.

"Quiet," a voice said. But it was Darid's voice, and a moment later he came into view. Bindy scrambled forward and—yes, in the gunwale of the boat was a long, dirty-white bundle. The magus. Her magus.

"Is he breathing?" she said, as Darid pulled the boat up and stood, carefully, to lift the still-shrouded magus onto the embankment. "Is he still alive?" Because what if the magus had landed facedown in the water? What if he'd drowned before Darid could retrieve him? What if it had all been for nothing and he really was dead?

"I think so." Darid hoisted himself up onto the embankment. Bindy was already pulling at the sodden shroud she'd sewn not an hour before, wriggling a hand through her terrible loose stitches, fingers finding the magus's chilled nose, stubbly chin, throat. The pulse was fluttery, quiet. But it was there.

"He's alive," she said. "We need to get him inside and warm, quick."

Darid had stashed a barrow nearby, filled with rags and broken boxes and old factory committee bulletins. He dumped the scrap onto the ground. Then into the barrow the magus went, and back on top of him, as gently as possible, went the trash. Bindy hated that, but maybe at least it would be warm. Then Darid picked up the long handles of the barrow and with a mild expression that Bindy suspected he'd honed during his years inside the Wall, began to make his way back toward the main avenue, just as if he didn't have an escaped prisoner who was supposed to be dead hidden inside his cart. Walking next to him, Bindy was jittery and so nervous she wanted to scream. But she kept her face, too, blank and inoffensive.

Please, magus, she begged silently in her mind. Please don't be dead.

They made their excruciatingly sluggish way through Brakeside, weaving back and forth across the border between Paper and Tannery. The air in Tannery—or anywhere near Tannery—reeked of all sorts of things Bindy didn't like to think about, but because Tannery was filled with lots of small workshops instead of one big factory that flooded the streets with people at shift change, the streets were quieter there than in Paper. Also Tannery was full of derelict warehouses, including the one where Darid lived. That was where they were taking the magus. In a narrow alley, Darid paused. Looked around. Then, unceremoniously, dumped the cart's contents onto the broken cobbles, magus included. The debris on top of him joined the debris on the street. The magus's body rolled against a wall.

"Oh, grab him!" Bindy said, but Darid already had. A filth-strewn staircase led down from the surface of the street to an ill-fitting door, and then into the warehouse itself.

In a dramatic contrast to the deserted alley outside, the warehouse practically vibrated with life. The cavernous interior had been carved up in every possible way, a crazed web of scavenged material that reached up into the very rafters and made the attaches built out over the street in the rest of the city look stable and safe. Lots of people lived here; when Bindy looked up she could see the twinkling of lantern flames as far as she could see. None of the residents would bother them. Like most places where people were forced to live with no privacy, the warehouse dwellers had learned to close their eyes and ears to what didn't concern them.

Darid carried the magus down a long corridor, over a rickety footbridge where the warehouse's original floor had rotted away, and around a corner to another corridor. The walls of the passage were pieces of fabric sewn together or planks torn from shipping containers or other buildings. What little light there was in the corridors leaked through the places where the improvised materials didn't quite meet. The hall was filled with smells of tobacco and bodies and cheap, starchy food. They could hear quiet conversations hidden away but saw nobody.

Nobody, that is, except Saba, who stood, blazing with impatience, at an opening halfway down on the left. "Finally," he said, when he saw them, and stepped back to allow them into Darid's room. Usually the small tidy chamber smelled like cinnamon tea, but when Bindy had left it that morning, it had smelled like Saba's floral cologne and, underneath that, the sour scent of the powder he'd boiled into the potion for the magus. Now it smelled like Brake water, too, from the magus's shroud. Before Darid had even dropped him to the floor, Bindy had pulled a pair of scissors from her pocket and was cutting away the shroud stitches. Saba was doing the same with a knife, at the magus's feet, and the two of them soon had the sodden shroud peeled away like a fruit rind. Inside it, the magus was filthy, bits of muck and river sludge sticking to his ghost-white skin. He looked dead. Bindy knew he wasn't, but her eyes filled with tears anyway. She took a cloth and began to wipe the magus's face clean, as she'd done so many times before.

"Forget that." Saba was cutting away the magus's shirt. The magus's arms were thin, and lined with narrow, neat scars. Bindy had seen the scars before, when the magus had still lived in the manor, but had mostly forgotten them in the darkness of the cell. Now they stood out like bright white lines, and Bindy was horrified to see that Saba was using the same knife he'd used to open the filthy shroud—dear gods, had he even cleaned it first?—to add yet another scar to the row, another wound to that flesh they'd done so much to save.

"No!" she cried, and grabbed for the knife.

Saba pulled it back. "Stupid girl. Do you think I'd go through all this to kill him?" he said, angrily, and Bindy recoiled at his sudden harsh tone.

Darid stopped the man's hand with his own enormous one. "Our magi stopped bleeding people twenty years ago," he said, coldly. "And watch your tone with my sister."

"Your magi are only slightly better than the Elenesians, and the Elenesians are butchers. Anyway, I'm not bleeding him." Saba shook Darid off and made a small cut on the heel of his thumb. There was a small mirror Bindy had never seen before waiting on the table, and as the Dovetails watched, horrified, Saba smeared the shining surface with first his blood, then the magus's. Then, with the tip of his little finger, he drew a mark of some kind in the mixed blood, and another on top of it. The first mark was all curves, the second straight lines and sharp angles. Something about both of them made Bindy feel like she was watching something she shouldn't be.

Saba's fingers stilled. His eyes grew faraway. Bindy felt Darid at her shoulder. "Do you know what he's doing?" he whispered.

Bindy shook her head. Saba's brow furrowed. The magus made a small noise and Bindy's heart leapt. Then, as if a tether was cut loose, Saba's eyes opened. The magus jerked once, twice—and then his eyes flew open, too, staring wildly around the room, as if nothing he saw made sense to him. His eyes slid over Darid and moved to Bindy, where they stopped. For a moment she could scarcely breathe. He was seeing her. For the first time in months, he was *seeing* her.

She took a step forward. "Magus," she said, barely able to speak.

But his gaze had already moved on, pulled as if dragged to

Saba. As the two men stared at each other Bindy felt like all of the air had been sucked out of the room. Then Saba said, "Well, Nathaniel Clare," and the magus licked his lips and, with some effort, said, "Yes."

It was the first word Bindy had heard him speak in months. She fell on her magus, weeping, throwing her arms around him and not caring one bit that he smelled of prison and Brake water and blood and filth.

She felt one of his arms go around her, tentative and insubstantial. "It's okay, Bindy," he said, and that was tentative, too, as if he had to figure out words again. And for all she knew, he did. "I'm okay."

She pulled back. "Are you?" she said, staring at him. "Are you, really, magus?"

He managed a smile. It was a wan smile, but it was his. "I don't think I'm a magus anymore, Bindy," he said. "You should probably call me Nate."

Later that night, after Bindy left for home and Darid went with her to make sure she got there safely, Nate washed himself as well as he could. Noticing, as if from a great distance, his wasted muscles and protruding ribs. When his hair fell in front of his face he could see the distinct line between blond and copper, where he'd stopped bleaching it.

Saba noticed, too. "Your hair looks absurd. Sit on the stool and I'll cut it."

So Nate sat on the stableman's stool, and Saba cut his hair. At least then he couldn't see Saba's eyes. They were cold eyes, dark. Like a snake's eyes. It was Saba himself, not the color, that made them cold. Judah's eyes had been just as dark, and Nate had found them beautiful.

But the thought of Judah brought with it a wave of feelings that were too complicated for him to process, rage and grief and frustration and shame, so he pushed those thoughts away. He thought instead about Bindy. He didn't remember much about his time in prison, but he remembered Bindy telling him about the potion, as warm and cheerful as always. He could have made such a potion in six different ways. He didn't know which one had been used for the potion Bindy had brought him, but he didn't think Saba had made it. Because to make things from plants you had to—maybe not love plants, but understand them. To heal you had to understand living things, to care for them.

And from the moment that Saba had broken through the fog in Nate's mind, his unfamiliar sigil burning like a brand in the unfeeling darkness, he had known that Saba didn't care about living things. Nate's teacher Derie had been fierce and determined and terrifying, but he had never felt anything like the harshness with which Saba had dragged him back to awareness in the Work. He had found himself standing in a scrub desert, all low bushes and dust. Night. Nate knew this desert. He knew there should have been a grand sweep of stars overhead, but Saba was not a man to notice the stars and so they weren't in his memory. Nate was not a strong enough Worker to make him see them.

A caravan stood a few feet away, its once-bright paint worn and peeling, but there was no horse, and no people. That was wrong, too. A small fire gave off a flickering light but no warmth. *Nathaniel Clare*, Saba said. *Time to get back to work.*

Who are you?

I'm the one who's going to make you get back to work. You're a failure and a coward, but you're linked to the Daughter of Maia, and we need you.

The Daughter of Maia. Judah. *No*, Nate had said. *My mother is dead and Charles is dead and Derie is dead and Judah is gone and I don't want to do this anymore. I don't want to be this anymore.*

Saba had only laughed. Then—and this was something Nate had never seen in the Work before, never even imagined— the man's ugly sigil unwound into a long, barbed chain. Nate watched, paralyzed, as the sigil drew back like a snake about to strike. There was a moment of pause, of gathering. Focus radiated from the stranger like static.

Suddenly the sigil-chain struck, driving itself straight through the center of Nate. The pain was searing, agonizing. Nate dropped to his knees, gasping.

You don't have any choice, my idiot friend, Saba said. *Have you figured out what I am yet?*

The barbed chain trembled inside Nate, the slightest quiver torture. Somehow, he managed to say, *You're a compeller.*

Different people used the Work in different ways. Some, like Nate's mother, Caterina, used it to heal. Others used it to send information over great distances, or to find lost objects. Compellers, though, were rare. Most people with the necessary talent preferred to become mediators, joining two peoples' minds to heal misunderstandings and animosity between them, but a few—a very few, possessed of a particular indifference of heart—used it to control others, whether they would be controlled or not. No regular Worker would willingly join in Work with a compeller, so those who made compelling their life's work had to accept the loss of the network of minds on which most Slonimi Workers relied for knowledge, power, and communication. Nate himself had lost that connection when everyone he loved in the Work had died, and the loss had driven him deep inside himself. He couldn't imagine choosing that pain voluntarily.

A compeller's work is ugly, but necessary, Caterina had told him, years ago. *Sometimes there's no other choice.*

Sitting in the stableman's tiny warehouse room as locks of his own hair fell to the floor around him, Nate knew that he, too, had no choice. The feeling of Saba's fingers in his hair, on the back of his neck, was unpleasantly intimate. With each touch he felt the unraveled chain of Saba's sigil inside him, barbed and ugly, lying in wait to hurt him. "We'll get you some new clothes tomorrow," Saba said, when the haircut was finally done. "I'll give you a day to get your strength back before we start. You should eat."

Some of the Warehousers survived by cooking humble meals for their neighbors. Before she left, Bindy had dashed to the nearest and come back with a bowl of beans, with some sort of meat and something green stirred into it. The bowl sat on Darid's table now, white streaks of fat congealing on top of it as it cooled. "Before we start what?" Nate said, feeling like he was speaking a foreign language.

"Finding the Daughter of Maia. Since you were incompetent enough to lose her."

"I didn't lose her," Nate said. "She's gone. She jumped from the top of the tower. I felt it. It's why I was—why—my mother—" The barbed chain inside Nate flexed and pain shot through his body. With a strangled half cry, he found himself on his knees, bent nearly double.

Saba looked bored. "From all reports, your mother was a wonderful healer and her death was a huge tragedy for the caravans, but honestly, I don't care. And the girl isn't gone. She jumped, but she never hit the ground. The power bound up in the tower saved her."

"By draining my mother's life," Nate said, and the pain shot through him again. He cried out.

"Stop that noise." Saba sounded bored. Nate felt his jaws slam shut, the big muscles at their corners tensing, his vocal cords stiff with stress. The noise stopped. The pain continued. The corners of his vision turned white, then gray.

Then, abruptly, the agony was gone. Saba sighed. "Look,

I hate this city. I don't want to be here. So let's get this done as efficiently as possible, shall we? Take a day, eat a few decent meals, and breathe some fresh air if there is any, and then we'll dig into that memory of yours and find the girl. I'll do all the thinking. You don't have to do anything but obey." The compeller gave Nate a stern look. "I do insist on obedience. Understood?"

Nate wanted to object. Thinking of Judah brought up a loathsome collection of memories that he did not want to confront. He had watched his best friend kill himself, doing nothing to stop Charles as he opened his veins at Nate's own kitchen table. He had killed Elban's younger son, Theron, in cold blood. He had cared for Judah and he had hurt her anyway: he had let her believe Darid was dead when he knew differently, he had let her believe he was helping her when he knew differently. He had lost his mother, his health, his freedom, his decency. He had given them all to the Unbinding, and it was all for nothing, because this terrifying compeller was right. He had failed. He remembered waking in Elban's study with the Seneschal, and he remembered sliding back into darkness, glad and relieved and hoping he would never emerge. He did not want to be the person he had become. He was ashamed and angry and miserable and tired, so very tired.

But, as Caterina had said, sometimes there was no other choice. "Understood," he said.

"Good," Saba said. "Now eat."

Nathaniel Clare ate, and wished he were dead.

When Bindy returned the next morning, she found Nate sitting by himself in Darid's chair, wearing clean clothes. His hair had been cut close to his head, so that both the blond hair she'd known him with and the queue that marked him as a magus were gone. He looked exhausted, but he smiled when he saw her. "Hi, Bin," he said, and he sounded so much like her old magus—weak, sad, but himself—that she wanted to hug him.

She didn't. "Where's Saba?" she said.

"Out taking care of some things."

"Is he really your friend, magus?" she said.

"Nate," he said. "Please, Bindy. Nate."

There was a funny feeling in her throat, like she might cry. "Nate," she said, and remembered the night he'd told her his name. She'd laughed, even though it was the night of the coup and nobody felt like laughing; she'd told him that it sounded like it belonged to a little boy with a slingshot, and he'd laughed, too, and said he'd once been a little boy with a slingshot. "Is Saba really your friend?" she said again, and the words tumbled out of her in a shambling pile. "He said he was, and he could get you out of prison. He did get you out, but—is he your friend? Is it okay that I did what he told me?"

He was silent for a moment. Then he said, "You didn't do anything wrong, Bindy."

That sounded to her like a sidestep. The funny feeling got sharper. "I was afraid you were going to die," she said. "You would barely eat. You didn't even know who I was. I got that job at the prison so I could take care of you, and I did the best I could, but—when he came, I didn't feel like I had a choice, magus, I really didn't." Then, belatedly, "Nate." She almost spat the last word at him, and even as she did it she wasn't sure why she was so—angry wasn't the word, not exactly. But she really had done the best she could, and it had been difficult, and she could not escape the bitter feeling that it hadn't been enough. Meanwhile, the magus stared at her as if she weren't speaking Highfaller plain as plain, as if nothing she said made any sense.

"Why would you do all of that for me?" he said, barely audible.

Her chin went up. "Why did you help Canty, and all those other people in Marketside? Because it needed to be done and there was nobody else to do it, that's why. And because who's going to help those people when you're dead or rotting in that prison. And because you're my friend."

That made him wince, for some reason. He reached out a hand to her, and she took it. "I don't deserve you, Belinda Dovetail," he said. "And you don't deserve me. You deserve far better."

"I disagree," she said.

He smiled. It was nothing but a shadow of his old smile, but it was a smile, nonetheless. "I'm not surprised." His grip on her hand tightened. "Bindy—you did all of that for me. If I ask, will you do one thing more?"

"Anything," she said, and then thought better of it. "Well, almost anything."

She saw his throat move as he swallowed. "You're right. Saba isn't my friend. And he isn't yours. Don't trust him. I'm bound to him, for reasons that are complicated to explain, but—" He faltered, then seemed to gather strength. "Nothing would make me happier than if you walked out that door and never came back."

Walk out. Of her own brother's room. After all those long months. She hadn't expected thanks; she hadn't expected him to be grateful—not to her, anyway. For his freedom, maybe. His life. But her spine, her arms, her fingers, her legs were all charged with a hot, prickly feeling. If she'd been a year younger, she would have stamped her foot. "We're friends," she said, finally. "And you don't walk away from a friend and never come back. I don't. And I won't."

Nate gave her a long look. She wished she knew what was

happening in his head, now, what it was that kept him so carefully blank. What he didn't want her to see. "I really don't deserve you, Bindy," he finally said.

"Tough," she said.

F I V E

THE SENESCHAL TOOK KORSA STRAIGHT FROM THE prison to what appeared to be a fairly prosperous Highfall lodging house, where he was allowed to bathe and given plain clothes in the Highfaller style. When he looked in the room's reflecting glass he was shocked to discover that he still looked much the same as he had before prison—maybe with a few more lines around his eyes, but that didn't matter. The Seneschal gave him back his earrings, which helped. He found himself missing the green kohl he'd always favored. Which seemed ridiculous, given the circumstances.

He was fed again, and allowed to sleep for the night in a clean bed. In the morning came yet another meal, and strong tea. As he finished, the Seneschal returned and from there, they went straight to the orphan hall so that Korsa could choose the children to use for the Seneschal's experimental *kagirh*. And if Korsa had thought he could not feel worse than he had sitting in that dank hole in New Highfall Prison, away from sun and *kagirh* and waiting to die, he learned his error then. Room after room they walked through, and each room full of beds, and each bed assigned to a child with nowhere else to live—a concept that Korsa still found perplexing, that a child could be uncared for in this huge city full of adults perfectly capable of caring for them. Most such children, the Seneschal explained, were sent to work in trades or factories, and lived with their masters or in the factory barracks. The only ones remaining in the orphan house were those deemed unsuitable for work, either by deficit or disposition. They would be more than suitable for Korsa's purposes, the Seneschal assured him, and said, "I'm sure they will be relieved to be able to finally contribute something to their city."

And, no doubt, relieved to be out of the orphan house, which was grim and filthy and nearly as dark, in its central rooms, as Korsa's cell. The smell of the place brought bile up in his throat. He swallowed it and thought once again about how utterly bereft a people had to be, to accept a place like this. When the orphan mistress, a worn-looking woman with tired eyes, asked how old a child they were looking for, the Seneschal had looked to Korsa, who had still been too stunned to speak. "How about our thirteen-fourteens?" the mistress suggested. "That's a nice middling age."

Korsa had entered *kagirh* at twelve. "Fine," he said, but when they reached the ward, the thirteen-fourteens looked impossibly young. Thin arms and thin legs sticking out of thin smocks—except for one girl, who had no legs at all—with thin faces above them, wary and stiff. The Seneschal told him to choose three of the girls, and then they would go to the boys' ward and choose three boys. Korsa had intended to choose the ones who seemed the worst off, but the more he walked up and down the cramped aisles between the beds, the more he realized that there were no worst-off. This place was dire. Everyone in it was at risk. So he chose almost at random—making sure he selected the girl with the missing legs—and then, in the second terrible room, he chose at random again. The chosen six were brought downstairs, where a wagon waited for them. One of the boys saw the wagon and immediately began screaming. Nobody—including Korsa—tried to reassure the boy. Nobody said a word to him. The Seneschal merely waved a hand, and the boy was taken back into the orphan house.

"Five will do, won't it?" the Seneschal said, as he and Korsa entered their carriage again. Korsa, too stunned to speak, nodded.

The coachman had a bell that worked with a pedal, to warn people in the street of the carriage's approach, and the sound of it was harsh and piercing. It was the second time Korsa had been pulled through the streets of this city, although the first time he had been in a cage. He still remembered the agony in his shoulders as the cobbles jostled the cage and the cage jostled the chains that held his arms over his head. He still remembered the sick despair of being without his *kagirh*, how frantically he had tried to reach into the place where they should be.

When the carriage stopped at the massive Wall surrounding Elban's palace, a deep rumble filled the air. Korsa remembered that noise, too. It was the sound of the gate in the massive Wall opening. Beyond it, instead of being dragged out of his cage in chains, he stepped down from the carriage and crossed the courtyard under his own power. Walking up the grand staircase, his Highfall boots clipping merrily against the marble, he felt dazed, almost drunk with the dislocation of it all. The Seneschal led him down a narrow corridor and up a narrow staircase and through a dozen other turns and switchbacks, the smocked thirteen-fourteens herded behind them by guards.

Finally the Seneschal stopped at a door, opened it, and gestured Korsa and the thirteen-fourteens through. The room on the other side was large and sunny, with a bank of windows along one wall and marks on the wooden floor where furniture had once stood. Evenly spaced holes in the wall looked like they'd supported cupboards or shelves. Whatever the room's previous life had been, only the sink in the corner remained of it. The sink itself looked old, but the pipes looked new. Also new were the six cots that filled the room. One more than they needed, because of the boy who had refused to come. Korsa hoped he had not been punished.

"There's an anteroom off to the side, there," the Seneschal said. "You should have plenty of space. Food will be served in the room across the hall, and next to that you'll find a bathing room. Farther down this corridor is a staircase that leads outside. Feel free to have a look around the grounds. I would suggest that you keep the children to the agricultural areas."

"They are not children," Korsa said. "And they will need real clothes."

The thirteen-fourteens had each found their way to a bed, except for one girl who had drifted to the window. The Seneschal looked at them. "I suppose so. I'll have things delivered. We'll talk more after you're settled."

With that, he left, and Korsa was alone with the thirteen-fourteens. Five pairs of eyes—well, four, since the drifting girl was still at the window—stared at him. He stared back with his one pair of eyes and wished, neither for the first time nor the last, that his *kagirh* was here. Kind Meita would soothe the young peoples' souls, charming Faolaru would make them laugh. Unfortunately, all they had was Korsa, and he did not know how to talk to them. He would be a poor teacher. Even if he managed to form them into a *kagirh*, he would not be able to teach them to live in one.

One of the boys stood up. He was tall and handsome and

bore no immediate defect. "The man said something about food," he said, clear and strong.

"Yes," Korsa said, "go," and stepped back as the five of them rushed out of the room, the girl from the window pulled along by the others and the legless girl moving as quickly on her hands as the rest did on their feet. He followed, and found himself in a smaller, windowless room, where a large table was laid with bread, cheese, bowls of cooked vegetables, and some round yellow grain. Simple food, and cheap. The thirteen-fourteens were as excited as if it had been a feast. And didn't he know what that was like? Hadn't he had his own feast the day before, as simple as this one and just as welcome? Watching from the doorway as they eagerly filled wooden bowls, he realized that while there might be no making a *kagirh* here—in this dead place, out of this ragtag group of mistreated adolescents—he could feed them, and keep them warm and safe. That was worth something, at least.

Suddenly the handsome boy dropped his wooden bowl with a clatter, spilling grain and cooked carrots across the floor. His arms and legs went tense and rigid, his head canted back and to the side at an awkward angle. A high, stifled noise came out of his throat, and then his body went after his lunch, dropping heavily to the floor. His back arced. One of his legs kicked out, repeatedly.

Korsa, alarmed, had no idea what to do. But the thirteen-fourteens did. The window girl, who apparently didn't speak, kept eating as if nothing had happened, but the legless girl swung herself down to the floor and calmly rolled the handsome boy onto his side. The other boy, whose legs hung stiffly from his hips and who used crutches to walk, now used one of them to push the seizing boy's chair out of the reach of his kicking leg, and then clambered awkwardly down to the floor next to him and began to clear away the spilled food.

The remaining girl—who also used crutches, although she seemed to have more control over her legs than the boy did—squinted up at Korsa. "Is there something soft we can put under his head?"

"There were pillows in the other room," the legless girl said. "On the beds."

"I'll get one," Korsa said, and, heart pounding, did.

The boy who'd had the seizure was named Liam. He had them several times a day, the others told Korsa, some worse than others. By the time he'd come out of it, the bowl of food the others had put aside for him was no longer hot. Korsa tried to learn the others' names, and some identifying thing about them other than their differences. The legless girl, who had freckles and curly hair that constantly escaped her braids, was Ida. The boy on crutches was Jesse, who had a round face and a voracious appetite; the girl on crutches was Anna, who went around the room every morning and made everybody else's beds whether they wanted it or not. The window girl, Florence, never spoke or looked directly at anyone. By the end of the first day she had amassed a collection of small objects—a cherrystone, two buttons, an empty wooden spool—that she arranged and rearranged, and never let out of her hands.

He learned their names by asking, directly. None of the thirteen-fourteens volunteered any information about themselves or each other. When he was in the small antechamber—which, with another bed and a desk, became his sleeping and work room—he heard them talking and even laughing, but the moment he arrived they all went still and silent. He told them his name, but they didn't use it. Nor did they ask him any questions about himself, or about why they had been taken from the orphan house. He knew enough to understand that they were all waiting for the next thing to happen but he did not know how to tell them that there was no next thing, that he had no idea how to join their minds into a *kagirh* so there was only this, until the Seneschal grew bored of the entire project and sent them all back where they'd come from.

On the second day, by the time they sat down to the bread and butter and jam that was their breakfast (Jesse cut the butter into slices and nibbled it like cheese), the thirteen-fourteens were all dressed in clothes the Seneschal had brought—plain but serviceable, like those he'd given to Korsa—and combed or brushed where they needed to be. Without any intervention at all from him they distributed plates and cups of water, and made sure the food was shared around equally. The way they cooperated with and tended to each other was impressive, but it wasn't *kagirh*. The more he watched them, so very Highfall and so very not Nali, the idea of forming any kind of *kagirh* with them seemed even more ludicrous than ever. They were pleasant to be around; he liked watching Anna move from bed to bed, folding up the covers and arranging the pillows, and he liked watching silent Florence lay out her tiny collection of bits in patterns that made no sense to anyone but her. He liked the way Liam seemed to have appointed himself their leader, silently positioning his own body protectively between Korsa and the others. He liked the deft way Jesse used his crutches as extensions of his hands, and he liked the way Ida laughed. He liked all of them. But they were not a *kagirh*.

The second day passed. Liam had another seizure, this one smaller, and Florence's collection grew by two more buttons and a thimble. Korsa grew restless, and remembered what the Seneschal had said about the grounds. After so many months in prison, the idea of being able to merely stand up and walk out of the room felt like it belonged to another life. "I am going outside," he said, to the room at large, and waited to see what would happen. None of the thirteen-fourteens looked at him.

But it was the kind of not-looking that was its own kind of awareness. They, too, were waiting to see what would happen.

Frustrated, uncertain, Korsa went outside. At least he knew how to get to the courtyard. Raghri the pragmatist, Meita the kind, Faolaru the charming, and Giorsa the farseeing; and Korsa himself, the tactician, the rememberer. He'd never been lost in his life. The Seneschal had said to continue down the corridor, but Korsa didn't want to see what the gray man wanted him to see. Halfway to the great front hall he heard footsteps behind him, turned, and saw Florence following ten paces behind him. "Hello," he said, surprised.

Florence said nothing. She had stopped where she stood. Her blue eyes stared fixedly at something that apparently lay over Korsa's right shoulder and a very long way away. Only her hands moved as she passed her collection of buttons and oddments from one hand to the other.

"Are you coming for a walk with me?" Korsa said.

Florence said nothing. One of the girls had braided her hair for her that morning, but it was already falling out, and the plain dress the Seneschal had sent had cobwebs trailing from its hem. He wondered where they'd come from. "Well, it will be nice to have the company," he said to her. Then he turned and continued on.

The girl trailed behind him the whole way. When they stepped outside, the sun was shining and Korsa watched as Florence turned toward the warmth and light. The courtyard was empty, save for some crates and barrels tucked into a corner. "It is good to be outside," he said, because he was thinking it. "Which way shall we go?"

Florence said nothing.

"This way, then," Korsa said.

So they went, passing one abandoned building after another. The dusty bowl they crossed seemed to have once been a training ground, with stables and pasture nearby for horses and an outbuilding with nooks where one might store equipment. Florence stayed ten paces behind Korsa. They saw nobody. By the time they returned to the workroom, lunch had been laid out. Korsa asked who brought it.

"A girl," Ida said, tearing apart a piece of bread.

The next day Korsa announced again his intention to go outside, and once again, Florence followed. Slightly closer this time. They found orchards on that day, leaves bare so early in the year. On the other side of a high stone arch in a brick wall, the cramped fruit trees were replaced by wild trees, and the cultivated rows by unruly natural growth. Squirrels ran up and down the trunks of the trees and in one place they stepped over a pile of deer scat. And yet, Korsa could still feel the great Wall surrounding the forest.

"It's strange to see an entire forest walled in like this," he said to Florence. Florence said nothing.

Every day, he went out exploring the grounds. Every day, Florence followed. The girl who brought the food told him how to get to the kitchen gardens; from the gardens, they explored the outside of the House, which seemed to be the working parts of the grounds. Most of the buildings were identifiable by smell—the brewery, the piggery, the sheepfold—but all of the men working there looked the same. They wore gray smocks not unlike those the thirteen-fourteens had worn in the orphan house. All of the men seemed tightly focused on their work and Korsa understood why, because every group of workers was watched over by an armed guard on horseback. They passed fields, oats and rye and hops, and in these, too, gray-smocked men worked under guard. Finally they came upon a few low buildings with a wood-fenced corral outside one of them, and in the center of the corral was a gallows, and hanging from the gallows was a body that had been dead for several weeks. Crows perched on the crossbar of the gallows. The hands and features were gone.

"Don't look, Florence," Korsa said, surprised by the sudden protectiveness he felt for his silent companion. But Florence was already looking, placid in her unending equanimity.

When they returned, Liam was sitting on the floor with Jesse and Anna, teaching them to write their names. Ida was nearby, pretending not to pay attention. He should ask for books for them, Korsa thought, still dazed by the body on the gallows, and wondered if he should tell them not to go outside. But they would want to know why. They would ask questions that he did not want to answer. Or maybe they wouldn't ask, because they already knew the answers—and that disturbed him, too.

Still, the next day, still thinking about the corpse, he managed to make it outside without Florence following. Finally, he followed the Seneschal's directions, down the corridor and the stairs, and found himself on the other side of a small, nearly hidden door. He could see the stable buildings and the gallows in the distance, and chose a path leading in the other direction. Straight toward the great Wall itself, as it turned out, and then along its base: bare dirt, grassless from the passage of generations of feet, and screened from the rest of the grounds by tall overgrown hedgerows. He didn't care where he went. He was depressed by the hanging body, by the downtrodden smocked men, by their bored guards. He had merely traded one prison for another, and brought five others along with him. The hedgerow fell away and the path curled back toward the house. He passed a patch of land that had been burnt, and tried to be cheered by the veil of bright green new growth over the black char. But all he could think of was the fire. He wondered what had stood on the burned place, and who had set fire to it.

Then he came to a gate that hung askew from broken hinges in a stone wall. Since it was open he walked through it into a wild, overgrown garden. Silent Giorsa had been the one in his *kagirh* who understood plants, and would have been very interested in this strange outdoor room. For a while Korsa lost himself in memories of his four lost *kagirhi*: Raghri and Giorsa, Faolaru and Meita. Where were they now? Did they mourn his absence as he mourned theirs, the emptiness like a missing tooth where he should be? Did they think of him in this dead place, where a rock felt the same as a tree and a tree felt the same as a gallows with a corpse hanging from it?

You are lost, Korsa, Raghri said in his head. *You are gone from us.*

The despair threatened to overwhelm him. When he found another door he pushed that one open, too.

And found himself on a wide green lawn, beautifully manicured and unlike anything else he had seen behind the Wall. A wide marble path beckoned, but it wasn't long before it dove in between two well-trimmed hedges. The hedges had been trained to form tiny plazas and nooks, some with fountains and some with benches and some with graceful arbors where trailing vines hung like curtains. He could hear laughter, high and merry and (perhaps) a bit drunken. An ecstatic wail. Those noises, this place, were so unlike the labor that happened on the other side of the walled garden that he found himself curious and wary at the same time.

He was trying to decide if he wanted to investigate the sounds more than he wanted to flee them when he turned into another of the small plazas, and came upon a woman. Her hair was white-blond, her eyes blue and thickly surrounded with lash blackener. Her round cheeks were an artificial pink. And while he didn't have much experience with Highfall clothing, her clothes were the strangest he'd ever seen. Instead of sleeves, and despite the spring chill in the air, the dress was held up by two bands of wide lace over her shoulders. What should have been the neckline was so low that he could see the tops of her nipples. The hem fell to her ankles in the back, but the front was cut high above her knees to reveal bright high-heeled shoes and green-and-yellow-striped stockings that looked to be made of silk. She had one leg hiked up onto a bench so she could adjust the garter that held the stocking up. Her painted lips were set in a scowl.

All this Korsa saw in a moment, before she sensed him, and looked up. He saw the way she put on a pleasant, coquettish mask as her head moved up, and also the way that mask fell away when she realized he wasn't who she'd expected. Her brow furrowed; she looked him up and down, taking in the plain clothes he wore, the tattoos on the backs of his hands, and his black hair. The guards had shaved it when he'd entered the prison but it was long enough now to tuck behind his ears. "You're strange-looking," she said, in a broad High-fall accent. "Where are you from, then?"

He was silent. He had not had enough contact with the people of Highfall to know their opinion of the Nali. The prison guards had called him barbarian but they had called the other prisoners unpleasant things, too. Idiot. Ugly. Maybe barbarian was as nonsensical as those words were. Or maybe it wasn't, and this woman would attack him or scream for help. Finally, he said, "Far away."

She laughed. Sort of. At least, she made a sound, sort of rough and bitter. "Bet you wish you'd never left there. Did you come through the walled garden?"

He nodded, extremely confused. She assumed (incorrectly) that his confusion was geographical, because she put down her leg and said, "Don't feel bad. This place was built to be confusing. Come on, now. I'll lead you back."

"Back," he said, and she said, "To the work side. That's where you came from, isn't it?"

She didn't wait for him to answer, but let her absurd skirt fall and walked briskly by him in a cloud of sickly-sweet perfume, down the path he'd come. He caught up with her. "What is this place, if it is not the work side?" he said.

"The House of Repose," she said, dry and sarcastic. "Where the wealthy of Highfall take a break from their arduous lives of being incredibly shitfuck rich. The best of food and drink and the most obliging of company."

He finally understood. "That's you. The obliging company."

"At your service." She gave him a sidelong look. "Although maybe not. You don't look quite the part, Mr. Far Away. Now, there you go. Across the lawn, there."

"Thank you," he said.

"Don't come back here," she said.

That afternoon, the Seneschal came. He stood in a corner and watched the thirteen-fourteens for what seemed to Korsa an unreasonably long time. They clearly remembered the scarred man in gray from the day they'd arrived, and were cautious. Korsa could feel their awareness. They were like rabbits in a field, waiting for attack—except for Florence, who was arranging her buttons.

Finally, the Seneschal looked at Korsa and indicated the corridor outside with a tilt of his head. "You asked for books," he said, when they were alone. "Can they read, then?"

"Liam can. He's been teaching some of the others."

"Is that wise?"

Why would it not be? Instead of answering the Seneschal's question, Korsa asked one of his own, and was *that* wise? "Seneschal, where have you brought me?"

"The House. It used to be Elban's palace," the Seneschal said. "Specifically, your room was the weaving shop. Now it's a place where you may conduct your experiments in peace. I trust you are, in fact, conducting your experiments."

Korsa chose to ignore that. "And the workers in the fields and the women in the gardens—are they conducting experiments, too?"

The Seneschal stared at him, and then shook his head with a faint smile. "I did say you had the run of the place, didn't I? Well, Korsa, the factory managers who run this city work very hard. They supported me when my men and I took the city. They are used to thinking of the House as a paradise, a place where anything can happen, and they feel that they deserve a reward, a privilege. The men you saw in the fields are people who had a difficult time adapting to life in New Highfall, and could not stay there, so instead they came here, where all of this land merely waited for someone to work it. And as for the women—" He shrugged. "Everyone needs a purpose, do they not? Theirs is not a purpose that everyone would like, but it is a purpose, nonetheless."

"Are they free to go when they please?"

"They are bound here for a certain length of time," the Seneschal said. "Both the entertainers and the laborers. Why do you care?"

"Because," Korsa said, "I want to know what kind of place this is." He looked up and down the corridor, with its scuffed floors and narrow, dirty windows. "*Kagirh* needs—" He had trouble finding the words, in this ugly language, and so spread his fingers wide and then brought his hands together, as if gathering up all of the everything. "I cannot do it in a poisonous place. I cannot do it in a dead place."

"And is this house a poisonous, dead place?" There was something dangerous in the Seneschal's tone.

"Yes," Korsa said.

"That's troublesome."

"I did not say I wouldn't try," Korsa said. He heard his own bitterness and remembered the way the woman in the garden had laughed. "I am sure my prison cell waits for me."

"You're fortunate that it does," the Seneschal said. "There are no beds waiting in the orphan house for your young charges."

Korsa stared at him. "What?"

"Didn't I just say that everyone in Highfall needs a purpose? If the children were suited to factory work they would have been hired already, and they're obviously no good to me in the fields." He looked thoughtful, as if something had occurred to him. "We could always find work for them in the House of Repose."

Repulsion filled Korsa. "You would not," he said, the words merely a breath.

"I will not have to," the Seneschal said, "because you will fulfill *your* purpose. If you don't—" He shrugged. "Would you rather I put them out on the street to starve?"

Would he? At least on the street, the thirteen-fourteens might find somebody in this city who recognized them for what they were, and helped. Then again—he pictured Liam, lying in a dark alley with limbs tense and askew. Ida's strong arms wading through the muck he'd seen in the streets of Highfall. Florence—silent Florence, with eyes only for her buttons. "There is an herb called *kagirha*," he said, reluctantly. "We use it for the initial bonding, but I don't think it grows here."

"And this herb helps you—what's the phrase? See from the other side of the water?"

Somehow, Korsa kept from rolling his eyes. "An extremely poor translation. Rather, it lifts the mind."

"We have such substances here. I'll have some samples brought to you. Perhaps one of them will work." The Seneschal gave Korsa an appraising look. "It would be unfortunate if you were merely stalling. I hope you don't think I'll wait a lifetime for results."

Korsa held his ground. "Creating *kagirh* is not like lighting a candle or digging a privy. The process is very subtle, and it has never been tried with someone who is not Nali."

"You're Nali."

"Those in the room behind us are not. Obviously."

The Seneschal's gaze was steely, piercing. Korsa felt as if he were staring down a snake. You were not supposed to stare down snakes. You were supposed to look away, and let them slink off about their business. But this entire city was the Seneschal's business, and Korsa knew that even had he had the run of it, he could not have escaped him.

The next day, the Seneschal brought two vials and an assortment of dried herbs. "This herb is chewed," the Seneschal said, with clear distaste, as he touched one of the herbs. "The others are smoked, although this one can also be eaten. The vials are drunk in small quantities."

Korsa looked at the herbs first. He picked them up, smelled them, broke off tiny pieces to nibble, and put them back down. "None of those."

The gray man touched one of the vials. "This one is difficult to find. The other is very popular."

Korsa tipped a drop of the difficult-to-find liquid onto his finger, lifted it to his tongue, and recognized the bitter taste immediately. "This is not it. We have this, too. It comes from a desert plant." Then he picked up the other vial, and tasted its contents. His heart sank. It was not quite right—there were too many other ingredients added—but at its heart, he recognized the slippery, quicksilver feel of the *kagirha* fern on his tongue, and the faint aromatic bubble at the back of his throat. "What is this?"

"The people take it, copiously. They merely call it the drops. Will it work?"

Would it? This was not the gentle lifting of *kagirha*; this sensation was crude and blunt. Raw, unformed rock, when he needed a fine-honed knife. "It will need to be refined," Korsa said, with great reluctance.

"I'll send you more, then. Be careful, too much will render you a drooling idiot."

When the Seneschal was gone, Korsa went back into the main room. The thirteen-fourteens stopped talking immediately, as they always did, and he was conscious of their eyes on him as he crossed to his own small room.

"That looks like a drop vial," Liam said, coldly.

Even Florence was watching now. Korsa looked down at the dull metal vial and said, "That was what the Seneschal said it was called, yes."

Anna shook her head. "Drops are bad. My brother took drops. Made him a screaming lunatic."

"Best throw those right out the window," Ida said.

"Why do you have drops?" Liam said, a note of challenge in his voice. "What are you doing with them?"

The way they stared at him. None of them had asked, still, why they had been taken out of the orphan house and brought here. None of them had asked what they were to do. Even as he had marveled at this, it had filled Korsa with dread. Because he knew they would ask, eventually, and did not know what he would tell them. "I am going to use them for an experiment," he said, now.

"What experiment?" Ida said.

"It had better not be on us," Liam said.

The space of the converted workroom suddenly felt as alive with tension as *kagirh* ever had. "Wait," he said.

Then something small hit him painfully on the cheekbone and landed on the floor with a clatter. A button. He looked up in time to see Florence hurl another one at him. He turned his head, feeling foolish, but then Liam said, "Jesse, loan me a crutch?" Jesse passed him one. Liam shifted it in his hands so he was holding it like a club.

Korsa stopped feeling foolish. An icy battle calm came over him and he reminded himself that they were nearly children. "Give Jesse back his crutch," he said. "The drops are not for you."

"You trying to swipe our minds clean, so we'll work like beasts at whatever ghastly job they give us?" Liam took a single, menacing step, the crutch gripped tight in his hands.

Would the drops do that? No wonder the Seneschal allowed them. "I have not mistreated you," Korsa said. "I live in here with you, do I not? I am not free, any more than you are. But I am not in prison and you are not in the orphan house, so while we are here, we are all better off."

Liam's eyes narrowed. The crutch did not waver. "You were in prison?"

Korsa nodded. "It was a terrible place. I don't understand the place we took you from, but it seemed to me like it was also a terrible place. Was it?"

"I've been in worse," Jesse said, glumly.

That was unpleasant to think about. "But now we are in the same place, and there is sun and fresh air," Korsa said. Then, more gently: "I am a fighter, Liam. I was taken in the war, but I was not taken easily. Six of Elban's men, it took, and I stopped counting after that so there might have been more. That crutch will do no good against me, and Jesse needs it to walk. I don't want to break it."

Liam's mouth fell open despite himself. "Six of Elban's soldiers?" he said, at the same time that Jesse said, "You fought against Elban's army?" They sounded awestruck. Boys hearing about battle often did, even Nali boys, because they knew nothing about it.

"He attacked my home," Korsa said.

"Wait," Anna said. She sounded scared. "I knew you weren't from Highfall, but—you're Nali? You're the Nali prisoner?"

"I am," Korsa said, wearily. "Liam, are we going to fight, or not?"

Liam stared for a moment, his mouth working. "I suppose not," he said, and handed the crutch back to Jesse.

"The Nali are magicians," Ida said. "Demon worshippers."

Korsa shook his head. "No."

"Show us your tattoos," Jesse said. "I heard the Nali prisoner's arms were all up and down tattoos."

Korsa put the vial down on the desk and rolled up his sleeves. The thirteen-fourteens crowded around, as well as they were able. Even Florence came closer. And they were so exactly a crowd of young people seeing something new that Korsa would have smiled, except that Liam's eyes were still wary, his body tense.

"What do they mean?" Ida said, staring down at the black lines of ink, some crisp and some blurred with age.

"Not necessarily anything. This—" Korsa pointed to a flower below his left elbow "—was the favorite flower of a girl I loved, when I was very young. This leaf...there was a raid on a village, and many of the survivors wear this. This bird, I just liked." He grinned, remembering the day he'd seen the bird, flying over a softly waving plain on a perfect day. Then the grin faded, and he touched the fir tree that grew down his right arm, ending in a soft point on the back of his hand. "This is the symbol of my *kagirh*."

"What is a *kagirh*?" Liam pronounced the word perfectly.

"A group of people who join together to live and work, for their whole lives." He was grateful that they were keeping to simple questions, the kind he could answer. If they asked what the Seneschal wanted of them, things would become more difficult.

"Like a family?" Ida said.

Korsa shook his head. "We are born to our families. We choose our *kagirh*."

"I thought it was *a kagirh*," Liam said.

Korsa almost smiled, because Liam had gone from threatening him with a crutch to pinpointing his grammatical inconsistencies. "One is part of a *kagirh*. One is also in *kagirh* with one's *kagirh*, which is made up of one's *kagirhi*. It can also be an epithet: *kagirh*, you ask a lot of questions."

Ida giggled. Liam didn't. "What do you mean, join?" he said.

"In the mind," Korsa said. "A *kagirh* thinks as one, sees as one, acts as one. You are still yourself," he added, quickly, when Jesse frowned. "You know and control your own thoughts. But you know your *kagirhi*'s thoughts, as well. They are different, but the difference doesn't matter." He was explaining this so badly. He had never tried to explain it in words before. He had never known anybody who didn't understand. He drew a deep breath, and decided that it would be easier to simply tell the whole truth. "You are here because the Seneschal wants me to try and form *kagirh* with you. I will be honest. I don't know if I can do it. I don't know if I should. I have mostly decided that I will not even try. I only agreed because I was in prison. I did not want to live anymore, and I had no way to kill myself."

A few of them nodded. Florence had not drifted away;

who knew if she was listening or not? "What are the drops for, then?" Jesse said.

"My people harvest a fern that they brew into tea. It's called *kagirha*."

"Of course it is," Liam muttered.

Korsa smiled faintly. "We use it for the first joining. It loosens the mind, makes the connection possible. After the connection is formed, the tea is not needed anymore." He looked down at the vial he still held. "Somehow, there is *kagirha* in your drops."

"Drops are bad," Anna said, decisively.

"A knife can kill. It can also cut an apple from a tree." He gestured toward the vial on the table behind him. "Anyway, I am supposed to distill the *kaghira* from the drops. I don't even know if that's possible."

"But if it is possible," Ida said, "and if you do manage to make the tea, will you make us take it?"

"I will not make you do anything," Korsa said. "The nature of *kagirh* is that it will not work if you aren't willing."

"But if we don't take it, it's back to the orphan house for us," Ida said, resigned.

"Doubt it. They've filled our beds by now," Liam said.

"That is what the Seneschal said, yes," Korsa said, and the words sounded as heavy as he felt. "I do not know what will happen to you, then."

Silence fell over the small group. Finally, Anna said, "Well, what if it works?"

"Then you will be able to see through my eyes, and know what I know. We will not be able to lie to each other. We will know each other's hearts." He was surprised to feel the prickle of tears in the corners of his eyes.

"That's not what she meant," Ida said, and Korsa said, "I know it wasn't. I'm sorry. The Seneschal mostly seems interested in the communicative aspects of *kagirh*. But I don't know exactly what he has planned, if the binding works."

"Nothing good," Liam said, and Korsa nodded.

The silence returned. Finally, Anna said, "Florence can't agree. She doesn't talk."

"I don't have an answer for that," Korsa said. "But I will not try it on anyone without knowing that it is something they want. I'm sorry. I feel like I'm saying the same thing over and over, like a trained bird. I do not know, I do not know. I will try to take the best care I can of you while we are here."

"Provided you can keep the Seneschal happy," Liam said, and Korsa nodded.

"He calls you chieftain," Jesse said. "Is that the same as a chief?"

"I suppose. It is not entirely accurate."

"Do the Nali go naked and eat meat raw, Chief?" Ida said.

Korsa smiled. "We do not. Still, I imagine we do other things you would find strange, just as I find Highfall strange."

"What's the strangest thing you do?" Ida said, eagerly, at the same time that Liam said, "What's so strange about Highfall?"

To Ida: "Probably *kagirh*." To Liam: "You lot, for one."

Liam's lip curled. "Everyone in Nali born perfect, then, are they? Never get sick or hurt?"

Korsa spoke carefully. "Nobody is born perfect. Not in my home, and not here. But if a child is born, somebody always takes care of it."

"Even if it's not from their family?" Anna said.

"A child is a child," Korsa said.

Liam scoffed. "Not us. We're liabilities. We can't work. But we still need food." Liam looked around the circle of nodding heads. "I don't imagine there's one of us here whose parents could afford to keep us, even if they wanted to."

"Then the problem in Highfall is bigger than one child," Korsa said.

There was a long silence. Ida broke it, saying, "Did you have a *kagirh*?" and after that the questions came like midges at evening, so fast and quick he could barely focus on one before another buzzed in his ear. He told them everything he could, which felt like opening his own veins. Raghri and Giorsa, Faolaru and Meita. He had known Raghri and Giorsa since childhood, which is probably why he always named them first, but his memories of his first meetings with Faolaru and Meita shone like crystal in his mind. They'd laughed over that so many times, how Faolaru and Meita wished they'd met the others earlier, and Raghri, Korsa, and Giorsa wished for that lovely moment of meeting, for the sweet chime of recognition. But in truth they all had each other, and that blistering hot day by the lake when Korsa had first seen Faolaru held the same love as his earliest memory of crawling in the dirt with Raghri.

"Love," Liam said. "It's like being married?"

Not at all. Marriage was a different kind of bond. Chosen, yes, but tended and watched over like a sapling. More complicated, in some ways. A good many *kagirhi* married but his *kagirh* had decided they would not until the wars were over, because it did not seem fair to a spouse to leave them when you might die.

"Your *kagirh* is all men, then," Jesse said.

No to that, too, but Korsa had to think a moment to remember exactly which mind went with which body. The thirteen-fourteens found that funny, and so he explained to them that people were made of the bodies they inhabited, yes, but also of their minds and lives and experiences, and when those lives and experiences were shared for long enough the bodies began to matter less. This brought nods of agreement.

"It doesn't sound so bad," Anna said, and was he only imagining that she sounded a bit wistful? "You think you'll be able to make the stuff you need?"

Korsa lifted his hands, and dropped them again. "Who knows? My skill is memory. I can go anywhere I've ever been without a map, but I don't know about plants and elixirs. How I'll make *kaghira* from that—" he gestured to the vial "—is as great a mystery to me as to you."

They all stared at the vial. Korsa did not need *kagirh* to know they were thinking about how their lives all rested on his ability to make something useful of it.

"My da was a painter," Anna said finally. "I mean, he was mostly a drunk, but painting was his trade. He used to say, there was a solvent for everything—something that dissolves other things. Water, or oil, or alcohol."

"Is there one that dissolves giant stone walls?" Ida said. "Because if there was, we could get out of here," and they all laughed, the tension breaking a little. Not too much, but enough.

That night, after the thirteen-fourteens were asleep—mostly; Florence sat up in bed, arranging and rearranging her buttons on the surface of her cot—Korsa tried to enter *kagirh* once more. It was empty. It was dead. And for a moment he wished again that he had died in prison, but then he remembered the five young people in the other room, and felt a bleak surge of determination. Perhaps he would die in this place. Perhaps all the thirteen-fourteens would die, too. But they would not die without his trying to save them.

SIX

AS THEY HIKED AWAY FROM THE BURNING RUIN OF the winemaker's house, Cleric told Judah that her name was the botanical equivalent of being called Thorn Bush or Poison Oak. "Says the man who calls himself the guild equivalent of Smith," she said. Her lungs hurt from the smoke and her mouth tasted like godswill. "I know about the Judah vine. Parasitic. Tears down buildings. I've heard it all before."

"It grows in the north," he said. "Did you, as well?"

"Whose north? Your north? My north?"

"She's from a place called Highfall," Lukash said.

Cleric frowned. "But that's on the other side of the Barriers."

"So the winemaker said." Judah's brain could barely process that particular piece of information. How had she jumped from a tower and ended up on the other side of the continent? She had thought Elban's empire the whole world, but Cleric and Lukash had only vaguely heard of Highfall, and never heard of Elban at all. And she had never heard of this north where people who looked like Cleric lived, with his sharp features and dark hair, or the brown-skinned Morgeni who—according to Lukash—lived on mountaintops, dug gems out of the rock, and studied the stars. Then again, her education hadn't been a priority in Highfall. Maybe Elly and Gavin would know the places the two men came from.

Gavin, I brought food.

At least Elly and Gavin were alive. It was something, to know that, even if thinking of them caused her pain that was nearly physical. She didn't try to reach out to Gavin again, much as she wanted to. She had always known that the only reason she had been kept alive was to protect him, but on that last awful day in the tower, when poor mad Nathaniel Magus had begged her to actually kill Gavin and thus somehow complete what he called the Unbinding, she had realized that the only reason she existed at all was to hurt him. What a god-awful mess it all was, and she could see no way out of it, then or now. She could not forget the eerie feeling of staring through Gavin's eyes at the rust-colored rocks, of something—many somethings?—turning toward her. Whatever those things were, she wanted to avoid drawing their attention. She told herself that it was enough to know that he still existed, somewhere. A hard grace if ever there'd been one: to live herself, but with that part of her that lived in him cut away as if with one of those swords he was so fond of.

"Highfall," Cleric said, as if tasting the name, and made a face. "Terrible name for a city. Why would you put *fall* in your city's name? Doesn't that seem like asking for trouble?"

"Don't ask me," Judah said. "They named me Thorn Bush."

Cleric snorted. It was almost a laugh and she didn't take it as a criticism. "Well, regardless, I still think we should take you to Black Lake and let the guards figure out what to do with you. Wherever Highfall is, they're more likely to be able to get you there than we are."

He looked for confirmation at Lukash, who remained silent. "The winemaker said she was special," he finally said.

"Are you special, Thorn Bush?" Cleric said.

Judah chose not to respond.

Cleric shook his long hair back. "See? Nice enough girl, but she's not special."

"I'm not all that nice, either," she said.

"I wish you were prettier," he said. "It'd be easier to find someone to take you off our hands if you were prettier."

"Take me off your hands? What am I, a goat?" Now it was Lukash who snorted a laugh, but Judah was unamused. "Let's get to this Black Lake place and I'll take myself off your hands."

The woods thinned and vanished entirely. They began to pass other travelers, some on foot and some pulling carts behind them. A few were even on horseback. Those they passed had hair of all colors, skin of all colors. None gave them more than a single, cursory look. On either side of the road were broad green fields where workers crawled like ants. Each field came with a blue-uniformed man on horseback pacing its perimeter, looking bored and officious. Ahead of them lay the town of Black Lake, brown roofs barely peeking over the battlements. One towered building reached above the others into the sky. They couldn't see the lake anymore, but when the wind blew from the right direction Judah could smell it, damp and alive as a breath.

The gates in the town wall stood open, but staffed by guards in the same blue uniform as those in the field. The guards swiped the back of each of their hands with black ink. It didn't smear when Judah rubbed at it and left no mark on her other hand. "Two-day pass," the guard said in a clipped accent. "After that, the ink will fade and you'll be illegal. Nasty scar."

This last was to Cleric, whose rippled purple hand wouldn't absorb the ink properly. "I'm clumsy with fire," Cleric said, genially, and gave the guard his other hand to mark.

Through the gate, they found themselves in a wide square. In front of them and to their right were rows of neat wooden buildings. To the left was the lake, as dark as its name, extending as far as the eye could see with not even an island to break the vast smoothness. Looking at it made Judah feel nearly dizzy. A wooden ship was moored at the dock, along with other smaller, flatter vessels that were probably for fishing. As for the buildings, the tower she'd seen from outside the town turned out to be the central and tallest tower of a three-towered building, directly in front of them. The two smaller towers both appeared to be equipped with bells, and the huge doors leading into the building were at the top of what appeared to be a wooden version of a grand staircase. The other buildings on the square seemed to be shops and inns. It was all incredibly...tidy. Oppressively so, even. Judah could not remember ever walking the streets of Highfall, but she had the distinct impression that it wasn't like this. The wood-plank sidewalks looked freshly swept, and the buildings were neat and trim, all straight lines and obedient angles. The streets leading away from the square were broad and orderly. Even the carters calling to their donkeys did so quietly. There was a grass park in the middle of the square and not a tree to be seen anywhere.

"Let's find an inn," Lukash said. "I want some real food."

Cleric was staring across the square, his jaw clenched, at a large building painted white with a blue symbol over the door that looked to Judah like a weeping willow. A wide covered veranda stretched in front of the building, where a man in a drab-colored robe shuffled slowly with a broom. Another man, in a slightly finer-looking robe, stood nearby, holding a long pole and looking bored. When the sweeper reached the end of the veranda, he walked directly into the wall of the building that bordered it, continuing to sweep as if insensible. Then the man with the pole leaned over and used it to nudge the sweeper's shoulder until he turned back in the direction he'd come. The motion of his broom never stopped.

"Not here," Cleric said, cheerlessly. He turned down another street, away from the building marked with the blue willow.

In a slightly less tidy part of town—which is to say that there were fewer flowerpots—they found a round-shouldered jeweler who was more than happy to give them a small purse of coins in exchange for two of the jewels Lukash had taken from Sevedra. He also gave them directions to a nearby inn, where single figures sat perfectly still at the few occupied tables, each with some sort of bulbous apparatus in front of them. Despite the open windows, the air was heady with a fragrance that gathered in the back of Judah's throat and made her eyes water. As they came closer, Judah saw smoke twining up from one of the devices, and the smell grew stronger.

But the innkeeper—as round-shouldered as the jeweler, and at least his cousin if not his brother—could promise them food, and the room he showed them seemed more or less clean. It came with hot water down the hall, and that was all they needed to hear. The men told Judah to bathe first, because she smelled the worst. She didn't argue. The bathing room was small but the water was, indeed, hot, and it was lovely to settle into the beaten copper tub and feel all of the sweat and grime and smoke and godswill soak out of her. The tub wasn't long enough to stretch out in, but it was deep enough to let the heat penetrate the travel-sore muscles of her back and shoulders. There was a jar of thick soap, sweet and faintly gritty. She washed, then leaned back as well as she could, and for what felt like the first time since finding herself in the Ghostwood, relaxed. Closed her eyes.

In Highfall, the bathing rooms had deep, sunken pools, big enough for several people to share. The water there was infused with woody, aromatic herbs, eucalyptus and lavender and thyme. Here the water smelled like copper, with a faint living smell that Judah guessed was the lake. The rim of the bathtub was chilly against her back. She raised her arms and watched the water fall in a sheet off her skin, which was still perfect except for the cut the winemaker had made. She could still picture the curlicue scars that should have been there, one on each arm, their surfaces raised and shiny. Not rippled like Cleric's hand. Cleric had fallen into a fire; Elban had branded Judah's arms with a hot poker. She could still see his smile as he pressed the hot metal against her, still remembered the sound and smell of her own flesh searing. And on her back, where she'd been caned, she knew that when she reached over her shoulder she should have been able to feel a knotted lump where the lash had cut deep. That lump was gone now.

She remembered the pain so clearly. Losing the scars made her feel dislocated and slightly insane. Her eyes stung as strongly as if there had been aromatics in the lake water and she was afraid she was about to cry. She tried to concentrate on the heat of the water, the sting of it in the cut the winemaker had made. Abruptly, she laughed. Gavin had loved Sevedran wine. Everyone in the House had. After the coup he'd found a cache of it, deep beneath the aquifer, and one afternoon the two of them had snuck down to the crypts and got thoroughly, luxuriously drunk on the ledge that had been carved out of the living rock for Gavin's own coffin. And now she'd killed Sevedra. If there was any wine left in that cache, it would be worth a fortune.

Eventually, she climbed out of the tub and dried off. She'd grown used to the feeling of the boy who'd died in her road-filthy clothes but as she put them back on she felt him anew, just as she felt the dirt anew. Now she could sense the place he'd died, filled with the smells of rot and disuse and that sweet, herbal perfume, whatever it was. Back in the room, she stood at the window while the men took their turns. The air was warmer here than it had been in the mountains, but the breeze off the lake held a knife's edge of chill. There didn't seem to be any factories in this town; no fires burning in the distance, no spires, no wall but the wooden one—and that seemed tiny, almost playful, compared to the massive Wall around Elban's House. It was entirely unlike Highfall. She had never considered that somewhere so entirely different could exist in the world.

Finally, Lukash and Cleric returned, neither looking like the road-worn travelers she knew. Cleric's hair was neatly combed. Lukash's beard was trimmed, his ropes of hair bound back in a leather thong. With them came a drift of a sweet, herbal, horribly familiar aroma. Judah went still. "That smell," she said. "What is it?"

"Oil for his hair," Cleric said, nodding at Lukash. "The Morgeni are secretly a very vain people."

"You have clearly never been to Morgou," Lukash said, lightly. Judah said nothing about the smell, or the dead boy, because what could she have said? And she sensed a tension underneath their banter that had never been there in the Ghostwood. When they went downstairs to eat she saw the way both of the men's eyes darted around the room and realized that their tension was with Black Lake, not each other. The innkeeper gave them bowls of rice and greens, with rosy slices of fish and a dark, spicy sauce to pour over the top. Cleric ordered wine, Lukash ale. Judah asked for water—after her experience at the winemaker's, she wasn't interested in being drunk—but the innkeeper frowned and one of the men kicked her under the table. So instead, she asked for ale, and ignored it when it came.

"I hate lowlander towns," Cleric said, and poked at his rice. "What's the point of rice, anyway? It tastes like nothing."

"Fills a belly," Lukash said.

"It's better than those damn mushrooms," said Judah, who was actually enjoying the meal immensely. The fish she knew was dry and strong and oily. This was delicate and fresh. "What was that building in the town square, with the blue tree painted over the door and the man sweeping out front?"

"It's not a tree," Cleric said, grimly stabbing at a knot of greens. "It's a scourge."

"They don't have Elenesian Refuges in Highfall?" Lukash asked, and when she shook her head, he said, "They're healers."

"Among other things," Cleric said, "and the reason you don't have Elenesian Refuges in Highfall is because somebody who lived there was wise enough to banish them." He nodded at Lukash. "The Morgeni were the same way."

"The Morgeni have their own healers," Lukash said.

"Why would Highfall kick out a guild of healers?"

Cleric's mouth did something strange, as if he were both smiling and wincing at the same time and trying to suppress both. "Because they're also zealots. The Elenesians believe that the god Eleni sends us the life we're meant to have. If it's winter, we're meant to feel the cold. If it's raining, we're meant to be wet. If we catch fire, we're meant to burn."

"Is that what happened to your hand?" she said.

Cleric put his hand under the table and didn't answer. Lukash said, "The Elenesians run Refuges in nearly every town west of the Barriers, and many towns east of them. They're good healers, and they'll heal anyone who needs it."

"Their healing comes with a price," Cleric said. "A hearty dose of godswill for everyone that walks through the door."

She frowned. "You told me the godswill saved my life."

"It kept you from dying. There is a distinct difference. *God's will*, you understand? It's Eleni's will that you're hurt, or sick. It's His will that you feel pain. Any other healer, the Slonimi or the Apothecary Guild or any common herbwife from any common village, they'll give you opium or willow bark or whiskey first thing to stop the pain. But the Elenesians want you to feel it. Doesn't matter if you have a broken leg or you've been speared through, they think if it happened, the god Eleni meant for you to feel every moment of it. Your brain might want to pass out, shut down. But the Elenesians won't let that happen." Cleric shook his head. "Godswill keeps your brain and your body together, whether they should be or not. That poor wretch in front of the Refuge back in the square? Maybe he came into the Refuge with a broken arm. Or—there's this tiny organ in your body, like a finger off your gut. It doesn't do anything, but sometimes it gets infected. Any healer with basic surgical training can go in and take it out. But only the Elenesians will make sure you're conscious and feeling while they do it. And if it breaks you—if it sends you mad, like that poor man with the broom—guess what they call that?"

"God's will," Judah said, horrified. "I see."

"You don't see," Cleric said, his tone glacial. "You can't see, until you've experienced a pain so terrible that you would rather die—that you *should* die—rather than feel it. Until you've begged to be allowed to die, and the people taking care of you patted your head and chastised you for not being appropriately grateful for the suffering Eleni has given you." Then he clamped his mouth shut, as if there were further words inside him, and they needed to be bitten back. Judah could see his jaw muscles working. Then he stood up. "I'll see you in the morning. Leave the room unlocked, eh?"

Lukash nodded. Cleric turned to Judah. "There's a vial for you on the windowsill upstairs. Take it before you go to sleep." Then, as bitter and nasty as the elixir itself, he added, "It's god's will."

He left. "I guess I shouldn't have asked," Judah said.

Lukash took a long pull on his ale. "He would have gone out anyway. Whenever we find civilization, he goes in search of trouble. Are you done eating?"

She looked down at her fish. "I seem to have lost my appetite."

"Pass it over," he said, and finished it off in three big bites. Then he said, "You were dying. The godswill was the best chance you had. Just because the Elenesians use it in an evil way doesn't make it inherently evil."

Right then, the innkeeper approached, holding one of the bulbous things. It looked like a very small, odd samovar, with the flame on top, and, on the bottom—where the flame should be—a glass bowl of what looked like blue peppercorns. The whole thing was framed in brass, with loops on the outside holding tongs and delicate, long-stemmed glass bulbs. "Glory?" the innkeeper said. His smile was friendly, satisfied, as if they shared a secret.

"Thank you," Lukash said, before Judah could say anything, "but no. We're tired."

"Glory will help you sleep," the innkeeper said.

"We've been on the road for nearly a month. I don't believe we'll have any trouble." Lukash stood, and looked at Judah. "Shall we go upstairs?"

The innkeeper's gaze was decidedly unfriendly now. Judah nodded.

Their room was small, with a bed pushed against each of the three walls. One was a trundle bed the innkeeper had pulled from underneath one of the others. Lukash dropped to sit on the smaller of the two cots and had his boots nearly all the way off before he noticed that she was still standing. "Take whichever bed you like. By the time Cleric comes back he won't care where he sleeps." He peeled off a woolen sock. His toes were long, and the one in the middle was missing.

Tentatively, Judah sat down on the largest bed. "What's glory? Bad?"

He curled his long toes tightly, spread them out again, and shrugged. "It's like godswill. Not inherently evil, but the cartel uses it in evil ways."

"So glad you brought me here, then."

"The next closest town was a month's travel away," he said, with a wry, tired grin. "Do you like us that much?"

"I feel like I can safely say that I like you both better than anyone else I've met this side of the Barriers." As she took off her own boots, the bed rustled and compacted under her, but not very much. Straw, or sheep clippings. Still better than a forest floor. Lukash stretched out, his eyes closed and his hands laced together on his stomach. She could smell that faint herbal aroma again, the same one in the dead boy's memory. She was almost certain that it had been Lukash's arm that snapped the boy's neck the night he died, but she wasn't afraid. If Lukash—or Cleric, for that matter—had wanted to hurt her, they would have, long before now. And for all she knew, the dead boy was a vestige of the godswill, or the near-death state they'd found her in, or some weird echo of those watching multitudes she'd sensed in her contact with Gavin. "So what should I say tomorrow when I go to this evil cartel for help?"

"Will anybody in Highfall pay to have you back?"

Gavin, I brought food.

Gavin wasn't in Highfall. But she was quite sure the Seneschal was. "Not that I want to see."

"Then lie," he said, eyes still closed. "Say you don't remember anything. Tell them you were hit in the head and we rescued you."

"Does Cleric use glory?"

"Alcohol is cheaper." He was silent for a moment. She wondered if he'd fallen asleep. But then he said, "Something builds up in him. Enough pebbles make a rockslide. Been that way as long as I've known him."

"How long is that?"

Lukash considered. "Five years? Maybe more. I met him in the north. He was cheating at cards."

"So naturally you befriended him."

"I was cheating at cards, too. The other men we were playing with objected. We discovered that we fight well together. I'm going to sleep now."

Then he rolled over, and did just that. It took a long time for Judah's muscles to relax so she could follow his example.

She was jerked awake in the middle of the night by a loud crash. The candle was out and for a moment she was too confused to do more than stare into the darkness. She sensed movement, heard voices, and scrambled across the bed, head swimming, to throw open the wooden window shutters and let in the light of the streetlamp outside.

Lukash was holding Cleric upright, one of the Northerner's long arms draped over his shoulders. The healer didn't seem able to stand on his own, lurching from side to side as if the room was a ship and the waters were stormy. The innkeeper scowled in the doorway. Quickly, Judah went to Cleric's other side and took his free arm. The smell of alcohol—not anything as refined as ale but cheap, rotgut whiskey, the kind Gavin used to buy from the guards before he discovered wine—was so strong that Judah's eyes stung. "Bed," Lukash said, and they carried him the three steps it took to drop him down onto the thin mattress Judah had just vacated.

Cleric cried out. Lukash lit the candle, and Judah saw that Cleric had been beaten. His jaw was distended and his nose bloodied. One of his eyes was swollen nearly shut. But it was his chest he clutched at, moaning.

"Too much noise," the innkeeper said. "If he's hurt, take him to the Elenesians."

Quickly, Judah pulled her satchel out from under the bed and found one of the coins she'd taken from the winemaker. "He'll be quiet for the rest of the night. Take this for your trouble," she said, trying to sound as much like a courtier as possible as she passed it to the innkeeper.

The innkeeper looked reluctantly at the coin, and then at the man writhing on the bed. Lukash was trying to pull Cleric's shirt over his head so he could see the injury. Cleric fought him. "You'll leave in the morning," the innkeeper said.

Judah wondered how disapproving the innkeeper would be if Cleric was off his head on the inn's gloryseed. "Most assuredly." She nudged the man out the door, then closed the door behind him and locked it for good measure. Meanwhile, Lukash had successfully removed Cleric's shirt. Judah drew in a harsh breath. The left side of his chest was covered by a huge purple-red mark, and the rest of his torso was dotted with smaller bruises that looked, to Judah, exactly like boot prints.

Cleric pushed Lukash away. "'S just a broken rib," he said, slurring, and letting himself slump down onto his side. "L'keep 'til morning."

"I hope it was worth it," Lukash said.

Cleric's eyes were already closed. He smiled dreamily. "So

worth it," he mumbled, or something that sounded like it. A moment later he was snoring.

Lukash yawned and turned back to his own cot. Judah stared at him. "That's it? You're not going to do anything?"

"I did do something. I made sure he hadn't been stabbed. Go back to sleep. He'll be sober in the morning." Lukash blew out the candle. Judah curled up on the trundle. Cleric's snoring was loud. When she finally slept again, it was thin and restless.

As Lukash had predicted, Cleric was sober in the morning. He was also in a terrible mood. When Judah woke, he was sitting shirtless on the edge of the bed, wrapping a long strip of cloth around his bruised chest. "You're staring," he said.

"You look terrible," she said.

"I feel even better." He stood up, gingerly. As he turned around to pick his shirt up from the bed, she saw that his back was crossed with long scars reaching diagonally down from each shoulder. They looked old. At some point in his life, Cleric had been whipped, or caned. She had been caned, too. Before she realized what she was doing, her hand lifted, touched the place on the back of her shoulder where the tip of her own scars should have been.

"Where's Lukash?" she said.

"Downstairs eating breakfast," Cleric said, trying to work his arms into his shirt. "More delicious rice, no doubt."

"Here." Judah stood up to help him. He flinched when her fingers made contact with his skin, but let her guide his shirt over his scarred shoulders. His apothecary box lay open on the bed, its contents scattered across the blanket. When his shirt was on, and buttoned, he leaned down stiffly to pack it up again. Judah moved to help again and he pushed her hand away.

"I can do it," he said, crossly. "Lukash said you paid off

the innkeeper last night to keep him from sending me to the Refuge."

"It was nothing."

"Thanks for nothing, then."

She sat down on the trundle and began to put her own boots on. "What happened last night, anyway? Who did that to you?"

"Where does your rich family live?" he said.

"I don't have a rich family."

"And nobody did anything to me." He closed the apothecary box and slipped it into his satchel. "Isn't sharing nice?"

Downstairs, the largest bowl on the table in front of Lukash was, in fact, filled with rice. But there was also bacon and boiled eggs and three tiny plates of dark red jam, each holding no more than a spoonful. "Eat," Lukash said, by way of greeting. "We paid for it already. How are your ribs?"

This last was to Cleric, who only said, "They'll heal."

Judah saw a coffeepot on the table. The smell of it mixed with the bacon and eggs and it all smelled delightfully breakfastish. She hadn't had coffee since before the coup in Highfall. It tasted burned without milk or sugar. After he'd picked at some bacon, Cleric reached into his pocket, pulled out a small flask and handed it to Judah. "Here. Enough godswill for a week. You're at a half dose now. Keep that up for a day or two and then wean yourself off it. Gradually, mind you."

She grimaced and pocketed the flask. "You're not going with me to the town hall?"

"Nothing in it for us," Cleric said. "There's no reward. Highfall's too far away."

"We'll walk you there, at least. After we're done eating," Lukash said. From the way he seemed determined to eat everything in the inn's larder, that might be a while. His copper-colored eyes darted up to her and he seemed on the cusp of saying something else.

But then the door opened, and sun streamed in. Or would have, were it not blocked by six large human shapes. Men, as it turned out. Guards, as it further turned out, wearing Black Lake tunics. Cleric went silent. Across the table from her, Lukash stiffened. When the guards came straight to their table, she was the least surprised she had ever been.

"The Town Master has ordered you brought to the hall," said the one in front, wearing the most heavily decorated uniform.

Neither of the men moved, so Judah didn't, either. "What's going on?" Cleric said, his voice once again as syrupy and pleasant as her earliest memories of it. "We're just travelers. We've done nothing wrong."

"Then you have nothing to fear," the guard said.

The Town Hall was the building with three towers, opposite the main gate. They passed under the lintel—it was, somewhat incongruously, carved with three-petaled flowers—and were taken into a small room, the single door of which was locked from the outside. Their packs and satchels were taken away from them, as were their knives and the flask of godswill in Judah's pocket. Then they were left alone.

"If you see an opportunity to save yourself," Lukash said, "take it," and Cleric nodded.

"Save myself?" Judah said, startled. "You think we're in actual danger?"

"Almost certainly," Lukash said, and then they said no more.

After an interminable amount of time, the guards came for them. The room where they were brought was wide and unfurnished except for a wooden desk, behind which sat a man wearing a velvet tunic and a heavy gold chain. He was older and clean-shaven, with hair thinned to almost nothing on the top of his head. When they entered, he ignored them. The guards merely waited, doing nothing to draw his attention. Judah realized that the room wasn't unfurnished at all, but was being used exactly as intended: so that a crowd had plenty of room to stand in uncomfortable silence while waiting for this man—clearly the Town Master—to attend them. Which he was apparently in no rush to do. He was writing something on a piece of paper in front of him. Judah noticed that he had a faded tattoo of the same three-petaled flower from the lintel on his hand, in exactly the place where their two-day marks were. Sneaking a look to either side, she saw that the guards did, too.

On the desk in front of the Master, she saw a bottle of wine with Sevedra's tag, Cleric's apothecary box, her own satchel, and a piece of red cloth she knew had come from Lukash's pack. Eventually, the Master put down the thin bone sliver he was writing with. "Well. A Morgeni, a Northerner, and a woman."

"Town Master," Cleric said, with a warm, ingratiating smile that seemed incongruous with his bruised face. "Surely there's been—"

"A mistake?" The Master smiled. "Perhaps. We keep a tight watch over our visitors here in Black Lake. We have a reputation as a safe, comfortable town in which respectable people can experience the relaxation and comforts of gloryseed, and we intend to keep that reputation intact. To that end, I'm sure you won't mind a few questions. May I ask what happened to your face?"

Cleric's expression turned serious and sad. "We were waylaid outside the Ghostwood. My cousin—" he indicated Judah with a nod "—suffered a blow to the head. We are lucky that she did not suffer more."

Cousin. Judah kept her face blank, but apparently, the Master wasn't convinced, either. "Your cousin," he said, flat and unimpressed.

"On my mother's side."

"Shall I call a healer?" the Town Master said. "Our local Refuge is one of the best."

Cleric gave the man a broad smile. "Thank you, but no."

The Town Master picked up the bottle of wine and examined the label. "This is a fine vintage. How did you come by it, may I ask?"

"It was given to us as a gift," Cleric said.

"Before or after you were waylaid?"

"After. We were lucky enough to come upon the winemaker's house, and took an evening's rest there. A lovely man." The liar's first rule: stay as close to the truth as possible. Cleric, Judah noted, lied like a virtuoso musician at his instrument.

"Yes. He was. And very talented. A great loss."

Cleric's brow furrowed. "A loss, Master?"

"I'm afraid the vintner was found murdered yesterday, his house and vineyards set on fire."

"How do you know he was murdered if his house was burned?" Judah said, without quite realizing she was going to speak before she did.

The Town Master surveyed her. "Enough of his body remained to see that his throat had been cut. What is your name, please?"

"Judah," she said, because she was not as good at lying as Cleric was, and had no other name immediately at hand.

"And where are you and your cousin from, originally?"

"The North."

"Master, her memory suffered in the attack," Cleric said, smoothly. "Our village was called Findhorn. Very small."

But the Master was still looking at Judah. "You don't look Northern."

"So I'm told."

"Why are you wearing men's clothing?"

"Have you ever tried to travel on foot through heavy underbrush in a dress?"

One corner of the Master's mouth twitched. "I have not." He reached out and touched the red scarf on the table. "Is this yours?"

"It is mine, Master," Lukash said.

"And where did you get it, Morgeni?"

"I can't remember." The disinterested way Lukash said the words spoke volumes. It does not matter what I say, it said; you will hear a lie.

Now the Town Master's hand moved to Judah's satchel. "And this satchel?"

"Mine," Judah said.

"And I trust you also do not remember where you came by it. Because of your head injury," the Master said pleasantly. "Perhaps you had a past life as a gloryseed merchant. Because here—" he lifted the flap to reveal the small three-petaled flower inked in blue onto the leather, which Judah had never noticed "—is the mark of our Merchant's Guild. The number next to it is a license number. The merchant bearing this particular number disappeared several years ago."

"The satchel was a gift from Sevedra." It was almost not a lie.

"And perhaps the red sash was a gift from a Harkerstown Guardsman, who wear identical sashes as part of their uniform," the Town Master said, conversationally. "The sheriff of Harkerstown and his son were also murdered recently, did you know that? They were both found in the woods with broken necks."

The sheriff's son. The dead boy.

The Town Master continued. "And the Harkerstown payroll has vanished. Two men were seen in the area before the killings, but not afterward. A Northerner and a Morgeni."

"Not exactly iron-clad descriptions," Cleric said.

"Aren't they? The Morgeni aren't known for their wanderlust." The Town Master picked up Cleric's herb box. Judah realized he was enjoying himself. "This is also interesting. It looks very like the ones the Elenesians carry—ah, yes, see here?" He pointed to the edge of the box, where the willowlike scourge was carved into the wood. "That's the mark of Eleni. And if we look inside—" He opened it, examined the contents briefly, and then pulled out the small bag where Cleric kept the godswill powder. With two fat fingers he pulled the bag open and sniffed deeply. "Yes. This is godswill. Only Elenesians carry godswill, which means this is, indeed, an Elenesian apothecary box. Show me his hands, please."

Roughly, the guards standing on either side of Cleric grabbed his wrists and forced his hands forward. The Town Master nodded. "Nasty burn. And right where the Elenesians put their guild mark, isn't it? Are you an apostate, Northerner?"

Cleric's eyes went flinty and his chin went up. The guards let his hands go and they fell to his sides, clenched into fists.

"I've seen enough." The Town Master yawned. "All right. The three of you sold gems last night, which you claimed to have inherited, but which were obviously stolen. You are furthermore in possession of Sevedran wine, a Harkerstown Guard sash, and a Merchant's Guild satchel, which makes you thieves at best and murderers at worst. You are hereby sentenced to five years labor in the gloryseed fields, at the end of which you will be extradited to Harkerstown and, if necessary, to the Elenesian Guildhall, to answer charges for crimes you've committed there." He waved to the guards. "Take them to the prison barracks."

The guards moved. Strong hands grabbed Judah's arms. "Wait!" she said.

The Town Master lifted a finger, and the guard's grip on Judah loosened. "Have you decided you're not the Northerner's cousin, after all?"

Judah didn't bother answering that. "If you found the winemaker's body, you found his storeroom, didn't you? The one full of traveler's equipment and goods? Gold, jewels? Clothing? Satchels?" She nodded at the satchel that had so recently been hers, which still lay on the Master's desk. "Like that one. That's where I got it. The scarf, too." Might as well throw everything in. "Did it occur to you to wonder where all of those things came from? Did you wonder what happened to all of the travelers who'd carried them? The winemaker killed them. His wine might have been good but the way he made it was nothing but evil. He tried to kill us. We had no choice but to defend ourselves."

"I'm sure," the Master said, drily.

The man's lack of interest made Judah angry. "He fed his grapevines on blood."

The Town Master blinked, indifferent as a cat. "I've changed my mind," he said, and Judah felt her shoulders slump as relief flooded her. But then he said, "Take them to the wetlands, cut off their heads, and dump them. Except for the apostate's," he added, as if in an afterthought. "The Elenesians will pay a good bounty for his. Take his hand, too, while you're at it."

"Wait," Judah said, again, and the Town Master smiled.

"Do you know how much a bottle of Sevedran wine is worth, girl?" he said, and leaned forward. "Enough that if I were to take you to a brothel and try to trade you for one, I would need at least four of you. And even then, I'm not sure

I'd get more than a sip." The guards laughed, obedient, servile chuckles. The Master smiled. "Take them away."

Something flashed in front of Judah's eyes and she felt a tight, remorseless stricture around her neck. Her hand moved instinctively to reach up and touch it but a guard was tying her hands in front of her. Next to her the guards had slipped wire garrotes around each of the men's necks, too, and held them taut enough that Lukash's eyes were wide and Cleric's face began to redden. Any fight went out of them with their air, she saw. Leashed that way, with the threat of suffocation at any moment and their hands bound in front of them, they were taken to a dingy courtyard behind Town Hall, where a group of hollow-eyed workers in metal collars picked over a huge pile of empty gloryseed sacks, plucking away each stray blue grain, and where one of the guards picked up a wicked-looking axe. From there they passed through a locked door and down a narrow alley that smelled of piss and through another locked door that turned out to be set into the city wall, and the whole time the guard holding Judah took every opportunity to bump against her, to grab at her, to laugh. The first time his rough hand landed on her breast a flash of helpless white-hot rage filled her and she twisted away, throwing her upper arm against his arm. Instantly the garrote tightened and she could not breathe. Her whole body was instantly panicking and his hand didn't matter; all that mattered was air. She froze. The garrote relaxed. His hand came back, squeezed her flesh painfully. "That's better," he said in her ear, and the other guards guffawed. She could see cords standing out on Lukash's forearms. His fists were tightly clenched. Cleric's lips were turning faintly blue.

They were dragged, pushed, and pinched across an empty field to a ragged patch of ground, simultaneously rocky and soggy. A forgotten place, a look-away place. Green rushes spread in a thick carpet out into the lake to their left and through them she caught glimpses of the dark, murky water, which smelled dark and murky, too. A scarred wooden block stood at the edge of the solid ground.

"Down we go," Judah's guard said, and pushed her onto her knees.

"Let's do this one first, so we don't forget to save the parts," the guard holding Cleric said. Lukash's guard kicked at the back of his knees and he dropped down next to her in the muck.

"I'm sorry," Lukash muttered, as they watched Cleric being dragged to the block, helpless. The guards forced the Northerner's neck down onto the scarred wooden surface and Judah didn't know if it was because the end would be coming soon or if it was because he could breathe again, but she could swear the look on Cleric's face was almost relieved.

The guard with the axe was rolling his shoulders as if to loosen them and stretching his arms across his chest. Judah slumped down, her hands falling to the muck and the garrote hanging loose like a macabre necklace. The memory of the man's hands on her was too vivid, too alive. Next to her, Lukash's jaw was clenched as tight as his own garrote, but he did not take his eyes off his friend. Because friends did not abandon each other. When the Seneschal's guard had caned Judah in Highfall, Elly had not looked away, either. Judah wasn't as strong as Lukash or Elly. She could not watch Cleric be murdered. The mud squished between her fingers and she looked at that instead. The ropes binding her wrists were thin and shaggy and cheap. If only there was a knife here, buried in the muck. If only somebody had dropped a knife here and forgotten it. It didn't have to be a big knife. It didn't even have to be very sharp. Just sharp enough.

The guards were discussing if they should take Cleric's head first, or his hand. They were discussing what would happen to her, after. Her guard called something out to her. She chose not to hear the exact words but she heard the guffaws that came after, and could guess what they were. She did not want to be the last left alive. Judah felt—something. Like a lifting, or a letting go. Both. Neither. Her vision was beginning to go white around the edges, her hands seeming almost to glow in the filth, and she understood that the stress and horror had knocked something loose in her brain. She wished that she could take the tiny stones in the dirt and gather them together, fuse them into a blade. Squeeze them together like clay and draw them to a point, make them lethal. The whiteness took over and she closed her eyes, imagined the feel of a knife in her hand, long and solid and tapered to an edge—

Her fingers touched something solid. Her eyes flew open. A shard of something? A broken bottle? Whatever it was, underneath all the mud it was sharp enough to prick her hand if she pressed against it. She cleared the mud away, saw a blunt mud-covered handle and a long mud-covered blade.

The guard with the axe, adequately limbered, raised the weapon over his head.

Instantly, the world was crisp and clear and bright. She grabbed the knife, twisted her body again—exactly like she had to avoid the guard's horrid groping fingers—and plunged it deep into the thigh of the guard holding Lukash's garrote. The guard screamed and the garrote fell loose.

"Lukash!" she cried, and his head snapped toward her. With her tied hands, she yanked the knife out of the guard's thigh and tossed it toward the Morgeni. It wasn't much of a throw. It wasn't much of a knife. But when it fell at Lukash's feet, he didn't hesitate. In one quick motion he was up, mud coating him from midthigh down, hands still bound. But those bound hands held the knife between them and plunged it straight into the throat of his former captor, who was still clutching his thigh and screaming. All of this happened in seconds. The guard who held Cleric on the block stayed where he was but the other two—including the one with the axe—charged toward Lukash. The axeman swung the axe at Lukash. By the time it dropped, Lukash was no longer there; the momentum of the swing pulled the heavy blade around in a circle, and the axeman with it. Before the man could reorient himself Lukash was there to send the knife into the axeman's groin and cut him open. A gleaming mess of pink and red fell out of the wound. The axeman screamed, and dropped.

Then Lukash had the axe. Still on her hands and knees in the mud, Judah could only watch as he swung it straight toward the center of her guard's skull and then that man dropped, too. Lukash put a foot on the dead man's shoulder to retrieve the axe. Cleric's guard abandoned his post and charged Lukash but suddenly he dropped, too, and Judah saw the knife she'd thrown to Lukash sticking out of the base of his skull. Cleric stood behind him. A deep, bloody groove in his long white neck marked where the garrote had been, and his face was an unhealthy mixture of red and gray. Lukash must have tossed the knife toward his friend after gutting the axeman.

With a wet, sticky sound, the axe came free. Lukash slung it behind him and held out his hands to Cleric, who pulled the knife from the back of the guard's head, cut Lukash's bonds, and then sank down to sit on the very block where he'd nearly met his end, looking unsteady. Lukash took the knife and cut his hands free, too, then turned to Judah. She was glad he wiped the blood off the blade before freeing her hands. She was the only one of the three without blood on her.

"Swamp," Cleric said, hoarsely, and struggled to his feet.

Lukash stuck the knife into his belt, picked up the bloody axe, and pulled Judah up. She felt strange, sort of faraway, but then again she'd never seen four men killed in rapid succession before, so maybe strange and faraway was how she was supposed to feel. The three of them splashed into the murk next to the executioner's block, probably the exact spot where the Town Master would have ordered their bodies thrown. Judah could not see the top of her trousers, much less her feet, so it was better not to think about the nature of the solid things her boots found in the muck. The water was deep enough most places that their heads were well below the rushes. Sometimes they had to swim. Sometimes they had to crouch. Soon they heard shouts and cries behind them as—presumably—the dead bodies of the execution party were discovered. Judah's legs itched. Midges buzzed her eyes and something bit the side of her neck. Her legs bumped against things. Things bumped against her legs.

But they were leaving the sounds behind them. Soon the swamp quieted entirely. The bushes grew taller and turned into trees, gnarled and feral-looking and sparse. Judah was exhausted and her mouth tasted of swamp water. Finally, as the sun began to sink toward the horizon, the trees opened up entirely and they found themselves on the edge of a small lake. It was long and narrow and they could see no bridges or boats or other signs of life on it. The sun glittered hot orange fire on the gently rippling surface. They paused at the edge of the trees. The water was shallow enough for Cleric to stand, easily. Lukash could, too, water lapping at his chin. He'd somehow secured the executioner's axe so the blade protruded above his head and stayed out of the water. Judah was shorter than both of them and had to tread water.

"What now?" she said, and got a little water in her mouth as she did so. She didn't mind. The lake water was fresher than the swamp water, which had tasted musty and somehow lived in.

"We swim," Lukash said. "They might have dogs."

So they swam, down the length of the shimmering water. She had to take several breaks to rest. Marveling at the way Lukash managed the axe, she couldn't imagine what it would have been like to make this long, wet trek with her satchel. She supposed the Town Master had done them a favor, in that way. It wasn't until they reached the other side of the pond, clambering over the rocky shoreline to the blessedly solid ground on the other side, that she realized that without their supplies, they had no food and no way to start a fire. So maybe not so much of a favor, after all.

The light was turning silver. The trees here were stubby and drab. After a few moments to catch their breath, Cleric led them up and through the foliage until they emerged on a wide plain, thick with scrub. The sky was dark in the east by then, and as they trudged ahead stars began to flicker in the blackness. The empty space in Judah's stomach had long since shriveled into queasiness and she felt like the rest of her had shriveled, too. She was shaking with cold and her wet trousers were chafing the insides of her legs. Finally, they reached a clearing, and stopped. Judah wanted to take off her sodden boots more than she wanted anything else in the entire world.

"Do you think they're coming after us?" she said.

"I'm sure they think we're dead. And they might be right," Cleric said. A bit of muck was stuck to his chin. He pressed the heels of his hands into his eyes and moaned. "My herb box."

"My knife," Lukash said, calmly. He still had the one Judah had given him stuck in his belt. "And all our food. Everything. Don't take your boots off." Because Judah was doing that, or starting to. "Look for wood. Dry brush. Anything that will burn."

So they did that by starlight, stumbling through the dark on their numb feet. By the time they returned to the clearing, shriveled hands filled with sticks, Lukash had assembled a pile of twigs and dried grass and was crouched next to a small collection of jagged-edged rocks. He had something in his hand and was methodically striking it against each of the rocks in turn, until finally, he opened his hand for a moment and Judah saw that it was a firesteel.

"Where did you get that?" she said.

"Keep it on my belt. Looks like part of the buckle. They look but do not see." The last part sounded like a quote. Judah was too tired to ask about it. He picked up another rock, examined it, and then struck the steel against it experimentally. A spark flew into the pile of dead grass and she found herself holding her breath as he blew gently at the tiny orange ember. His focus reminded her of Theron in his workshop. But Theron's fingers were nimble and thin and Lukash's were strong and tough. Tough enough to hold the ember as it caught, and to lay it gently in the nest of kindling he'd made.

"It's a miracle," Judah said.

Half of his mouth smiled. "It's a skill. I'll teach you."

"I have never loved anything as much as I love this fire," Cleric said, dropping an armload of wood next to Lukash.

"Then feed it, and love it, and sing to it gently." Lukash stood up. "I've got to get these boots off."

Cleric said they should take off as many layers as they could. So they took off their waterlogged coats and boots and stockings, draping them around the fire. The men left on their braies, and Judah left on her shirt; they were all thin linen and would dry soon enough. Judah was blazing hot in the front and freezing in the back. She could smell herself, the reek of mildew and sweat and swamp water. Her eyes were gritty with exhaustion and as she stared at the fire it blurred. It blinked. Was it going out?

No. She was.

SEVEN

THE CUT ON ELLY'S CHEEK HADN'T HURT WHEN IT happened, but it hurt now. Eduard assured her there was a magus who was good with a needle at his camp, where he'd take her as soon as his men were done cleaning out the guild-hall larder. They'd stripped off the black coverings they'd been wearing, and green-and-black Tiernan livery was everywhere. The sight of it made Elly ill.

There were new creases in the corners of Eduard's eyes now, and a deep scar on his chin, as if he'd been cleaved in the jaw with an axe. She could sense that he wanted to talk to her and she wanted none of it. She stuck close to Gavin as they were covered in dark capes and bundled onto the backs of horses, a change in circumstances that Gavin accepted calmly. But his eyes were watchful, taking the measure of each of Eduard's men, and of Eduard himself.

"Is this the brother you hate?" he said, under his breath, once they were underway.

"I hate them all," she said. Then, grudgingly: "Eduard isn't the worst."

Angen was the worst. Of her five brothers, Angen and Eduard were closest in age; the oldest, Millar, had teased Eduard by calling him Angen's lapdog. The two younger, Raymond and Lorens, had been small boys hanging on Millar's every word—until, that is, Millar had been thrown from his horse and killed. He'd been twenty-three; Elly had been four, and he'd barely noticed her existence. She remembered little of him other than the cloud of noise and beer-smell that surrounded him and his death. Their father had grieved terribly. Angen had moved all too easily into his dead brother's place as eldest and heir. She'd sensed something different among her brothers after that. It felt like hearing a wolf howl on a dark night and knowing all the doors were open.

Eduard's camp was several hours' ride away. Elly, who could count her horseback experiences on one hand, was miserable for most of the trip. When they finally arrived, Elly and Gavin were led to a tent with two cots, a small oil lamp, and a jug of clean water. Gavin sat down on one of the cots. His hands kept clenching and unclenching, his fingers rubbing together as though there were cloth between them. Elly hadn't even had time to slip her boots off before the tent flap opened, and a large man with a neatly trimmed beard stuck his head in.

"I'm the magus. You have a cut that needs stitching?" he said, in the Tiernan way, with some vowels pinched tight and others stretched out. The sound of it made Elly want to twitch. Then he saw her cheek. "You certainly do. I have a good lamp in my tent."

Gavin—still clenching and unclenching his fists—said, "Do you want me to come with you?"

Elly hesitated. The magus said, "You're welcome to come, Lord Gavin. But no harm will come to my lady on my watch."

There was something in his voice as he said *my lady*. Something she didn't associate at all with his accent. Something... respectful. It made her wary, but also curious.

"I'll be fine," she said, to Gavin.

He nodded. "Find me a pair of gloves, if you can?"

The camp was new enough not to be terribly muddy. In Highfall, the last House Magus, Nathaniel, had been a slender man, his predecessor Arkady withered and old. Eduard's magus was like a wall with legs. He led her to a tent that was slightly larger than the others, bowed, and pulled the flap back so she could enter. Then he turned up his lamp, the light from which was indeed very bright, as well as slightly purple. "That's Wilmerian gas," she said.

"Yes. I only have the one tank, but it's marvelous for surgery." He sat down on one of the two stools and gestured for her to take the other. "I'm Ambrose. Do you want opium before I get started?"

She most certainly did not want opium. Not in a camp full of her brother's men. "No, thank you. I'd rather not."

He studied her for a moment. "Want to keep a clear head, do you? All right, then." He pulled a small table near to him, and began to set out supplies. One glance at the long, curved needle was all Elly needed. She looked away. Humming slightly, the magus dabbed something cool and wet on her face. "This will numb you a little. Not much, but better than nothing."

She closed her eyes and felt the needle, a bite of agony in the duller pain of the wound, and drew in a harsh intake of breath. "Sure you don't want that opium?" the magus said. "The Elenesians find benefit in suffering, but I never have."

"No, thank you," she said, through gritted teeth. "What's an Elenesian?"

"Healer's guild. Not one I'd go to, unless I was desperate. Now maybe stop talking while I finish?" That sounded good to Elly, but the stitching seemed to last forever. Finally, Ambrose sat back. "All right, my lady. You have a choice to make. If you were one of the guards outside, I'd stop there. You'll have a scar, but no little children will cry when they see it. If you have slightly higher standards than a guard, another five stitches would get you a thinner scar. One you could cover with cosmetic."

Ambrose's gaze was steady. She liked him. She had not met a magus she liked in a long time. Nathaniel Magus had turned out to be a traitor and a liar, and his predecessor Arkady had been a cruel old lecher. Although not to Eleanor. Never to sweet, biddable Eleanor, bought for a song with the promise that she'd be no trouble at all, from the same family that had now come to her rescue.

Some rescue that was. Her brothers were all lechers, too.

"Would you like a mirror?" Ambrose said. She nodded, and he produced a small piece of polished metal. There had been no looking glasses at the guildhall, and the face she looked at now was thinner than the one in her head. But her lashes were still long, her skin bright—except for the gash along her left cheekbone. The black ends of the magus's thread stuck up like the legs of something insectile. (She wondered if the thread had come from the same mills as the floss for the famous Tiernan blackwork.) The flesh around the gash was swollen. It was not the kind of fine seam she'd been taught to sew as a child in the women's salon. A pretty little thing, they'd called her. Except for Angen, who'd called her his pretty little kitten.

The tent flap opened. Eduard entered, holding two steaming mugs. His eyes went straight to the gash on her face, and that decided her. "Leave it," she said to the magus, and stood up.

Eduard passed a mug to her, and they stepped outside together. The mug held tea, Tiernan-style. Anise and nettle with lots of honey. Elly hadn't tasted it since she was eight years old. "You were very quiet while he stitched you," Eduard said.

"No point in screaming," she said. A little stiffly, because of the stitches. "Speaking of points, Eduard, what's the purpose of all this?"

"To rescue you. No Lady of Tiernan should be held prisoner, no matter who she's betrothed to." But Eduard didn't look at her as he spoke, and she didn't believe him. The men they passed were busy with the sort of tasks that kept a camp and army going—fletching arrows, mending armor—but she could sense that they *were* looking at her, out of the corners of their eyes.

"How did you know we were at the guildhall?" she said.

"Angen has his sources. Information is the only currency anybody has, these days. And not everyone supports the Seneschal, Norrie."

Elly stopped where she stood. "My name is Eleanor."

"Eleanor, then," Eduard said, looking confused.

"Yes. Eleanor." She took a breath—easy, easy—and began walking again. "Would it be possible to get some gloves for Gavin?"

"Absolutely. I was told his hands have been kept bandaged. Why? Is there something wrong with them?" Eduard said, and—when Elly felt her eyes narrow—added, "The kitchen boy was ours."

The dead kitchen boy, that Elly had stepped over in the hall. "Nothing is wrong with Gavin's hands," she said.

"I thought perhaps they'd been bound to keep him from killing himself," Eduard said, bluntly. "The boy seemed to think he was less than healthy, mentally."

"He's lost nearly everything in the last year. His brother, his city, his future—" Not to mention Judah, and was it this that Judah had been sorry for? Leaving Elly to deal with Gavin as

141

he bore the weight of one more loss? "How healthy, mentally, would you be? And why does it matter?"

"Because Angen wants to put him back on the throne of Highfall." Eduard's tone was flat and blunt. "If he's lost his mind, I need to know. Not that it will make a difference. You remember how Angen is when he wants something."

"My memories of Angen are quite clear, thank you," she said flatly. But inside, she was boiling and sick. For everything they'd lost, for Theron and Judah and all the long, hungry months in the House and the gloomy guildhall—at the very least, this Lord of the City, Lady of the City nonsense was supposed to be over, and it was not until this very second that Elly realized what a relief that had been. "Exactly how does he plan to put Gavin on the throne?"

"I'll let him give you the details. Gavin's brother is dead?"

The boiling sickness doubled. "So I'm told."

"You're not sure?" Now it was Eduard who stopped walking. "Eleanor," he said, "I'm sorry. I was unkind to you when you were a child. And I let Angen—be horrible to you."

Was that what they were calling it?

Eduard went on. "He's Lord of Tiernan now, but he hasn't changed. You won't trust him, when you see him, and you're right not to. You can trust me."

And all of the sick roiling anger burst out of Elly in a short, brutal laugh. "You? You always did everything he said. Every single thing. Without hesitation."

Eduard's jaw clenched. "Can Gavin take the throne? Can he keep it?"

She didn't answer. But something small and ferocious had been set ticking inside her. Once they had been going to rule Highfall, she and Gavin together. They were going to fix what was broken, heal what was sick. Make everything better. Then Elban had been killed, and the Seneschal had taken over, and since then she and Gavin had done nothing but survive. She didn't know if he could take the throne. She didn't know if he could keep it. She knew better than to trust Angen—or Eduard, for that matter. Leaden exhaustion fell over her. She would have to be very careful.

Eduard stepped closer. She didn't step back. "The Seneschal wrote to Angen. He said there was a fire in the House." He hesitated before adding, "He said you set it."

"It was the Safe Passage. Not the House." She didn't add that sometimes she dreamed of the screaming men on the other side of the locked door. The sick feeling in her stomach eased. She was not the small scared girl she'd been, the last time Eduard had seen her. She had held off the Seneschal and all his guards. She would hold off Angen and all his, if she needed to. "Are gloves a possibility, or shall I go back to the tent?"

Eduard stared at her for a moment. Then he stripped off his own gloves and handed them to her. They were sheep's hide, not fine but well-made, and they smelled like tobacco smoke and lanolin. "Try these."

"Thank you," Elly said.

She made her way back to the tent. Surely the sun would be up soon. Surely this night couldn't actually be endless. Inside the tent, two covered bowls sat on a small tray on a folding table, and the starchy aroma of porridge was thick in the room. Gavin, lying on one of the cots, seemed to be sleeping, his hands still making that strange motion. Fitful, almost compulsive. She sat down on the empty cot. The wooden frame creaked, and Gavin's eyes opened.

"They brought porridge," he said, and then, "Elly, your poor face."

"Here," she said, and held out the gloves.

He sat up, swung his legs over the edge of the bed, and

took them, immediately sliding them on. His chest rose and fell in a sigh. "Thanks. It feels strange, having my hands free."

"I'm sure it does. They've been bandaged for months."

He made fists. The leather at his knuckles grew tight. Then he let them go. "So, which of us do they want? Long-lost sister or deposed heir?"

No point mincing words. "They want to put you on the throne again."

Gavin's mouth curled. "Curious to hear how they plan to accomplish that."

"So am I. Would you do it?"

"Depends on the terms."

The tent was large enough to be comfortable, but small enough for her to reach across and take one of his gloved hands. Gently, she turned it over, pushed up the sleeve of his coat, and exposed the inside of his arm. His scars had faded since she'd last seen them. Although they weren't his scars. They were Judah's, almost all of them: the raised curlicues Elban had seared into her with his fireplace poker, the neat cuts the magus had made in the tower (and why had Judah let him do that? Elly wondered). But she was looking for the pink welts of the scratches he and Judah used to send messages back and forth, and there were none. She was so used to seeing the scratch code's inscrutable curves and crosshatches that even after all these months, Gavin's arm looked naked, almost vulnerable, without them. Elly had assumed that while she was gone, Gavin would take advantage of the first bandageless privacy he'd had for months, and reach out to Judah. But he hadn't.

He gave her a wan smile. "I didn't try."

"Why not?" she said.

"Because she might not have answered." He pulled his sleeve back down. "Is that cowardly?"

If she could reach out to Judah, she would have done so the moment the bandages hit the floor. "No."

"I know she's not dead. I can feel her. My arm feels like it's been cut, even though there's no mark. She's out there, somewhere. But I don't know where, and I don't know why she hasn't tried to contact me." He sighed. "Anyway, tell me about this brother of yours."

Which one, she wondered, and then realized it didn't matter. "Angen's Lord of Tiernan, now. Eduard is the one you met—he's Angen's man, through and through, or at least he was when I was a girl, and Angen is terrible. They have some Highfall source who knew where we were, apparently."

"Probably some courtier who survived the coup." He lay down again and closed his eyes. "Thanks again for the gloves, El."

His hands were still working, his fingers stretching and palms pressing together as if for reassurance that the thick leather was still there. "You're welcome," she said, and took a bowl of porridge from the tray. It was rich with butter and still warm. She'd survived the day. She would eat and sleep as well as she could; tomorrow, she would wake up and survive another one.

Eduard and his men headed north, bringing Elly and Gavin with them. The farther north they traveled, the colder the air became and the more familiar the land looked to her. The rusty outcroppings she'd seen from the guildhall were replaced by smaller, grayer outcroppings; the rolling hills grew more pronounced. They stuck to roads when the roads were going in the right direction and traveled overland when they weren't, passing through a few villages but stopping in none of them. Eduard seemed to prefer camping as far away from civilization as possible. Whether this was because of the townspeople's tired, jaded gazes or because of Eleanor and Gavin, Elly didn't know. Would Gavin be recognizable now, with his long hair and dirty traveling cloak, miles away from anywhere people would expect to see him? Eduard had not spoken to her since that first night, so she couldn't ask him about his motives. Not that she would have, anyway.

After a week, Ambrose took Elly's stitches out, and told her that the men had been very impressed by her silence as he put them in. That afternoon they saw their first sheep pasture. A young, wind-burned shepherd sat on a rock nearby, his shaggy dog raising its head to watch as the troop passed. Elly was so stiff she could barely move. She hated her horse. He was nice enough, but she would have sent him on his way with all the good wishes in the world if she'd never had to ride him again.

Gavin was a better rider than she was but it had been months since he'd been on horseback. When they stopped, she could tell he was stiff, too. He flexed his shoulders, then caught her watching him and managed a grin. "We'll reach Tiernan in a few days," he said.

"How is that possible?" she said. "It took five weeks for me to travel from Tiernan when I first came to Highfall. The guildhall was only a few days away from the city."

"When you came to Highfall, you were traveling by carriage, on roads. Carriages are slower than horses, and roads are less direct. Also, you were a child."

"Believe me," Elly said, "when I came to Highfall, there was absolutely no consideration whatsoever made for the fact that I was a child."

He said nothing.

Four days later a vague grayish outcropping in the distance grew unnatural edges and distinct corners. Eduard fell back between Elly and Gavin, smiled at his sister, and said, "Welcome sight, isn't it?"

It wasn't. Elly said nothing. Gavin said, "That's Tiernan?"

"It is," Eduard said, and clucked his horse back up to the head of the procession, where he could look successful and triumphant.

Elly felt like she was being dragged backward through time. The sky was overcast and heavy, like the skies she remembered from her childhood. As the round cupola on top of the weaver's guildhall and the blocky crenellations of the manor grew distinct, she remembered that the manor had felt overcast and heavy, too, the ceilings low and dark with old smoke. There was nothing like a town in Tiernan; only the guildhall and the manor, jutting like teeth above the gray-green horizon. Wool was the only currency and wool was the only trade: shearing it, carding it, spinning it, dyeing it. There was no need to build a town over precious grazeland. After years of staring out over the jumbled roofs and spires of Highfall, Elly found the two lone buildings sad, pathetic, and deeply terrifying.

Except that now, where there should have been nothing but pastureland, the ground was plowed into neat rows of dark green plants. As they approached the manor hall, they came upon a new field being cleared, women and children bending over the soil to cut sod and dig rocks. And there was a lot of activity around the base of the hall itself: tents, people, horses. A market? It wasn't market season.

She tapped her heels against her horse's sides the way Gavin had taught her and caught up with Eduard. "What are they planting?"

"Angen's newest passion. It's called glory," Eduard said grimly. "He's convinced it'll make Tiernan rich."

"And what's outside the hall?"

"That's the army encampment."

She blinked. Tiernan men might be shepherds or dyers or

weavers, but they were not soldiers. "Tiernan doesn't have an army."

"We do now."

That same grimness in his tone, still. Somewhat nonsensically, Elly said, "Who's watching the sheep, then?"

"The same people working the fields," Eduard said, gesturing at the workers cutting sod and hauling rocks. "The women and children."

The tents at the base of the manor looked a bit ramshackle, as if they'd been put up in a hurry. A herd of horses grazed nearby. Never had she seen so many horses in Tiernan, or swords. The Tiernanese, slight and small statured, seemed to be training under the watchful eyes of wide-shouldered men who had clearly grown up with better food. All of the tents had small banners flying from the ridgepoles. Most of these were Tiernan green and black, but scattered among those was a different flag, dark and light blue in wide bands. Elly didn't recognize it.

"These men aren't all from Tiernan," she said, quietly, to Eduard.

"No," he said, curtly.

Gavin, she saw, had drawn up his hood and lowered his head. Not a terrible idea. She reached back to do the same, and Eduard said, "Leave it down. Let them see that the Lady of Tiernan is returning."

Eleanor wasn't the Lady of Tiernan. That title belonged to Angen's wife, whoever that unfortunate woman was. Eleanor had no title. The young Lords of Tiernan and their sister: that was how they'd been presented, on those few occasions when they had all been presented together. Sometimes whoever was doing the presenting had even remembered her name. Still, she left her hood down, and as they entered the bivouac, activity around them gradually dwindled until nothing was happening at all. An eerie silence fell. She heard the whuffing of horses, the thuds of their hooves on the road, and the jingling and creaking of their tack. In the distance she heard the lilting croon of a shepherd calling his sheep. Dozens of hungry eyes stared up at them as they passed through the camp. She wondered if they'd recognized Gavin, after all.

But the men weren't staring at Gavin. They were staring at Eleanor. She was unexpectedly very aware of the cut on her face, which throbbed and stung.

The bulk of Eduard's men peeled off to the side, calling greetings to their fellows; Elly and Gavin and a few others followed Eduard into the courtyard, which was small and crowded with bales of wool. Not as many bales as Elly remembered, maybe, but the last time she'd been here, she'd been a child, and things had probably seemed bigger than they were. More of the space seemed to be taken up with small wooden chests. The boy who came to take Elly's horse was pure Tiernanese: the harsh cheekbones in his too-thin face, the watery blue eyes fixed on her. She remembered the staff children in the House, and smiled at him. "Thank you," she said, as he took the reins. The boy's eyes went wide and he scurried away, the horse following placidly behind him. Elly turned to Gavin. "They're all staring at me," she muttered.

"You're very pretty," Gavin said. "And they haven't seen you in fourteen years."

Eduard summoned a girl to take them to the guest rooms, and told them they would see Angen at dinner. The girl might as well have been the horse boy's twin, with the same watery blue eyes and the same underfed frame. Elly doubted they were related. It was hunger that carved them so thin, and ill health that brought their shared pallor. Tiernan had not been prosperous when she'd left, and it didn't look like anything had improved. The guest rooms were incongruously well-appointed, with thick rugs and warm running water. Eduard had ordered their scanty wardrobes brought from the ransacked guildhall, which meant they had cleanish clothes. Those clothes were the ones they'd had in their rooms in the House when the coup happened, nearly a year ago. Unpacking them, the girl ran her thin fingers over a hurried patch on Elly's dress and frowned.

"Lady Eleanor," she said, finally, "perhaps I may bring you clothes from the common store? They won't be fine, but—" They will be better than these, the girl didn't say. Instead, she said, "I can send a seamstress up, to make sure they fit."

The common store was where extra clothes were kept. Sometimes they were outgrown or outmoded, but most often the owners were dead. Elly had not cared about her clothes in a long time, but now she looked at the girl's own worn dress, considered Angen, and said, "Yes, please. That would be very helpful."

"The scar isn't that bad, you know," Gavin said when the girl was gone, as he splashed water over his hair.

A full-length mirror stood in the corner, its surface rippled like water and stippled with dark spots where the silver had worn away. Elly looked. The scar was a rose-colored seam along her cheek, from her jawline to her cheekbone, and she found she didn't mind it. The life a person lived should show. It was unnatural, the way the courtiers erased every imperfection and glossed every dull spot. "No, it's not," she said. "But if I know Angen, it'll be better for us if we look a little more—"

She hesitated. Gavin finished her sentence. "Like the Lord and Lady of Highfall?"

Elly smiled. The scar pulled. "Less like their serving staff, maybe."

He was combing his wet hair back, his movements relaxed and even. Facing provincial dignitaries was, after all, what he'd trained for: that, and occasionally killing them. She'd had the same training, without the killing, but she felt neither relaxed nor even. With his hair combed back, he almost looked like the Gavin in her memory. "Tell me about Angen," he said.

"He's cruel, and ruthless. And not as smart as he thinks he is. But he's good at terrorizing people into doing what he wants them to do."

"Most ruthless people are. You're scared of him, aren't you?"

"Yes," she said, simply.

"But you weren't scared of Eduard."

"Eduard can't decide what to wear without orders."

He finished his hair, turned to face her, and took her hand. He still wore Eduard's gloves. "I just realized," he said. "I'm not sure I've ever seen you scared before."

She half smiled. "I was scared when Theron was poisoned." Theron had never been the same after that, which was its own kind of dreadful, but that first long night when they didn't know if he would ever wake up—that had been terrifying.

"You didn't seem scared. You seemed angry."

"That, too. And I'm afraid of high places, remember?" Because when she was a child, Angen had chased her up trees, and then shaken them until she begged to come down, until she'd promise anything to have her feet on the ground again. "I couldn't climb the tower."

"You did, though," Gavin said.

Theron had helped her. Standing between her body and the edge of the staircase, holding her up. *Breathe, El. You can do this.* But Gavin thought Theron was dead. He thought she'd climbed the tower on her own. "I suppose I did," she said, and managed a smile.

The clothes the girl brought were better than Elly expected. Gavin's tunic was a rich brown, a more somber color than any he'd ever chosen for himself, but she supposed it suited a deposed City Lord. She'd even brought him some finer gloves that might almost be appropriate for a state dinner. The dress she brought for Elly was Highfall-style, all in one piece, which Elly was grateful for. Tiernan dresses were made up of three pieces—sometimes more—all pinned together in a way that left one unable to move quickly or even breathe without being poked. After a few minutes from the seamstress's calloused fingers, both the dress and the tunic looked, if not made for them, made for two people nearly their size.

While the seamstress worked, the girl rubbed lanolin into Gavin's boots until they shone as well as could be expected, and then turned to Elly. She had brought concealing cream for the scar, but Elly told her no. She insisted on doing her own hair, as well. The girl's own hair was in the two looped braids that young Tiernan girls had worn when Elly was a child, and apparently still did. Adult women braided their hair in a single loop, which the Tiernanese called a handle. Elly wanted no part of that. She braided her own hair and twisted the braid up, pinning it close to her head while the girl trimmed the ragged edges from Gavin's hair and pulled it back in a neat tail at the nape of his neck. Silly, simpering slippers were brought for Elly, absurdly pointed and with bows on the tips. They pinched, of course. Such shoes always did.

The pinching shoes, the tight bindings of the dress, and the long walk through the corridors on Gavin's arm—another accessory, like the bright buckle of the belt the girl had brought for him—it was like being in Highfall again. And Elly felt like she had in Highfall, when she'd been dragged to meet one courtier or another. Dread, disgust, resignation. She was grateful for the girl and the seamstress. But she missed her old boots, which had been—Theron's by way of Judah? No, Judah's had been lost. Theron's by way of Theron, the imprint of his feet inside them nearly worn away by now.

She and Gavin were still betrothed. She hadn't thought about that in ages.

The girl led them to a small, slightly shabby parlor where Eduard waited. He wore a clean tunic of Tiernan green with a gold rope around one shoulder to show that he was Second Lord. She would have to remember to tell Gavin what the rope meant. When he saw them, her brother looked relieved. "I told Moira to see you made presentable. I see she took the instruction to heart." He smiled at the girl, who blushed and ducked her head. But Elly saw the hint of a smile on the girl's lips. A shrinking feeling came over her.

"She is skilled, for one so very young," she said, emphasizing the last two words in a way that Eduard couldn't miss.

He didn't. His face tightened. "You may go, Moira," he said to the girl, who curtsied and left. Then he turned back to Elly. "I understand that you can only judge me by your memories of the callow boy I used to be, but I am not that boy anymore."

"So you don't jump when Angen calls, these days?" she said.

"Angen is the Lord of Tiernan. I step carefully around him." His eyes flicked to Gavin. "I would advise both of you to do the same."

"I always step carefully," Gavin said, without concern, and Elly managed, somehow, not to roll her eyes. Because arrogance was called for now, wasn't it? And hadn't Gavin grown up around courtiers? Hadn't he spent two decades stepping carefully around his father? The first time Elly had met Elban, she had been a child younger than Moira, but she had recognized his viciousness immediately. It was in the way his kind words never reached his eyes, in the way he had slid a ring on her finger—looking not at her, to see how she'd received the gift, but at all the other children, to see how they liked *not* receiving one.

The corridor Eduard led them down was familiar to Elly: the blackwork banners on the walls, the iron sconces, and the greasy sheep's tallow candles. When she was a child, her mother had scented the candles with lavender from her greenhouse and the manor had smelled of it, always, woodsy and friendly. Clearly that tradition had gone by the wayside, and now the manor smelled of sheep. It was a gray smell, somehow, like the stone walls and the light and the sky outside.

Then they walked into the main hall, and nothing about that had changed at all. It still smelled like wood smoke, sour sweat, ale, and overcooked meat. The dais at the end was barely worthy of the name, and the blackwork tapestry hanging behind its overcarved armchairs was the same one that had hung there when Elly was a child. It was moth-eaten now, a bit faded. In front of the dais, talking to a woman whose back was to them, stood two men, and one of them was her brother Angen. Seeing him was a million icy spider legs running up and down Elly's spine.

Be still, kitten.

Eduard led them toward Angen and she had no choice but accompany him on numb feet, feeling like a child again. Gavin offered her his arm and she took it; how she wished for some of his old insouciance, his imperviousness to tarnish. A single glimmer of it, to arm both of them against Angen. She drew herself up as straight as she could. She was not the scrawny child who had been sold out of this room when she was barely eight years old, and she was not the scared kitten promising her brothers anything if they'd let her down from the tree. She was Eleanor of Highfall, nearly the Lady of the City (twice over, if she counted those horrible weeks when she thought she'd have to marry Elban). After the coup she had kept the four of them alive, and after they lost Judah in the tower and Theron who knew where, she had single-handedly kept the

Seneschal's men out of the tower for nearly two weeks. She would not be afraid of Angen or anyone else.

Suddenly Gavin's arm clamped her elbow tight against his ribs. His eyes were fixed on the woman speaking with Angen. Elly assumed that the woman was Angen's wife, despite the slightly-too-glossy braided handle in her hair, for a Lady of Tiernan, and the slightly-too-grand gown. She didn't understand why Gavin was reacting so strongly. But then the woman turned around, and she was Amie of Porterfield, and Elly understood everything, all at once.

"Lord Gavin!" the horrible woman cried, and rushed over to him. She stopped short and curtsied, as if they were all back in the solarium in the House, surrounded by courtiers and perfume and fakery. Then she threw her arms around his neck, and Elly was forced to choose between pulling away from Gavin and stepping back, or being pulled into the embrace with them. She stepped back.

And found herself face-to-face with Angen. "Sister," he said, and took her hand. Pressed it to his mouth. He had a beard now, and a mustache. They were stiff and rough against Elly's hand and his lips were moist and yes, she was afraid of him, after all.

Dinner was predictably terrible. They sat, the four of them and Eduard, at one end of a long, empty table, along with the second man, who had been introduced to them simply as Burim, with no title or home province. Whoever the gaudily dressed man was, Angen considered him important enough to sit at his right hand. Serving girls—all young, and all with the same coltish prettiness as Eduard's pet Moira—brought food, one dish after another. Mutton stew, roast lamb with potatoes, nut bread, pickled onions, and melon. Sheep's cheese with everything. It was not a casual meal. It was, in fact, exactly what was served at the feasts of Elly's childhood. She wondered if this was deliberate, if Angen was trying to trigger some sort of nostalgia in her: some memory that didn't involve his sneering, his grasping fingers, the sweat-and-leather reek of him. Everything smelled too rich and too heavily peppered and it turned her stomach. She could not eat.

It didn't help that Amie of Porterfield had talked, incessantly, from the moment they'd been seated. "We went to our country houses, didn't we?" she was saying now. "Everyone did, after that awful Seneschal drove us out of our city. I was so worried about you, Lord Gavin, all those months when you were supposedly under house arrest. I knew the Seneschal couldn't be trusted, we all did. And then I heard he'd taken you out of the city, sneaking you out in the middle of the night like a common criminal!" Amie's cheeks flushed with outrage. She was still pretty. Her hair was thick and glossy, her skin like cream. Not a word had she spoken about the betrothal ball, when she'd so obviously expected Elly to be pushed aside in her favor. Nor had she mentioned the moment of silence after her expectations had not been met, when Elly herself had heard a thin high crack and only known when Judah told her later that it had been Amie's fan, breaking in half.

Angen, at the end of the table, watched Amie's performance with a smug half smile. He'd had the pox since last Elly had seen him, and his pitted cheeks probably explained the beard. That smile hadn't changed, though, and Elly did not need Eduard to tell her that he was still not to be trusted, and neither was Amie. None of this was.

"Then," Amie continued—her smile dazzled, how were her teeth such a pure white? "—I heard a rumor about that dreadful old guildhall where the Seneschal took you. Porterfield doesn't have much of an army, not really. All we have are a bunch of dull-witted metalfiber miners, and even they're all full of ideas, thanks to the Seneschal. As if we haven't been taking care of them for generations." Now, for the first time, her eyes went to Elly, and she smiled a beautiful, ersatz smile. "When I heard that poor Lady Eleanor's father had died, I realized that Lord Angen and I had mutual interests. The Seneschal had robbed both of us of people who were important to us."

Angen's gaze rested on Elly, and she thought, I am not small, I am not weak, I am not insignificant. Gavin said, "If Porterfield doesn't have an army, who did we see outside under the Porterfield banner, training the Tiernanese?"

Amie blushed prettily. "Why, Lord Gavin, you recognized our colors. Mercenaries, I'm afraid. Most of them used to work for courtiers, and liked it better than working for the Seneschal in New Highfall." Amie said the last two words with immense contempt. "They made their way to my father's country house, once I put the word out. Tiernan is really very beautiful, in a stark sort of way. And Angen and I get along famously." She turned to Angen. "If only you'd taken rooms inside the Wall, Angen, like the rest of the courtiers. We could have been friends for years. But I know you're too devoted to Tiernan to leave."

Angen was also too broke to ever leave, much less take a courtier's room inside the House. That had been true when she was a child, and judging by the stingy pours allowed from the one bottle of Sevedran wine Angen had brought to the table, it was still true now.

"You must be so relieved, Lady Eleanor, to finally be home safe with your family," Amie continued.

Safe and *with her family* were not concepts that Elly categorized together. Angen said, "It is, indeed, good to have our sister back where she belongs." His voice, like his skin, had roughened with time, but it still held the same nasty little purr.

"So much has changed since I was last here," Elly said. "What are the fields being planted outside? Eduard said it was something called glory."

Angen and the man Burim exchanged a smile, as if she were a child who'd said something amusing. "Ah, yes. It's a western crop. We are the first to grow it here. It's used to make the drops."

"It is very profitable," Burim said. "And very easy to grow."

"The drops the courtiers took?" Gavin said, frowning.

Angen laughed. "Everyone takes them these days, Lord Gavin. And soon, Tiernan will get a cut of every vial." He inclined his head toward Burim. "With our friend Burim's help."

"You're a dropmaker?" Gavin said.

"No, Lord Gavin. I am a broker." Burim held up his left hand, and turned it so that they could all see the tiny blue flower tattooed there. "My guild mark. We are quite an established guild, in the West, but as far as I know, I am the first to cross the Barriers. The Seneschal has a stranglehold on glory traffic into the city. My guild is exploring as many alternate markets as possible."

"Is the food to your liking, Lady Eleanor?" Amie said, in what was surely the least adroit change of subject Elly had ever witnessed.

Elly looked down at her nearly untouched plate. "I am merely tired." She made herself look directly at Angen and forced her face into the same pleasant vagueness she had reserved for courtiers, back in Highfall. "And I am sorry not to meet your wife, Lord Angen."

This was not a lie. Surely any woman married to Angen for any period of time would hate him as much as Elly did. Also, it had not escaped her notice that Amie sat in the seat traditionally given to the Lady of Tiernan, and she did not mind reminding the lady courtier that she didn't belong there.

That smug look the woman had worn at the betrothal ball, ridiculous butterflies bobbing on wires around her head—how sure Amie had been, that night, that she would take Elly's own place.

"Lady Yana prefers to take her meals privately," Angen said. "You will meet her soon enough."

"I look forward to it," Elly said.

Amie put another slice of roast mutton on Angen's plate, as his wife would have done had she been there. Another deliberate act. "Lord Gavin," she said, "more for you?"

When the food had been served, Elly's rusty training in dinner-party diplomacy had her thinking in circles. Should she serve Gavin, like the wife she would have been, had their lives turned out differently? Serving him could be taken as a sign of unity, capitulation, or subservience. Unity was fine, but Elly bristled at the other two. Before she could decide, Gavin had put a slice of mutton on her plate, a few chunks of potato, a pickled carrot. All of the things that were nearest to them. How that had been interpreted, Elly didn't know.

Meanwhile, Amie still held the slice of meat aloft, between a serving fork and a knife. A drop of blood fell from it to the wooden surface of the table. "No, thank you, Lady Amie," he said, and Amie put the slice on Angen's plate, instead.

Angen raised an eyebrow. "You eat with your gloves on, Lord Gavin?"

"You remember, Angen," Amie said, slightly chiding (and without the honorific, Elly could not help but notice). "We had word that Lord Gavin's hands were injured. Is it your bleeding condition, my lord?"

"Bleeding condition?" Gavin said.

"That afternoon, when we were—having coffee." Amie's pause was ever so subtle; the purr in her words, significantly less so. "Your poor hand began to bleed, and you had to rush away to call the magus."

Elly nearly laughed. Amie was talking about the time that Judah, angry at Gavin for ignoring her scratched requests to come talk to her, had driven a knife through her hand. Gavin had come to talk to her, all right, shirt mostly unbuttoned and bleeding hand wrapped in one of Amie's flimsy silk scarves. It hadn't been at all funny at the time. Elly had been furious. How she wished Judah were here now. How she missed meeting those dark, dark eyes across the room, and knowing that somebody else was watching, and finding the proceedings as absurd as Elly did. The corners of Gavin's mouth twitched. Elly knew he was suppressing a smile. She hoped he was smiling at the memory of Judah and not the so-called coffee he'd shared with Amie. "Right," he said. "My bleeding condition. Yes, the gloves help."

"Nobody mentioned a bleeding condition to us when Eleanor was promised to you," Eduard said, frowning.

"It's manageable," Elly said.

Angen waved the whole issue away with one crudely jeweled hand. "Hardly matters now. I was sorry to hear about Lord Theron's death, Lord Gavin."

Amie clucked her tongue. "Poor thing. He never was healthy, was he?"

Gavin didn't look at Elly. "He was brilliant," he said, instead, biting down on the consonants.

"We have no proof that he's dead," Elly said. "For all we know, he's still being held in Highfall."

"And what became of the Foundling?" Amie said, spreading butter on her nut bread. Nut bread was dense and dry and Elly hoped she choked on it. "It's such a challenge to get reliable news out of the city."

"Judah is gone," Gavin said. His tone was so cold it burned.

Amie gave him a sad, fake smile. "I'm so sorry. Is she dead, too? Forgive me for asking. You seemed so attached to her, back in the House."

"She's gone," Gavin said, and in the words Elly could hear the utter bereavement under the ice.

Amie heard it, too. For a bare second those pretty blue eyes studied Gavin. Then she smiled. "Well, the important thing, Lord Gavin, is that you're back with us, and safe."

"And now that we've freed you," Angen said, "we can take back Highfall, and put you on your father's throne where you belong."

Angen clearly expected the words to be a surprise. Elly refused to consider that she and Gavin might owe Eduard any gratitude for the forewarning. "Hear, hear," Burim said.

Gavin ignored the broker. "My father's throne doesn't exist."

"Of course it does. You don't think the Seneschal could hold the city if the courtiers rise against him, do you?"

Calm and collected, Gavin leaned back in his chair. "Do you think that's something they're likely to do?"

Angen lifted his chin. "Tiernan will."

"And Porterfield, as well," Amie said. "There are others, believe me—plenty of others—who aren't content to be mere merchants, as the Seneschal would have us be. We were taken by surprise when Lord Elban died, that's all. Now we wait only for the opportunity to reclaim what's ours." She reached a hand across the table. "And you're that opportunity."

Gavin looked at Amie's hand, lying on his gloved one as if it were a small animal that had crawled there. "And Eleanor?" he said.

"After all that my poor sister has been through," Angen said, "I'm sure she will want nothing more than to stay in Tiernan and live a quiet life. Even if you managed to get as far as an actual wedding, I think we can consider that contract void." He looked at Elly, a small smile curling under the beard. "I'm sure Lady Amie is better suited to help rule Highfall than Norrie is. From what I've heard, the Seneschal kept her so sheltered that she's completely ignorant of governance."

Ah. Elly understood, now. Lord Gavin and Lady Amie. It was the betrothal ball all over again. Gavin took his hand out from under Amie's. The lady courtier let him, and folded her hands neatly in front of her as if it were no consequence. "Elly has done nothing for the last fourteen years but learn governance," he said.

"Dinner parties and childbirth," Angen said. "Both of which will be useful, in my wife's household."

"A lady's maid?" Gavin laughed. "Eleanor?"

"Lord Angen is very wise," Amie said, chiding. "I've found his counsel invaluable. I'm sure he'll make the right decisions for Eleanor."

"Eleanor," Elly said, scarcely able to believe the words coming out of her mouth, "can make decisions for herself. And if you're relying on Angen's wisdom, you've backed the wrong horse, Lady Amie. Eduard was always the bright one."

Angen's lips pressed together. "You've picked up poor manners in Highfall, sister."

"The Foundling's influence, probably," Amie said.

"Her name is Judah," Elly said.

"Her name doesn't matter," Amie said.

"Let me make sure I've judged this correctly," Gavin said, sounding impossibly composed. Elly's own heart was pounding, her cheeks burning. "The two of you joined forces to rescue us from the guildhall so that Amie and I can be Lord and Lady of Highfall, and restore the courtiers to their former prominence?" He looked at Angen. "With you, I presume, as our trusted counselor, while Elly helps your wife pick out dresses in the morning."

Eduard shifted uncomfortably in his seat. "Rescuing you from the guildhall was no minor matter," Angen said. "Nor was it inexpensive. Have I not proven my loyalty?"

"Absolutely," Gavin said. "And we're grateful to you for breaking us out of the guildhall, aren't we, El? It was unbelievably boring there. No scenery to speak of. Nothing to do." This was Gavin at his most regal. All of Elban's lessons, all his example. "Tell me, how long do you expect me to live after we all work together to retake the throne?"

Angen blinked. Amie did not. Elly could only look at her plate. Because he was right. Obviously he was right. Angen and Amie wanted the throne. They had no interest in Gavin sitting there.

Gavin continued. "I'm guessing it won't be very long. A wasting illness, that's how I'd do it. Or maybe I'll be driven mad by tragedy and loss. That's romantic."

"You might find yourself filled with a desire to retire quietly, after all the fuss and bother of retaking the throne," Angen said, calmly.

"And let you take over?" Gavin said.

"Gavin, don't be silly," Amie said sternly. None of this Lord Gavin nonsense, now, Elly noticed. "We didn't go to all this trouble—"

Burning with anger, Elly said, "Yes, you did. This is exactly why you went to all this trouble." She looked at Burim. "And you? What's your stake in this?"

"I merely sell glory, my lady," the broker said, but there was a faint smile around his lips. He seemed to be enjoying himself.

"Eduard," Angen said, "take our sister back to her rooms. She's overtired." Eduard stood.

Gavin did, too. "We'll both go," he said. "I appreciate the

rescue. But even if I wanted to rule Highfall, which I'm not sure I do, it's not going to happen the way you're planning it."

"I'm sorry to hear that. I was hoping we could discuss this like men." Angen nodded at his guards, who moved to take Gavin by the arms.

Eduard had a hand on Elly's shoulder. "Lord Angen," he said, "shall I—"

"No," Angen said. "Let her watch."

"Wait," Elly said.

"Oh, dear," Burim said, and Amie said, "Don't damage his face, please."

Eduard's hand was stern on Elly's shoulder now, pressing her down into her chair. Squeezing gently, as if to reassure her. But she was not reassured. The two guards held Gavin while a third began to hit him: smashing fists into his stomach, delivering savage kicks to his shins and the big muscles of his thighs. Gavin did not even seem to fight back, although what could he do, pinioned as he was? The sound of boots and solid fists connecting with his flesh made Elly want to scream but she didn't want to give Angen the satisfaction. She couldn't stop the tears trickling down her cheeks. She thought: nothing will get better, ever.

Finally she could stay quiet no longer and managed to stammer out, "Stop this. Stop it, Angen."

"Hush, kitten," he said, and the beating went on, and on, and on.

EIGHT

WHEN JUDAH WOKE, THE SKY WAS THE SINGULAR blue of early morning, bright and dark together, and the rich smell of dew on the skeletal desert brush filled her nose. She was deliciously warm. It took her a moment to realize that the warmth came from her position sandwiched in between Lukash and Cleric. Her face was pressed against Lukash's back, which was heavily muscled and covered with soft, tightly curled hair. A long scar across his shoulder looked to Judah like a wound from a knife or a small sword. Behind her, she could feel Cleric. A lock of his hair had even fallen across her neck, still damp from the swamp. Stretched over the three of them was Cleric's long, wool-lined coat. Judah's every indrawn breath was thick with the reek of mildew and sweat. Both men seemed to be sound asleep. She didn't want to wake them. She also didn't want to be snuggled between them when they woke.

Carefully, she wriggled out, like a snake from its skin. The fire was burned down to coals, but she knew how to fix that. In a few minutes it was crackling merrily away again. Her trousers were dry, if stiff. Shivering, she pulled them on, and then cringed as she put her feet into her clammy boots. She was starving and itched all over, and she had to pee.

She found a place away from the clearing. By the time she was done, the sun was coming up in earnest. She pulled her trousers back up and looked around. Not far away, she could see the stand of trees that marked the edge of the lake where they'd left the swamp, and beyond that the green haze of the swamp itself. The primary color of the place where they'd come to rest now was dusty brown. The dirt under her boots was dry and sandy. Some of the bushes that dotted the plain were almost high enough to be considered small trees, but their gray-green stems were leafless and thorned. There was no grass here, except in tall clumps with stiff, bulblike tops. When she crushed one of the stiff bulbs between her fingers it was dry and hollow, crumbling to nothing.

Before she went back to the camp, she knew, she had to figure out the knife.

The world was more than what her eyes saw. She had always known that; her earliest memories were of Elban watching as the Seneschal and the old House Magus, Arkady, tested the bond between her and Gavin. Cut the child Judah, the young lord bleeds. Put Judah in the snow, Gavin's lips turn blue. And after the coup, in the tower, Nathaniel Magus had taught her about the Work, lifting her to a place where she could see the violently purple web of power that connected everything in the tower, filling the room like air. She could even see her bond with Gavin, a thick-woven rope of Work connecting her chest to his, no matter where they were. Toward the end, she had discovered that Nate had been stitching the stuff into her, too. Ripping those stitches out had hurt worse than any pain she'd ever experienced, bad enough that she hadn't been able to finish. He'd said, that last terrible day, that the tower wouldn't let her die. Maybe the stitches had been part of that. If so, she supposed she should have been grateful. Except that as part of the same ritual, he'd killed Theron, and tried to convince her to kill Gavin. So gratitude was not on the agenda.

But the Work had been more than the purple webbing, and for that, Judah *could* find gratitude. Because there had been other rituals, hadn't there? Nate had taught her to draw blood and, in that blood, to draw sigils: symbols that functioned like names or fingerprints, each unique to the person it signified. Through that messy, ridiculous ritual, she had been able to step into Nate's head, to see the world through his memories. In that other life, before she'd jumped, she'd never set foot outside the Great Wall, but through the Work in Nate's mind she'd seen oceans and mountains and ruins and prairies. She had seen campfires and villages, marvels and wonders. She had seen the first girl Nate had ever loved. She had watched his best friend die.

She had asked him why, if this power was so marvelous, she couldn't use it to fly or start fires with her mind, and he had told her it simply wasn't that sort of thing. Meaning, she guessed, the sort of thing that affected the outside world. But she *had* used it to step through Nate's memory and talk to his mother, Caterina—not his memory of her, but the woman herself. She had used it to find Gavin in the kitchen garden after the coup, tracing her way down the thick rope that bound them, and that had been real, too. When he'd hugged her she could smell the sweater Elly had made him. And later, in the tower, Nate had somehow used Theron's blood to paralyze Gavin, to hold him while Nate tried to convince her to take his knife and open Gavin's throat with it. Begged and wept and pleaded with her.

So clearly, despite what Nate had said, this power *could* be the sort of thing that affected the outside world. She also knew that she had done things in the Work that he had not expected. And, kneeling in the mud outside Black Lake, waiting for the executioner's axe (the same axe that Lukash had used to cut firewood the night before, and that called to mind the countless other necks that axe must have hacked its way through)— listening to the guards joke about what would happen to Cleric after he died and what would happen to her before she did— she had made the knife. She knew it. She had felt the tiny bits of rock, and wished that they were a knife, and felt in her hands—in her mind's hands? in her hands' mind? that didn't make sense—what that blade would feel like, and then it had been there. In the white she had thought about trees and they had formed in the mist, she had thought about her gown for Elly's betrothal ball and she'd been wearing it. Later she'd wished she'd thought about a practical coat and some sturdy boots, but by the time she'd realized she needed them she'd been firmly in this world, not the white, and it was too late.

White. Not purple. Her vision hadn't gone purple, there in that muddy field when she made the knife; it had gone white. Was it still Work, the white? Or was it something else? Could she do it again, or did she have to be afraid for her life? More important, what lie could she tell Lukash and Cleric to hide the fact that she had done it at all?

When she finally gave up and made her way back to the fire, the two men were nowhere to be seen. The executioner's axe lay in the dust next to the fire and the men's outer clothes were draped over the nearest bush. Had she thrown her lot in with these two? Had they thrown theirs in with her? Was the white the same as the purple, was the knife made out of Work? Could she do it again? Should she do it again? There had not been the sense of watching multitudes in the field that there'd been at the window overlooking the moor.

A burst of laughter from the bushes, and then the men were back. Lukash had two birds like small chickens, and Cleric carried a bundle of something slung over his shoulder. "Well, Thorn Bush," Cleric said, when he saw her. "I guess we find out now if you need the godswill or not, don't we?"

"I feel fine," she said.

"That's nice. I feel terrible." He looked terrible. The bandages wrapping his bare chest were tattered and filthy. She'd grown used to his split lip and black eye, and had completely forgotten that everything they'd done yesterday, he'd done with at least one broken rib. "I'm filthy and starving and smell like a dredged corpse. But I have good news." Carefully, Cleric put the bundle down and let it fall open. "Roots, eggs, and—" he touched a bundle of waxy leaves "—this, which is either a useful stimulant or a powerful purgative."

"Let me know when you figure out which," she said. "What are the reeds for?"

Because along with the eggs, roots, and leaves, he'd brought several large reeds, the kind she'd seen at the edge of the lake the day before. They grew in segments, closed on either end. "Canteens, eventually," Cleric said. "For water. You do like water, don't you?"

"I like it better than dying of dehydration," she said.

Meanwhile, Lukash was gutting the birds he'd caught, using the knife Judah had made. "How did you catch those?" she asked.

"They're stupid. Throw a coat over them, they think it's nighttime, you can scoop them right up. I didn't have my coat, so I used my braies."

"As if I didn't have enough nightmarish images haunting me," Cleric said.

Lukash grinned. "You've seen my ass before," he said, and handed Cleric the knife.

While Lukash speared the pieces of bird on sticks over the fire, and nestled the eggs and roots in the ashes around the edges of it, Cleric used the knife to bore two holes into the top end of each reed. Then he began to braid some of the long stiff grasses into what turned out to be a carrying strap. Judah sat, and watched. How bizarrely peaceful it all was. Yesterday they'd been running for their lives, and now they were making breakfast, as if they hadn't all nearly been executed the day before. The birds sizzled and smelled delicious. The last time she'd eaten was—breakfast at the inn. Tiny spoonfuls of jam, and rice, and eggs. The night before that, she'd had a bath. She wondered, idly, when her next bath would be. Then another thought struck her. "What happens now?" she said, to the two men.

Who looked at each other, and had one of those silent conversations that always gave her a tiny pang of missing Gavin. Lukash was the one who answered. "Now we head east, and get as far away from Black Lake as we can," he said. "The closer we get to the Barriers, the less power the cartel will have. You staying with us?"

Something in her chest eased. "Probably a better idea than striking out on my own, at this point. At least until we get to the next town."

"While we travel," Cleric said, "maybe you can tell us about this." He tossed the knife down on the ground in front of him. "Not that we aren't grateful for the tool, given the circumstances. But we'd love to know where it came from."

Judah's relaxation vanished. The thing in her chest grew tight again, and a prickle of warning ran up the back of her neck. She liked Lukash and Cleric. Maybe they were thieves and murderers, but they hadn't murdered her, and they might cheat at cards but they'd always played her straight. Still, there was no denying that they had saved her life in the Ghostwood not out of the kindness of their hearts but because there might have been profit in it. What would they do if they knew she could make weapons out of mud? "Found it," she said, and set her attention on the quarter of a wildfowl that dripped fat into the fire at the end of her stick.

"So somebody just happened to drop a knife on the Black Lake execution field, and the guards just happened to not notice it, then or afterward, and you happened to find it exactly when you needed it." Cleric's tone was dry enough to suck the moisture from the air around him.

Judah shrugged, hoping it looked more casual than she felt. "When you put it that way, it does seem unlikely. But that's what happened."

There was a silence. She still didn't look at them, but she could feel them looking at each other. "It's a funny sort of knife," Lukash said, finally. "I've never seen anything quite like it."

"Ugly as sin," Cleric said.

"And the balance is all wrong." Lukash picked it up, moved the blade back and forth as if testing it. "Almost as if it were made by somebody who'd seen a fighting knife, but never actually held one."

"Interesting that you say that." Cleric reached into his coat pocket, and pulled out a scrap of green fabric. "That's what I was thinking about this fabric from her dress. It's sort of like—if I were to describe cloth, without giving any indication of how cloth was made. Soft and flat, sure, but it's one solid piece. No warp. No weft."

He passed the scrap to Lukash, who examined it, and then held it out to Judah. Not knowing what else to do, she took it. Cleric was right. It was soft and flexible like fabric, but it was also a solid thing, as if it had been carved from marble. The real dress—the one she'd worn to the ball, taken off and never touched again—had been made for her by the House seamstresses, the first ever made specifically for her. Elly had fought the seamstresses to make sure it fit, and then put diamonds in Judah's hair, and later that night Judah had found Darid in the pasture and kissed him. "Odd," she said, and passed it back.

"Where did the dress come from?" Cleric said.

"I don't know," she said.

"Where did you get the knife?" Lukash said.

"I don't know." The juices dripping from the bird looked like blood. The juices dripping from the bird were blood.

"Did you take it from the winemaker's when we weren't looking?" Cleric said. "Neither of us would blame you for wanting a weapon we didn't know about, given the circumstances."

"Yes," she said. "That's what I did."

"There were plenty of good knives there," Lukash said, and held her knife up so she could see it. It was very clearly *not* good. The blade was uneven, the handle was awkwardly angled, and from where she sat it almost looked as if there was a pebble protruding from the hilt. "Why choose this one?"

"Lukash had a very special relationship with his knife," Cleric said. "I don't know if you noticed."

"I did. I really loved that knife. I'm also very curious about this one," Lukash said, and she could hear in their rapid, easy banter that this was a thing they did, this back-and-forth, to put people at ease. It didn't work with her. He flipped the ugly knife in his hand—the balance was so strange, it almost got away from him—and extended it, hilt out, to her. "Here. Take it."

"I don't want it," Judah said.

"You took it from the winemaker. You must have wanted it then." Lukash continued to hold the knife out to her. She continued to refuse to take it. A very long second passed.

Finally, Lukash flipped it back around. "You didn't take it from the winemaker, did you?"

She said nothing. She did nothing.

"Did you steal it on our way out of the Town Hall?" Cleric said. "Because if you're that good a thief, we should discuss a more long-term arrangement."

Quietly, Lukash said, "Give her a moment."

His golden eyes never left Judah. She felt pinned under his scrutiny, like the dead butterflies in a case some long-ago tutor had shown her. Why did things have to be so damned difficult? She should have left them in Black Lake as soon as they arrived. At least then, even if she'd still ended up in the Town Master's office, she would have had the tiniest modicum of control over what happened to her. Now here she was, in some nameless scrub desert west of the Barriers, and she had no control whatsoever. She trusted Cleric and Lukash not to murder her, or rape her, or poison her food. She did not trust them with the Work. For that matter, she didn't trust the Work, which had yanked her out of midair and dropped her in the Ghostwood with what seemed to all appearances to be a brand-new body and no boots. (Unless that had been the white, and she didn't know, so she didn't trust that, either.) The knife didn't feel like the Work, exactly. And it was such a sad, misshapen thing. They had needed it so badly. They would all be dead without it. The fat from the bird dripped and fell into the fire with tiny sizzling hisses that were gone as soon as they'd come, that were barely noises at all. She stared fixedly at it. "They were going to kill us," she said, staring at the bird. Drop. Sizzle. Vanish. Her voice was so controlled it was nearly shaking. "We needed a knife. I found a knife."

Lukash stood up. Three steps brought him to her side, where he crouched down next to her. Gently, he picked up her right hand, placed the knife into it. The misshapen hilt was grooved, she saw now, and as Lukash wrapped her fingers around the thing, her fingers slid into the grooves neatly. "It fits your hand like it was made for you," he said. "Or by you."

Very consciously, she rolled her eyes. "With what? Mud and the force of my charming personality?"

"I once saw a man who'd been chopped nearly in two kept alive by godswill," Cleric said. "He kept turning his head to look at his legs. The world is strange, my little foundling."

A fierce anger swept over Judah. She fixed Cleric with her gaze. "Do not," she said, "call me *foundling*."

Whatever he saw in her made him pull back, a tiny flicker of something—fear?—on his sharp features. Then her anger faded, and she was tired. Tired and hungry. The cooking birds smelled good. She'd had enough. "Fine. It's stupid, but if you want to see me try to make a knife out of mud, I'll try. Back up."

They both moved back. Not too far, and was she actually going to try to do this? No. Not in front of them. Not until she'd figured it out. Not that kind of thing, Nate had said, and yet. She put her hand down to the dirt and felt the prickle of pebbles under her palm. Calling to mind the white, remembering it until it began to creep around the edges of her vision. No, this wasn't Work, with its sigils drawn in blood and its reflective surfaces to draw the moon and the tide, with Nathaniel Magus and his small silver knife. It had been elegant, that knife, with a short, thin blade that folded into the handle. Not a weapon but a tool, made for straight, deliberate cuts in soft flesh. For cutting Nate's own arm open, and hers, and in his wildest deluded dreams, Gavin's throat—but most of the time it lived in its own special pocket in a leather satchel, and the leather satchel spent most of its time over Nate's shoulder. She could see the magus, as he'd looked that last day in the tower, slender and sickly, with a long straw-colored braid of hair down his back. He had drawn the sigils in blood on his own dirty arm, that day, and Gavin had gone unnaturally still, and the magus had held the knife out to her in the tower, weeping.

Take it. Let all his blood.

And Gavin, kneeling on the ground in front of her—

All at once her vision blazed purple, as if a veil had been thrown over it. And no, this was nothing like the white. She had slipped from the white to the Work without meaning to. She felt strong hands gripping her arms, like they had in Black Lake, and—Elly, she could see Elly, sitting in a gray room at a table with a tall, unfamiliar man standing behind her with a hand on her shoulder, and Elly looked horrified, and someone Judah didn't recognize said, *Oh, dear*, and someone else that she almost recognized said, *Don't damage his face, please*, and there came again that sense of countless eyes turning toward her, multitudes of observers, all attention drawn—

She forced her eyes open and in a moment of extreme disjointedness saw Cleric and Lukash crouched in the dirt and also Elly in the gray room, terrified, and the tall man holding her in place. Then pain pounded into her, a fist driven into her stomach. She cried out, curled double. Vaguely, she was aware of Cleric and Lukash staring at her, dumbfounded, and her fists were clenched so tight they hurt, and the invisible blow came again. This time in the ribs. Then in the thighs. Over and over. Elban and the Seneschal had trained her not to react to pain but it was as if all that training had washed off in the swamp, as if it had dissolved like smoke into the white, and she couldn't stop screaming. Cleric was bent over her, saying, "Let me see. Good gods, what's happening to you?" and she could hear Lukash saying, "Help her," and Elly saying, *Stop*, and the blows came and came and she could not stop them, she could not fight back, she could not escape. All she could do was lie on her side in the dirt, invisible hands like chains on her arms, and be tossed by the pain as if by one of the great furious waves in the ocean Nate had shown her. White crashing water on rocks below a broken ruin. The waves came again and again. Crashed. Splintered. Cataclysms of violence, cold as ice and bitter with salt.

Finally the blows stopped—faded?—and Judah lay where she'd fallen, pain pulsing from two dozen places on her body. She couldn't move. She could barely breathe. Cleric pulled at her clothes, extended each of her arms, and said, high and loud with frustration, "Damn it all, I don't see anything wrong."

"Can you sit up?" Lukash said, concerned.

Slowly, Judah pushed herself up on her hands. As she opened her fists something fell to the ground.

A knife. A small, silver knife: warped and slightly distorted, as if through memory.

The two men stared.

"Sainted Eleni," Cleric breathed.

NINE

LONG WERE THE DAMP HIGHFALL NIGHTS WHEN Korsa worked in his tiny chamber off the room where the thirteen-fourteens slept, trying to isolate what there was of the *kagirha* in the drops the Seneschal had sent. He tried to extract it with water and alcohol, with heat and distillation, and finally succeeded, to a degree, with a combination of orange oil and wine. But it still wasn't right. When he drank it, it did as he expected. It unmoored his conscious mind, let him move into someplace that was almost—but not quite—*kagirh*-space. Half a *kagirh*-space. Like riding in a cart with one square wheel, uncomfortable and wrong. And he was alone there, which was horrible and wrong. It also made him sick afterward.

"The drops do that to everyone," Anna said, after one such experiment, as she watched him dump a basin of vomit out the window.

"Cursed stuff, cursed place," he said, in his own language. The words felt like liquid on his tongue and made his heart hurt.

Anna blinked. "That sounds like what you say in your sleep. What does it mean, Chief?"

They had started calling him this of their own accord, a few days before. He didn't feel like the chief of anything but he found it oddly endearing. "In my own language, they mean, I am glad to have you as my friend."

"It's pretty," she said. "I wish I could understand it."

With a flash of inspiration, he said, "That is what *kagirh* is. Imagine that in an instant, you understood. Not only my language, but everything. The trees, the birds—"

Her eyes widened with shock. "You understand what the birds are saying?"

"No. But I understand them. All the living things. Because we are all alive, you and me and the birds and the grass. *Kagirha*, the herb, opens the door to *kagirh*, where we are all the same. And you can join with others there, and if the joining is true it will stay when the *kagirha* fades. You will still be yourself, but you will not be alone anymore."

"So I take this drug, and then I can understand the grass, and also I can see in your head," she said. "And then the drug wears off, and I can still see in your head?"

"More than that, we would understand each other." He shook his head. "Still. I won't let any of you take it until I'm sure that it's safe and I'm sure you're willing."

Was this deceitful, what he was doing? This careful choice of words. *I will not* let *any of you take it*, as if it were a great privilege. He was telling the truth. He would not force any of the thirteen-fourteens to take the drug. But he was also not telling the truth, because the more he came to know them, the more he was afraid of what would become of them if the Seneschal decided his plan wasn't working. And the more time he spent in that awful empty half a *kagirh*-space the more he missed his own *kagirh*. Life without them was terrible and lonely. Alone, he felt like a fifth of a person. He did not fully trust himself not to encourage the thirteen-fourteens to take the drug, to try and heal that terrible wound.

"Say more in that other language," Ida said, coming near with bright, greedy eyes. "I've never heard another language before."

So he said in Nali, "If I leave this place alive I will take all of you with me," and the girls laughed, and kept him sitting with them, saying any phrase they could think of, until food came.

The next day, after breakfast, Anna came to him again, her crutches tapping softly on the floor. "You know," she said, which was how all of the thirteen-fourteens said good morning, and hello, and how are you, "I used to be able to walk."

Korsa, who was exhausted and depressed from another long night moving in and out of the horrid empty *kagirh*-space and had been staring blankly out the window at a fallow field, turned to look at her. "Did you?"

She nodded. "I got a fever. When it went away, my legs wouldn't hold me up anymore."

"How old were you?"

"Four. Five. But I remember walking. Sometimes I dream about it." She hesitated. "If I took this drug you're talking about—"

"It wouldn't help you walk," he said.

"But I could feel you walking," she said. "What would it feel like? Not walking. The herb. And I want to know what it would *really* feel like, not all that loosy-goosy stuff you were saying before."

He chose his words carefully. "If it worked correctly—

which it doesn't, yet—you would feel strange. Not unpleasant. It goes away."

"Like being drunk?"

"Much like that. But while you are in that space, while your mind is untethered, I will connect us. Or try to."

"I've been drunk. I've even had drops. Can it be undone?"

"Yes. It would be very difficult, and very sad, but it's possible."

"All right, then," she said, decisively. "I'll try your *kagirha*, Chief."

"Anna," he said, alarmed by the twisted bloom of hope within him, "are you sure?"

"The worst that can happen is that it won't work, right?" she said. "And I'll be no worse off than I am right now. Sure, I'm sure."

"All right," he said. "When it's ready," and she said, "When it's ready."

Soon after that—the days all blurred together, an endless flow of meals and games and walks and finally, when the thirteen-fourteens had exhausted all of the things they could usefully do, sleep for them and experiments for Korsa, along with headaches and nausea and loneliness and misery—the Seneschal came to the workshop for a progress report, and as they always did, he and Korsa walked up the corridor, where the thirteen-fourteens couldn't hear. He asked Korsa how he was faring with the drops, and Korsa hesitated. The moment he did, he knew it was the wrong thing. Charming Faolaru, who knew the workings of human minds better than anyone Korsa had ever met, would have groaned and torn at his lovely hair.

Frown, Korsa, he would have said. *Smile. Laugh. Anything. But never let them see you deciding what to tell them.*

And, sure enough, the Seneschal's eyes went keen and incisive. "What has happened?"

"I have made progress," Korsa admitted. "But it is not there yet."

"Not there yet?"

"It is wrong." Korsa used the metaphor that had occurred to him earlier. "It is like riding in a cart with one square wheel. Rough and unpleasant." *Purple*, he almost said, but didn't, because it made no sense.

"A cart with a square wheel still works. Perhaps it moves slowly, and tires out the horses pulling it. But it still works."

"Yes," Korsa said, "but we are not dealing with cart wheels and tired horses. We are dealing with human minds."

"True enough." The Seneschal rubbed the back of his neck, his hand drifting toward the rippling scar on the side of it. "Chieftain, I must admit. I feel a bit like a tired horse myself. The city is running efficiently, thanks to the factory managers, but the city is only one part of the empire. Trying to pull along that one part without the others is also like trying to pull a cart with a square wheel. Do you know how I plan to solve that problem?"

Korsa said nothing. He didn't need to.

"I'll solve it one step at a time. When a material is unavailable, I look at what is available and adapt. The managers grew restless, felt that they were working too much for too little return. So I created the House of Repose, and now they are willing to work a bit more. Perhaps you can take the same approach with your problem. One step at a time."

"I have done so," Korsa said. "I am doing so."

"Then perhaps you are walking in the wrong direction," the Seneschal said. "You have only tested your *kagirha* on yourself, I assume? Perhaps you have come to the end of that particular road. Perhaps it is time to begin testing it on others."

"It is not ready," Korsa said.

The Seneschal gestured to him. "You've taken it. You seem fine."

"I am Nali. My mind is different from theirs."

"If we opened your skull, I think we would find otherwise," the Seneschal said, his voice hard. Then he sighed, and looked tired again. "That was not a threat. Or at least, not a serious one. But I'm afraid our circumstances have changed. I've lost access to Gavin, which means that I am now missing two pieces of this puzzle."

"What do you mean, you've lost access?"

"The hall where I was keeping him was raided." The muscles in the Seneschal's jaw were tight, and Korsa sensed a deep well of anger in that tightness. "There were no survivors, except presumably Gavin himself. We didn't find his body, at least."

Korsa did not mind seeing the Seneschal so discomfited. "You do not know who is responsible?"

"I am investigating," the Seneschal said impassively. "Meanwhile, your work has become more important than ever. I cannot keep those children here forever. The staff are beginning to talk, and the managers are beginning to ask questions. Difficult questions, some of them." Now the man's gray eyes were steady on Korsa. "Perhaps we overestimated the number of children you need. Are there any that you feel will be less useful to you than others? What about the silent girl?"

Florence. Korsa felt as if the man had opened his stomach and pulled out some vital organ. "I will need them all," he said, through numb lips.

"Then I suggest you put them to work," the Seneschal said.

He stayed up all night after that, working. The *kagirh* was not quite there, not quite right, no matter how he changed it. What the Seneschal had said was abhorrent. Talking about opening skulls—Korsa would have relished the chance to open the gray man's skull, if it came to that, and that *was* a threat. Or would be, if Korsa ever had the means and opportunity. (And what would happen to the thirteen-fourteens then?) But he had to admit that there was at least a chance that the Seneschal was right. *Traveling the wrong road will only bring you farther away*, Raghri the pragmatist had said, more than once, and Giorsa, who could make an herbal salve that would numb any pain and prevent any scar, had said the same thing. To the point, in fact, where it had become a kind of slang among them, for the kind of reckless decision that occasionally needed to be made, in life or in battle. *I am going to travel the wrong road.*

Now Korsa was so turned around and alone and bereft that he didn't know what the wrong road was. He heard the thirteen-fourteens rise in the other room, the yawns and giggles and petty squabbles of too many people trying to accomplish the same washing-and-dressing tasks in too small a space. He heard the tap of Anna's crutches, the louder *thunk* of Jesse's cane, somebody—maybe Liam—saying, crossly, "Would you move, already?"

Korsa sighed, and stood up. All the roads were wrong. He supposed there was some consolation in that.

In the eating room, rolls and honey were laid out. The diet in the orphan houses had been sparse—"Gruel, gruel, and more gruel," Ida had said—and now the thirteen-fourteens ate greedily, licking every sticky drop from their fingers. Even Florence, who sometimes had to have food spooned into her mouth because she couldn't be bothered, was feeding herself this morning. Korsa took a roll from the plate. They were soft and white and only slightly dry.

"Did you sleep yet, Chief?" Ida said, passing him the pot of tea. "You look exhausted."

"Not yet." He put the roll back down.

The room grew quiet. They were staring at him, all of them. Except for Florence. They were perceptive, these thirteen-fourteens. They had grown up in a precarious world, where any stability could be snatched away from them as easily and cruelly as a crutch. Finally, Liam said, "Well, either you figured out the mind-stuff, or we're all going back to the orphan house. Which is it?"

Neither. He could not lie to them and tell them otherwise. "The *kagirha* is not quite right. But—"

"It works?" Jesse said.

"Will it make us throw up?" Ida said.

"I want to try it," Anna said.

A hush fell over the room. Liam leaned forward. "Are you sure, Anna?"

"Sure, I'm sure," she said, with a tremble of bravado. "Somebody's got to be first, don't they? Let's have it, Chief."

"Is it that simple?" Ida said. "You just drink the stuff?"

"In my country, there were words said," Korsa said. "But only for the sake of ritual. In emergencies, a *kagirh* could be formed without them."

"What counts as an emergency?" Jesse said.

"War, or disaster."

Jesse broke into a thin smile. "I don't know about war, but New Highfall's pretty much a disaster. Can you do more than one of us at a time?"

"I do not even know it will work for one of you," Korsa said.

"Back off, Jess. I'm first. Next time, stand up faster," Anna said, and poked him with her crutch. Then she turned to Korsa. "Can we do it now? I don't want to wait, and get nervous."

She seemed nervous already. He certainly was.

Are there any children who will be less useful to you than others?

He was a very long way down the wrong road.

He fetched the small bottle he'd prepared from his work-room back to the eating room, and poured out a careful measure for her and a careful measure for himself. The stuff wasn't the right color. *Kagirha* should be the clearest of greens, and the liquid in the two glasses was a murky brown. It smelled strongly of oranges and vinegar. Anna wrinkled her nose. "Yuck," she said, then picked it up and drank it, all in one go.

Quickly, Korsa did the same. For a moment the room was filled with tension, the taut moment between the lightning's flash and the break of thunder. Then he felt his mind lift out of his body. Real *kagirha* would have raised him gently, like an infant from a cradle, but the degraded stuff in his bottle had no gentleness about it, no care. He was spilled upward, somehow. Or out. The room, the table, the bread and honey, the circle of watching thirteen-fourteens dissipated like smoke blown away in the purple wind. But there was no wind. There was nothing.

Kagirh-space was supposed to be pure being, a white sea of potential waiting for whatever the *kagirhi* chose to create. The place where Korsa found himself now was the break of thunder. It was the maelstrom, nebulous and dark. He had no words there. The simplest of thoughts had to be wrenched from his mind and even then it took everything he had to hold them. He had to find his *kagirh*. Raghri and Giorsa, Faolaru and Meita—

No. It was Anna he had to find. And as he thought of her, he saw her, through the spinning violet darkness. Her drab dress, a shiny spot of honey below her lip. And under each arm, a wooden crutch, worn smooth where they pressed against her body and where she gripped them with her hands. She seemed startled. He managed to say her name and she looked up at him through the purple storm with wide-eyed delight. She raised her arms. The crutches drifted away like feathers.

Chief! she said, the word coming to his ears garbled but intact. *Chief, look!*

I see you, he said, or thought he said, and then Anna's form blurred, and was gone. Smoke, blown away in the wind.

He cried out her name, even though speech was of no use here, and reached for her, to bring her back. But Anna was not there. Anna was nowhere.

Anna was gone.

Her body lived only a few minutes once she was no longer in it. "You got it wrong," Liam said, angry, and Korsa could not speak, could not move, as Ida wailed and Jesse called Anna's name and Florence stacked her buttons, endlessly, endlessly.

The Seneschal came with the men who took her body away. He pulled Korsa aside. "What happened?" the gray man said. "What went wrong?"

"What went wrong," Korsa said, tuneless and blank because he was unable to muster any feelings except anger and grief, "is this place. Everything is dead here. The air. The water. Now Anna."

"I'm sorry," the Seneschal said, not unsympathetically. "Progress is not always easy or straightforward. Sometimes there are losses. Perhaps she was simply the wrong child for the experiment. Perhaps she lacked—something."

Anna had lacked nothing, save for good health and a family that could afford to take care of her and a life far, far away. It was on the tip of Korsa's tongue to say so, but then he saw the Seneschal's eyes, the chill there at odds with the sympathy in the rest of him, and knew that the Seneschal would have him work through every one of the thirteen-fourteens, and only when they were all dead would Korsa be allowed to die, too.

He did not know what they did with Anna's body. He did not know how, or if, Highfall honored its dead. The remaining thirteen-fourteens retreated into themselves, grieving and afraid. Ida lay on Anna's bed, clutching the other girl's blanket and weeping. Jesse, who had volunteered along with Anna, now would not meet Korsa's eyes, but Liam would not let them go. His gaze was dark and threatening.

Korsa went into his small antechamber and did not come out. Outside, the sun climbed high in the sky. When it had risen, Anna had been alive.

There was so much he hadn't told them.

He had told them of the marvelous parts of *kagirh*: how wonderful it was never to feel alone, how glorious to see through another's eyes. To know someone completely. To trust them completely. So that he, Korsa, whose mind worked in maps and diagrams, knew the graceful flight of Meita's imagination and the clarity of Raghri's perception. He, who had always felt the right words slip out of his grasp like so many fish, could know what it was to be Faolaru, to play words like music, or to see plants not as markers on a scroll but as their own living entities the way Giorsa did. He had told Anna that through him, she could walk, and he had said so in front of all the others. As if the different ways their bodies worked were wrong, were his to fix. The way Ida moved was beautiful, the way her strong arms worked in concert with the momentum of her body—did she even want to see the world from his height? He hadn't asked. He had merely assumed, and held the assumption out in front of her like one of the sweets she so loved.

And he had not told them the loneliness of *kagirh*. The anguish when one of your *kagirhi* died, and how some, having seen those left behind go mad with grief, chose not to risk entering *kagirh* at all. He had not told them how as those in *kagirh* aged, they often made plans to kill themselves together rather than suffer the pain of losing each other one by one. He had not told them of the way that *kagirh* could separate mothers from children and lovers from each other, because no relationship would ever be as primal, as necessary, as those one had with one's *kagirhi*.

Anna. Oh, Anna.

He had given her the liquid. He had let her swallow it. He knew it had not been exactly right—how could it be, here?—but it had never occurred to him that it would kill her. And now that the Seneschal knew the stuff existed, he would force Korsa to give it to them all, one by one. And they all would die like Anna.

So there would be nothing to give. Not until he got it right. The rest of the elixir sat in front of him, in an old wine bottle. He grabbed it and drank it. No careful measurements this time. All of it, every foul drop. Perhaps it would kill him, too, and so what if it did? At least he wouldn't have to watch the thirteen-fourteens suffer.

And then the stuff was inside him, and he realized how selfish that was, but it was too late to go back.

It hit him like an iron club. His mind was not so much lifted out of his body as it was brutally ejected. The space on the other side of the water was purple, swirling, turbid. He was buffeted and tossed about, as if in a flood. The storm tossed him from side to side. He could almost feel the power trying to nibble at him, to erode him—and meanwhile the thirteen-fourteens were on their own, back in the real world, and if he was going to do this stupid thing he should at least have figured out a way to keep them safe first.

Then, unmistakably, he felt the sensation of two hands gripping his wrists. They were not of his memory. They were other, and they were from elsewhere. There was a wrench, a tearing that was somehow thick—

And then the air was calm around him, and fresh. His cheek was pressed against something rough that felt like a rug, and he was warm, as if he lay in a patch of sun. The scratchy wool, the vague smell of dust, the heat—these felt real.

But Korsa had been working in *kagirh*-space since he was thirteen or fourteen, himself, and he knew when he was there and when he wasn't. He was there, now. Full *kagirh*, not the broken semi-*kagirh* that had killed Anna—but also not the stable, comfortable space his own *kagirh* had built. This was somebody else's mind. Under the calm air he could feel a constant pull—toward death or something else, he couldn't tell. It was like fighting a current in water. He couldn't think clearly here. Thorns snagged at his mind, his thoughts. The thorns, somehow, were purple.

He opened his eyes. He did, indeed, lie on a rug, a faded and flowered one. In front of him he could see a turned furniture leg, made of some dark wood. Beyond that, a glass door opened onto a sunny terrace made of the same white stone as the Wall.

He lifted his head, turned it the other way. The room seemed to be a sitting room, with sofas and chairs as faded as the rug. It was no room Korsa had ever seen before. On one of the sofas sat a young man, lean and lanky, with long sandy hair. He was leaning forward, peering intently at Korsa through dirty eyeglasses, his elbows propped on his knees and his hands loosely laced in front of him. "Are you conscious?" the young man said, in perfect Highfaller. "Can you think?"

Odd questions. But perhaps not here, wherever this was. Korsa pulled himself to sitting. A door stood open on either side of the room, but through them he saw nothing but blankness. There was nothing to see over the terrace wall, either. He could feel the unsteadiness, the faint shimmer, of *kagirh*-space.

"I can," Korsa said. The words sounded right enough.

The young man leaned in, more intently. "Tell me something I don't know."

Korsa stared at him. "How do I know what you don't know? I have no idea who you are."

"Then it should be easy. You should have lots of memories without me in them." The young man spoke with command, but at the same time there was something tremulous in him. As if command was not his normal state, and he was only brought there through some stress. His lower lip was trembling, and so were his long-fingered hands.

Korsa defaulted to the way he would have introduced himself to another Nali. "My name is Korsa. I am joined in *kagirh* with Raghri, Giorsa, Faolaru, and Meita, but they are far away, and I am here alone. And I have done something terrible."

The young man frowned. "Well," he said. "I don't know what very many of those words mean, so I guess you're not something I made up. And I don't know about terrible, but if you're here, you've certainly done something very interesting." He stood, and reached a hand down to Korsa; who took it, and then found himself standing, as well, without making any effort to do so. This young man, whoever he was, had a slippery sort of control over this place, and of him, as well. He would have to be careful.

"It's nice to meet you, Korsa," the young man said. He was very thin, with a long face. "Although at this point, it's nice to meet anybody. My name is Theron. And I'm pretty sure I'm dead."

TEN

ON VITRIOL STREET IN MARKETSIDE, NEAR WHERE Highfall's Textile District met the Dye District, stood a four-story house made of red-brown brick. Because it was more difficult to knock a hole in brick than plaster and lathe, the temptation to knock out an exterior wall of one of the upper stories and build a rickety wooden attach extending out over Vitriol Street had been resisted. This made the brick building one of the most stable in Marketside, and therefore one of the few worth investing in. The building had glass in the windows and pipes that ran water to every flat. The topmost flats had flush toilets, the waste running through more pipes down to the pit privy in the back garden. The larger flat even had a skylight. In the morning the light there was fresh and clean, and in the afternoon a warm burnished gold.

Firo of Vitriol Street—formerly Firo of Cerrington—lived in that larger flat, and he loved to watch the light change. He loved the flat, the two small rooms that were the closest thing he'd had to a home since he was a child. He loved the wooden floors, rubbed to silkiness by who knew how many years of feet, and he loved the creamy milk paint on the walls, and he loved the bright rag rug William's mother had made for them. He loved the enameled teakettle that sat on top of the tiny woodstove. Like most of Marketside, William drank cinnamon tea, and the whole flat smelled warmly of it. Sometimes on winter nights they steeped the tea in warm wine and drank it with honey. Sometimes in the morning they ate sweet bread and cheese for breakfast without even leaving bed.

Firo of Cerrington had woken each morning in his grand rooms in the House, surrounded by a riot of color, and had dined by his window or in one of the retiring rooms on meat with rich sauces, too much butter, strong coffee. Dressing had taken him an hour. His hair and cosmetics had taken another hour, getting the swirl of his oiled hair right and the kohl and lash blackener around his eyes perfect. Firo of Vitriol Street owned two plain linen shirts, one coat, and no perfume. He hadn't changed his earrings in weeks, although he still liked a little kohl and lash blackener.

Firo of Vitriol was much happier than Firo of Cerrington.

Part of his happiness came from William, who worked for an inker, pulling in the rafts of pigments that floated down the Brake from the factories in the Dyeing District. He was strong and capable of many things and very delightfully simple—not simple like the man who worked the midden heap in the House had been simple, but simple in the way the flat was simple. Clean and straightforward and pleasant. Life in the House had been laborious, all the time: the layered courtcraft of every conversation, the faceted calculations behind every decision. It had taken Firo some time after the coup to learn to say what he meant without dousing it in subtext and innuendo. Simple things like, *Yes, I would like more tea*, which had carried such weight inside the Wall but in Marketside only meant that he wanted more tea. It had taken him even longer to be able to stand William's gaze and his bright, genuine affection without squirming. Finances were slightly complicated, but the inker paid steadily if not luxuriously, and Firo's skill at double-talk and bargaining made him useful to people who needed that kind of thing. Most of those people were as unsavory as any courtier he'd ever strolled the Promenade with, but in Marketside he was free to walk away if he wanted. He had never been free to walk away from anything before. Come to think of it, he had never before found himself in a situation from which he so assuredly, definitively didn't want to walk away.

When, however, he turned the corner onto Vitriol Street and saw the three people waiting in front of the solid brick building, he very much wanted to walk away. The girl was only vaguely familiar, and the tall man he didn't know at all, but he recognized the former House Magus instantly—for all that he was thinner than when Firo had last seen him, his long blond hair now short and dark and his spectacles missing. Firo knew him from the way he carried himself. He had found the magus interesting-looking, back in the House corridors. A type that Firo liked, slightly boyish and not too pretty—but then he'd had a conversation with him, and the magus had turned out to hold the same loathsome opinions that Firo's own father did, and that made him significantly less attractive. In short, he had no positive associations with the magus and was not happy to see him standing outside his place of residence.

At the same time, the not-quite-dead courtier inside him perked up like a cat who'd caught a whiff of mouse. The last he'd heard of the magus, he'd been taken to Highfall Prison to die. That he was now standing on Vitriol Street with his bones showing under his skin and his magus's queue cut off was intriguing to a degree that the non-courtier Firo found dismaying.

Before he'd figured out what to do next, the girl noticed him. She tugged at the magus's sleeve and pointed in Firo's direction, and when the magus looked up Firo was shocked to see the utter defeat in his eyes. The man standing with them, the one Firo didn't know, looked at him, too, and it turned out that Firo did know him, after all. Not his name, his story, or where he'd come from, but the core of him, because Firo knew a predator when he saw one. And the stranger was, without a doubt, a predator.

There was something ineffably non-Highfall about the stranger, the cut of his coat or the bottle-green color of his trousers. Perhaps, as with the magus, it was the way he held himself. If the magus looked defeated, this man looked as if he'd won. Firo took his time walking down Vitriol, observing them, learning. The girl was at that awkward liminal stage that came after childhood, wearing a body that she no longer found quite comfortable. She hovered protectively near the former magus, her slender shoulders angled like a barrier between the two men. Marketside through and through, her boots were worn and her hair braided against her head like a servant's. Now Firo remembered where he'd seen her. She'd worked for the magus in those last weeks before he disappeared, when Firo was helping Vertus, the black marketeer, with his little drops enterprise. Firo had been tasked with picking up the drops from the House Magus's manor house on Limley Square, and the magus had kicked up an annoying amount of fuss if Firo knocked before she'd left the house.

The closer he drew to the small group, the more Firo felt the calculation of the apparently-still-living courtier creep back over him. It felt like slipping into bed with somebody you didn't particularly like but still wanted to fuck. "Why," the courtier said, through Firo's own mouth, "it's my lovely magus. What a delightful surprise. I'd heard you were in prison."

"I was," the magus said. He had always been quiet, but now he was the kind of quiet that had all the life leached away. "I'm out now."

"Legitimately?" Firo said, as though it were a perfectly normal question. As though escaping from Highfall Prison was the sort of thing a person could actually do while still possessing a heartbeat.

The girl laced her arm through the magus's. It was sweet, this tiny almost-child, so protective of the sad, broken man. The magus himself said nothing. The stranger stepped forward. "My name is Saba," he said, smiling brightly. "I'm an old friend of Nathaniel's. I'm afraid he's a bit the worse for wear, after his time spent at the Lord Seneschal's pleasure." Courtiers had used the phrase *Lord Elban's pleasure* to describe a certain kind of extremely well-appointed detention, but Firo had never heard the Seneschal's name substituted in. His guard, already well up, doubled as the man went on. "We would like to talk to you about reviving a business arrangement you and Nathaniel once enjoyed. Is there somewhere we could talk privately?"

A business arrangement. That would be the drops. Firo had found that arrangement extremely beneficial, and since the magus had vanished, he had felt the lack of it. He was still able to negotiate occasional imports of specialized, usually illegal goods, and Vertus appreciated that, but none of his current schemes were as profitable as the drops had been. "Perhaps over a cup of tea upstairs," he said.

Still smiling, Saba said, "Most welcome, yes."

And that was how Firo of Vitriol Street ended up leading

them up to his beloved rooms, his precious sanctuary away from every sordid thing that happened on the street below: the broken former magus, the half-starved Marketside girl, and the predatory foreigner. He gestured them inside with a feeling of distaste, as if they had the pox. But he pushed the feeling down. "Tea, then," he said, and put the enameled kettle on to heat.

"This is a lovely room," Saba said, his eyes devouring the details of the room with a specific attention that Firo remembered from the House, from painted and adorned courtier eyes sweeping every corner for information. Were the wall hangings growing thin? Was there a stray roll wrapped in cloth on a shelf, put aside for a hungry moment, or a half-full bottle of wine? Which drawers had no locks, which looked hastily shut? But he and William had nothing to hide in this room. They were poor. This was Marketside. Everyone was poor.

"I like it," Firo said. "So, reentering the drop trade, are you, magus?"

The magus's shoulders slumped. "My name is Nathaniel. Nate."

"All right. I know who's living in your old manor house, Nate, and it's not you. How do you propose to make drops without your lab or your herb garden?"

Nate, standing awkwardly in the middle of the kitchen, looked as if Firo had kicked him. Quickly, Saba said, "Perhaps you and your associates might be willing to help us find supplies. Surely Nathaniel's skill would be worth that much of an investment."

"Maybe. But you say he's the worse for wear, after his time in prison. How do I know the tattered parts aren't the ones I need?"

Saba smiled again. Firo didn't like his smile. There was

something too knowing about it. "Nathaniel will not disappoint you."

"I would like to hear that from Nathaniel," Firo said.

The girl still held the magus's arm as if she were holding him up. His expression was morose, distant, like a man being led to the gallows. The girl, though—her eyes licked everything in the room as greedily as Saba's had. Less calculation and more desperation, perhaps. Now she shook the magus's arm gently, as if to wake him up. "Magus," she said.

"I can do it," Nate said, without any emotion. "If I have the materials. I can make you a list."

Firo shrugged. "I don't even know if Vertus is interested. Perhaps he's found other herbalists who don't require an investment." But Vertus would be interested. Nate's drops, in their dull silver vials, had been Vertus's best sellers. Firo had heard him complain more than once about their loss.

"Surely the skills of the former House Magus are superior to those of other herbalists in this city," Saba said.

The door opened and William entered, his hair wet and dripping on his shirt from the public baths down the street. The baths weren't particularly clean, but they were enough to wash off the smell of the ink vats. His eyes widened with surprise when he saw the visitors. "What's this?" he said in the voice Firo found so charming, musical but with the faintest of rasps.

"You remember the House Magus, William, my love," Firo said. "Apparently we're to call him Nathaniel now. And these are Saba, and—" He realized he didn't know the girl's name.

But William was already nodding. "One of Nora Dovetail's girls. I'd recognize that hair anywhere. Which one are you? Rina?"

The girl gave him a cautious look. "No, Rina's my sister. I'm Bindy. You're Will Ember, right?"

"That's me." William grinned. "My ma has the bakery two streets over from your house."

Saba watched this exchange with mild interest. But a spider knew a spider, and Firo recognized the impatience simmering under Saba's surface. "We just came to talk with Firo briefly. We're almost done," Saba said to William.

The words were a dismissal. The teakettle shrieked and William smiled. "Finish your conversation, then," he said, mildly. "I'll pour the tea."

"I'm afraid it's rather a private conversation."

"Well," William said, "you're having it in my kitchen, aren't you?" He put a hand on Firo's shoulder, which Firo covered with his own.

Saba's eyes darted back and forth between them, and then fell back into placid pleasantness. "Well, in that case," he said, as if it were a complete sentence. "Are you interested in our proposal?"

"I'll speak to our friend about it." Firo stood. "Now, if you don't mind—"

"Of course," Saba said, and stood, as well. But as he moved toward the door, the girl grabbed the magus's arm and clung to it, keeping him behind.

"Please," she said. "Could Nate stay here while you wait to hear from your friend? He's not well, and his lodging situation isn't really good for him. He won't be any trouble."

"Absolutely not," Firo said, at the same time that Saba said, "Don't be silly, Bindy, he's fine where he is," and William said, "Well—"

The girl ignored all of them. "Because you'll want him to get to work straightaway once you speak to your friend, won't you? And to be where you can find him, and make sure he's working. Plus, lab equipment won't be safe where he's staying, now. It'll get stolen before it's even unpacked."

"Where's he staying?" William said.

"One of the warehouse warrens in Brakeside."

William gave Firo an imploring look. Under no circumstances, Firo was about to say. Under no circumstances. Abominator, this man had called him, and looked at him as if he were a contagion to be burned before it spread. "Bindy," Saba said, "don't pester the man. Nate's fine where he is."

There was a blade behind the words. Both Nate and the girl flinched as if cut with it. Something was happening among the three of them that Firo didn't quite understand, and like all things he didn't understand, it intrigued him. "Nonsense," William said, and Firo was surprised to hear a blade in his voice, too. "Those warrens are no place for a sick man. We can certainly try it."

"I can help," Bindy said, eagerly. "I can come and clean, and do your shopping—I'm still working at the prison, but I could come straight here after."

Firo stared at her. "Dear gods, girl. You're working at the prison? You're a child."

Her chin went up. "I needed to take care of the magus. But he's out now."

"And, as he keeps trying to remind you, not a magus anymore." Saba's edge was softer now, but still there. A stiletto instead of a longsword. "You don't need to take him in, Lord Courtier. The warrens will be fine."

And that did it. *Lord Courtier.* The blatant, insincere flattery of it; the craven appeal to Firo's vanity. "Here's fine, as well," Firo said. "Honestly, I'd take in Elban himself if he came with housekeeping."

The girl broke into a wide, relieved smile. "You won't regret it. I promise. We'll go get his things. There isn't much," she added, hastily, as if Firo might expect them to return with a wagonload of furniture.

When they were gone, William brought two cups of tea to the table where Firo sat. "Bindy seems like a sweet girl," he said, sitting down. "Don't much like that Saba. Something about him."

"Indeed," Firo said. "It's all very interesting."

"You and your interesting things," William said, and Firo said, "None more interesting than you, my love." He picked up William's hand, and kissed it.

"Get off," William said, "you're full of it," but they both knew he was pleased.

Downstairs, stepping back out onto Vitriol Street, Bindy's heart felt lighter than it had in months. But no sooner had the street door latched shut behind them than Saba took her by the elbow. "It doesn't matter where he is, you know. He still belongs to me," he hissed into her ear. Then he looked at Nate and said, more loudly, "Tomorrow. First shift bell."

First shift bell rang at six in the morning. Nate nodded. Saba's reptile eyes lingered a moment on Bindy. Then he turned, and disappeared into the crowd.

"Never mind him," Bindy said to Nate.

Nate gave her a weak smile. "If only it were so easy."

He didn't seem as relieved as she would have expected to be leaving the warehouse behind, but she didn't care. Her mind had started working the moment she'd set foot in the cheerful little flat, trying to fit the pieces together. When Will Ember had walked in, she'd known, instantly. The Embers were good people, everyone knew that. And this room would be good for Nate's lungs, which were still bad from the prison air, and good because there would be two other people around. She would not be the only one. She would have help.

She led Nate through the streets of Marketside, where strolling vendors called their wares and carters pulled barrows of goods and factory guards lurked on the corners. Bindy could remember a time when the Beggar's Market had been an actual market and not an empty place where the factory squads practiced drilling, and she could remember when the carts had been fuller and the carters hadn't had to hire guards for themselves. But what had once been unthinkable had become ordinary, and it was only when she made the effort to remember the way life had once been that she realized how bad it was now.

Today, she looked at all of the new-normal Marketside life being lived around her and marveled at how simple it all looked, how vast and faraway even the new normal seemed. Because her life and Nate's life now seethed with disquiet, and the disquiet's name was Saba. Even in a crowd, where all she had to do was turn and walk away, she could not figure out how to escape from him. And it was her fault. She was the one who had let Saba into their lives, into the warehouse, into Darid's room. Now here they were.

Saba had ordered Nate to tell him every detail of his life in Highfall before being imprisoned, and Nate had done so, in intimate, horrifying detail. Nate had asked Saba to send Bindy out of the room, but Saba had told her to stay. "We need someone with a working brain who knows their way around this place," he said, and she was afraid of Saba, of what he would do to Nate if she disobeyed him, so she stayed. And that was how she learned everything that Nate had been through, everything he'd done. Some of it—everything to do with Judah the Foundling, mostly, and Lord Gavin, and some tower somewhere and something called the Unbinding—made no sense to her, like Saba's hold over Nate made no sense, but some of it made all too much sense. She hadn't known Nate made the drops. She hadn't known he'd watched his friend Charles die at the kitchen table and done nothing to help, and she hadn't known that he'd poisoned the old magus, Arkady. She wouldn't have thought her magus, so kind and wise, capable of such things. But she wouldn't have thought one person could so deeply control another, and from the sound of it Nate had been under the control of that awful old woman long before Saba had hooked him. Bindy had met her a few times in the manor house. She'd seemed harmless enough, but Nate told horrible stories of the old woman beating him with her cane. He spoke flatly and without emotion because Saba had told him to quit whining, but Bindy could see the grief and misery in his eyes.

She hadn't known. She'd believed he was sick with some wasting disease, all those times she'd found him collapsed on the floor. All those times she and Charles hadn't been able to wake him. The months when he'd grown less and less sure of himself, more and more confused. She hadn't understood then and she barely understood now, but she knew that Nate needed her.

She also understood that Darid didn't like Saba, he didn't like sharing his room with the two men, and he didn't like sharing his sister with them. He was ramping up his work with the Warehousers—she was pretty sure they'd set the Iron Master's new manor on fire—and he didn't want her hanging around the warehouse, in case it was raided. "Nate needs me," she'd told him, and he'd said, "Bindy, you need you." Even though he owed Nate, too, even though Nate had helped him escape the House when the Seneschal ordered him killed for being with the Foundling (and that was something else Bindy hadn't known, but Darid would not talk about it).

But Darid hadn't been there, had he, on the night of the coup, when Bindy and Rina had brought the littles through the dark, terrifying streets and the magus had let them in? Darid hadn't been there when Nate had let them take over his house, spoken so kindly to Kate, bounced Canty on his knee. Darid hadn't been there when the magus had told her how to cure Canty's sun-starvation, and let Bindy bring him to work with her, and when he'd given her money for new clothes to keep the courtiers she delivered medicine to from sneering at her. She'd never told him about the sneering court-iers, or about the kitchen boys with their hands that groped and wandered and pinned, but he had seemed to know, any-way, and had never sent her to make deliveries to those houses again. That was her magus. The Nate she knew now was sad and weak but she had decided that this was a temporary sick-ness, and if she could only nurse Nate through it, her magus would come back.

When Nate told him about the drops, Saba's eyes lit up. He told Bindy to go out into the city and find out whatever she could about the man who had paid, Vertus, or the courtier who had been the go-between. She had not much relished the idea of wandering the streets of Marketside asking where she could get drops, so instead she asked Alva. Alva said she knew a man rumored to be a former courtier who'd been somehow involved with the drops. The courtier lived on Vitriol Street, Alva had said, so Bindy had gone there after her shift at the prison and waited. She'd known Firo the moment she saw him. He'd come to visit the magus a few times, back before everything had gone so horribly wrong, but she would have known him for a courtier even if he hadn't. He wore work-er's clothes, a plain shirt and jacket, and steel hoop earrings like the dockworkers did. But he walked like a courtier, tall and confident. So much so that she wouldn't have been sur-prised to see a servant walking in front of him, ringing a bell to warn people to step out of his way. Honestly, she didn't know how the man had survived the purge, worker's clothes or no worker's clothes.

The only thing the magus needed to collect from the warehouse was a small leather pouch, which Saba had given him. It held a knife, a mirror, and a cheap handkerchief. He put it in his coat pocket and looked around the room, as if for something else.

"What's wrong?" Bindy said.

He gave her a small, embarrassed smile. "I was just wishing I had my old satchel back. Not for any reason. You know that man, William?"

"Will Ember? Sure. I mean, I don't know him personally. But I know his mother." For Bindy, that was the ultimate testament.

"Does she know he lives with another man?" Nate said.

Baffled, Bindy said, "I don't know. Does it matter?"

"Where I come from, it does."

"Well, it doesn't, here," Bindy said, with as much cheerful finality as she could muster. "And that flat's far nicer than the warehouse, and safer, too. Healthier. We just need to get you a little stronger, magus. So we can kick that old Saba back to the Brake where he belongs, huh?"

Nate said nothing.

She walked him back to Vitriol Street, where Will Ember had made him a pallet on the kitchen floor, apologizing for it not being a bed. Firo had pencil and paper and when she left, he and Nate were discussing lab equipment, and prices, and other things she wasn't particularly interested in. It was getting late. The gaslamps were being lit. That was something the Seneschal had done, running Wilmerian gas to all the streetlamps and hiring children to light them, Bindy's sister Mairead among them. Mairead was barely even ten. Her friend Jethro had been one of the first lampers hired, because he'd always been able to scramble up anywhere like a squirrel. But they hadn't gotten the gas right yet and one evening it had exploded as he'd opened the valve, so now half of his face was all rippled and pink, with the eye melted shut. He was also missing two fingers on his right hand, where he'd been hanging on the streetlamp's crosspiece. But he could still scramble like a squirrel, and so could Bindy's sister, and the job paid in city scrip that could be used at any factory store. Ma didn't get paid well enough to turn that down, even if it was dangerous. None of them liked it, but it was what it was.

The Dovetail family lived in a tiny house on Winder's Alley, which was more of a leftover space than a deliberate thoroughfare. All of the cottages on Winder's Alley were built underneath attaches from the bigger streets that surrounded the alley. Because of the risk of collapse, these cottages were extremely cheap, and because of the buildings overhead, they were completely dark for most of the day. But, because of the haphazard way they were built, these cottages came with oddly shaped empty spaces outside them where the cottagers could keep a pig, or some chickens, or even grow plants if there was enough light. The Dovetail cottage had one sunny wall, where Nora had planted berry vines that grew up the walls. It made a cheerful place for the littles to play, and they were there now. Kate, at a bit of a loss since Mairead had started working, was trying to cajole the barely-big-enough Canty into some game or other. When they saw Bindy, they attacked her legs.

"Rina's here!" Kate said.

"Rina!" Canty echoed.

Right. She'd forgotten. Tonight was Rina's night, not Darid's. She would find Darid later, to tell him about the magus. "That's exciting," Bindy said, with more cheer than she felt. "Shall we go say hello, then?"

Inside, her older sister sat at the small kitchen table with their mother, a pot of beans boiling on the stove. The beans smelled like there might be meat in them, and a new paper-wrapped cake of yeast sat on the shelf. Rina's doing, both of those. "Hi, Bindy," Rina said. "They keep you late at the prison? Thought you got off at third shift."

"Well," Bindy said. Careful, because you always had to be careful talking to Rina. She'd risen high on the Paper Committee, and held the regulations above pretty much everything else. "Actually, I have news. I got another job."

Nora, cupping a steaming mug of tea, blinked. "You what?"

"Got another job."

There was a moment of silence. Then Rina said, "Do you have papers for it?"

Rina's tone was easy enough, but Bindy still didn't trust her. "I will have. It's housekeeping. For Bess Ember's son and his live-with."

"His live-with can't keep house on her own?" Rina said.

"He's a man," Bindy said, and Rina didn't say anything else. Nobody expected a man to do housework, no matter who he lived with. Not when there was more profitable work to be done, and people like Bindy who could be hired to do the drudgework for him.

"How'd this come to happen?" Nora said, her eyes steadfast on Bindy.

Bindy hadn't exactly made up a story to tell about that, but it didn't matter. Ma was used to Bindy lying around Rina, to avoid mentioning Darid. "I met him—Will, that is—on the way home. He recognized me from the neighborhood. They're looking for someone, a few hours a day. Sweeping up, fetching laundry, the like."

She could see Ma sifting through that, finding the truths in the lies. Canty crawled up on her lap and Ma bent her head down to kiss his ear, pressing her nose into his soft yellow curls. "Well," she finally said, "I suppose you're three-quarters grown, and can make at least that many of your own decisions. I worry about you working so many hours."

"And who'll watch Canty and Kate at night, with Mairead lamping and you keeping house for Will Ember?" Rina said, biting. "Did you consider that?"

"I considered the money," Bindy said, but as the words left her mouth a chill ran down her spine. There would be no payment from Will and Firo. She'd offered to work for Nate's room and board. Well, she'd find it somewhere.

"Stupid," Rina said. Not an accusation, exactly; more of a comment. "All those years of schooling Ma paid for, so you can slop buckets at the prison all day and for the baker's boy all night. You ever want reasonable work, I can get you on at Paper."

"But I'd have to start on the night shift, wouldn't I?" Bindy said. "Who would watch Canty and Kate then?"

"Now," Ma said, and that ended the sniping. "You don't worry about that. If nothing else we can put them in the Paper crèche for a few hours." Bindy grimaced. She hated the factory crèche, which was a corner of the basement formerly used for storage. The women who worked there tried to be kind—they were too old, injured, or pregnant to work—but there were too many children and not enough hands. Bindy knew Ma didn't like it, either, but there were too many children and not enough hands at their house, too.

After Rina and Bindy helped Ma feed Canty and Kate, Bindy said she had to go back out. "I'll walk with you," said Rina, who ate and slept at the factory barracks now. The arrangement freed up food and space that were in short supply in Winder's Alley, but the more time Rina spent at the factory, the more it seemed to get its claws into her. She wore her sash all the time now, and grew more aloof every time they saw each other. Rina had always been hard-nosed but it was as if the factory gave her a space, and she was growing into it.

Outside on the street, Rina said, "Now, Bindy. You and I are going to have a talk about the direction your life is headed."

"Oh, are we?" Bindy said. "Which direction is that, Rina?"

"Sideways," Rina said, decisively. "I was absolutely serious about all that schooling of yours. You know how many people at the factory can read and write? Not a lot. You sign on at Paper, you'll be off the floor in a year. Two, tops. Why, you might even end up in administration, keeping the books and shipping tallies and so forth. And that'd be a solid job. Even after your committee dues you'd still be making twice what Ma ever did, and she was as near to a foreman as a woman can get."

"I don't want to work at Paper," Bindy said.

"I guess you'd rather empty slop buckets for prisoners and wash out Will Ember's chamber pots."

"They have a privy."

"Aye, and you'll be scrubbing it."

"Come off, Rina." Bindy was very tired. "If Ma has no problem with it, why should you?"

"Because I know why you took that prison job in the first place, and Ma doesn't," Rina snapped back. "It's because that crazy magus of yours was there, and you were hoping he'd get out and take you on as an apprentice again. Should only have taken a week in that place to know that wasn't going to happen, but you spent months there anyway, didn't you? So maybe you're not so smart, after all."

"People get out," Bindy said, stung.

"Not your magus. He's dead." Rina stopped short, her mouth clamping shut almost audibly. If she'd been anybody else, Rina would have slapped her hand over her mouth in shock at what had come out of it. But she was Rina, so she did nothing of the sort.

Bindy's mind was moving like lightning. How had Rina learned of the magus's fabricated death? Had her sister been keeping tabs on her? "Yes," she said. "He died last week. How did you know that, Rina?"

"I'm on the committee. I know a lot of things." Rina shook her head. "I'm sorry, Bin. But I'm also not sorry, because it means you can go on with your life. It's all well and good for Mairead to scamp around lamping at her age, but you're three-quarters an adult, like Ma says. And women can't be magi, so you need to find something else to do with yourself." She blew out a huff of air. "If you're going to keep house for a living, at least get married so you can keep your own house."

"I'm done talking to you about this, Rina," Bindy said, quietly. "The law says I have to have work. Well, I have work, and the papers to prove it. There should be nothing else for you to complain about."

"Fine," Rina said, and "Fine," Bindy said, and then Rina stormed away like they were two children arguing over a doll. Bindy stared after her, angry and sad. Her sister had always been fiercely determined, with not a shade of gray in her. She supposed that if Rina hadn't found the factory committee, she would have created it. Just to have a place to feel important, and rules to live by.

Bindy found Darid at Alva's. The tavern was full and raucous, but he saw her across the room—Darid was always watching—came to meet her, and pulled her outside where it was quieter. She still must have looked sad, because he frowned at her and said, "What's wrong?"

"Rina," she said. As if that was enough, and it was. Darid shook his head, but only asked her if she wanted a meat bun. She said no. There was no real money anymore in Highfall, only factory scrip, and Darid never had enough of it. But he ducked in through Alva's back entrance, anyway, and returned in a moment bearing two paper-wrapped buns, one of which he handed to her.

"Well, I can't eat in front of you," he said, when she protested. "Keep it for later if you don't want it. What was Rina on you about?"

"She wants me to come work at the factory." Bindy had no intention of saving the bun for later. It smelled delicious, and it was.

Darid chewed, and looked thoughtful. "It's steady work. Decent wages, too."

"Until you get hurt," she said. "Or old, or until there's a bad quarter and they cut you loose. I'd rather scrub privies. At least then I know what I'm dealing with."

Darid laughed. "You're no fool, Bin. The Seneschal and the factory owners pretend the jobs exist for you to live off. They're not. They're for them to make money off. Once all you know is paper cutting or pulping or how to fix that one machine that does that one thing, you're theirs forever, no matter what they do to you." He shook his head. "Say what you will about the House, at least it was honest. They told you going in that you weren't ever coming out."

She stuffed the last of the meat bun into her mouth and crumpled up the paper. "Well, anyway, I have good news. We found the magus somewhere else to live. You get your rooms back."

Instantly he looked relieved. But then he frowned. "What somewhere else? And what do you mean, we?"

"Well, Saba and me," she said, reluctantly. "But he's staying with this courtier. This used-to-be courtier, I mean. Someone he knew before he went to prison."

Whenever courtiers, or Elban, or anything to do with the

House came up, Darid's eyes went dark and hooded. Like now. "I thought all the courtiers were run out of the city."

"Not this one. He's living in Marketside with—do you remember Bess Ember? The baker's wife?" Darid nodded. "Her son, Will. On Vitriol Street." Something occurred to her. "Doesn't vitriol mean anger? Why would they name a street that?"

"It's a chemical," Darid said absently. "They use it in dyes and inks. What's the courtier's name, Bin?"

"Firo. Seemed okay, for a courtier."

But Darid was staring at her. "Tall man, with big gems in his ears?"

Bindy frowned. "He wears earrings, but not gems. Like the ones the dockworkers wear. Did you know him, inside? Was he one of the rotten ones?"

"They were all rotten," Darid said. "They were courtiers."

But he wouldn't say anything else.

ELEVEN

THE FARTHER EAST JUDAH, CLERIC, AND LUKASH
traveled, the flatter the terrain became, but it was still full
of the desert birds Lukash could catch by throwing his coat
over them. Judah's pains continued, several times a day, with
no warning or provocation. They appeared in different ways,
in different parts of her body: her cheekbone, her jaw, her
thigh, her stomach. One night, while they were eating, the
first two fingers on her left hand shrieked with pain, like the
bones within them had snapped, and then went numb. She'd
dropped the piece of bird she was eating into the dirt (then
picked it up and finished it anyway). Some part of her always
hurt, now, to some degree. Sometimes she could hide the pain.
Sometimes she couldn't.

"It's not the lack of godswill. You'd be fevered and puking.
I don't know what it is. As far as I can see, you're absolutely
fine. So you'll either get better or die," Cleric said. Apparently, not understanding things made him peevish. They both

knew there was little he could do for her without his satchel (or even with it, to be perfectly honest, but Judah kept that to herself), so *get better or die* was pretty much all he had to offer.

Still: she wasn't absolutely fine. For one thing, the pain was excruciating. For another, she knew exactly what each kind of pain was. They were familiar pains, from being kicked or hit or burnt, and none of those things were happening to her, which meant they were happening to Gavin. Somebody was doing awful things to him, wherever he was, and they were doing them over and over again.

The pains that started when she made the silver knife were the first real sensations she'd had from him since she'd come awake in the Ghostwood. Other than that brief flash through the window at the winemaker's, she hadn't felt hunger or cold or a stubbed toe or a stab of pleasure. It had been enough, after the winemaker's, to know he was alive, and part of her had hoped that their physical connection had vanished with her scars. All those watching minds she'd sensed scared her. The magus had told her, in the tower, about the great Unbinding that his people had been working toward for generations, the ritual that needed Gavin's death to complete. She was afraid that the magus's people were the watchers, and that reaching out to Gavin would draw their attention. The last time she and Gavin had been in the same place together, they'd both nearly died. Theron actually had died. She would deal with the pain, if it meant keeping them all alive.

But the connection was clearly intact, or at least some part of it was. She thought she understood why she felt Gavin's injuries but didn't bear the marks of any of them; if this unscarred body she inhabited really was new, somehow, the physical link might have vanished with her old one. But her mind hadn't changed, and she didn't understand why she couldn't push the pain down anymore. She hated the way it forced itself out of her in embarrassing shrieks and moans and doublings-over. Lukash and Cleric had been watching her like she might combust at any moment, ever since she'd made the second knife. When her pain was on the better side of awful, Cleric pelted her with questions. How big a thing could she make? Did it have to be something she'd seen? Did it have to be dirt? She didn't know, she told him. The ugly knife was the first thing she'd ever made. He didn't believe her.

By day they wandered east across the scrub plain, which was slightly lusher than a desert but nothing so lush as a prairie, and pocked with mineral-crusted puddles of bad water that burned the tongue like acid. The fresh puddles were rarer by the day. With no map or compass, they were looking for civilization, Lukash told her. Any civilization. Preferably before they died of exposure. "But that'll be a long time yet," he added, as if to reassure her. "The weather will get warmer soon."

"Yes, we have summer where I come from, too," she said, and then felt bad for speaking so curtly. But he didn't seem to be offended.

Cleric was offended, though—deeply offended, by her refusal to spend her evenings with her hands in the dirt, forming one useful item after another. Make a firesteel, make a file, make a hammer. She would not. She was not, she told him, a trained dog. Finally one night, exhausted and sore, she said, "You know what I wish I could make?"

His eyes lit up. "What?"

"A sandwich."

Across the fire, Lukash made the slightly forceful exhalation that meant he was amused. Cleric said, "Try a gold piece."

"There's no gold here, you craven thief."

"Don't flatter me. How do you know there's no gold here?"

"The same way I know there are no sandwiches," she said.

"I wouldn't mind a sandwich," Lukash said, and Cleric swore but, blessedly, gave up.

Honestly, Judah, too, wondered how she knew, but she did. When she touched the dirt, reached into the white and thought about gold, she didn't get an answer. She couldn't do anything with living plants; they were themselves, somehow, and could not be anything else. And she couldn't change something she'd already made. She couldn't draw the blade of the silver knife finer between her fingers, or round the hilt. It was modeled on the small folding knife Nate had used for Work, but her knife didn't fold. Couldn't, she supposed, because she had never looked closely at Nate's knife, and didn't have a mental image of the hinges. And now that she had asked the metal to be a knife, it was a knife. She wasn't sure why she had tried to make a knife and ended up with Elly and Gavin. Maybe it had been an accident; maybe she'd fallen too far into the memory of that last day in the tower, and somehow made contact. But the uncertainty made her reluctant to try again.

But Cleric's endless rambling about gold had put something in her mind, which was this: when—if—they eventually reached civilization, she was going to find herself standing in a town or a village or a city with the two men, surrounded by a thick and heady cloud of *Now what?* And she had no idea what would happen, then, but she knew that whatever it was, she wanted a choice in it. If she had gold in her pocket, she would have a choice. The next time they stopped to rest, Cleric immediately pulled his hat down and fell asleep, and Lukash went hunting. She walked a short distance in the opposite direction, to a clearing in between the gray-green bushes. She knew these bushes, by now. They grew to her midthigh, woody and stiff and dotted up and down the stalks with flowers like soft yellow stars. When they burned, the smoke was fragrant, almost friendly.

She crouched down. Pushed the dead grass out of the way, and lay her hand flat on the ground. She would be very careful, and stop at the slightest hint of purple. Closing her eyes, she reached into the soil. Her mind went white. Inside the earth, she could feel—hear?—a chaotic jumble, like a crowd (but not the multitudes she'd sensed earlier, she was relieved to find). There was something solid; something flowing like water that wasn't water; something flowing like water that probably was. The solid thing was probably a mineral vein. She seemed to remember learning, at some point, that minerals came in veins. There was no purple. There was also no gold, she was very sure of that, but—she focused, and formed, making sure to keep her mind as firmly in the white as she could.

Something pressed against her palm. She picked it up, rubbed away the dust: a thin ring of metal, too big to fit any finger and too small to fit any wrist. It was bright and warm; slightly misshapen and extremely beautiful in her dirty palm. Copper. As bright as any pot in the House kitchen.

"Good enough," she said, satisfied and relieved, and slipped it into her pocket.

Sometimes in the thick of Gavin's beatings, Judah saw flashes. Boots. Stone walls. Nothing she could understand. One morning, about an hour after they'd broken camp, a searing pain shot through her fingers, from the tips to her palms, one after another, in sequence. As if they'd been thrust into a fire, or were being smashed with hammers. Her vision went grayish-purple, as it always did when the pain came, and she tried not to gasp but did anyway.

Cleric heard her breathing through her teeth like a scared horse. He slung the staff Lukash had cut for him over his back and stopped. "Show me," he said, and she extended her fingers. It was pointless. They looked fine, her fingers. They did not feel fine. They felt like her fingernails were being torn off. Cleric and Lukash looked, and had one of their silent conversations, and whatever was said made Cleric shake his head and grit his teeth.

They kept walking. The pain intensified. She felt like her fingers were candles, lit at the ends, and followed the two shapes of the men in front of her nearly blinded by the pain. When they came upon a puddle—one of the bad ones, with red and yellow and white crusted around its edges—all she could see, through her pain-blurred vision, was the lovely, unnatural blue of the water itself, jewellike among all the gray and brown.

"Wait," Lukash said, as she pushed toward it, but she ignored him. The pain in her fingers was louder than anything Lukash could say. She dropped down to the discolored crust at the edge of the water and thrust her fingers in. For the slimmest margin of an instant, the coolness and relief was lovely.

Then the acid burning started. A different kind of pain: this was her own pain, coming from outside her skin instead of inside it. She retreated into the white, where the water was a cacophony of off-key notes, as sliding and sibilant as the colored film that swirled on top of the liquid. Cleric and Lukash were crouched next to her, one on each side. She could feel them trying to pull her wrists out of the water. But stronger than that was the memory of that one blissful moment of coolness. The men were swearing. "Why is she so strong?" Cleric said, and Lukash said, "Why are you so weak?" but he couldn't pull her away, either, and suddenly they both stopped, and went still and silent.

Because something was happening in the water. The liquid was turning gritty. She turned her hands over and tiny grains of something drifted down to rest in her palms, like flecks of snow. The water grew clearer. The slick on top of it began to disappear, the swirls dwindling and dwindling into nothing. And—wonder of wonders—the burning was disappearing, too. The coolness was coming back. Whatever she held was growing heavy, and large enough that she had to hold it with two hands, so she lifted those two hands out of the water and discovered that the something was a gray-white, amorphous lump, about the size of an apple.

Cleric and Lukash were watching, open-mouthed, their fingers limp on her wrists. "What is that?" Cleric said.

Judah dropped the lump on the ground next to her. Her fingers were burning again, in the open air. She plunged them back into the water, which was clean and fresh and felt wonderful.

Lukash crouched next to her, dipped a hand in the water and touched it to his mouth. "It's clean," he said, wonderingly.

Cleric picked the lump up gingerly and turned it over. The sun glinted off its crystalline surface. "Useful trick," he said, but that impatient edge of not-knowing had disappeared.

Her hands still plunged into the now-clean, now-refreshing water, Judah felt the confusing, hopeless weight of it all slide onto her. Her pain had eased. Wherever Gavin was, his hadn't. "Not useful enough," she said, sad and heartsick and very, very tired, and Cleric, with unusual discretion, said nothing.

"What about gems?" Cleric said.

Her fingers felt fine. No new pains had appeared. Their makeshift canteens were filled with water from the newly clean pool, and the stubby thorn bushes were sparse enough that hiking was easy, and Judah would have been very nearly happy if Cleric hadn't been grilling her again about her—talent? Ability? She didn't know what to call it. "I don't know," she said. "I don't think so."

But Cleric persisted. "Have you tried, or are you assuming?"

This was annoying, and Judah was about to say something extremely rude, but then Lukash said, "It wouldn't be a bad assumption. She works metal, but metal starts out as ore. You can mine it, melt it down, refine it. You can't melt down a gem."

"Yes, yes," Cleric said, dismissively. "You Morgeni know everything there is to know about all things mine-related."

"We Morgeni know a lot of things about a lot of things," Lukash said.

"The point is, if she can make diamonds, I'll marry her," Cleric said.

As if Judah wasn't even there, walking beside the two of them under the wide clear sky, listening to every word they said. "If I can make diamonds," she said, "I'm not marrying anybody, ever. Least of all you."

Cleric laughed. "Fair enough, Thorn Bush."

"Do you think the—" there was a brief pause, during which Lukash chose his words "—making of things is what's causing your pain?"

"Doesn't seem to be," she said. And didn't say that she knew exactly what was causing the pains, and that she thought they were different because one was purple and one was white.

Lukash nodded. "I wondered if that was why you were reluctant to test it."

"I'm reluctant to test it," she said, "because I don't trust a certain greedy healer not to lose his mind."

"Don't worry. I'm lazier than I am greedy. Forcing you to fill my pockets against your will is too much work. You're too stubborn," Cleric said with a grin. "But unless I miss my guess, our Morgeni friend here is working his way up to asking you if you'll make him a better knife."

Lukash's answering grin was almost shy. It was incongruous and entirely charming. "Maybe you could improve this one," he said, took the ugly knife out of his belt, and held it out to her.

The knife really was a clumsy, awkward thing. She hadn't been thinking about aesthetics when she made it. She shook her head. "I'm sorry. I don't think I can do anything with that."

"Why not?" This was Cleric, who always wanted to know the whys, and the hows, and every explicit detail. It reminded her of Theron. It was the only thing about him that reminded her of Theron.

"Because it's already what it is. It was a bunch of dirt and rocks, and then I made it a knife, and now it can't be anything else. Unless you have a forge, but I suspect then it would break apart, anyway. Fine steel, it isn't."

"Could you make me another? A better one?" Lukash said.

She smiled. He was such an enormous wall of a man, and he'd asked so tentatively. "You really do miss your knife, don't you?"

"It was a very good knife," Lukash said.

"If I made you another, there's no guarantee it'd be any better than that one," Judah said, and pointed to the ugly weapon in his hand.

"There would be if I taught you about balance, first," he said.

He didn't have a decent knife to show her on, so they ended up hunched over a flat place in the ground while he used the ugly knife to draw pictures in the dirt, to explain what made it bad and what a good one would be like, instead. At her suggestion, he used the bad knife to carve a piece of wood into a hilt that felt right in his hand, and she held it for a while, to get the sense of it. She had never tried to create something so detailed. Even the copper ring in her pocket was just—round.

It was an interesting exercise. Even Cleric, who professed no interest in knives whatsoever, kept an ear aimed toward them.

She asked Lukash how he knew so much about making knives, and he said, "Knives are tools. The Morgeni make excellent tools."

"I thought the Morgeni were miners."

"And toolmakers, and astronomers," Cleric said from the other side of the fire, where he was pulling the feathers out of a desert bird Lukash had caught earlier in the day. "Irritatingly well-rounded."

"Not a lot to do on the mountain besides dig in the dirt and look at the stars," Lukash said.

"Is that why you left?" Judah said.

Across the fire, Cleric's plucking hands paused ever so slightly. But all Lukash said was, "I'm not good enough at astronomy and too good at fighting. Morgou is better off without me."

His manner didn't invite any further questions. She went back to the knife. It was different, convincing the chaotic jumble of metal in the dirt to be not only a knife shape but a very specific knife shape. Holding the image of the knife in her head, remembering how the wooden hilt had felt in her hand, remembering all Lukash had told her about grip and balance; forming the handle, drawing the soil gently into something shaped like a knife.

She was pleased when the knife formed in her hand, confident and friendly. *Thank you*, she thought, with no real sense of who deservered her thanks, and handed the weapon to Lukash. "How's that?" she said.

He took the knife from her gingerly, as if it might bite. Held it a moment, turning it over in his hand; testing the blade, moving it through the air as if carving invisible circles out of nothing. Then he smiled. "You're getting better," he said, and Cleric said, "Are you sure you don't want to marry me?"

"Completely sure," she said. But she was pleased.

Early the next morning, the pains hit her again. Her stomach this time. Gavin, poor Gavin, who was hurting you? Why? Clutching her midsection, her hand strayed to the inside of her wrist. So easy to scratch in the message, a few lines, a curl. They burned bright in her head, she saw them on her squeezed-shut eyelids. *Who why how can I help. Where. Where where where.*

But she didn't. Even thinking about it brought back the feeling of the multitudes again, all of those staring, searching eyes. Instead she cast her mind back to all those long painful hours in Elban's study, learning not to show any pain. She tried to remember how to push the pain down, to dismiss it as nothing to do with her, but it felt like trying to remember how to fly because she'd done it in a dream, once. The purple throbbed at the edges of her mind and it was all she could do to keep it away.

The pains continued, off and on, all day. They'd never lasted this long before. Lukash, new knife strapped to his belt just where the old one had been, suggested they stop and rest, but she insisted they press on. The sun began to sink. Waves of pain came over her and her surroundings receded. She couldn't tell if the purple in her vision was Work-purple or the natural purple of twilight. She opened her eyes enough to see her feet, to make sure she wasn't stepping into some animal hole or walking into a thorn bush, but that was as much as she could do. The air grew dimmer around her. Once she had been able to keep the pain inside, completely. Once she had borne any level of agony without even blinking. She had been trained that way and every moan felt wrong, weak, pathetic—but also satisfying. Because it wasn't normal, was it? To be beaten and make no noise?

Cleric held out a hand. They stopped. Judah managed to focus her gaze enough to see that Lukash had his new knife out, and ready. "What is it?" she said.

Cleric pointed into the dusk. "A campfire."

She squinted. Yes, she could see it. A tiny orange flicker. All three of them stood and stared at the distant fire, as if staring alone could answer any of the questions they all had about it.

Finally, Cleric said, "Well, we've been looking for civilization."

"Maybe they have a map," Lukash said.

"Or opium," Cleric said, with a glance toward Judah.

"I don't need opium," Judah said.

"You," Cleric said, "need opium more than anybody I have ever met."

They stepped quietly—or, in Judah's case, tried to—in case there was danger. But only one figure sat by the fire when they approached it. The person wore a brimmed hat, low on their head, obscuring their face. There was nothing inherently threatening about them, but Lukash's shoulders and head were down, his mouth tight and eyes wary. His new knife was still in his hand.

"Peace." The figure's voice sounded like a woman's. Roughened, as if by years of smoking, but a woman's, nonetheless. "Come forward, if you like."

Cleric put an arm in front of Judah, letting Lukash and his knife be the first to step into the circle of firelight.

The woman looked up at him. Judah was startled to see that she was smiling, faintly. "What do you plan to do with that knife?" Her cheeks were weathered, as were her trousers and jacket, but Judah didn't think she was more than ten years older than Judah herself. Under her brimmed hat, her hair was cut short in a way not unlike Judah's own. It was less of a style and more of a what-happened-when-you-cut-all-your-hair-off. A flare of pain shot through Judah. Bad, this time. She pushed Cleric out of the way and stumbled forward.

"What are you doing?" he hissed.

"Sitting down," she said. *Before I fall down*, she didn't say. Then, to both him and Lukash, "There's one of her and three of us. Put that stupid knife away."

"Did I say *peace*, or only think it?" the woman said, as if wondering aloud to herself, as Judah dropped clumsily to the ground next to the fire. Her language was clear but accented, as if her tongue were tripping over itself. A little extra flutter in the middle of *only*. In the dusk, Judah could not tell if the rich brown of her skin was natural or the work of the sun.

"They're not listening," she said, and winced. Lukash glared at her. She didn't care. "You're not with the gloryseed cartel, are you?"

The woman shook her head vehemently. "I want nothing to do with gloryseed, or anyone who sells it. I'm only a traveler, headed home. I realize that's how all stories start, and misadventure comes after. But in this case, it is the truth." She had not moved from the fireside, but cocked her head now, to look up at the three newcomers. "Also, I would like to point out that it is the three of you who have come to my campsite, not the other way around. So, I say again, peace. And perhaps, Morgeni, you should listen to your friend, here, and put your knife away."

There was a moment of pause. Then, with deliberate movements, Lukash slid his knife back into his belt and dropped to sit next to Judah. A moment later, Cleric did, as well.

"Merrit Idris," the woman said, by way of introduction.

"Cleric. Lukash," Cleric said, pointing to each of them in

turn. Then he gestured toward Judah. "And somebody who needs to be more cautious when traveling in the wilderness."

"If I were a cautious person, I wouldn't have ended up in the wilderness," Judah said. "And I definitely wouldn't be traveling with you."

The woman—Merrit—smiled broadly. "Are you hungry? My dinner isn't interesting, but it's edible. You're welcome to share."

"We have no way to pay you," Lukash said.

"Pay me in company, then," Merrit said. "I've been traveling alone longer than I'd like to say."

So they sat as she took a quantity of dried biscuits from her pack, and some green flakes of something, and some brown shards of something else, and put it all into a pot of water that was nestled next to the fire. In a remarkably small amount of time, they were all eating a sludgy but not unpleasant porridge from pieces of waxed paper, cupped in their hands to make bowls. It wasn't the best meal Judah had ever had, but it was certainly the best she'd had since Black Lake. The green flakes turned out to be some sort of savory dried plant, and the brown shards were meat, which softened in the hot water. They had been living on roots that Lukash dug out of the soil and the occasional desert bird or small animal. Sometimes they came across streams with fish in them. They weren't starving, but Judah had long ago—she'd lost track of time—stopped thinking of food as anything other than a necessity.

While they were eating, Merrit asked if they had come from Black Lake. Cleric lied and said they hadn't. "I wondered, because you mentioned the cartel," Merrit said. "But the cartel's reach grows broader every day. I hear they're even making inroads across the Barriers, now."

"And you?" Lukash said. "Where are you from?"

"All over. I am a—well, a mapmaker, sort of."

"You have maps?" Cleric said sharply.

"I keep most of them in my head. I have a good sense of direction."

They continued talking, about landmarks and distances and places Judah had never heard of. Meanwhile, her pleasantly full stomach began to shift and tilt toward nausea. The pain had not entirely left her, this time. It was rising and ebbing like a tide. She was glad to be sitting, glad to have a warm fire, glad to not be hungry. But the gray was pulling at the edges of her vision and she hoped that whoever was making a hobby of hurting Gavin was done for a while, that all she was feeling were the aftereffects.

Until her stomach muscles seized. She hunched over, trying to hide the pain. It was one thing to groan and whine around Cleric and Lukash, but quite another to do so around a stranger. Even a pleasant enough stranger, who had invited them to share her fire and fed them and had now taken an ocarina out of her bag and begun to play a high, ethereal tune that was lovely and lilting and went through Judah's head like a knife. She could feel Lukash and Cleric stealing glances at her. She pulled her knees closer to her chest. If she forced herself into a tight ball, if her muscles had no latitude to move, then all she would have to focus on was keeping quiet.

The music stopped. The night went still. Judah was grateful. The pain twisted and wrenched and then, blessedly, eased. She opened her eyes.

Merrit Idris was staring at her, but not unkindly. "You are ill."

"I'm fine," Judah said.

But Merrit turned to Cleric. "This is why you were so curious about villages and towns nearby. You are looking for help for her."

"Or perhaps I don't want to live my entire life wandering

around in the desert," Cleric said, but Lukash said, "Can you help her?"

"I do not know," Merrit said. "I do not know what's wrong with her."

"She is right here," Judah said, through gritted teeth. "She does not particularly like being talked about as if she's not."

"She suffers pains," Lukash said, ignoring her.

Merrit nodded. "That much, I can see. How often?"

"It's nothing," Judah said.

"Once or twice a day," Cleric said.

"More." Lukash didn't look at Judah. "She hides it well."

Cleric shook his head. "I don't understand it. I can't figure out what's wrong with her, and I'm a trained healer."

"Yes, I see where your guild mark was." Merrit's stare was fixed on Judah. "There are no villages within a week's walk of here."

"Thanks so much for your concern, then," Judah said.

Merrit's mouth twitched. "There are healers among my people. I am on my way to meet them now."

"Who are your people?" Judah said. "The godswill healers from Black Lake?"

Merrit frowned in puzzlement. Then realization dawned. "You mean the Elenesians. No, my people are traders. They have many names, but the Morgeni call them—" The woman said a word that Judah didn't know, in a language she didn't recognize. But it sounded like Lukash, like the music that hovered around the edges of his words.

Cleric's eyebrows shot upward, and his face came alight. She knew that look. It was the same one he'd worn when she'd first met him, back in the Ghostwood, and it was the same one he'd worn when he'd learned the winemaker's name. It was greed. "You're serious," he said, and Merrit nodded.

"They might actually be able to help you," Lukash said,

reluctantly. "They are supposed to be very skilled at treating all kinds of illness. Not just the physical."

Judah wondered if he thought she was crazy, her pains all in her head. "I'm not exactly ill."

"I think you are," Lukash said.

"Even if I were, we have nothing to trade. Why would traders help us?"

"I'm sure we can figure out something," Cleric said, eyes still bright with avarice. Merrit's people would have herbs, she realized. Herbs and oils and little bags full of mysterious powders. All the things he'd lost in Black Lake.

And then he said, "Perhaps they need knives," and she thought, Oh, no. Merrit lifted her ocarina again, and began to play.

Merrit was tall, solid, and strong. There was a grace about her, but it was a horse's grace, not a bird's. In the morning, learning that their reed canteens were empty, she offered to show Judah the spring where she'd drawn water for their porridge the night before. Judah glanced at Lukash, to make sure he would be listening while she was gone, and he nodded, ever so slightly.

Merrit showed Judah a spring underneath a creosote bush, where the water gathered in a small, sandy puddle and then sank back down into itself. Judah wondered if she could pull water from the soil, if she needed to. Merrit filled her skins first. "Your Morgeni friend is protective," she said, as bubbles flowed up from the mouth of her skin.

"No. Just not stupid."

"How did you three come to be traveling together?"

"I was lost in the Ghostwood and they found me."

Merrit frowned. "How did you come to be lost in the Ghostwood?"

"How does everyone know Lukash is Morgeni?" Judah said, instead of answering.

"His hair. His skin. The way he carries himself." Merrit cocked an eyebrow. "Do you not know about the Morgeni, and the gem wars?"

"I'm from a long way away."

"You know Black Lake, and the cartel that runs it," Merrit said. It wasn't a question. "A similar cartel took control of the Morgeni gem mines. That cartel no longer controls anything. They no longer exist. The Morgeni killed them all." She said it casually, as if talking about the weather. "They are kind, studious people, for the most part. Known for their hospitality. They have a—not a religion. A philosophy, I suppose. They call it the Quiet. As in, one should move quietly through the world. Not cause pain or harm to others. The gem cartel took advantage of that. They thought that because the Morgeni chose to be quiet, that was all they could be." She shook her head. "Most war is the product of lazy, selfish people who prefer to beat their problems with a stick rather than solve them, but in the case of the gem wars—the Morgeni fought fiercely for their freedom, and won it. But the fight went against everything they believed. That is difficult, to go against everything you believe. Many of those who did the fighting never went back to their regular lives. Many of them were very young. Are they good men?"

For a moment Judah was confused, and then realized Merrit was asking about Cleric and Lukash. Something in the older woman's inflection told her that Merrit was well aware of the other kind of men, who were not good enough, or good at all. "I think they are, yes."

"The Northerner seems a little shifty, but if he is fleeing a guild, he might have reason to be. I get the feeling from them that they've traveled together a long time. They have that way about them." Merrit slung her filled skins over her shoulder. "You don't."

"I've been with them a few weeks." Judah dipped the reed canteen into the water. Then something invisible hit her in the ribs and all the breath went out of her in a muffled grunt. She fumbled the reed, almost dropped it.

Merrit caught it. "The pain again?"

"I'm fine." There was a stabbing pain about the size of a fist on the left side of Judah's chest, but it was not the worst she'd suffered.

"You don't think my people can help you," Merrit said.

"I don't need help," she said. And that was true. In Highfall, Gavin's injuries had been her injuries. She had bled when he bled, and bruised when he bruised, and the person who hadn't sustained the original injury healed faster but they still had to heal. Now there were no injuries. Only pain. She could bear pain. Gavin was the one who needed help. Whatever was happening to him was terrible, and it was ongoing. That knowledge—that idea of Gavin, broken and in pain and alone—sat in her stomach, twisted and unbearable. Maybe it wasn't safe for her to be near him, but that idea was starting to feel hollow. He wasn't safe, anyway. And if he wasn't safe, what had happened to Elly? The very question made her feel ill.

She didn't know where they were, she told herself. She couldn't go to them even if she wanted to. But that made it worse.

Sometime in the middle of the night she woke. Her back was to the fire and the front side of her body was frozen. The sky was dark but the moon was full and bright. She rolled over, so that her chilled nose could warm again—

And saw Merrit, across the fire. She wasn't asleep, either.

She was sitting up. Her eyes were open, and glittering in the firelight, and staring directly at Judah.

Judah's breath caught. She pushed herself up on one arm, cautiously. Merrit did not move, or react in any way to the movement. Judah lifted a hand. Merrit still didn't react.

She saw Lukash and Cleric, or at least the shapes of them; they were still asleep. Judah knew they'd awaken at the slightest noise. She lay back down and watched Merrit for what seemed like an hour. The strange woman didn't move, or speak, or do anything at all. The moon moved across the sky. Merrit held something in each hand, but Judah couldn't see what. She was working up the nerve to go look when Merrit's eyes fluttered closed and she inhaled deeply, as if waking up.

Startled, Judah squeezed her own eyes shut. And then opened them, just enough to see Merrit tucking something into her coat. The woman rolled her head as if her neck were stiff, and then lay down, pillowing her head on her pack. In a few moments, she'd fallen asleep.

It took Judah much longer.

The next morning, Lukash put out the fire. Nobody spoke. After they'd eaten, the strange woman simply set off into the desert, and the rest of them followed. Judah was tempted to tell Lukash and Cleric what she'd seen the night before—but what had she seen? Merrit, sitting awake in the middle of the night, and being still? Not exactly a murder plot in the making.

And anyway, Merrit turned out to be a good traveling companion. She kept them entertained with her ocarina and with stories from her own travels: near escapes, clever evasions, unexpected windfalls. Cleric said, out of her hearing, that her stories reminded him of the trickster stories he'd heard as a child. Judah couldn't imagine him as a child. The best she could do was a boy-sized version of his long coat, topped with his frowning face and his long hair.

Two waves of pain broke over her that morning. She did her best to ignore them. When the third came, Merrit had just passed around sticks of pemmican from her pack, and Judah's fell right out of her hand into the dirt. Which was for the best. Somewhere, Gavin was being punched in the stomach repeatedly and she might never eat again.

Lukash, behind her, picked up the sticky piece of meat, brushed away the dirt, and handed it back to her. "If Merrit Idris is telling the truth about who her people are, they can help you as well as anyone can."

"Not to mention resupplying Cleric."

One corner of Lukash's mouth turned up. "That, too."

Merrit and Cleric, about twenty feet ahead of Judah and Lukash, had paused, waiting for them to catch up. From this angle, she couldn't see either of their faces.

"What if she's not telling the truth?" Judah said quietly.

Lukash shrugged. "Where else would we go? Once we cross this desert, we'll reach the Barrier foothills. The land there will be slightly more hospitable. And there are trading towns near the passes. Has she done something to make you suspicious? Or do you not like healers?"

"I like Cleric," she said. "Most of the time, anyway. He doesn't make it easy."

"I think he'd be very proud to hear you say that. What about Merrit Idris?"

"She was awake last night," Judah said, reluctantly. "Just—staring. I don't even think she noticed when I sat up. At least, she didn't react." She stared at her grubby stick of pemmican. "It's not really anything to be suspicious about, is it? I'm being silly."

"No," he said. "You're being vigilant. But, as I said—"

"Nowhere else to go," Judah said. "I get it."

They walked through that day and made camp when the sun went down. Merrit brought out the ocarina again and the high, wistful music drifted through the air, as much a part of the night as the buzz of insects, the rustling scrub, and the crackle of the fire. Judah's head ached. She lay on her back and stared up at the sky. She had never seen so many stars, before coming here. There was no part of the sky that didn't hold a glimmer of light. She couldn't decide if the stars made her feel like a very big thing trapped in a very small space or a very small thing adrift in a very large space. How strange it was that she, Judah the Foundling, foster sister of Lord Gavin and Lord Elban's most unsolvable problem, lay on the hard cold ground of a western desert with two criminals and a strange woman she didn't trust. Suddenly and clearly, she thought, I don't belong here. She was so acutely conscious of being in the wrong place that her right hand strayed to her wrist. Her fingernails were long enough to make a scratch, now.

Gavin, my frustrating, bothersome, suffering other half, where are you and where is Elly and how can I help you without giving us both away?

Merrit's ocarina warbled across the fire. Quietly, without calling attention to the movement, Judah lay the flat of her hand on the same hard cold ground on which she rested, and reached inside it. Not for an object this time, or for a mineral—but for Gavin. Because this dirt was next to other dirt which was next to other dirt and if she could reach far enough surely there was dirt wherever Gavin was, too. Perhaps she could reach him through that dirt, the same way she had once reached him through the purple rope of Work-stuff that bound her to him. Tentatively, she extended her reach. She had to focus more intently on him, because while the Work had run in lines of purple—however jagged and webbed—each fragment of stone was next to hundreds of other stones, and the possibilities were endless.

But only one possibility led to Gavin. Nate had told her about sigils, symbols in the Work that every human was born with, that never replicated. A song sung once and never again, he'd said. She did not know Gavin's sigil, but she knew the essence of him; knew him inside and out, and had for her entire life. She focused on him, on the Gavin she knew, and let her reach flow toward him. Finding the path of least resistance, like water. Making its own paths where there were none, like water.

And she found—

a splintered board under a heavy head.

the smells of urine and sweat and dirt and blood.

a locked door.

a woman, speaking.

There was a clatter. The music of the ocarina stopped. Judah twisted back to the fire. Merrit had dropped the instrument, and was currently fumbling to pick it up. "What happened?" Lukash said, sitting up.

"Nothing," Merrit said, recovering both her instrument and composure. "I am tired, perhaps. We are almost to the meeting place."

Changing the subject. Judah found Lukash's eyes across the fire.

"How can you tell?" Cleric sounded annoyed. "Every day looks the same in this damn desert."

"No," Lukash said. "The ground is growing softer. There's more grass. And we are moving uphill."

It was true, Judah realized. She had begun to feel the strain of the slope in her hamstrings. "How close are we?"

"One day. Maybe two." Merrit, seemingly recovered, put her ocarina aside and picked up a twig waiting for the fire.

With it, she drew a long line in the dirt. "Here are the Barriers. This is the flatland. We are here," she said, making a small divot in the dirt, and then another. "The meeting place is here, in the foothills."

The second divot was close to the line of the Barriers, but not on top of it. Judah moved closer to see the map more clearly. Cleric and Lukash leaned in, too. Judah said, "Where is Black Lake?"

Merrit pointed, with her twig. "Here. You see, you have already traveled almost all the way across the western half of the continent."

Judah looked at Lukash. "And where is Morgou?"

He plucked a wildflower from the grass and dropped it along the western side of the Barriers, but farther to the north. Then he looked at Cleric, who scowled, but reached out one long leg to jab a booted toe at the makeshift map, level with the top of the Barriers but far to the west. "There. Where they have both kinds of weather, fog and snow. What about you, Thorn Bush? Where's the exceptionally poorly named Highfall?"

Judah tore up a piece of grass, alternately running it through her fingers and wrapping it around them as she stared at the vast unmarked expanse to the east of the line that represented the mountains. She hadn't been allowed to look at maps since she was a child, but she remembered them. She put the limp, crumpled thing on the spot where she thought Highfall would be. "There," she said.

"You are a long way from home," Merrit said, and Judah said, "Yes. Yes, I am."

They found Merrit's people two days later. By then, they could see the Barriers in the distance, blue-gray and immense. It was early; the sun had barely appeared over the peaks. The faint smell of wood smoke was the first sign. "When we crest that hill, you'll see our camp," Merrit said, and Cleric and Lukash hiked up the hill with renewed vigor. Anticipating breakfast, maybe. They'd eaten the last of the pemmican the night before and their stomachs were empty, or at least Judah's was.

Her legs, however, grew heavier with every step she took. She had grown stronger since those early days in the Ghostwood, but the long trek through the desert with not quite enough food had left her soles and ankles permanently aching. Still, the closer she came to the top of the hill, the more the heaviness in her legs began to feel like dread. She stopped. "Wait," she said.

Merrit turned around. "Not much farther now."

"I don't want to," Judah said. Although it was unclear even to her why.

"Don't be ridiculous," Cleric said. Lukash merely waited. What was Judah supposed to do? Turn around? Go back through the desert with no food or water? So she took the last few steps to the top of the hill, and looked down into the valley. The campsite was larger than she'd expected it to be. She could see the horses tethered off to one side, and half a dozen fires, and children playing among the wagons.

The wagons. The colorfully painted, appallingly familiar wagons.

She turned to Merrit, horrified. "You're Slonimi," she said. It wasn't the word Merrit had used to describe them.

Lukash and Cleric looked at her and then at each other, their confusion clear. Clearer than anything else that was happening. Clearer than how, in the vastness of the desert and the whole of the western continent, Judah had been brought to exactly the people she didn't want to see. The high grass rustled and all at once there were men everywhere, surrounding them on the crest of the hill. None of them looked anything alike. Some were pale as Elban and some darker than Lukash.

One of them stepped forward and held up his hands. "Daughter of Maia," he said, respectfully. "We have found you at last."

On one of his upraised wrists, Judah saw an all-too-familiar cuff of worked leather. She knew if he flexed his wrist just so, a blade would pop out of the cuff on a smooth, clever mechanism. She had seen Nate use one, in his memories. He had called it a springknife.

"Please, lady," Merrit said.

But Judah was already running. She was weak from the trek, though, and the Slonimi caught her. They caught all of them.

TWELVE

IN THE DUNGEON BENEATH THE TIERNAN MANOR, Gavin had plenty of time to ruminate on pain, and violence, and the art of beating someone only to hurt, and not to injure. Because—as Gavin had learned at the hands of his father's combat master, back before the coup in Highfall—it was an art: leaving bruises but not breaking bones, leaving wounds but ensuring that they'd heal. The art was in controlling your own strength, measuring each blow perfectly, not letting the twin rushes of adrenaline and power overtake you. Gavin had never been good at it. He could control his face, his carriage, the pace of his steps, and the timbre of his speech, but once it came to a physical fight he fought to win, always. Angen's guards were very good at hurting without injuring, but they'd made some mistakes. Two fingers on his left hand were broken, and he was pretty sure that a rib on his right side was, too.

As prison cells went, his wasn't terrible. A single splintered

plank of wood fixed to the wall served as the cell's only furniture, but the cold stone floor and walls of the cell almost felt
good, sometimes. One of the cell walls was warm, for when
the cold stopped feeling good. There must have been a furnace
or a laundry boiler on the other side. He was only occasionally conscious, anyway. He woke up when the guards came
in—or when the cowardly one who wouldn't come into the
cell alone hit the damn bars with his infernal rod—and once
he thought he'd heard a woman's voice speaking, but it was
possible he'd been dreaming that. He'd been dreaming a lot
of things, slipping easily from the cell to the training field,
the training field to the parlor, the parlor to the guildhall.
Sometimes Theron was there, or Elly. None of these dreams
bothered him. They were better than the cell.

More interesting still was what happened when the guards
came in. The first blow would hurt, and the second, and the
third—but then his mind would begin to drift, sort of, and
everything would seem very far away. It wasn't ordinary un-
consciousness. It was somewhere else. He was not sleepy in
that place. If anything, he was more awake. Because, wherever that place was—Judah was there. In a blurry, very, very
drunk way. He couldn't actually see her, but he could feel her
nearby. He saw a blue pool of water, unhealthy rings of white
and orange crusting at its edges, the sun bright and brutal on
its surface. He saw a boundless ocean of stars, draped across
the blackest black sky in graceful waves and bright clusters. He
saw the inside of a dark wooden room, that same brutal sun
streaming in through the slats, and he saw chains, and dust.
None of this was clear. He couldn't focus on any one thing long
enough to really see it. Like the images that came to him on
the cusp of dreams, endless stairways and half-glimpsed figures,
these images slipped away as soon as he tried to catch them.
And sometimes he couldn't be sure—the feeling of Judah in

his head was so familiar, he couldn't always detach his mind from hers, he'd never been able to. He heard high thin music, strangely accented words. He felt ruthless hands gripping her arms—or his? He couldn't tell.

Maybe the dreams and the cell blurred into one, but the impressions he had from her were real. He knew that, just as he'd known on that terrible day when she'd vanished that even though she could not be found she was without a doubt *somewhere*. He had not been able to reach her. He'd tried and tried and been met with nothing, over and over again, but he knew she was there.

Now, though. Now he could reach her. And all it took was being perfectly, exactingly beaten.

Life was funny.

He heard the lock on the cell door open and as always felt a sick surge of mixed terror and anticipation, racing each other through his pain-addled brain. He didn't bother opening his eyes. But instead of the heavy bootfalls of Angen's guards, he heard a soft swish, and then the gentle whisper of silk, and he smelled—perfume? The scent was incongruous, almost nauseating. A hand touched his shoulder, gently. "Lord Gavin," a soft female voice said. "My poor love."

He knew that voice. It was Amie, the lady courtier he'd once found delightful; Amie of the soft skin and softer sighs; Amie of the very capable hands and the viper's heart. She didn't love him any more than he loved her. He heard gentle sloshing, and then something warm and fragrant and damp touched his cheek, where one of the guards' rings had scraped it. It had been a long time since he had felt anything so pleasant. The panic receded. In its place was nothing but dull disinterest. Amie would go away. The guards would come back. They would hurt him. He wondered where Judah was. The last sense he'd gotten from her was a smell of damp wood and urine, but his cell smelled like urine, too. So that was no help. Judah had fled to the tower because they'd argued, and he had gone up to the tower to bring her down, but in between, he'd seen her only once. It had been late autumn. He'd been chopping wood, alone and hating everything, and then he'd heard her say his name and she had—been there. Not in person. Not exactly. It had something to do with the tower. She'd tried to explain but it hadn't made sense and they'd never had another chance to talk about it.

But she had been able to hug him, that day in the kitchen yard. He'd felt the wild tendrils of her curly hair against his cheek, the beat of her heart against his. She was short and round and only now, as Amie cooed nothingnesses and daubed at all of his hurt places with her stinking rag, did it occur to him that all of the women he had pursued had been her exact opposite, willowy and lithe. Elly. Amie. All the others. He had always assumed that willowy and lithe was his type and short and round was not, but now it occurred to him that maybe it had nothing to do with that, that the specific feeling of hugging Judah was its very own thing and he had walled it off from all of the conquests he was expected to make. To keep her special. To keep her—his. Exactly what they'd argued about, in the first place.

"I brought you a clean shirt," Amie was saying, now. Almost purring. Her fingers pulled at the filthy tattered one he'd been wearing ever since the guildhall, which he'd puked on and bled on and who knows what. It came apart as much as it came off and he heard her suck in her breath. When the perfumed cloth touched him again the hand that held it was shaking. Who knew what his body looked like at this point, that one broken rib and all the other, more minor marks, left by kicks and clubs and gauntleted fists? Distantly he wondered what she had expected, how she had thought this would go.

That purr. Had she thought that the mere act of taking his shirt off would be enough to rekindle whatever it was they'd had in Highfall? He supposed he must have liked her, once, but he mostly remembered later, when he'd hated her for the plans she'd made as his father tightened the noose around his neck. Rekindling? He had never felt less kindled in his life.

Except that then the cloth touched the broken rib and pain flared through him, so he dove into it—

she was scared, sick-scared and filled with self-loathing, and I'm trying, *she said to somebody, gritty with frustration, and an unknown man said,* Try harder, *and a third, young and female, said,* You're all crazy, the lot of you.

The shapes of the words were wrong. Where was she, where was she? Why was she scared? Who were those people?

But then the pain faded and he was back in the cell. Amie was pulling the clean shirt over his shoulders. She had recovered, he guessed, because she put a hand on each side of his face. The left one landed exactly on the spot where they'd broken his tooth. They'd sent a magus in after that, to take out the jagged root that remained. Amie turned his head toward her and she swam into blurry focus. There was her clear soft skin, her huge blue eyes. Her lashes were not as dark as they'd once been—maybe lash blackener was difficult to find now—and she wore her hair in that ridiculous braided loop the Tiernan women favored.

"Now, Gavin," she said, firmly, "you're being very silly about all of this. All Angen wants is to take you back to Highfall and make you Lord of the City, like you were supposed to be. And we'll be married, like we were supposed to be." He said nothing. Her hands were soft. One of them stroked him, gently. He wished it wouldn't. The stroking hurt; not enough to bring him to Judah, but enough to be unpleasant. "Unless you don't want to marry me, anymore?"

He pulled back from her, to make the pain stop. The shirt she'd put on him was soft white homespun, with tiny nubs where the thread had been spun unevenly. The cuffs hung loose. Where the fabric fell away, he could see his scars under the bruises on his arms: the curlicue scars from Elban's poker. The short straight scars from Judah's time in the tower. The faint symbols where he'd scratched himself bloody trying to reach Judah, in the weeks before the Seneschal had broken through the melted door in the Wall. When she was missing, when he'd lost her. What a terrible time that had been. What a lonely, terrible time.

"Gavin?" Amie prompted, gently.

She seemed to be waiting for an answer. He'd already forgotten the question. "It's the strangest thing," he said. "I can feel her, but I can't reach her. I can't talk to her. I can't see her."

Amie's huge blue eyes blinked. "I'm right here, Gavin. Can you not see me?"

"Not you. Judah," he said, and from the way her eyes widened and her brow furrowed, he realized he'd said something wrong. He shouldn't have mentioned Judah. Not to Amie. He was getting to be like Theron. His head wasn't working right.

"Gavin." Now Amie sounded firm, not coy at all. "You need to get out of here."

"Why?"

"Because you're in a dungeon. A dungeon is a place where you put people to die." She stood up, grabbed his arm, and pulled. "Come on. Stand up. I'll go get the guards and we'll tell Angen you're ready to cooperate, okay?"

He had been trained in wrestling. He slipped her grip easily. Pressure on the thumb, that was the trick. "No."

Her pretty little fists clenched. Her pretty little chin jutted. "What's wrong with you?" she said. "Why are you being like this? Don't you want to go back to Highfall, to live in the

House with all of your pretty clothes and lovely things? Don't you want to be Lord of the City?"

He shrugged. The shrug turned into a curl, and the curl into a lethargic slide, as he slumped bonelessly back down on the bench. "I wish I could talk to her."

"Who? Eleanor?"

"Judah," he said.

She stared at him. Finally, she said, "Judah's dead."

"No. Theron's dead. But Judah's alive. I just don't know where she is." He looked up at Amie. She was angry, he could see it. She could be withering when she was angry. Not like Elly, whose anger came in arctic politeness. "How is Elly? Is she okay?" he said, and then remembered that Amie was angry. That was the whole reason he'd thought of Elly in the first place. She and Elly hated each other. His brain was definitely not working right.

Amie closed her eyes. Took a deep, deliberate breath. Let it out again. "Gavin," she said, finally, "we need to go back to Highfall. You don't know what the city is like under the Seneschal. It's not only the courtiers. People starved to death last winter. There were—burial pits, and the factory managers—" She shook her head. "We need to take it back."

He was very tired. "You can do that without me."

"No." Amie sounded baffled. "No, we can't do that without you."

"I'm tired," he said, and closed his eyes. Pressed his arm against his broken rib. But he couldn't get back to Judah, he couldn't find her again. At some point later he opened his eyes and Amie was gone.

THIRTEEN

"WHAT IS THIS PLACE?" KORSA SAID, LOOKING AT the room where he'd found himself: the rug, the sofa, the faded silk on the walls. A room that he suspected was not exactly real. The young man named Theron—who was also not exactly real, and who in fact claimed to be dead—looked around, as well.

"It's the parlor. Where I used to live," Theron said, and then, as if reconsidering, "When I lived."

"It is in the House?"

Theron nodded. He gestured toward the terrace. "Go take a look. I usually don't bother making anything I'm not specifically looking at, but I'll show you."

Korsa stepped uncertainly out onto the terrace. For a moment, he was looking at—nothing. The nothing was a faint lilac color, and somehow more blank for that than it would have been, colorless.

Only the part of the floor visible from the parlor, as the boy had called it, existed. Then Theron joined him, and an entire world coalesced swiftly around them. To the left were several comfortable-looking chairs, one with a bow and quiver propped in it. To the right was what looked like a block of straw wrapped in some kind of coarse cloth, crudely painted with a series of concentric circles. A target.

Over the terrace balustrade, Korsa could see the same impossibly tall white Wall that surrounded the House today. But the space below them, which Korsa knew to be full of plowed fields and midden heaps, was instead rolling green pasture, dotted here and there with sheep. In the distance he could see trellises full of green plants that he thought were hops, and a small building with a smoking chimney that was probably a brewery. He could also see a pond that was too perfectly round to be natural, and dense thickets of ivy at the base of the enormous wall. It all looked real, but his nose told him the truth. The world outside the terrace had no smell. It didn't exist.

"Like I said," Theron said, "I don't bother making it if I can't see it. But I can make it look like anything, which is interesting." The grass turned purple, then blue, then green again. "I can even put people in it, if I want to." Workers appeared, springing out of the ground like drab flowers: pulling carts, hauling bundles, herding the sheep. "But they're not real. You're the first real person I've met since I woke up here. Who are you?" Theron gave Korsa a considering look. "You look sort of familiar, but you're clearly not from Highfall."

"I am Nali," Korsa said.

Theron snapped his fingers. "The chieftain! The one who was taken prisoner when my father was hurt, right? The Seneschal brought you to Elban's chambers, to see Gavin and Judah."

Korsa didn't remember him, but he'd had a bag over his head at the time. It had only been taken off once he was in that horrible room full of pain, where he'd met Elban's son and the purple-haired girl. "You are one of Elban's sons?"

"I was." Theron seemed remarkably composed. "Like I said, I think I'm dead. And I know for a fact that Elban is. Thank the gods he didn't end up here." He shuddered. "That would have been horrible. Trapped in—wherever this is— with my father."

"It is *kagirh*-space," Korsa said. "An empty space that you can form to your will." But even as he spoke, he realized it wasn't, exactly. It was somewhere else.

Theron shook his head. "I don't know that word. But you are the Nali chieftain, right? The one they brought here in a cage?"

"I am. I don't remember it well. I was half-crazed with despair and anger."

"I was more or less insane myself, at the time," Theron said, cheerfully. "Gods, I'm happy to see you. I want to hear all about this *kagirh*-space. But first—how did you get into my parlor?"

So Korsa told him about the prison, and the Seneschal's plan, and the children. He told him about the dead, strange feel of the city. Theron listened without interruption. Korsa didn't know what he'd been like in reality, but here, even as Theron stood motionless, there was a palpable sense of movement coming from him as he listened. When Korsa was done speaking, Theron stared off into the distance, over the edge of the terrace, and the sense of movement intensified. It was, Korsa realized, what happened when Theron thought.

Finally he said, "So the practical motive behind all of this is that the Seneschal wants to make more people like Judah and Gavin?"

"That seems to be so, yes."

"Does he know that Gavin's kind of an idiot?"

That made Korsa smile. Apparently brothers were the same, Nali or Highfaller. "All he cares about is the bond. But I can't seem to make it work. And now—Anna—" The smile was gone. "I don't want to try again, after Anna. But if I don't, I don't know what will happen to the thirteen-fourteens. I am afraid that the Seneschal will send them to the other side of the House."

"What do you mean, the other side of the House?"

"From what I understand, half of the House is a prison and the other half is a brothel."

"So nothing's changed." Then, seeing Korsa about to speak, Theron waved his hand. "No, no. I'm sorry. Bad joke. Look, I don't know anything about this bond of yours, or the herb—what did you call it?"

"*Kaghira.*"

"Right. I was never very interested in botany." And he wasn't that interested now, Korsa could see. "My question is, though—is it purple? Your *kagirh*-space?"

Korsa blinked. "It's no color. It's white. But the place I have found here is purple."

Theron nodded. Korsa experienced that sense of motion again, as Theron's mind turned over and over. Then, with a blink, something clicked into place. Nearly audibly. "This is an odd question, but—the Nali are human, right? I mean, despite all of Elban's attempts to convince us otherwise?"

"That is the first step toward war," Korsa said. "Convincing one group of people that another is less than human. Yes. We are human."

"Then there's no innate reason why the thirteen-fourteens, as you call them, couldn't learn to use *kagirh*-space the same way you did."

"The purple place is not my *kagirh*-space."

Theron pointed at him, his eyes alight with excitement. "Exactly. But it's close enough that you can use it. I can, too."

"Because you're dead," Korsa said.

But Theron surprised him. "I don't think so. I think it's because somebody tried to poison me a few months before I died. My body recovered, but my mind didn't." He shook his head. "I went a little nuts, frankly. I remember seeing cats, hordes of them, everywhere I went. And trust me when I tell you that there were not hordes of cats roaming the House. I remember telling Judah that they seemed extra, like pieces left over from a puzzle. But now I think they were stray fragments of the purple. Like sparks coming off a bonfire. The point is, I could *see* them. I could even feel it, I think—the purple—"

Suddenly his face went blank, and Korsa would have thought he was still what he'd called *a little nuts* were it not, again, for that incredible sense of movement, somewhere unseen. Then the blankness snapped away, and Theron looked around the room where they sat as if seeing it for the first time. "Before I died, I spent all of my time in my workshop, in the old wing. But after I died, when I could live anywhere I wanted—when I could *make* a place for myself—I didn't make it the workshop. I made it here. I thought it was because I missed the others. Judah and Elly and my thickheaded brother." A small, fond smile touched Theron's face. It vanished as soon as it appeared. "But that was wrong. I didn't make it in the workshop because the workshop was too close to the tower. The purple stuff—that place where your Anna drowned—it's in the tower."

His eyes slid away. His voice trailed off. Korsa waited.

And, sure enough, a heartbeat later, Theron came back. His gaze now was sharp and focused. "You know how to use the purple because it's sort of like the *kagirh*-space you've used all along. I know how to use it because I had—sort of a half step, between life and death, where I could see it, and sense it. It might even be part of me. I might even be made of it."

The boy stared down at his hands, holding his fingers out and staring at the space between them. Korsa said, "A half step. I do not want to half kill the thirteen-fourteens."

"Good. I don't recommend death," Theron said. "But I do recommend bringing them to the tower. If we can get the tower to—I don't know, recognize them, maybe it won't drain the life out of them."

"I don't understand. What tower?" Korsa said.

"Judah's tower," Theron said. "Ask the Seneschal. He'll know."

Through all of that day and the next, Korsa considered and reconsidered the strange interlude in the parlor. It had not been a dream. He was too familiar with *kagirh*-space to think that. But it was also not entirely like any *kagirh*-space he had ever experienced. He had never heard of a person dying and finding themselves there, had never encountered anyone there who claimed to be dead. And yet, Theron himself seemed utterly real. At dinner, as he sat in the dining room with the thirteen-fourteens—none of them, including Korsa, eating very much—he said, "Did Lord Elban have more than one son?"

It was the first full sentence any of them had spoken since Anna's death. The thirteen-fourteens looked up at him, startled. Jesse said, "Yes. Lord Gavin and Lord Theron."

"But Lord Theron was always sick," Ida said. "Before the Seneschal took over, everyone was saying he was going to die."

"Far as we know, he did. Far as we know, they all did." That was Liam. The words fell heavy on the table. Three pairs of eyes looked back down at their plates of food. Only Florence seemed unconcerned.

"They all?" Korsa said. "Who is 'they all'?"

"The Children," Ida said, sounding depressed. "Lord Gavin, Lord Theron, Lady Eleanor, and Judah the Foundling. None of them have been seen since Lord Elban died. I heard they're in prison."

"I heard they're living under fake names in the city," Jesse said.

"They're dead," Liam said, with finality. "The Seneschal has no reason to keep any of them alive."

That might have been true for Theron and Eleanor, but the Seneschal had a very good reason to keep Judah and Gavin alive. Still, the fact that Theron had existed at all, and wasn't merely a figment of the drug Korsa had filled himself with, gave him a small measure of hope. The next morning, when he heard the girl setting up food in the next room, he asked her to take him to the Seneschal. He did not tell the thirteen-fourteens where he was going. He did not want Florence coming along. The girl led him up one staircase and down another, all dusty and unused-looking, until finally they came to a heavy, iron-bound wooden door. From down a narrow staircase to the side came the clatters and shouts of what was surely a kitchen, but the girl turned the handle on the huge door and pushed through it.

The other side was a completely different world. There were thick-woven carpets under Korsa's feet and heavy tapestries and paintings lining the walls. Down this hall they found another staircase, which led them to a similar hall lined with doors. From behind the closed ones, Korsa heard moans and laughter and cries. Only one door stood open, and inside that one, Korsa saw an assortment of couches and gilded tables covered with wine bottles. A man lay on one of the couches, surrounded by a flock of women who seemed to be wearing more jewelry than anything else and one delicate-looking boy who reminded him horribly of Liam. The reclining man's eyes were closed. He was smiling, faintly.

After that corridor came another, lined with gleaming gas sconces and the same draperies and thick rugs. A soft place to do hard, unpleasant things. It was as if every beautiful thing in the city had been brought here, and the effect was like a child's vision of wealth.

Finally, they reached a part of the house that was not so gaudily decorated, a place where the floors were clean and polished but bare. There, the girl stopped, and pointed down the corridor. "Thank you," Korsa said, but she was already running away.

Halfway down the bare corridor, he found a door that opened onto a small cluttered office. The Seneschal sat inside behind a large desk, staring out the window. The gray man looked bone-weary, the kind of weariness that called not for sleep but for ease. A plate of bread and cheese sat in front of him on the littered desk. It looked untouched.

"Seneschal," Korsa said.

The man looked up. "Chieftain. What a surprise. How did you find your way here?"

"The serving girl showed me."

The Seneschal smiled. "You saw some of the House of Repose, then. I'm guessing that you disapprove. Come in, then. Sit down and tell me about it." Oddly, the man seemed energized by Korsa's presence, as if he were happy for the distraction.

Korsa did not want to sit down or tell the Seneschal anything. But he sat down, anyway, and took a piece of the cheese the Seneschal offered him. It was deep orange, with tiny crystals that crunched pleasantly between his teeth, and tasted good enough that he felt guilty not sharing it with the thirteen-fourteens. "The Nali tell our children that a game is only fun if everyone is playing," he said. "I think it's only the rich men who play, here."

"Women, too, sometimes." The Seneschal picked up the cheese plate and put it to the side. "Life is not all play. Each of us must work, in whatever way we can. This is what Elban and his courtiers never understood." For a single moment, something blazed in his eyes: anger, satisfaction. Korsa couldn't pin it down, and then it was gone. "Anyway," the Seneschal continued, "all of the House of Repose staff have made their own choices, along the way, and now this is their work. It's useful. There's a demand for it."

"You told me you would send the thirteen-fourteens there." Korsa's anger was impolitic, but he didn't seem to be able to rein it in. "They have not made any choices."

"It's important that everyone contribute, somehow," the Seneschal said, evenly. "And it's equally important that the factory managers have a place to relax. They're responsible for a great many lives and a great deal of money. It keeps them happy. I need them happy," the Seneschal said, and now the weariness was back. "What can I do to help you this afternoon, Chieftain?"

"I do not think the rooms we are in are suitable for my experiments."

"What's wrong with them? They're quite large and airy, if I remember correctly."

"They are dead," Korsa said.

The Seneschal's eyes didn't actually roll, but they did close briefly and open again, and the intention came through. "I'm afraid that's not much to go on. Lighter rooms I can find you. Less dead rooms will be difficult, since I have no idea what you mean."

Korsa had planned for this. "Humans do not make *kagirh*. *Kagirh* exists, whether humans make use of it or not. It is everywhere. But it is sparse in this city, and in the rooms where you've put us. I don't know why. But I know that I cannot work with something that is not there."

"There was enough of it to kill the girl with the crutches," the Seneschal said.

Korsa pressed his tongue against his teeth a moment to keep from speaking until he had control of himself, and then said, "I think it was the lack of *kagirh* that killed her. The drug lifted her out of her body, but there was nothing for her to grab hold of once she was there. It is very frustrating," he said, and that was true, at least. "I can feel the power somewhere in this House, like a fire burning in another room. But I can't find it." Korsa stopped talking, then, as if something had occurred to him. Or at least, he hoped it seemed like something had occurred to him. He was not a good liar. Faolaru had lied for them all, when there was lying to be done. "That red-haired girl, the one I met in the room that day, with Elban's son. She is the only person I have met in this place who felt—alive. Did she have a room? Somewhere she seemed drawn to?"

"She had rooms with the young lords and Lady Eleanor. I can show you those."

Korsa shook his head. "It feels—higher than that. Perhaps a tower?"

Even as he made the gambit, he knew how clumsy it was. He was almost relieved when the Seneschal's eyes narrowed. His tone was edged with frost, like a pond in early winter, when he said, "How do you know about Judah's tower?"

"*Kagirh,*" Korsa said, simply. "Knowing these things is why I'm here, is it not?"

The Seneschal watched him for a long moment, and eventually nodded. "I suppose it makes sense. Judah did seem to be drawn there." A faint smile touched the man's lips. "Do you know, there's a story among the guards that she's living on the roof? The House is huge. There's a lot of roof, and it would be difficult to search all of it. Every time some small thing goes missing, people say it's her. It's not, obviously. It's one of the staff, that's all. But I like the story. Judah was a difficult person, and stubborn enough to survive a winter on the roof to spite me." He shook his head. "I warn you, there's no running water in the tower. We rebuilt what we could, but we didn't add any pipes. You'll have to fetch water from one of the modern sections of the House. And if you find out that Judah really is living on the roof, please tell me immediately."

That last was said so lightly that there was no doubt whatsoever in Korsa's mind that the Seneschal was entirely serious. He nodded.

The Seneschal nodded back, and then shuffled among the things on his desk until he found a piece of paper and a pen. "None of my guards will go there. I'll draw you a map."

Korsa loved maps and understood them, but his grasp of written Highfall wasn't great. Back in the workroom, he showed the Seneschal's map to Liam. At first, the boy was surly, barely responsive. But as he looked at the map, Korsa saw Liam's natural curiosity emerge, as he'd hoped it would. "What are all these places?" Liam said. "The old wing? What is that?"

"I know as much as you do. Probably less. You've been hearing stories about this place your whole life."

Liam's expression grew bitter. "Stories about it being a beautiful place of plenty."

"There is food," Korsa said.

"A prison is a prison." Liam stood up. "Come on. I think we start this way."

So Korsa followed him through the corridors, up and down stairs, around unlikely-seeming corners. Finally, they reached a broad passage that didn't appear to have been used recently, and at its end, an enormous door, pulled from its hinges and propped against a wall. The place where the lock should have been was splintered and broken. What looked like construction debris was piled nearby: broken chisels, buckets crusted over with dried mortar, a few loose bricks. Liam pointed at the map.

"Old wing," he said, and they stepped through the empty space where the door should have been.

On the other side, a trail of spilled mortar on the floor dribbled off to the left, which—according to the map—was the way they were meant to go. The trail led them to another door, this one propped open with a piece of broken brick. Inside it was a perfectly round room, which seemed to have once been set up as a workshop. Shelves and work surfaces and cabinets lined its interior. Korsa tore away the greasy curtain covering the room's one window and the room filled with thin, much-diluted light. In the middle of the room was a chest with a broken lock that, when Liam opened it, proved to be full of pieces of scrap metal, some as big as Korsa's fist. In another cupboard, they found more scrap, as well as a number of vials of liquid and bags of powder. All of the containers appeared to be scavenged, but they were neatly labeled in the same clear, precise hand.

"This is a laboratory," Liam said. "I wonder whose."

Theron had said something about a workshop. But Korsa wasn't ready to talk to the thirteen-fourteens about Theron yet. "The Seneschal called it Judah's tower."

"I never heard anything about the Foundling working in a laboratory."

"What did you hear about her?" Korsa said.

Liam picked up a notebook and flipped through it. Dust rose from the pages like smoke from a pipe. "Everything I know comes from children's stories and puppet shows. She was supposed to be mischievous and brave. And nobody knows where she came from." He tossed the notebook aside. "What's through there?" Because a second door stood open in the far side of the laboratory. Liam walked through it, and looked up. "Stairs. Is that where we're going? Now I see why you brought me."

"I mostly brought you because you can read Highfaller," Korsa said, and they began to climb.

The narrow stone stairs spiraled up and up, nearly out of sight. The higher they climbed, the brighter the light grew. They had done two circuits when Liam stopped and pointed ahead. "Look. The stairs have been mended."

"Not very well," Korsa said, looking to the place where there were dusty planks put across a gap in the steps. Two tall metal spikes had been driven into the top and bottom of the gap, and a piece of rope tied between them served as a handrail.

They passed several more broken places before finally the stairs came to an end on a tiny landing. Yet another wooden door—also with a broken lock, although this break looked older, the jagged surface of the exposed wood gray with time—hung open. Liam, breathing heavily, said, "Why would you put anything at the top of a staircase this high? Who's ever going to bother coming up here?"

"Us," Korsa said, and went inside.

And found he couldn't breathe at all. He felt as if he'd walked into a solid block of—something—like the vast kelp forests that grew off the Nali coast, thick waving fronds where a person could tangle themselves and drown in the slick brown leaves. All of the life that was absent from the dead, evacuated air in Highfall was here. In this room. Burning, writhing, alive. Fighting. Straining. He understood why Theron had likened it to a thorn bush because it felt like a thousand prickly fingers grabbing at him, pressing into him. Trying to work their way inside. The strange lilac of the void was here, too, but stronger. Darker. More—*alive*.

Calm, Korsa. That is the point. This time it was Meita that he heard. Caring, soothing. Utterly imaginary. But it was enough to help him clear his head. Standing next to him, Liam said, "This is very strange."

He spoke the truth. The room held a smashed table and a settee with a stack of books replacing one broken leg. Its edges were littered with dry leaves, and Korsa couldn't figure out how they'd gotten into the room until he realized that the wall straight across from him was new. Most of the room was lined with shelving, like the laboratory downstairs had been, but halfway around the room on either side, the shelves abruptly stopped. A distinct line of demarcation crossed the floor and looped up to the place where the wall should have met the ceiling. The House was built with gray stone, but the repair was done with crude brown brick.

Meanwhile, Liam was exploring the rest of the room. "This room is bizarre," he said. "There's a tree growing over here."

"I see," said Korsa, staring at the tiny, determined sapling. But his mind was already working. He would need an intact table, and a stove, so that he could make an actual fire. If the thirteen-fourteens were going to be spending a lot of time here, he wanted them to be warm and comfortable. Jesse was going to have trouble navigating that staircase. Ida, too. Picturing either of them crossing the improvised bridge made Korsa feel vaguely ill.

He pushed the ill feeling down. "All right. I suppose the first thing we'll need is a broom."

The thirteen-fourteens were delighted by the dusty rooms and empty corridors of the old wing. The Seneschal had drab workers in gray set up their four cots in the abandoned work-shop, and Korsa made himself a pallet in the tower room. Sleeping there would be difficult, but he hoped the natural unmooring of his mind during sleep would help him understand the prickling force in the tower.

After they moved to the tower, they fetched their supplies from the old wing's entrance. The first delivery came with more vials of drops, which Korsa distilled immediately and took, the second night. He had hoped that he wouldn't need to take as much as he had the day he'd found Theron in *ka-girh*-space, and he was right. No sooner had he felt the lift of mind out of body than he found himself standing with the young lord of Highfall. This time, they weren't in the parlor but in the laboratory beneath the tower. It looked completely different than the room where the thirteen-fourteens slept, which was disorienting. The work spaces were piled with half-built devices and notebooks and more odd pieces of material, like the ones they'd found in the chest. The greasy curtain was back over the window, and a tattered tapestry covered the door to the stairs.

Theron looked faintly guilty. "I'm sorry. I should have taken us up to the top of the tower." He shook his head. "I don't like it up there. Even here—look." He pointed at one of the empty shelves. It was webbed with cobwebs, more thickly than it had been in reality. But these cobwebs were a sticky-looking, unhealthy purple. "That purple stuff is everywhere up there. I can't do anything with it."

They spent the rest of the night talking about the drops and about the way Korsa was distilling them. Theron had suggestions—a great many suggestions, in fact; a preponderance of suggestions, an endless torrent of suggestions—and in the morning, when Korsa came back to himself, he was exhausted but had an idea of how to make the false *kagirha* better.

Meanwhile, the thirteen-fourteens explored the house. They returned dusty, covered in cobwebs, and bearing things they clearly found marvelous. Things like half a sky blue eggshell, a green piece of cut glass, or a tiny carved cat. Florence was the only one who didn't wander. She was more interested in digging around among the assorted tools and scraps. Some of the scraps she collected, and put into a box she'd found, and after that—buttons forgotten—she spent long hours going through the box over and over again, picking up each piece of dirty metal and turning it over in her hands until whatever need she felt had been satisfied, and she could put it aside to pick up the next one.

In a guest room near the old wing door, there was a water tap that still worked, and they'd been getting their water from there. Liam and Florence usually made the trip, moving in a companionable silence. Those trips had started because they were the two most mobile, but they had evidently grown used to each other. Liam was protective of Florence. She, unsurprisingly, seemed outwardly indifferent, but she also tended not to wander out of a room he was in, or stay in a room where he wasn't. When he had one of his seizures she would sit next to him until it was over. Human beings were surprising. Their body might be male, but their mind female. Or perhaps, like Florence, they hid active, vibrant minds inside quiet bodies. Like Korsa's lost *kagirhi* Giorsa, who was a tall, thick-bodied woman who rarely spoke—but her mind was a festival of music and color. She remembered every plant she'd ever seen, and every bird, and all of their songs. She remembered birds and plants she hadn't seen, except in her imagination. Those birds had made charming, handsome Faolaru wild with excitement and the two of them had spent hours together, Giorsa imagining birds and Faolaru drawing them.

How Korsa missed his *kagirh*. He didn't know whether it was better or worse to watch as the young people formed their own, not in the ethereal reaches of *kagirh*-space but in their shared experiences, Highfall and the orphan house and the inherent challenges in their particular bodies. It was not the kind of *kagirh* he was supposed to form of them, but it was not that different, either. What one could not do, another did for them. What they had, they shared. Perhaps they had learned this in the orphan house.

He said as much to Ida once, and the girl laughed. "Don't go getting pretty ideas about the orphan house," she said. "It's easy to share here, because there's always enough. But I think if you look under Jesse's mattress, you'll find that some of us are a little better about sharing than others."

Korsa didn't look under Jesse's mattress, but he did start paying closer attention while they ate. And rolls did, in fact, find their way to Jesse's plate and then disappear before they could possibly have been eaten. He hoped Jesse would have time to realize that he didn't have to hide his food, that there would always be enough, but he and the thirteen-fourteens all knew there was nothing secure about their situation. If ever he needed a reminder, the Seneschal always seemed to be there to supply one. The gray man came to observe, a week or so after they moved into the tower. Korsa showed him the beds in the lower-level workshop, the boxes of materials that Florence was constantly sorting and rearranging, the collection of interesting things the young people had brought back from their explorations. They had started to put them under the window, where the thin light could catch them.

"This is very charming," the Seneschal finally said, the scar on his neck berry-pink in the light from the workshop window, "but it's unclear to me how it helps you progress toward your goal."

"It sets them at ease." Korsa knew full well—with the exception of Florence, who sat quietly with a box of scraps in the corner—the children were waiting in the empty room across the hall, to hear what came of the conversation between the two adults. Ida, who could move more silently on her hands than most did on their feet, was probably listening outside at this very moment. "They are still recovering from the loss of their friend. That is progress."

The Seneschal shook his head. "I understand that they are saddened by the girl's death, and so are you. But you have to understand that these children were never going to live lives of ease, no matter what happened to them. They were always going to suffer grief and sadness. We all do. I was an orphan myself, many years ago," he added, almost as an afterthought. "These children were always going to suffer, simply because of where they were born, and how."

Korsa felt his teeth clench. *Calm, kagirhi*, Faolaru said, inside his head, and Korsa neither snarled nor trembled when he said, "This is your city. You should not be proud of that."

"I am neither proud of it nor ashamed of it. It's merely a fact. This city runs on its factories, and these children are not suited for factory work. They're not suited for work at all, really."

"They're smart and resourceful," Korsa said.

"Then they'll find a way to survive. I did," the Seneschal said, with a hint of humor that Korsa found abominable. "They've already charmed you, haven't they? So it's even more important that you not fail them."

A skewer of anger drove up through the center of Korsa and he said, before he could think better of it, "Which reminds me—have you had any luck locating your missing lord, yet?"

The Seneschal's humor vanished. "Be very careful, Korsa," he said, quietly. "If your little project does not succeed, I am exactly no worse off than I was before."

The two men stared at each other. Korsa had been a warrior once, before being brought to this horrid place, and for a moment he could not help but consider that in other circumstances, he could have killed this gray man who stood before him. Easily. Without thinking twice about it.

But then he heard footsteps on the stairs. Liam—who had ostensibly been upstairs tidying in the tower but was more likely standing at the bottom of the stairs listening—came through the stairway door. The skewer of anger in Korsa froze and turned to fear. No, he couldn't kill the Seneschal. Not while the thirteen-fourteens depended on him.

As if he'd read Korsa's mind, the Seneschal's mouth relaxed. He turned to the boy. "Will you please find your companions? I would like to speak to all of you."

Liam glanced at Korsa, and then went across the hall. In less than a minute, the thirteen-fourteens were filing into the room. The gray man waited until they were each seated on their own cot. Silence fell. The only sounds were the faint clinks of metal on metal from Florence and her box.

"You all seem to like living here, with our Nali friend," the Seneschal told them. "You seem happy, and I'm glad of it."

With Florence unconcerned, the three remaining thirteen-fourteens watched the Seneschal warily and said nothing. Korsa stood frozen, afraid to move or speak or do anything that might risk them.

"I wish you could stay here forever," the Seneschal went on. "But unfortunately, you're here to do a job. We all must do our jobs, mustn't we? A factory that didn't produce wouldn't last long. Then all its workers would be unemployed, and their families would starve. I am very sorry for the death of your friend, but now it's time to get back to work. If any of you are unwilling to do that work, please tell me now. We will try to find other work for you."

"What kind of work?" Ida said.

The Seneschal smiled down at her. Korsa was glad she took

it without reaction. "What do you think you can do here? Can you work in the fields, or the kitchen?"

"I probably could," she said, defiantly.

With her strong arms and the smoldering determination that always burned in her eyes, Korsa would not have been at all surprised. But Liam said, "Quiet, Ida."

"Everyone must find something they can do," the Seneschal said. "This place exists because the factory managers saw a need for it, but all who live here must contribute, in one way or another. I would rather see you work here with Korsa, because you all seem happy here. But if he continues to make no progress, I will have to reassign you, whether we like it or not." He looked at Korsa. "I wish you the best of luck," he said, and left.

"What was he talking about?" Jesse said, sounding uncertain, when the gray man was gone. "I kept waiting for the threat to come. It sounded like there was a threat coming."

"It was all a threat." Korsa sighed. "The other side of the house. It is a—" He stopped. He was unable to say the word to them.

"A brothel," Ida said, and then, when Korsa looked at her in surprise, "The girls who bring the food always have makeup around their eyes. Like they tried to wash it off, and missed some. Kitchen maids don't wear makeup." She gave him a sad smile. "The orphan house is still in the real world, Chief. Why do you think we're all so humble-looking? It's because the pretty ones got taken out early."

"Except Liam," Jesse said. "And that's just because they don't want him having a spell in the middle of—"

Liam gave him a dark look, and the younger boy shut his mouth hastily. But when Ida said, "Some things, you don't need legs that work for," they all nodded.

"I hate this city," Korsa said, grimly.

"Sounds like it's time to test your mind-herb again," Liam said. Korsa shook his head. "You could die. Like Anna."

There was a long silence. Ida, who was always the speaker of truth when truths needed to be spoken, was the one who broke it. Softly, she said, "How long do you think brothel girls live, Chief?"

When Korsa was their age, he'd thought himself immortal, brazen with the confidence of youth. He hated that these young people were able to speak of their own deaths with such equanimity. He knew they valued their own lives, but he also knew that most of the people they'd been around didn't, particularly. Their pragmatism horrified him.

"You are all important," he said. "To me, and to the world. There is more to your value than whether or not you can work a shift in a factory. You are not disposable."

He didn't know what he'd planned to say next. But before he could figure it out, Korsa felt a light touch on his arm. He turned and saw Florence standing next to him. Florence hated to be touched, and she never touched others. She would occasionally suffer one of the other girls to brush and braid her hair, if they cornered her and insisted very gently, but even then they were careful only to touch her hair, and not even to let their fingers brush the tips of her ears.

But now here she was, hand on his upper arm, wide blue eyes staring up at him. Her mouth, her jaw, her eyebrows were as affectless as always, but the piercing stare was new, and different. He could feel the warmth of her hand through his shirt. He could smell the residue of the oily metal on her fingers.

"I guess you have a volunteer," Liam said, awestruck, and Florence kept her hand exactly where it was, and there was nothing but silence for a while.

FOURTEEN

ANGEN'S WIFE, LADY YANA, WAS TALL FOR A TIER-
nan woman, and raw-boned despite being extremely pregnant. She had beautiful hair, thick waves of warm burnished
gold, but her eyes were nervous and there was a dour set to
her mouth. Like many extremely pregnant women, she was
miserable and peevish, but Elly suspected that she would have
been miserable and peevish even without the discomfort of
the child growing inside her. Whenever Yana looked at Elly,
she either held her head high, like the haughtiest of courtiers, or low, like a dog about to attack. When she spoke, her
jaw clenched.

And Elly belonged to her. Angen had given her to his wife
as a gift, after Gavin was dragged down to the prison beneath
the keep. "You've never been a lady's maid before," he told
Elly, "but I'm sure Lady Yana can train you." And with a
sweep of his soft, loathsome hand, Elly had been dragged away,
too. She'd been given a plain servant's dress to wear, and had

her hair braided in the dreaded handle at the back of her head. Yana did it herself, and, as the saying went, made sure it was tight enough to hang by. Elly's scalp hurt all the time, now.

Figure out a way to survive the day, wake up tomorrow, and do it again: wisdom passed on to Elly by her grandmother, who had once lived in the rooms where Yana slept. Now the air there rang with recriminations and criticism, as Yana barked gleefully at Elly to brush her dress, arrange her hairpins, fetch her water, and straighten her bedclothes. Elly didn't seem to be able to do any of it properly, but she moved as quickly as she could and tried to keep her wits about her despite the constant sniping. Going to bed, at this stage of Yana's pregnancy, was a complex affair involving an elaborate construction of pillows and cushions and as Elly arranged and rearranged them at Yana's orders, she made herself look again and again at the woman's swollen ankles and stiff fingers and remind herself that this woman was uncomfortable, and unhappy, and married to Angen.

Finally, Yana settled back in bed and demanded tea. Elly gladly went to fetch it from the women's salon. Her feet had known the way since childhood, but the familiarity was uncomfortable. It only grew worse when she arrived at the salon itself. Traditionally, the salon was the only place the women of the house held any sway at all. When Elly's mother had been Lady of Tiernan, it had been lovely and full of light. Elly remembered being taught to sew there, the feel of the linen beneath her fingers, the smell of the lavender in the candles. All of that was gone, now. The gracious sofas and armchairs were crowded awkwardly together, to fit in as much other, less comfortable seating as possible. The room smelled not of lavender but of black dye and stale breath.

Squeezed into one corner was a small tea table, and squeezed in next to that, arranging a tidy tray next to the samovar, was

Eduard's maid, Moira. She turned when Elly came in, and smiled. "Lady Eleanor," she said, with a warm smile. "Come see how Lady Yana takes her tea."

Gratefully, Elly went and saw. With a very precise amount of honey, apparently, and a few drops of valerian, to help her sleep. And a fine saucer holding one piece of the dry cracker that Tiernan shepherds carried with them on long grazes. "In case her stomach bothers her at night," Moira explained. "But it must be a perfectly unbroken piece, and it must be laid perfectly straight. See?"

The girl was so sensible and kind that Elly, exhausted and more frazzled than she wanted to admit, felt her eyes prick with tears. "You," she said, "are officially my favorite person in Tiernan. How can I possibly thank you for all of this?"

Moira grinned, and Elly almost gasped. Moira's smile was Elly's mother's smile, exactly. And now that she looked for it she could see something of Eduard around Moira's cheekbones, and the shape of her eyes. Or did she see it because she was looking for it? "You're welcome, Lady Eleanor," the girl said.

"Elly's fine," she said, and took the tray down to Yana.

Who promptly found fault with the temperature of the tea, the placement of the tray, and the speed with which the whole thing had been brought. "You aren't much of a maid. But we'll train the high-and-mighty out of you, Lady Highfall," she said, and waved her hand. "That's all."

In her own little closet of a room, Elly fell gratefully into bed, not bothering to undress. There was no door. Judah had slept in a closet like this throughout their childhood. Elly was heartstruck by how lonely that must have been, to sleep in a tiny afterthought of a room that didn't even warrant a door. But Judah almost never actually slept in that room, had she? She'd slept in the big room, with Elly, and how Elly missed her. She missed Judah's warm feet pressed on hers, the way

Judah always woke with her head buried under the pillow. How happy they'd all been, even in the worst of times. How stupidly, unknowingly happy. Because they'd had each other, hadn't they? And now they didn't even have that.

When she closed her eyes, all she could hear were the sounds of fists and boots hitting Gavin's flesh.

Moira shook Elly awake in the morning, a finger laid to her lips. Silently, she walked Elly through everything that needed to be done before Yana awoke. There was the fire to be stoked, the hairbrush and pins to be laid out in perfectly straight lines on the porcelain tray on the dressing table, fresh clothes to be taken from the press. All in absolute silence and stocking feet. Then Moira cocked her head, and the two of them headed toward the cramped salon, where breakfast was being laid out by other serving girls. Of course there was a specific way that Lady Yana liked her breakfast arranged. Of course she had a lengthy list of preferences. One piece of toasted bread, a boiled egg. No butter, no salt. Elly tried to remember, but she found herself distracted by the women filing into the room. Completely unlike the ladies floating gracefully into the salon in Elly's memory, these women, while well-dressed enough, trudged into the salon like workers onto a factory floor. Not that Elly had ever been on a factory floor, but the tired resignation in the women's eyes and the joyless exhaustion with which they trudged to their seats couldn't have been much different.

"I'm sorry, Moira," Elly said, interrupting as Moira explained exactly how Lady Yana liked her toast. "But what's happening here?"

Moira cast a puzzled look over her shoulder at the women. "What do you mean, Lady—sorry. What do you mean, Elly?"

Elly appreciated that the girl had remembered. "I mean, why are they acting like they're sitting down to work?"

"They are sitting down to work," Moira said, as if Elly were a bit stupid. "How else should they look?" The courtyard bell rang. Quickly, Moira picked up the tray and pressed it into Elly's hands. "You need to hurry. Lady Yana will be angry."

But Lady Yana was already angry. "You're late," she snapped, as Elly laid the tray down next to the bed.

"I'm sorry." Elly picked up the teacup to hand it to the woman.

Something black lashed out from under the bedclothes, and struck the back of Elly's hand with such a fierce sting that at first, she thought she'd been bitten by a snake, and yelped. The teacup clattered to the floor, greenish liquid splattering over the sheets.

Lady Yana bared her teeth in something like a smile, and held up a small riding crop with a knotted bit at the end. "Mind your duties," she said, "or the next one will be across your face. Not that you can get any uglier, with that scar of yours."

Elly was stunned into silence. She gripped her searing hand firmly in her uninjured one and stared at the woman in the bed. Noticed how the crop trembled slightly, and wondered if anyone had ever pointed out to the woman that it was easier not to be cruel. "Yes, Lady Yana," she finally managed to say, barely able to hear herself, and began to clean up the mess. A purple welt was rising on the back of her right hand. In her mind, she heard the thud of boot against flesh.

This was not going to work.

The next few days passed in much the same way. Yana waved the crop around a good bit but seemed somehow both panicked and elated about actually using it, as if she couldn't quite believe she had been given the power to hurt another person. However nasty Yana might be, Elly suspected she'd spent a good bit of time on the other end of the cruelty. Elly tried to think of her that way, as a woman ill-treated, rather than a monster. If she were a better person, she would be able to think of the tasks she did for Yana as gifts, not chores.

But she could practically hear Judah in her head: *Nobody is that good a person.*

The worst part was that things Yana wanted were quite small, and Yana would not have had to be nasty to get Elly to do them for her. She wanted tea three times a day. She wanted pillows for her swollen feet. She wanted water, endless glasses of it, with a touch of the coriander syrup that Elly remembered her mother giving Elly herself when she was ill. The smell of it was powerfully nostalgic, especially standing in Yana's room, next to Yana's bed. That bed, Elly realized, had been her own mother's bed, and her grandmother's before that. She had spent many an hour lying in that bed, running her fingers over the edges of the carved wooden leaves on the headboard.

The only other familiar object in the room was a piece of blackwork embroidery, hung on the wall in a dark corner. A single sprig of cornflower. Elly herself had made it, and she remembered being terribly proud of it. Now she saw that it was wobbly and uneven, like a cornflower viewed through water. Once upon a time it had hung over her mother's dressing table. It still hung in the same place, now half-obscured by a wardrobe. Elly was careful never to look at it, lest Yana notice. But whenever Yana harped at her until the words blurred into a single knifelike edge, she could feel it there, like a glowing coal. Elly had embroidered that cornflower with the feel of Angen's hands still on her, his laughter still in her ears. And she'd been willing to sew anything to keep from being sent outside for fresh air, because outside was where he and her other brothers were. The salon had been a refuge, then. Not a prison.

And not a factory. Not a place where the women of the house were expected to produce a certain amount of embroidery per day, or be scolded by Yana. The younger women, like Moira, were kept busy taking care of the house. Except for Elly, the older women worked in the salon, because they were the only ones who could still produce the blackwork. A few of the older women remembered Elly as a child, but the only one Elly remembered was named Margaret, called Peggy. Peggy was some female relative of Elly's, nothing as direct as an aunt. They tried to figure it out, one afternoon, but Peg had never been exactly sure what Elly's mother had been to her, and they soon gave it up, laughing.

Elly remembered a few girl cousins, back from the days before she'd been sent away. She asked about them, and Peg's lips pressed together. Mildly, though, she said, "After your father made such a good deal selling you off, he went through the rest of the girls your age fair quick. So they're married off, and away, most of them. Quite a few died. Childbirth, mostly."

"I'd be surprised he doesn't have a new match in mind for you, Lady Highfall. A good deal, to sell the same goods twice," one of the other women said. There was a note in her tone that Elly didn't like, any more than she liked the *Lady Highfall* nickname. Almost jubilant, as if Elly had been caught in the act of something. Peg glared at the other woman, who shut up immediately.

Elly said nothing, but bent over her blackwork despite the way it made her braided handle pull at her scalp. Inside, her head was whirling. Survive this day, survive the next one. From where she sat, Elly could see the exact window her grandmother had been sitting by when she'd given her that advice, so many years ago. But for the first time, Elly wasn't sure it was the right advice. *Sorry, Gran.* Elly wanted to do more than survive.

Yana, always exhausted, went to sleep early. Elly was supposed to sit by her, in case she woke and needed anything, but Yana had barely been asleep an hour when Moira appeared and told Elly in a barely-audible whisper that Eduard was waiting for her in the corridor. So Elly put the pillowcase she was mending aside and left the room with only the barest glance at Yana, asleep in Elly's mother's bed.

"Hello, Eleanor," Eduard said, in the corridor. "Come for a walk with me?"

"It's dark out," Elly said, bluntly, "and I need to be here in case Lady Yana wakes up."

Eduard looked at Moira, who scrunched her nose but said, "I'll sit by her."

"There are torches on the ramparts." Eduard stepped closer and, quietly, said, "It's the only place where there won't be ears to hear."

Elly had never been up on the ramparts before, and the very idea of it made her stomach feel wobbly. When she was a child, Angen had chased her up trees and shaken them to scare her. She'd hated heights ever since. But she was too curious about Eduard's motives to say no. The stairs leading up were steep but at least they were enclosed. When she actually stepped out onto the rampart, the wind caught her, and the sky reached so wide and empty before her that she could not breathe. The torches crackled and hissed, and the smell of them made her stomach sick. "Far enough," she managed to say.

"What's the matter?" Eduard said.

"High places." She remembered climbing the steps to the tower, Theron beside her. *Breathe in, breathe out, Elly. You can do it.* She wished the torches didn't smell so strongly.

"I'm sorry I didn't warn you about Amie," Eduard said. "I

273

needed to see how you two reacted to each other. You were both in the court at Highfall. You might have been friends." He leaned against the rampart and stared out into the darkness, as if the distance to the ground weren't at all terrifying, and Elly fixed her eyes on the rampart walkway. The stairs ended in a nook used for storing torches and arrows, and she gripped both sides of the entrance. She knew the floor wasn't swaying under her feet but still had to will herself to remain standing. "Giving you to Lady Yana was Amie's idea. I think she thinks it'll give you some incentive to get Gavin to cooperate."

Suffering as incentive. How novel, Judah said in her head, and Theron added, Breathe in, breathe out.

"What do you want, Eleanor?" Eduard said.

The question shocked some of the fear out of her. For a moment she could say nothing. Then she said, "I don't think anybody has ever asked me that before. It's incredibly irritating that it's you."

Eduard winced. "Nor—" He stopped, and corrected himself. "Eleanor. I know your life here was awful. It's not an excuse, but Angen was cruel to all of us. I thought that because he wasn't beating you—I didn't understand. It was worst for you." He looked at his boots. "I look at Moira now and I wish I had been braver."

Moira was Eduard's daughter, then. "I wish you had been, too, but you weren't," Elly said, as close to emotionless as she could get. "As for what I want: I want to get Gavin, leave this place, and find Judah." And Theron, too. But she didn't say that.

"The Seneschal told Angen that the Foundling was dead."

"The Seneschal lies like most people breathe. I'd like to see for myself, thank you. If she's alive, she's in Highfall."

"If you convinced Lord Gavin to go along with Angen and Amie's scheme, they might be willing to take you along."

Elly shook her head. "Too many *ifs* and *might*s. I don't know if I can convince Gavin of anything, these days, and even if I could, I'm not going to try to push him down a road with a headman's axe at the end of it, and you and I both know that's what will happen. I don't want to sign myself up for that, either." She sighed. "I'm not sure there's an alternative. It might be the only way."

"It might. It might not." In the flickering torchlight, his carriage was gloomy. "Angen has not been good for Tiernan. Glory hasn't been good for Tiernan. The people think it has, because it puts more money in their pockets than sheep farming, but it's killing us. The shepherds are all turning farmer, letting their flocks die off and planting glory on their pastureland. Even the artisans, the spinners and the weavers and the embroiderers—most of them work in the fields now. The guild is nearly empty. They're housing glory brokers there, now."

"And the women in the salon?" Elly said.

"Forced to work. Angen wants Tiernan to be known for glory instead of wool, but there are still rich women out there who want Tiernan blackwork to lay across their tables." Eduard sounded disgusted. "People starved in Tiernan last winter. Angen told them they'd be able to buy food if they stopped growing it, but the prices were too high."

Elly frowned. "But if they made so much money from glory—"

"The people don't know what glory is worth. How could they? Do you? I don't. I'd never even heard of the stuff, two years ago." Eduard spoke softly now, but Elly had the distinct impression that this was because he was trying to keep from yelling. "I think Angen is lying about how much he's able to sell it for. He says he's taking a tiny cut and passing the bulk on to the farmers, but I think it's the other way around. He's the one who arranged for the food imports, too. You saw the army camped outside the stronghold. We're shepherds. We've never had an army that well equipped. We've never needed it."

"And the people go along with this, while they're starving to death?" Elly said. "If Elban can be overthrown, anyone can be."

Eduard barked a laugh. "It's Angen. All it took were a few shepherds dead of unnatural causes, and now anyone who's not blinded by the vast amounts of gold that they think they could be making is afraid to do anything other than obey him. The guards won't organize without someone to lead them, and they don't trust me any more than you do. I've done Angen's bidding for too long. Never mind that I didn't have a choice. Never mind that I still don't. Moira—" Eduard's voice grew very soft and trailed away.

"Who was her mother?" Elly said.

He gave her a sad smile. "A weaver. Died in a plague when Moira was six. I couldn't have married her anyway. Angen doesn't want his heirs to have any competition but each other. I tried to get Moira into the house without Angen finding out she's my daughter, but I'm told her parentage is fairly obvious." He stepped closer to Elly. "If we could prove to the guards that Angen is stealing money from the people, and give them somebody to follow, I think they would turn against him. I really do."

"You're thinking of Gavin?"

Eduard cleared his throat. "Actually, I was thinking of you."

For the second time in the span of a single conversation, Elly was wordless. Eduard took advantage of the silence and plunged forward with a hint of desperation. "All these years, ever since you were sent away, the people talked about how much better things would be when Lady Eleanor was Lady of the City in Highfall. And now you're back, and the guards who were at the guildhall are telling everyone about you fighting off that old woman with a knife. And about the way you bore those stitches without crying out." His mouth twitched. "They call you Eleanor the Brave. I think they'd follow you, if you were willing to lead them. There's no future for you in Highfall, anyway. Not with Amie and Angen. You know that. Once Angen is gone, you can go to Highfall. You can even take the army with you."

"I have no interest in ruling Tiernan," she said, although the image of herself walking into Highfall with an army at her back was appealing. The image of herself telling Angen and Amie to go hang—perhaps literally—was even more so. "Even presuming you manage to get rid of Angen, which is a big presumption. If he's taking more than his fair share, there have to be records somewhere. A ledger, or something."

"I've never seen Angen with a pen in his hand longer than it took to write his name."

"Maybe he doesn't keep the records," Elly said. "Maybe Yana does."

Eduard's eyes widened. "Of course. Of course! How could I forget about her?" Elly had a fairly good idea what the answer to that question was. Eduard had forgotten about Yana because Yana was a woman, and already married, and therefore could not possibly have anything to offer him. "If you'll look for those ledgers—just look, that's all I'm asking—I'll do anything you want. I'll get you better food, more rest time, anything. I'll even tell the guards to go easy on Gavin."

Elly's breath stopped. "What do you mean, go easy on him? Have they—not been going easy on him?"

Evenly, Eduard said, "They have not."

Then Elly understood everything, all at once, in a flash. Angen wanted to prove that all of the power was his and none of it was Gavin's. It was the same thing Elban had done to the four of them, when he'd tried to force Gavin to choose between murdering Theron and yielding Elly herself to his own father. The same thing the Seneschal had done, when he'd trapped them in the empty House to be worked to death or starve. Suddenly exhausted, Elly wondered if there was any other way to lead.

"Take me to him," she said.

The air in the dungeon was relatively dry, considering that Tiernan soil was mostly wet clay and bogs. The walls and floor had been well mortared and didn't feel clammy under her fingers. Lanterns burned at regular intervals along the stairwell downward. The smell of the rendered sheep fat that burned in them wasn't pleasant—and what would Angen do when there were no more sheep to render, Elly wondered—but it was more pleasant than some dungeon smells she could imagine.

Then they reached the main hall, such as it was. There were only three cells, each covered with an iron gate. Elly's father had not gone in for long trials or imprisonments, and it seemed that Angen didn't, either. The first two cells were empty. Outside the third, a guard sat on a high stool with a large metal rod in one hand. As Elly approached with Eduard, he glanced into the cell, and slammed the rod against the bars. The clamor was hideous. He hadn't noticed them yet.

"Guard," Eduard said.

The guard stood up straight, startled. "Lord Eduard." Then he saw Elly, and his eyes widened. "Lady Eleanor?"

Elly summoned every bit of her Highfall imperiousness and swept past him to look through the bars. A figure sat huddled in a corner of the cell. If Elly hadn't known that this must be Gavin, she wouldn't have recognized him. He'd been in the cell for almost a week. It might as well have been a year, by the looks of him. She couldn't see his face, but the hair that hung over it was dark and matted with something that was probably blood. He had curled his arms around his knees, pulling himself into the smallest shape possible. Elly felt tears prick at her eyes as she imagined him strolling across Elban's Great Hall, tall and handsome and effortlessly confident.

The blood-matted head began to slump over the tucked knees again. The guard slammed the baton against the bars.

Elly wheeled on him. "Stop that. Let me into that cell."

The guard blinked. He was younger than she was, his beardless cheeks flushed red. Whether with embarrassment or anger, Elly couldn't tell. "Nobody is allowed in, Lady Eleanor. Lord Angen's orders."

"Who's been hurting him?" Elly was furious. Judah was missing. Theron was missing. Gavin was all she had. "Is it you? And why won't you let him sleep?"

"His father killed my mother's entire family," the guard said, his voice defensive, and cracking slightly.

"Is it his father in that cell?" Elly spat.

The guard's eyebrows lowered. "Come, Eleanor," Eduard said quietly.

By the time they were upstairs, all of the frustration and anger of the past few days was forcing its way out of her, streaming out of her eyes in salty streaks. "You have to help him," she said.

"I'll help him," Eduard said, "but you must help me," and Elly nodded, because there was nothing else she could do, and nothing else she could say.

Elly found Tiernan blackwork loathsome, the endless swirls and meaningless curlicues and leaves and flowers that grew from nothing, with no roots and no color and no life. And the symmetry, the hideous symmetry. Trust her family to take all the wild possibility of nature and drain it of all color and everything wild. Each half of a piece had to mirror the other, down to the very stitch, and after a few hours of work Elly's wrists would ache and her fingers would be necrotic-looking from the black dye.

Unfortunately, she was good at it. She'd been doing it ever since she could hold a needle. It had not taken long before her skill was recognized, and now she did nothing else while Yana napped. She would rather have spun, or worked the loom— but no. Still, it was better than waiting on Yana. It gave her time to think, and watch, and wonder where Yana kept Angen's ledger, through all of the long, sleepy afternoons. But she was unable to look for it, unable to go anywhere but this one room and the privy down the hall unless Yana called for her. And always the guard at the women's salon, watching to make sure none of the women wandered off. Had there been a guard there when Elly was a child? She didn't remember.

They were making wall panels. Elly didn't know who had commissioned them but she knew that a commission like this would have paid the wages of her father's guards for three months. One panel was already done, finished before Elly had arrived and now hanging on the wall, wrapped in paper. There were four to do in total. A seasonal theme. The one Elly was working on was winter, all snowflakes and holly. If Elly were designing a winter panel, she would have found a way to capture the variations of bark on the bare branches, all the lichen and scars and tangled squirrels' nests. Squirrels themselves. Cardinals. Yes, one blaze of red in all that stark black-and-white. Tucked away in a corner. How she wished she had pencils and paints. How she wished she was anywhere but here, stuck in this room, sewing this panel.

She was almost relieved when Amie came to see her. The former lady courtier was a plainer, drabber figure than the one Elly had seen from a distance in Highfall, albeit still wearing a dress as red as the cardinal in Elly's mind. But there were no enameled creatures in her hair, no opal powder on her cheeks. Her earrings were tiny gold drops, almost modest. Her hair was braided in a neat handle, like Elly's. Doubtless hers was not tight enough to make her scalp burn. She looked upset. Her cheeks were red and her fists kept clenching and unclenching. "Eleanor," she said, imperiously. "A word?"

"Lady Yana would not like me shirking my work," Elly said, and didn't move.

"Lady Yana will get over it," Amie said, as the woman herself appeared in the doorway. Barefoot, because so late in her pregnancy her feet did not fit into her tiny, impractical shoes; with her hair down, because Elly had not been there when she woke to braid it into a handle for her. A knitted shawl was wrapped around her shoulders. Despite the dark circles under her eyes, she looked very young.

"What will I get over?" Yana was trying to sound as imperious as Amie, but she couldn't quite manage it. She thrust her chin into the air. Her lips were trembling. "Why are you in my salon?"

Amie smiled, and it was such an oily courtier smile, in such incongruous surroundings, that Elly almost laughed. "I need to speak with Lord Angen's sister. It will only take a moment. Then she can return to—" Amie's gaze dropped to the panel on Elly's lap "—whatever it is that she's doing."

"I don't see what she could possibly have to say to you," Yana said.

"It's about Lord Gavin," Amie said, and Elly felt a lurch in her stomach. She put the panel aside, and stood up.

Yana watched, wild-eyed. "You'll be punished. Sit down. Do your work."

"In a moment," Elly said. As she and Amie left the salon, she could hear Yana shrieking invective behind her, calling her lazy and proud and a thousand other things, promising all sorts of evil upon Elly's return.

"She's unpleasant," Amie said, conversationally. "Come, let's talk in my room." So down the corridor they went to a lovely bedroom decorated in smoky blue and rose, with windows positioned to catch the light. Colored-glass hummingbirds were set at the corners of the beveled glass windows—imported, probably—and the bed looked soft. Amie gave her a faint smile. "You know, I don't think the two of us have ever actually spoken. Isn't that odd?"

Elly looked at the lady courtier. Whose perfume she had once smelled on Gavin's clothes, who had done everything she could to take Elly's own place in Highfall, and who had nearly succeeded. The last time Elly had seen Amie in Highfall was at Elly's own betrothal ball, smiling sweetly as she danced with Gavin, so confident in her own success—Amie was no less a pawn than the rest of them, then, but Amie had not been about to be traded away to Elban, and so Elly had hated her.

"What about Gavin?" Elly said.

The woman wasn't stupid. Elly saw the gears clicking inside her head, like one of Theron's machines. The friendly conversation track would lead nowhere, so the gears lifted, recaught. The faint smile vanished. All business now. "I went down to see him. I'm concerned about him. The dungeon is unhealthy."

"Most dungeons are. Perhaps you should have considered that when you allowed him to be sent there."

"Yes, well, I didn't expect him to be stupid enough to stay. If nothing else, his own sense of self-preservation—" Amie's lips pressed together, and her chin dropped. She almost looked—worried? Was it possible that this craven peahen actually cared about Gavin? "I'm worried about him. He's not himself. I think he's gone mad."

"If he hasn't, I'm sure Angen will make sure he does." But Elly's heart ached. She turned to go back to the salon.

Amie put a hand on her arm to stop her. Elly could not have been more shocked if the woman had kissed her. "I know we've had our differences, Eleanor. But surely we can agree that the best thing for him is to be out of that cell."

"So tell Angen to let him out. You've got his ear—or some part of him, anyway."

The corners of Amie's mouth twitched. "Angen is a clumsy instrument. He has to be played very carefully. Is Lady Yana treating you well?"

"Not particularly," Elly said. "But I feel sorry for her."

"She doesn't feel sorry for you."

"Yana and I have a lot in common."

Amie gave Elly a long, measuring look. "As do you and I."

"The only thing you and I have in common is going mad in Angen's dungeon."

"Not true. We've both survived," Amie said. "If you told Gavin to capitulate, Angen would set him free. He'll still need to marry me, but I can find a way to help you, too. Somehow."

Now it was Elly's turn to take the other woman's measure: the plain clothes, the plain hair, her very presence in this backwater stronghold. And was that true sympathy in Amie's eyes, or was it more playing of a clumsy instrument? "If you want to help me, get Gavin out of that cell, and away from Angen's guards."

"I can't do that."

"Play the clumsy instrument," Elly said. "You're the virtuoso, aren't you?" Then she turned, left the woman alone in her lovely room, and went back to work.

Thin soup that night for dinner, with gristly chunks of mutton. Yana, for once, had been invited to eat with Angen. Elly knew the woman would call for her the moment she returned, so when she had eaten as much of the soup as she could stand, she went down to the laundry to fetch a clean nightgown. The fabric was thick and lush against her fingers, the smell of the rose water the laundresses had ironed it with sweet and fresh. Once upon a time, Elly had worn clothes like this. Now she merely enjoyed their proximity.

As she passed the main hall, she could hear the sound of conversation and clattering cutlery inside. The women were still eating in their dining room, too. Assuming Yana wouldn't be back yet, Elly went into her bedroom without knocking.

But inside, she saw Yana sitting at her desk, writing in a slim book. Elly's breath caught. Yana's head twisted around, and she slammed the book shut. "Who do you think you are, coming in here without knocking?" she squawked. She hauled her ungainly self to her feet. Elly wanted to get a closer look at the book—the ledger? or just a diary?—but Yana was advancing now, the crop in her hand. She always kept it close. "I'll tell you who you are. You're nobody. You're nothing. Your father sold you for the price of a year's wool, what do you think about that?" Yana sounded triumphant, as if she'd scored a great victory.

Too much. Too much anger for walking in unannounced. Angen must have said something, or done something, to stir Yana up like this. Elly took a breath, and let it out slowly. "My mother," she said, "would have given me away for free, to get me away from Angen and my brothers. And if that child you're carrying turns out to be a girl, I'd advise you to do the same."

Yana cried out a word. It was a crude word, and an evil one, and Elly had never actually heard it applied to any woman, let alone herself. The crop rose and came down against Elly's upper arm. Her fingers released of their own accord and she dropped the clean nightgown on the floor.

"You are not worthy to say my lord's name!" Yana shrieked. "You are nobody! You are nothing!"

And the crop came down again, this time on the side of Elly's head. She dropped down next to the crumpled white puddle of the nightgown, hunched into a protective ball as the crop came down on her neck, her shoulders, her back, leaving hot stripes of pain everywhere it fell. Judah's caning, back in Highfall, had been worse than this, Elly told herself, dimly. Judah had survived. Judah had withstood it.

But still, against her will, a hitch and sob of pain escaped her. Yana laughed, high and nervous. The leather-wrapped rod came down three more times before Yana dropped it, winded. Elly's shoulders were shaking, her breaths coming in whimpers from her body. "Pathetic," Yana said, contemptuous. Elly heard her make her way across the room, shuffling on swollen feet, her breathing labored from the exertion. "Get up. Go get me another nightgown. That one's dirty."

It wasn't. But Elly hauled herself to her own feet, feeling as stiff and clumsy as Yana. "Yes, Lady," she said. Gathering up the fallen nightgown, and the crop, too, she bundled the nightgown in one arm and laid the crop on the bed, where Yana could easily find it again.

But in the hall, her tears stopped. Because while she'd been on the floor, watching from inside the cave of her curled body, Yana had opened an invisible panel in the side of the desk and slid the ledger inside. Pathetic, indeed. Elly wiped the tears from her sore face, and made her way down to the laundry.

FIFTEEN

LUKASH AND CLERIC FOLLOWED THE SLONIMI down the hill to the circle of caravans more or less willingly, but Judah fought all the way. She forced the guards to drag her bodily down to the clearing where the rest of the Slonimi waited, silent and formal. Men, women—there were even a few children, peeking around the legs of the adults. They didn't look like monsters. They looked like people, better kept than Judah's little party but equally as dusty. Their staring eyes were every color Judah had ever seen and many she hadn't; their faces were skim-milk blue and the soft dark of a starless night and every color in between. Nate had said the Slonimi collected people from all over the world—all that mattered was that they had power—and, among their practical traveling clothes, she spotted traces of what must have been the costumes of the places they came from. A bright bit of embroidery here, earrings there. One of the men even wore his hair in the same long ropes as Lukash.

The leader was a bearded man wearing a dark blue neckerchief who greeted Merrit with a solemn nod. Judah could tell he was in charge by the way the other Slonimi kept glancing at him, as if for reassurance. Next to him stood an older woman with a spray of flowers tattooed on her cheekbone, her eyes fixed on Judah. She alone didn't glance at the bearded man, so she must have been important, too.

The bearded man stepped forward. "Daughter of Maia," he said, and spread his hands out, as if in welcome. He wore a springknife, too.

Judah said nothing. Cleric shot her a scowl and stepped forward. "Please excuse my companion's rudeness," he said, with his warmest, friendliest smile. "She hasn't been well."

The man gave him the barest, most contemptuous glance. Then, to Judah, he said, "Merrit told us about your pains. We can help, Daughter of Maia."

Merrit had told them? When? Then Judah realized that the question was not *when* but *where*, and the answer was *in the Work*. Slipping away, stealing moments like the one Judah had seen by the fire. That was why Merrit had always kept her coat on, to hide the cuts from the bloodletting. "I don't want your help," she said.

The man gave her a patient smile, as if she were a cranky, overtired child. "It's not our way to allow suffering, when we can help it."

Cleric tried again. "Your reputation as healers—"

"She doesn't need a healer," the flower-tattooed woman said, curtly.

"She does." All this time, Lukash had stood silently, his copper eyes taking everything in. The Slonimi had taken the misshapen knife she'd made him, holding it gingerly as if it were unclean. He had yielded it without any argument.

"That's why we agreed to come to you. She has fits of pain, with no cause, and no sign of injury."

The leader stepped forward. "There's a cause. She's only forgotten it. You've been through a great ordeal, Daughter of Maia." He said that last directly to her, with a look on his face—the wide eyes, the parted lips—that she knew all too well. She'd seen Nate Clare wearing it often enough, hadn't she? *You are a miracle*, his mother had said, when Judah had slipped through Nate's mind to speak with her in the Work. And that—that *reverence*—shone out of the man's eyes now, and those of the flower-tattooed woman's, and all of the other Slonimi. Judah didn't want it. She didn't want to be anybody's miracle. She had jumped out of a tower to escape all of this. She had left everybody she had ever known and every person she loved and every place that was familiar. The fury with which she'd fought on the way down the hill wasn't feigned. She would fight to the death, but she would not be their miracle.

Still: *Maia*. Her mother had a name.

"Stop calling me that," she said, through gritted teeth. "My name is Judah."

"And mine is Daniel," the man said. "I lead this caravan. And this is Pavla, our best Worker." He indicated the flower-tattooed woman. "We are very, very glad to see you. We welcome you home."

Cleric stared at Judah. "You're Slonimi?" he said, stunned.

"She is," Daniel said, at the same time Judah said, "I'm not."

But she remembered, a literal lifetime ago, saying to Nate, *Your people are my people*. She'd been so warmed by the idea that she had actual family somewhere in the world. That was before she'd learned what the Slonimi wanted from her. Now, to Daniel, she said, "I won't do it."

"Won't do what?" Daniel said.

"You know full well what. I won't kill Gavin for your precious Unbinding." She felt a collective drawing-in of breath from the watching Slonimi and pushed forward anyway. "I wouldn't do it when Nate asked me and I won't do it now."

Daniel looked at Pavla. "Gavin?"

"Elban's heir," the Worker said, her lip curled in disgust.

"Ah." Daniel nodded. "Well, now that you're back with us—"

"You can stop saying that, too," Judah said. "I can't come back to a place I've never been. I'm not home."

"Let's not worry about it now," Daniel said. "It will all be fine, I promise." Then he looked meaningfully at Pavla.

Who, stepping forward, gave Lukash the barest glance. "The Morgeni has no power. Give him a piece of gold and send him on his way."

"The Morgeni cannot be bought," Lukash said. His face was impassive, but anger simmered under the surface.

"The Morgeni have strong ideas about money and honor. And this one's probably a former soldier, which makes it worse," Daniel told Pavla. "What about the other?"

The tattooed woman looked thoughtfully at Cleric. "Maybe. Hold him, Kendzi," she said.

The man who had first spoken to Judah gestured, and two big men grabbed Cleric, one at each arm. Cleric looked down with surprise at the huge hands gripping him and said, "Wait," but the Slonimi ignored him. Pavla brought a small knife out of her pocket. The moment Cleric saw it he swore and struggled, but the burly Slonimi holding him twisted his arms up behind his back, immobilizing him. "Don't be silly," Pavla said, scolding. "That hand of yours hurt more than anything I'll do to you." Then she pushed up her sleeve.

Judah saw the neat line of scars there, identical to Nate's. "You have to ask!" she said, quickly. Now hands were holding her and Lukash, too. One of the men had a springknife at Lukash's throat. "You have to have his permission."

"I'm afraid we don't have time for manners today," Pavla said, and made a small cut on the meat of her arm. She pushed up Cleric's sleeve and cut him, too; then she touched her fingers to her wound, and with bloodied fingers drew a mark over the wound she'd made in Cleric. His sigil. Even from a few paces away, Judah could see him in the lines of it—the hard-formed edges, the sweeping depths—and realized that it was familiar to her, that some part of her had seen it all along.

Then Pavla drew what must have been her own sigil on top of Cleric's, and Cleric's back went rigid. Except for those midnight moments by the fire with Merrit, Judah had never seen the Work from outside. From inside, it felt gentle, like a door opening. There was nothing gentle about what happened to Cleric. His jaw was clenched, his eyes squeezed tightly shut. It hurt Judah to see.

Pavla merely wore a slightly faraway expression. "What are you doing to him?" Lukash said. He sounded menacing but Judah knew he was worried.

"He'll be fine," Daniel said.

But Cleric didn't look fine. His body shook like a frightened rabbit's, and panic rose in Judah's throat. This was her fault. The men were only here because they were with her. This should not be their problem. None of this should be their problem. "Stop," she said. "Leave him alone."

"It will be over soon." Daniel watched dispassionately as Cleric's wrists flexed painfully, his fingers curled into hooks like he was clinging to a wall. "Pavla's very talented."

Even as he spoke, Pavla pulled her hand back. The men holding Cleric let go of him, and he dropped to his knees. Shaking, still. But the shaking was more rhythmic now, rippling through his shoulders and down his spine. He was sobbing. Lukash said his name, straining against the grip of the two men holding him, but Cleric didn't answer. Pavla wiped her fingers on her skirt, as if she'd touched something distasteful.

"Elenesian apostate," she said. "Burned off his own guild mark. You can see the scar."

Burned off? Deliberately? Judah felt ill. Daniel pressed his lips together. "Could we trade him for access to the pass, do you think?"

Pavla nodded. "They don't take apostasy lightly, the Elenesians."

"I'll send a runner." All this time, the other Slonimi had stood silently. Staring at Judah, most of them. Daniel turned to a thin boy in his early teens. "You go, Adam. Merrit will tell you the way."

Judah had almost forgotten Merrit, treacherous Merrit, who had led them here when all Judah wanted was to be left alone. Merrit, who stood away from the crowd a bit, frowning slightly. Good. Judah wanted her to feel bad. She wanted Merrit to feel terrible. But when Daniel glanced at Merrit, she only nodded.

The men holding Lukash dropped his arms and he crouched next to Cleric, who hadn't moved and was still sobbing silently. The Morgeni looked horrified, as if he were seeing something unnatural. Uneasily, he put a hand on Cleric's shoulder. "They'll kill him if you send him back there," he said to Daniel.

"Nobody is forced to join the Elenesians, or to agree to live by their rules," Daniel said. "You're free to leave, if you want to."

"Let them both leave," Judah said, and discovered that her voice was trembling with rage. What Pavla had done to Cleric—going inside his mind, breaking what she found there and rearranging it to suit her—Nate had done the same thing to Judah, or tried to. The arrogance and temerity and *wrongness* of it infuriated her. "They're not involved in any of this."

Lukash looked up at her, his copper eyes icy. "Any of what?" His voice was full of rage. Judah knew it was directed at her.

But Pavla was advancing on Judah, her eyes greedy and fascinated. "Daughter of Maia," she said, breathy and awestruck. "You look very like your mother."

"You hurt my friend," Judah said, coldly.

"I don't think this is the time, Pavla." Daniel looked at the man with the springknife, the one he'd called Kendzi. "Put them in with the girl. If the Morgeni refuses to leave, put him there, too. Daughter of Maia, we will talk later, when you've calmed down."

"My name is Judah," she said, defiant. But Lukash was already being herded away, Cleric carried as if drunk or ill, his feet dragging through the grass. The gripping hands were already back on her arms and there was no stopping any of it.

The wagon where they were brought was windowless and dark, with slits near the roof for air and a heavy iron hasp on the door. Iron cuffs were fixed to their ankles, and then to chains fixed to loops in the walls. A dozen more loops waited, empty, and that was a terrible sight because the caravan was not large. Judah stared at the empty loops as the man named Kendzi fixed her chain to one of them. How many people were the Slonimi willing to fit into this dark wooden box?

"I'm sorry about this," he said, sounding genuinely sorry. "Nobody here wants to hurt you, Daughter of Maia."

Judah spat at him. Nate had been sorry, too. Sorry as he'd killed Theron, as he'd held out his knife to her and begged her to kill Gavin. Sorry as he'd emptied all the warmth out of her memories of Darid, as he'd woven bits of the ghastly purple tower-stuff through her, making her lose track of time and lose track of herself. Kendzi gave her a sad, grim look, wiped his cheek, and left them alone.

The moment the heavy bolt slid home, Lukash exploded. He pulled the chain on his ankle to its length and kicked against the slats of the wall with his heavy boots, pounding the places where the slats joined with his fists. His face was set into a tense blank and his silent fury was terrifying. Cleric sat motionless where he'd been dropped, head slumped, arms propped on his knees, and burned hand hanging slack. That was terrifying, too. In the dim light, Judah's eyes kept being pulled back to the shadow of his hand. Whatever it meant to be an Elenesian apostate, it was bad enough that he had melted his own flesh to hide it. Cleric slumped and Lukash raged. The two men had done nothing but help her. What had she done to them?

A voice came from the huddled body at the far end of the wagon. She spoke with an accent that Judah didn't recognize. "Might as well give that up. They build things well, these witches."

Lukash stopped, instantly. He turned and looked toward the girl. Her feet were bare and dirty beneath her shackle, her dress plain and coarse. She had a broad nose, a pointed chin, and long hair that she wore in the remnants of a braid, although most of it had fallen out by now.

"Witches," Lukash growled. Judah had never heard him so angry. He looked at Cleric, still hidden behind the curtain of his long hair, who had not reacted when the girl spoke. Then he turned to Judah, and in that same dangerous tone, said, "What did she do to Cleric?"

The girl in the corner said nothing. Judah sat down on the floor. "I don't know, exactly. Something inside his head."

Cleric said nothing.

"It'll wear off," the girl said, reassuring. "When they mess with your head it always wears off, eventually."

"You know?" Lukash said to her.

The girl laughed. It was a bitter sound. "What, do you think I came in here because it seemed nice? I got a thing for spiders, maybe?" She shook her head. "But, yeah. It wears off. Your friend is a guildsman?"

Judah almost laughed, despite everything. Nasty, swearing, fighting Cleric—oh. Right. *Cleric.* And he had been a guildsman, once. "Cleric is only the name he uses," she said. "He's a healer. I'm Judah. This is Lukash."

"Onya," the girl said. "Might as well relax. They won't treat you too bad, other than locking you in here. Hells, they can be nice, even."

"So nice, they've got us all in chains," Lukash said, and Onya did laugh.

"So nice, indeed," she said. "The trick gets us in here, and the chains keep us. But you'll see. They'll be back as soon as you quiet down, sweet as pie. Keep telling me I can come out as soon as I agree to join up."

"So agree." Lukash sat heavily down on the floor, too. "Then run."

Onya shook her head. "Tried it. Didn't work, but maybe you're a better liar than I am. To hell with them, anyway. Me and Inek will get away from here sooner or later."

"Who's Inek?" Judah said.

"My brother. Only five years old, but they took him, too."

"Why?" Lukash said.

"They say we've got power, and it's not safe for us to live among regular people. Power, hah! I'm blind as a new kitten, practically, and Inek's barely got the power of wiping his own butt."

Lukash seemed to be thinking all of this through. "They said I had no power," he said. "They said I could leave."

"Then you should have," Onya said.

"They're delusional," Judah said. "All of them. You're not powerless."

He turned on her. "You certainly aren't. They were all but setting up altars to you, Daughter of Maia." He spat the words with contempt.

Judah wanted to shrink back, but there was nowhere to shrink back to. "They're especially delusional about me. But I'm not one of them. I never even heard of them until—gods, less than a year ago."

"So you say," Lukash said. He was looking at her as if he didn't know her, as if she were a stranger he already disliked. Which was terrible, not because she was afraid but because he had been—had he been her friend? Almost. She would have been very lonely, not to mention very dead, had Cleric and Lukash not found her in the Ghostwood. Lonely enough to even welcome the Slonimi, had they been the ones to find her. And she'd been right; they'd been looking. She remembered Nate telling her that for Slonimi, finding power was like following a song to its source. All of those watching multitudes she'd sensed in the purple—it hadn't been chance that she, Cleric, and Lukash happened upon Merrit in the desert. Merrit had been waiting for them. Waiting for her.

"Tell me what's going on," Lukash said. "Everything, this time. The whole truth."

Across the dark caravan, Cleric's eyes were fixed on her through his hanging hair, glittering with hatred and rage. Was the hatred and rage for her, or for something the woman Pavla had put in his mind? There was no way to know. "They sent—an agent, I guess you'd call him, to Highfall. He tricked me into thinking he was my friend. He said I was one of them, and they'd arranged it so I would grow up where I did. He called them the Slonimi. I didn't know that word Merrit used for them, or I never would have let us come here."

"Why did you care where you grew up?" Lukash said.

"So I could kill my foster brother." She raised her hands, and let them drop. "Don't ask why. I don't know. Nate—the agent—was pretty crazy by then. He wasn't making much sense. He called it the Unbinding, said it would bring the world back to life. I refused to do it. I still refuse to do it."

"How did you end up in the Ghostwood?"

This conversation felt like an interrogation. "I don't know," Judah said, wearily.

"Like you don't know how you're able to make the knives."

"Yes."

"Can you break these chains?"

She looked at the chains. Iron, heavy, old. "I don't think so."

"Try," Lukash said. It wasn't a threat, but it wasn't exactly *not* a threat.

Onya was watching, curious. Judah tried to ignore her. She put her hands around the chain that bound her to the wall. Closed her eyes, which felt right. The metal felt clammy and rough. The links of the chain were hand-forged, not machine-made. She focused on the white, and reached inside. Pulling metal out of soil or impurities out of water had felt—what had it felt like? Like gathering wildflowers, or herding chickens into a flock. The chain felt orderly, the substance of it lined up in stern, featureless rows. There was nothing to gather, nothing to collect. If the neatly regimented metal could have looked down its nose and scoffed at her, it would have.

She opened her eyes, shook her head. "No good. It's already what it is. I can't make it something else. I could try forcing it, but—"

"But what?"

"But I'm not strong enough. And I don't like forcing things," she snapped.

"It's metal. It doesn't feel," Lukash snapped back.

And that was wrong somehow. It shouldn't have been, but it was. She even thought he felt it: his words, lying in the middle of the dirty caravan floor like a sludgy puddle of wrong.

"Hey," the girl, Onya, said, and Judah turned to look at her. "You're the one they were all losing their heads about, aren't you?"

Probably. But Lukash said, "What do you mean?"

"When they first took us, seemed like there was always someone in here with me, talking at me, trying to tell me stories or get me to play cards or something. Trying to be my friend. Then all of a sudden—nothing. Like they'd forgotten about me entirely, except to throw a roll in once or twice a day. If not for Inek I probably would have starved. He said they were all excited and busy, because somebody special was coming." Onya looked at Judah. "I guess it was you."

"How long ago was this?" Lukash said.

Onya frowned. "Ten days, maybe? Hard to keep track, in here."

Ten days. Where had they been ten days ago? The wine-maker's?

Gavin, I brought food.

Judah despaired. It hadn't mattered whether she tried to contact Gavin or not. They had noticed her, the moment she'd made contact with him. They would have found her no matter what she did. Her hand strayed to her wrist then froze. The Slonimi had her, but they didn't have Gavin. As long as she didn't know where he was, they never would.

"You aren't one of them," Lukash said to Onya.

"Me?" The girl laughed. "No. They came through my village about a month ago. Traveling show, right? First night there, this boy offers to buy me a pie. I should have known, then. You never can trust the pretty ones."

"He kidnapped you?" Lukash said.

"He got me out walking on the moors with him, was what he did. Tried to dazzle my brain. And it almost worked. All, run away with me, my precious darling, and we'll have so many beautiful children. But I didn't want to run away. And children! There are ten in my family and my pa died last winter. If I wanted children I could stay at home. So I said no. Fine, he said. And off I go home to bed. But when I wake up, I'm here and my mouth tastes like flowers." In the darkness, her voice was sharp with anger. "Inek thinks he's on a fun little larkabout. They told him I'd been bad and that was how come I had to stay in here. Used to bring him to me every day, so he could tell me how he wished I'd be good so I could come play. And at first I said, sure, I'd love to play with you, Inek. I'll be good. Thinking I could wait and then grab him?" She leaned her head against the wall. The gesture was tired and hopeless and sad. "But they knew I was lying. The one with the tattooed face, the one who sold the pies at the market—she told me ever so kindly that it would need to be real, but not to worry, I'd get there." Then, bitterly, "Did she ever make it sound wonderful. But there's three boys for every girl in my village. I know plenty about people making things sound wonderful." She nodded at Cleric. "Whatever they did to your friend sure doesn't look so wonderful."

"It can be," Judah said, reluctant. "You see what people feel. You know what they know. But it's how you use it. Like anything, I guess."

"You can do what they do?" Lukash said, with disbelief. "See inside my mind if you cut my arm?"

"The cutting part might be superstitious bullshit," Judah said. "Otherwise, yes."

"But you say you aren't one of them."

"I'm not one of them. I'm not who they think I am."

"Who do they think you are?" Lukash said.

Judah leaned back, like Onya, against the caravan's dirty wall. "They think I'm a miracle," she said, disgusted.

"And who are you, really?"

That, she couldn't answer.

They sat in the caravan for hours, the passage of time marked only by subtle shifts in the color of the light, and its movement across the walls. The caravan didn't move—Onya said it hadn't, for at least a week—but they could hear the camp moving around them. They heard creaking wagons, snuffling horses, someone whistling as they passed. They smelled camp- fire smoke and, eventually, the charred rich smell of something roasting. For all Judah knew, the Slonimi were very quietly burning each other alive outside. That would be satisfying.

Cleric still hadn't spoken. She began to worry that whatever Pavla had done had broken something in him permanently, the way the poison Theron had been given had broken some- thing in him. Lukash didn't speak, either. He didn't ask her any more questions and she was glad, because the answers were all unpleasant and difficult. Onya disappeared into the silent place where she spent most of her time, head leaning against the wall, eyes unfocused and faraway. They actually were un- focused, Judah knew. She and the girl had spoken a bit, after Lukash had stopped interrogating Judah. Onya hadn't been joking about being blind as a new kitten. She could see their outlines, but would have to be in good light and very close to actually distinguish their features. From what she'd told Judah, she'd spent her short life taking care of nine children she could barely see. Judah wasn't surprised that a few weeks in a Slonimi caravan hadn't managed to break her.

This was not acceptable. None of this was acceptable.

Finally, when the light had faded almost entirely, the bolt on the door thunked open. Two huge Slonimi men entered. They unfastened Judah's shackle from its chain, taking care not to touch her. Cleric didn't even lift his head as the men pulled her to her feet. Lukash said, "Where are you taking her?" but not as if he were particularly invested in the answer.

The outside air was beautifully fresh and sweet smelling. There were easily twice as many wagons now as there had been when they'd arrived, and the people to go with them, all milling about a giant fire. The crowd was eerily quiet. Judah could hear the soft music of the breeze in the long grass, the crackling and popping of burning wood. A horse whuffed. The men pulled her toward the fire, where some sort of beast was roasting. Only one voice spoke.

It belonged to a woman with snow-white hair and dark skin. She was standing a bit forward from the crowd, her chin up and her stance angry and strident. "—was our best healer," she was saying. "We have her journals, but her knowledge is gone. My friend is gone." Tears glistened in her eyes. When she saw Judah, she stopped talking. The mix of raw emotions in her face was difficult to look at. Grief and awe and helplessness and—fear? Was that fear?

Daniel, who also stood forward, looked at Judah, too. For a moment, the clearing was silent except for the pop of flame and the hiss of fat dripping from the roast onto the fire. The two men holding Judah's arms let go; there was nowhere for her to run. The bonfire was surrounded by a circle of bodies many layers thick. Judah saw Merrit, and Pavla, and the man named Kendzi. Somewhere in the circle was Onya's brother, and somewhere else the pretty boy who'd bought the blind girl a pie.

The silence grew and swelled, and the fire crackled, and

finally Judah said, "Well? I'm here. Tell me what you want or let me go."

"Welcome, Daughter of Maia," Daniel said.

"Quit calling me that. My name is Judah."

A murmur went through the crowd. "The judah vine is an ignoble plant," Pavla said. "Those who gave you that name did not love you."

"As opposed to you, who chained me and my friends in a wagon," Judah said, and the murmur doubled back again, colored now with surprise and dismay. The dark-skinned woman shook her head.

"This has all gone wrong, Daniel," she said, hopelessly. "All wrong, and we've lost so much. So many."

"It has not gone anywhere yet." Daniel turned to Judah. "This is Gerda. She leads one of our oldest caravans. Tell her, Gerda."

"The Clares traveled with us," Gerda said. "Caterina, our healer. And her son, Nathaniel."

Judah went tense and still. "You know Nathaniel," Daniel said, and Judah said, "I know he's insane, and a murderer."

"He was not always so," Gerda said, at the same time that Pavla said, "He made many sacrifices for the Unbinding."

Which might have been true. In Highfall, in another life, Nate's mother had shown her the Nate she'd raised, and the merry-looking young man she'd shown Judah had looked nothing like the wan, worried magus Judah knew.

Wait.

Caterina, our healer. My friend is gone.

"Did something happen to Nate's mother?" Judah said to Gerda.

Gerda's jaw grew stiff. "Yes. She is gone, Daughter of Maia."

The dismayed murmur was quickly becoming a rumble. Daniel held up a hand to still it. "Please," he said to Judah.

"Tell us what happened in Highfall, at the beginning of last winter." Judah said nothing, and he added, "If you don't remember, Pavla can help you. She's very skilled."

Judah glared at him. "I saw exactly how skilled she is. My friend still hasn't spoken."

"Pah. You keep bad company," Pavla said, dismissive.

"Perhaps keeping bad company kept her alive," Daniel said, and then turned back to Judah. "We sent Nathaniel and a few others to Highfall to find you, open your eyes to the Work, and undo the wrong that Elban's ancestor did. He succeeded in the first two tasks. He failed in the last."

"So what happened to his mother?" Judah said.

It was Gerda who answered, her grief rippling her words, tearing at them. "A great wave of power moved through all of us. When it was over, Caterina's body was empty. She is not where she should be. She is utterly gone."

Judah felt a pang. She'd only met Caterina in the Work, but she'd liked the woman a great deal. The healer's love for her son, and his for her, had been like a small, private sun that shone only for the two of them. Still, she said nothing.

"Pavla thinks you tried to destroy yourself," Daniel said. "Did you know the tower would save you? Did you know it would come at the cost of three other lives?" He shook his head. "No action is without consequence. To save you from death, the tower needed a great deal of strength. So it pulled that strength from all of them: Nate, his mother, and the two others we sent with him. Derie Kulash and Charles Whelan. We think Nate survived because his own power was drained, so the tower used him as a conduit. But now his connection to us is broken. The others are lost to us forever."

I will not feel guilty, Judah thought, hopelessly, remembering the wavering tip of the knife Nate held out to her. Gavin frozen on the floor, tears pooling in his eyes. She'd never heard of Derie Kulash, but the name Charles Whelan tugged at her memory—and then, suddenly, she remembered a handsome, ravaged face, sitting in a plain kitchen. Bleeding to death, tidily, into a basin. Not her memory; Nate's. Nate had watched Charles die.

"Charles Whelan didn't die with the others," she said. "He killed himself. I saw it, in Nate's memory. Something was wrong with him. Nate just watched."

The murmur died out entirely. The clearing was so quiet, then, that Judah could hear the wind in the grasses again.

Somebody in the crowd made a noise. It sounded like a sob.

"Poor Charles," Gerda finally said, and shook her fine head.

A short, slender man, his dark hair shot through with gray, stepped forward. "I want to know, Daniel. What will happen after the Unbinding, to those of us who have lost branches of our bloodlines?"

"Nobody knows what the world will be like then, Jasper," Daniel said mildly.

"Power will still be power. And there she stands, blazing like a torch with it." He pointed to Judah. "My son is gone. My caravan deserves a child out of her bloodline for it."

Judah blinked. "My what?"

"Your son is still alive, Jasper Arasgain." Pavla sounded exasperated.

"But of no use to us," the man named Jasper said.

"Arguably, he was never of any use to us," Pavla said.

Gerda scowled and raised a finger to point at the tattooed woman. "Don't speak ill of Nathaniel, Pavla. I may be old, but I can still break your nose. That boy grew up in my caravan, not Jasper's. A good heart, he had, before Derie got hold of him. If anyone's to be compensated for his loss, it's us. And we lost Caterina, too. Haven't we earned a replacement?"

"Replacement?" Judah said.

But Daniel was nodding. "It's fair. The first to Gerda's caravan, because she lost the most. Jasper, your group can have the third. Let's agree to leave the second open, for now. Who knows what the world will be? Her line is valuable."

"We choose the fathers," Jasper said, and Daniel said, "Agreed."

A sick feeling welled up from the center of Judah. They couldn't actually be talking about what they seemed to be talking about, could they? The replacements, and the fathers—they had nothing to do with her.

"Twins run in Tobin's line, Daniel," Gerda said. "If she bears twins, they shouldn't be separated."

Daniel nodded. Judah looked from him, to Gerda, to the man named Jasper—who was apparently Nate's father, although Nate could at least pretend kindness, and this man seemed devoid of it—and said, "You're all monsters."

Daniel and Pavla exchanged a look. "You have been suffering, Daughter of Maia," Pavla said. "And you know why. It's Elban's boy."

Daughter of Maia. She had never *met* Maia. She had never had a mother, and she had no intention of ever being anybody's mother. "Elban's boy has a name, and so do I."

"From what Merrit says, it sounds as if he's being tortured," Daniel said.

"We can help him," Pavla said. "In the Work. You and I, together."

Judah looked from one to the other, all of those eyes staring at her around the campfire. "Last I heard, you wanted me to kill him. Now you're telling me you want to help him. Which is it?"

Daniel sighed. "You don't understand. How could you? You weren't raised with us. And Nate may have been a good man, but—" He looked at Pavla, who nodded, and pulled out her tiny silver knife.

"It would be easier to show you," she said. "If I may."

"So now politeness matters, does it?" Judah said.

"We're not your enemies," Daniel said.

"Every time somebody says that to me, they turn out to be lying," Judah said. But Pavla was right. There were things that were easier to see in the Work than they were to explain with words. Like intentions, for one, and she very much wanted to know these peoples' intentions. Nate had told her that she was an unusually strong Worker, that she had been bred to be. *Her line is valuable.* She shuddered. But she held out her arm to Pavla anyway—her arm that had been so perfect and unscarred in the Ghostwood, now marred by the thin line of the winemaker's cut. Soon there would be more. The world seemed determined to mark her.

"Go ahead," she said. Pavla did not need to be asked a second time. She cut Judah's arm, and drew their two sigils, and the world opened.

She was in a forest. Not a wintry forest like the Ghostwood, but a warm, sunny forest, with beams of light streaming through the leaves and setting the air aglitter with drifting motes. She stood with Pavla in a small clearing among lush green ferns that came almost to Judah's shoulder. Squirrels chattered overhead, and the air was thick with the scents of dampness and earth and growing. Judah could actually feel moss under her boots—the dead boy's boots—spongy and soft as a carpet. All five senses. Pavla was good.

See? Pavla said. *Nothing to fear here. Pretty, isn't it?*

Judah looked down at her own chest. Faintly, she could see the purple rope that bound her to Gavin, but it was faded and weak-looking, reaching barely an arm's length away from her body. She had complicated feelings about the rope (something else the Slonimi had done to her, like the evil stitching she'd ripped out of her body in the tower) but the sight of it petering away into nothing still made her sad. She steeled herself and turned back to Pavla. *You said you'd help Gavin*, she said.

I will. But first I want to show you something.

What?

Pavla gestured around them. *This. The world as it should be. Alive and lush. Look by your feet, Daughter of Maia.*

Judah looked. A tiny cluster of brown mushrooms sprouted between her feet.

Do you know about mushrooms? Pavla said, and then they were both crouched down over the tiny brown globes, without Judah even being aware of movement. Oh, yes. Pavla was very good, indeed.

I know they're tasty with butter.

Pavla smiled. *This,* she said, one bony finger touching the largest globe, *what we see, or eat with butter, is such a small thing. Pluck it, and it comes away easily.* She did so. The mushroom pulled away from the dirt as if it had been waiting for her. *But the organism itself lives deep underground. It reaches for miles. This thing I hold in my hand is like an apple plucked from a tree.*

Judah stood up. *Make your point.*

And Pavla, too, was standing. *My point is that human beings are like this mushroom. All connected, down deep where it can't be seen. Or we were, before that which connects us was bound by evil men in Highfall.* She shook her head. *They are always men, aren't they? Some of us have found our roots again, despite their best efforts. Some of us grow anew.*

Nate told me all of this.

If he had told you well, we wouldn't be here. As Pavla spoke, the world withered around them. The ferns shriveled, browned, and collapsed. The squirrels went silent. Even the sunbeams vanished. Now they stood in a thicket of death, white sky visible through leafless trees. The mushroom Pavla had plucked crumbled to dust in her fingers. *This is the world without the power. This is the world now. We can survive here, but can we thrive? Would you not bring it back to life, if you could?*

Unmoved—any skilled Worker could make anything appear in the Work—Judah said, *Not by killing Gavin. And speaking of surviving, what did you do to Cleric?*

Pavla's lip curled. *That is not his name. His name is Abominator.*

You people really *aren't great with names, are you?*

Pavla closed her eyes briefly, as if exasperated, and then opened them. *Daughter of Maia,* she said. Softly, and gently. *Beloved of all the Slonimi. You have been through the hardest of hard. You have gone into death and come back, and now you have found us here, and I know it was with the help of those two men with you. The Work brought them to find you so that you would stay alive long enough to find us. Brutal men were needed for that. Corrupt men, to help you navigate a corrupt world.*

Judah laughed. *If you think the world on this side of the Barriers is corrupt, you ought to meet one of Elban's courtiers.*

You do not need those men anymore, Pavla insisted. *You have us, now. We will protect you. We would walk through fire for you, to help you fulfill your purpose.* Judah felt a touch on her arm and looked down. The dead boy's coat was gone, the sleeve beneath it pushed up. Pavla's hand rested on her bare skin. *You are everything to us. You are our sun, our moon. You are the life that flows through us.* And slowly, from beneath Judah's feet, as if she really were the center of the world, color began to swirl into the clearing. Rich browns. Vibrant greens. The ferns grew, uncurled, reached. Warm light spread through her, around her. With the warmth came quiet, and with the quiet came the realization that she knew exactly what Pavla was doing, because it had been done to her before. Judah could feel the woman's fingers rummaging in her mind. Trying to smooth out the rough places, to make her easier, more docile. More amenable to this *you will be our everything* nonsense.

Anger swelled in her, for herself and for Cleric and even for Nate, who had driven himself mad trying to fulfill the expectations of these people and earned nothing but their contempt. In Highfall, she had learned to open her eyes and then open them again, to see the Work behind what Nate showed her; now she did it again and suddenly they were in the tower. Judah could see the bitten-away place where she'd jumped, yawning and open, the edges neatly sheared off. This was Judah's Work, nested inside Pavla's like two bowls stacked on top of each other. The purple rope extending from her chest looked slightly firmer here, but it still trailed away to nothing. No sign remained of her life here: no musty blanket, no bag of food. No Nathaniel Magus, weeping and shaking and begging her to kill Gavin. No Gavin himself, kneeling and paralyzed and despairing, waiting to die. There was only Pavla, eyes closed and fists clenched, beads of sweat standing out on her forehead. Her effort showed, here.

And still the fingers muddled, and probed. *Stop that,* Judah said.

Shhh, Daughter of Maia. Pavla was too immersed in her own Work to hear the warning in Judah's.

Well, Judah said, *I did ask nicely.*

She grabbed hold of Pavla with her own mind and pulled her. Forward? Up? It didn't matter. When Pavla saw the tower around her—the litter of leaves, the bitten-away absence, the gray Highfall sky outside—her eyes grew wide. *Oh, blessed power. Oh, Daughter of Maia.*

My name is Judah. Two syllables. It's not hard. She reached into Pavla's mind, which felt tangled, multiplicitous, like finding oneself in a flock of sparrows or starlings. Some mass of darting little things that flew as one. Judah didn't care. What Pavla had strained to do was easy for her. All she had to do was push.

She pushed. Pavla shrieked.

Then a dizzying, whirling drop, and Judah was back by the bonfire, out of the Work entirely. Pavla was lying curled on her side, body twitching, a weak moan drifting out of her mouth. The man they'd called Kendzi was crouched at her side with Gerda and Daniel. The rest of the Slonimi were motionless, as if unsure what to do. Daniel leaned over Pavla's crumpled body as her moans dwindled to whimpers. Only when she was lifted and carried away—eyes sightless, jaw slack—did he stand, and stare, bewildered, at Judah, whose initial burst of savage satisfaction at seeing Pavla on the ground had quickly faded to dismay.

"What did you do?" he said, querulous with horror, and in truth, Judah was horrified herself. She hadn't meant to hurt Pavla. She'd only wanted to stop her, to get those fingers out of her head. Everyone was staring, either at Judah or after the poor woman being carried away. Nobody spoke.

"Take her back," Daniel said, finally, choked and hoarse, and when Kendzi took Judah's arm again, she didn't fight.

Back in the wagon, somebody had brought a tray of soft pillowy bread and crumbly white cheese. Onya was eating. Cleric was still huddled against the wall. Lukash said, "What happened?" but did not press Judah when she silently took off her boots instead of answering. She didn't want to talk. What Pavla had done to Cleric was wrong. Judah had done the same thing to her. Arguably, the Slonimi woman had deserved it, but Judah still felt uneasy. Her arms hurt. Her head hurt. There was a very specific pain in her lower jaw; Gavin's pain, not hers. Someone had knocked one of his teeth loose.

He was suffering, and the Slonimi had never wanted to help him. They'd only wanted to get inside her head.

Because she could do nothing else, she wrapped herself in one of the thin blankets that had appeared with the food, turned her back on the others, and went to sleep—or at least to an anxious, sleeplike daze. She had uncomfortable dreams about the white, about trying to make Gavin and Elly and Theron from it the way she'd made her dress. Almost succeeding, over and over again, only to have them drift away in wisps between her fingers.

When she was awakened by the sound of the lock, she had no sense of having rested at all, but the camp was quiet. The door opened a tiny bit, and a dark shape slipped in before the bolt clanked shut. Then there was a flare of light. Judah watched as Merrit lit a lantern with the match she'd just struck. Heavy circles shadowed Merrit's eyes.

She looked at Onya. "Your brother is the boy named Inek?"

"Yes." Onya sounded grudging, unfriendly.

"He's well. They're taking good care of him."

"What's it to you?" And if Onya had sounded unfriendly before, now she sounded outright hostile.

"I thought you'd want to know." Merrit looked at Judah. "You've surprised me, Daughter of Maia."

"You surprised me, traitor," Judah said. "You knew who I was the whole time."

Merrit smiled. It was a sad smile. "In the same way I know what the moon is, yes. We had scouts looking for you all over the west. And all over the east, for that matter. Ever since the day we woke up knowing you were back in the world. You shine like a second sun." Her smile, faint as it was, faded. "I wish I could explain everything to you."

"Yes, if only we all understood each other," Judah said. "We wouldn't even need to put each other in chains, then."

Onya snorted, amused. Merrit didn't. "This has always been my least favorite part. This is one of the reasons I don't stay with the caravans."

"I don't think you get to be sad about things you made happen," Judah said.

Unexpectedly, Lukash said, "You do, but it does no good. Particularly not if you keep doing the same things over and over."

Merrit didn't answer. Instead she looked at Cleric, who was watching her. "The Elenesians control the southernmost pass through the Barriers. Daniel is going to trade you for passage through it."

Cleric didn't respond. Lukash said, "The Elenesians want him so badly?"

"I got away." These were the first words Cleric had spoken since Pavla had cut him. They sounded surprisingly normal. "Nobody is allowed to get away."

"What will they do with you?" Judah said.

"Kill me," Cleric said, flatly. "Slowly. Horribly. Pain purifies and is instructive for the clerisy."

"I don't see why you use the name *Cleric* when those who gave it to you would kill you for existing," Merrit said, and Cleric said, "No. I don't guess you would."

Merrit shook her head and took something out of her pocket. It was a soft leather pouch, the same kind Nate had carried. She looked at Judah. "I thought you would be happy to be found. Glad to be home."

"This isn't my home," Judah said.

"I am going to volunteer for the party going south, to the Elenesian stronghold. Kendzi trusts me. And he knows I don't like to stay in camp very long. I will try to help Cleric. It's the best I can do."

"It's a trick," Onya said. "They all lie, these witches."

"They do, indeed," Judah said.

Merrit removed a small knife from the pouch. She made a small cut in the heel of her hand and then extended both knife and hand to Judah. She wore a switchknife now, Judah saw. "Test me in the Work. I'm not much of a Worker—we scouts mostly use it for sending simple messages—but you'll be able to tell if I'm lying. You have nothing to fear from me. I can do nothing to you there, but you can destroy me."

The light from Merrit's lantern wasn't dim enough to hide the looks the others were giving Judah. Trying to ignore them, she said, "Fine," and took the knife.

Her hand was steady as she reopened the cut on her arm. Then she closed her eyes. Merrit's blood was warm and sticky and the other woman's sigil glowed purple on the inside of her eyelids. It was easier than Judah expected to draw their two sigils, one over the other.

In Nate's memory, Caterina had told her that there was a moment in everyone's life that fixed itself, a moment when a person felt the most themselves. This was the place she found in Merrit's mind. They were standing on top of a soft, rolling hill, golden grasses heavy with seed rippling around their knees. There was that same sense of multitude, of a great web of observers, but here it felt natural, nonthreatening. Like being anonymous in a crowd. Nobody was paying attention, now. Merrit herself was dressed as Judah had known her, in sturdy trousers and a wide-brimmed hat. Her hair was long and dark. The same wind that rippled through the grasses played in her hair. Something was caught there; a seed head, perhaps. Judah reached out. Touched it. The wind took it, and her with it, and

the girl Merrit, one of many girls, sat cross-legged on the dirt and listened as an old woman, face obscured by time, said,

When you are mothers, you will need to teach your own daughters about this, so listen carefully, and also

she ate sweet dough greedily by a fire with sugar-crusted fingers, and a boy with curly hair said to her, *Ma said you and me are for sure going to be matched, Merry,* but something about those words was the wrong size, something did not fit, and

the scout Merrit, one of many scouts but the only one here and now, crept through a desert toward a clearing where two men and a red-haired woman slept by a small, surly fire. Their swamp-sodden clothes hung from creosote and sagebrush and from the woman a great light shone and

the young woman Merrit, one of many young women and men, danced on a beach to lively music played on mandolin and ocarina, and the woman who played the ocarina had sparkling green eyes that watched Merrit as she spun, and later they found each other by a dune and the ocarina player ran fingers through the long silky black strands of hair and

the scout Merrit, younger now, stood with the man Kendzi, who strapped a springknife around her wrist and said, *The first thing is, does the person need to be killed, or do they only need to be stopped? Your primary focus should be surviving to send your message* and

the young woman Merrit was kissed by the ocarina player and

the scout Merrit, stonier now, crop-haired, stared through a spyglass at the two men and the woman again. The woman had short blood-red hair and as Merrit watched she and the men laughed together and Merrit's heart leapt and

the teacher told the girl Merrit and all the other girls, *Your responsibilities are to your line and your caravan and the Unbinding and that's all that matters,* and Kendzi told the scout Merrit, *The big vein is here and if you can't reach that, the liver is here* and

the curly-haired boy, now a young man, danced with the

young woman Merrit in a cheerful campsite, colorful banners all around, and he pulled her close and whispered, *Matching's in a month, Merry*, and she pressed against him as she pressed against the ocarina player as she pressed against a different boy with long golden hair and a different woman and the faces flashed and Merrit pressed them all, kissed them all, there seemed no difference and also

she said to a weeping woman, who shared her hair and chin and was clearly her mother, *I don't want to be matched, I don't want to be bred, I want to be a scout and Kendzi says I'll be good* and her weeping mother said, *It's only three times, Merry, that's all, if you don't they will expel you, they will strip your power away* and

the new scout Merrit slid a window open and slid her through it and picked a lock and filled her pockets with gold and

the not-so-new scout Merrit watched as the blood-haired woman put her hands in a pool of poison water in the desert and power blazed, power stung, power hurt and also

angrily, to Kendzi, she said, *The Elenesians will kill him, they will kill him brutally*, and Kendzi clenched his teeth and said, *There's no other way* and

the young woman Merrit who was also the new scout Merrit stood in a wagon that smelled like herbs, piling gold pieces, one atop another, in front of a woman with pitiless eyes. *You'll tell them I'm barren*, Merrit said, her eyes equally pitiless, *and you won't speak of this to anyone or I'll kill you*, and the woman nodded and swept the gold coins into a box and

the serious man Kendzi shook his head and said, *It's a shame, Mer, your blood is strong, but I'm not sorry to have you scouting for me* and

the woman who shared Merrit's eyes and chin wept and Merrit wept and the older woman said *It is unfair* and Merrit said *It is unfair* and they meant different things, they meant completely different things and

the blood-haired girl screamed, *No! No! No!* and she did not run to the circled wagons, she didn't even walk, she had to be dragged and it hurt Merrit to see, it was horrible, it was wrong and

the ocarina player slipped into the darkness and

and

and

Judah pulled back. Her hands were shaking, her breath quick.

In front of her, Merrit rocked back and forth, knees curled against her chest. She was laughing and crying and her wrist was shoved into her mouth to muffle the high, panicked sound. "Bucket," Judah said, and Onya kicked the bucket they used to relieve themselves toward her. Judah held it as Merrit lunged for it and vomited.

"What did you do to her?" Lukash said.

"She'll be okay." Judah couldn't keep her voice from shaking slightly.

"What did she do to me?" This was Merrit, still laughing, still weeping. She wiped her mouth on her sleeve and pulled herself up to sitting. "They're bringing in a Worker from another caravan, you know. The best we have, Daniel says. He thinks she'll be able to tame you." Tears still streamed down her face. "Tame the sun first. Tame the power-damned sun. Oh. Oh, what did she do."

She grabbed the lantern, lurched to the door, and rapped three times on it. The door opened and she fell through it. They heard the bolt slide home behind her.

Judah looked at Cleric, then at Lukash.

"We have to get out of here," she said.

SIXTEEN

THE SENESCHAL HADN'T CANCELED THE FEAST days. Old Highfall had celebrated one feast day a month, and New Highfall did, too. The feast days had names—Opatus, Bearsday, Marronmas—but nobody cared about what the holidays signified, any more than they cared about the gods whose shrines still sat outside every city gate. All that mattered were the festivities. Highfallers ate caramel apples on Opatus, decorated hats for Bearsday, burned paper packets of chemicals to make colored flames for Marronmas. And, always, they got drunk. Sugar might have been a trick to get since the coup, but alcohol was always plentiful.

Bindy loved the city on feast days. The factories never closed, so every feast day started a few days early and didn't end until everyone had a chance to wake up with a headache. For nearly a week, the streets were filled with music and streamers and the occasional spontaneous parade. The city was so gray and grimy, the other three weeks of the month, that nearly every celebration centered around color. Enterprising citizens, young and old, made and sold confetti out of whatever bright things they could get their hands on. Candles in colored glass jars burned in every window, where passersby could see them, and anyone who had any kind of a skill—playing a musical instrument, or dancing with bells, or puppeteering—set up on the street, license or no. On festival days, as long as you showed up for your shift, the factory guards wouldn't bother you.

As she made her way through Marketside on the Day of Ferina, surrounded by noise and fun and the smell of roasting honey nuts, Bindy almost managed to feel—not happy, exactly, but a faint glimmer of something. Happiness's morbid, depressed cousin, maybe. She didn't like to feel that way. It wasn't how she was built. Rina was the one who'd always been able to find the bleakness in any situation. Bindy was a laugher, a giggler, a jump-over-the-blood-to-the-candy-stall kind of girl. And she would be again, she told herself. This was not forever.

But right now, she felt like an unlit stove. She had walked to the Seneschal's office to drop off the latest shipment of vials, which was unpleasant enough, but when she'd met Nate to give him his share of the scrip, he wouldn't come to dinner at Ma's. He had to take the scrip to Saba, he said. He had to take it immediately. "Oh, hang Saba," she'd said, frustrated. "Why don't you stay away from him?"

He'd given her the weak smile that seemed to be the best he could do, these days, and said, "Why don't you stay away from me, Bindy?"

"Because I'm your friend. But Saba isn't, no matter what he told me and Darid that day in Alva's. He's a liar and I don't like him."

"He didn't lie about being from the same place I'm from,"

the magus said. "That's true. He has reasons for being here, and reasons for the things he does."

"I know, I know. Looking for the Foundling," Bindy said, and then, in response to his startlement, "Don't look so shocked. I'm not stupid. I've overheard things. But he doesn't have to be *evil* about it." Evil was a big word, a nasty word. A ridiculous word, when it came right down to it, made for puppet shows and ghost stories. But it was the word for Saba, right enough. And the magus had nothing to say about that, because even a baby Canty's age knew she was right.

He'd gone off to Saba's room in Fountain Hill and, angry, she'd let him. Now she was making her way through Brakeside, her feet crunching on oyster shells, and even when a bunch of girls off duty from the fuller's, traveling in a thick fug of cider-smell, whooped and showered her in confetti, she still couldn't manage more than a perfunctory grin. When Bindy didn't cheer and hurl confetti back at them they laughed and moved on. She didn't mind the laughter. It was friendly. She was glad somebody was enjoying life.

Snap out of it, Belinda, she scolded herself. Buy some honey nuts from that stall up there. You've got scrip in your pocket. So she did, but the nuts didn't make her feel any better. "Joy of Ferina to you," the seller said, and she said, "Joy of Ferina to you, too," but there was no joy in it. Not for her. Stupid Saba. Sometimes she thought it would have been better for Nate to die oblivious in prison than to be alert, and aware, and suffer from that evil man's foot on his neck.

The closer she came to the Brake, the quieter the streets became, and she was glad of it. There were a few children who lived in the warehouse warren, scrawny fearful-eyed things, but they knew her, and cried out *Joy of Ferina* to her when she entered. Down the dark hall from Darid lived a woman with two babies who'd been kicked out of her house when her husband had died in a foundry accident. She was sitting in her doorway, watching the children draw pictures in the dust on the floor. "Joy of Ferina," Bindy said to her, and offered her the nuts. She took them. There was plenty of pride in the warehouse warren, but it was a practical sort of pride. Particularly on a feast day, the woman—who wasn't that much older than Bindy, when it came right down to it—wouldn't turn down food.

Bindy made her way down the corridor, up a ladder, across a rope bridge to a set of spiral steps. The warehouse residents built networks of layers and scaffolding to make the most of their cavernous spaces. Sometimes the scaffoldings collapsed, and people died. But this one had a number of woodworkers and blacksmiths in it who had been independent before the coup, and unable to afford licenses afterward. They were angry about the turn their lives had taken, and eager to do something—anything—with their newly idle time. The craftsmen knew how to build things and they knew how to break them. They knew how to sink a barge, how to weaken a cart axle so it would break, where to set a fire so it would smolder quietly until the damage was done. The rope bridge Bindy crossed was strong and secure and barely swayed at all. The spiral staircase was built from unmatching bits of scrap wood, but it looked a lot more rickety than it was.

At the top of the building, under the rafters, where no factory or city guard would dare go, was a wide-open space. The warehouse residents called this space the roof, even though a person standing there could look up at the underside of the actual roof, to see the decades-old spiderwebs and swallows' nests. Tacked down in the middle of this space, where it could be rolled up and hidden if necessary, was a purloined piece of ship's sail, and painted on the canvas, in excruciating detail, was a map of the city big enough that Bindy could heel-toe down the larger streets without breaching the lines. The map was a composite of all of the Warehousers' knowledge of the places they'd worked and lived, with less familiar bits of the city filled in by scouting expeditions and conversations with other residents. Some of the details were crudely drawn, some beautiful, but they were all extremely specific. It would never be finished because the city lived and changed and evolved. Bindy loved the map. She loved to wander its lines when the roof was empty, to look at all the places she'd never been in the city she'd lived in her entire life. It made Highfall seem both large and small at the same time, and gave her a delicious feeling of possibility. She had never gone to the Steel District or Fountain Hill, but she could. Anytime, she could.

The roof wasn't empty now. She'd known it wouldn't be. She'd been looking for Darid and this was where he was, with the rest of the Warehousers, all circled around the map of the city. Lanterns were set up on the floor, with bricks piled around them to prevent some errant foot from kicking them over. A sturdy warren burned just as fast as a rickety one. The Warehousers were young and old, male and female. Some held long sticks to point with. Nobody had paper or pencil. Written records were too risky. As she pushed open the hatch, she could tell that the mood on the roof was dark. Tonight's discussion had become an argument.

"—give the workers notice that we're going to burn it down," somebody was saying. Not somebody she knew. She was careful not to look too closely at any of the Warehousers, when she was around them. Those who came in from other warehouse warrens often wore scarves over the lower halves of their faces at meetings, to hide their identities.

Somebody else said, "A fire here, in the northwest corner, will take out the machine floor."

"Tricky to get to that corner. Trickier still not to burn down the bakery next door. People need that bakery."

"But if we start the fire in the other corner, we'll just burn the stock, and the managers will force overtime to replace it. That won't help anyone."

"None of this helps anyone!" That was Darid. Bindy moved a little closer so she could see him. He stood with three others in the middle of the map, his arms crossed over his chest and his jaw tense. "This corner, that corner—does it really matter? This one shop is one of hundreds. Yeah, the owner's a craven ratbag. So are hundreds of others." Darid's voice was rising in volume. "We've done enough factories and shops and ship-sinking. It's time to hit them where they'll feel it. Where are Highfallers being kept as slaves? The House. Where have they always been kept as slaves? The House. Where are our people, the ones that vanished off the streets? The House, I'll bet you anything." He stepped back, and pointed at the thinly sketched space behind the Wall. "So let's take the gods-damned House."

There was a murmur. Bindy couldn't tell if it was approval, disagreement or plain surprise. "We can't get through that bloody Wall, and you know it, Darid," said the man who'd talked about burning the stock.

Darid threw up his hands. "So we keep sinking barges and fouling machinery and burning weaver's shops, while our own people are being worked to death inside? Marsh and Barney and Frank and Oswyn—Cecily and Susanna, for gods' sake. Have you considered what's happening to Cecily and Susanna?"

Now there was nothing but uncomfortable silence. Finally, the woman who'd said that people needed the bakery stepped forward, and put a hand on Darid's shoulder. "We'll get them back, Darid. You know we will. But we need—"

Just then, one of the people Bindy did know—a leather worker named Griff—spotted her across the room, and said, pointedly, "Hello, Bindy Dovetail."

Quickly, she stepped forward. "Not trying to listen in. I was wondering if Darid was done."

"I'm done, all right," Darid said. "Let me know when you lot feel like doing something that will make a bloody difference." He crossed over to the ladder, his scowl heavy enough to shake the scaffold. "Come on, Bin."

They descended the warren in silence. By the time they'd reached his tiny room at the bottom of the warren, Darid had found some of his natural even temper again. As he sparked up his little stove, he said, "Well, then, how's my smartest sister?" and even managed a smile.

"Surly," she said, sitting on his bed. "Just like you."

"I'm all right," he said. "Nate get the vials delivered?"

"Yes. Well, I did. To the Seneschal's office, isn't that odd? But that's where Firo said Vertus wanted them sent." Then Bindy burst out, "Darid, what am I going to do about Saba? He's got the magus doing some crazy project and I swear, he's worse off now than he was in prison."

"What crazy project?"

"Trying to find the Foundling," she said, and Darid—rooting in his little cupboard for something to eat—got the same strange look on his face he always did when somebody mentioned the Foundling around him: blank and focused at the same time, and with an unnerving intensity. "Sorry. I know you were her friend. But that's what they're doing, Darid, and it's making the magus miserable."

"Saba is making Nate miserable," Darid said, setting out a small pot of Ma's vinegar peas, another of soft cheese, and some flatbread. "Looking for Judah can't do any harm. She's not in Highfall anymore, anyway."

Bindy wasn't hungry, but she was unhappy, and she'd immediately picked up a flatbread and smeared it with the soft, creamy peas. Now she stopped, bread halfway to her mouth. "What do you mean?"

"The Seneschal sent her and the others out in the dark of night months ago, not long after your magus went to prison." He was making himself a flatbread, too. "At least that's the rumor. You know how it is. Somebody knows somebody who helped hitch the horses, or one of the guards got drunk and talked too much. What I don't know, is where they went. But I'm glad she's out from behind that Wall. Anyway, don't worry. Saba's project can't do any harm."

It was doing harm to the magus. Bindy didn't know how, but it was. She wasn't hungry at all anymore but took a bite of the flatbread, because she'd already made it. Her mother made excellent vinegar peas but she still wasn't hungry.

Darid asked how Mairead was doing lamping, and they talked about the littles for a bit. They didn't mention the Foundling again, or Saba, or the magus. But Bindy's brain kept chewing on the topic even as her teeth chewed the flatbread. After a while, she said goodbye and made her way back up into the street. The confetti-bearing children had mostly been called in for dinner, but the third-shift bells had rung so the second-shift workers were out celebrating now. Every feast day came with a moment where things sort of—tipped over, from fun and frolic to something darker. That moment hadn't come yet, but Bindy could feel it coming. The people crowding the streets now were older. There were fewer colors, more musicians, more dancing. More bottles of ale and wineskins. She didn't feel any of the Joy of Ferina around her, and apparently everyone else in Marketside did. It was a lonely feeling.

Back at Winder's Alley, she was glad she'd eaten at Darid's.

Ma's scrip would come a day late because of the holiday—funny that the paper factory floor didn't stop for Ferina, but the scrip office did—and the table held nothing but plain oatmeal and boiled mallow. There wouldn't have been enough for Ma if Bindy hadn't eaten at Darid's. Bindy helped make sure the littles were all fed, and that Mairead didn't take more than her share. As she helped Ma clean the dishes, Bindy said, "What's the point of having a sister high up in the Paper Committee if we're still licking the bottom of the porridge pot?"

"Hush it," Ma said, with unexpected savagery. "We're doing fine. Everyone on my floor is in the same spot, aren't they? How fair is it for me to take more than my share, just because Rina can give it to us?"

"Rina has it to spare," Bindy said, which was true. Since she'd gone to live at the factory dormitory, Rina's cheekbones had lost their prominence, and her coat didn't hang as limply. She, of all of them, was getting enough to eat.

"That's true, but Rina, much as I love her, is going to have trouble saying no to those who fill her belly." Ma turned and gave Bindy a fixed look. "There's a price for everything. I'd rather live on oatmeal scrapings and keep my conscience clean."

That burned, it did, since Bindy's pocket was still full of drop money from the Seneschal. Drying her hands, she said, "I'm off again. Got an errand for Will Ember."

"It's late," Ma said. "Be careful."

Most of the factory workers had gone home by now. The celebration was beginning to take on that dark, threatening edge. It felt like the kind of game Bindy remembered from her childhood, when the play got wilder and wilder until something—a word or a fist or a rock—landed wrong, and suddenly it was a fight, and afterward looking back it was obvious that the game had always been headed for a fight. Or maybe not always, but long enough that the toppling point was too far back to do anything about. The whole world felt that way. Things had gone bad, and the moment where it happened was so far back nobody remembered a time when it wasn't bad.

She really did have an errand—dropping off the ill-gotten money—but it was for Firo, not Will. Climbing the stairs at Vitriol Street, it occurred to her that the two men might be out celebrating Ferina. But on their landing, she smelled something spicy and lovely, and sure enough, when she knocked, Firo opened the door. His hair was tousled, he smelled strongly of beer, and he looked happy. "Belinda Dovetail!" He never called her Bindy, which he said was a name for a horse, not a girl. "Please do come in. William is making some recipe of his mother's called hotpot. I've never had it. It has rock pigeons in it, of all the disgusting things, but he swears it's delicious."

Bess Ember's hotpot was the envy of Marketside. The smell of it made her mouth water. Those pickled peas at Darid's had been too long ago. "I guess I'll have a tiny bit, if it's really okay," she said, trying to sound not particularly interested.

Will, standing over the stove with the titular hotpot bubbling in front of him, laughed. "Don't be silly, Dovetail. Grab a bowl and sit down. We're going to feed this ridiculous House fop some good solid Marketside grub." But Will's tone was fond and loving, and as he put two bowls down on the table—one in front of Firo and one in front of Bindy—he bumped against Firo's shoulder.

Bindy's loneliness and dissatisfaction tightened like a belt around her middle. "I can't eat your food," she said. Her mouth was watering.

"You can and you will, or I'll dump it over your head," Will said, sitting down with his own bowl. He gave her a puzzled look. "Why so dour, Bindy? It's Ferina. We've got sugar cakes for after."

And he sounded so kind and friendly that tears came to Bindy's eyes. She looked down to hide them, and since there was food in front of her she picked up a spoon and ate a bite. Rock pigeon or no, it was heavenly. "I only came to give you your share of the drops money, and to see if Nate was here," she said.

"He's off with Saba, doing whatever it is they do all night long," Will said.

"When you put it that way, you make it sound much more interesting than it probably is," Firo said. "Fun, even."

"Quiet, you," Will said.

Something was going on under the table, but Bindy didn't care. She scowled down at her hotpot, but kept eating, because it was good, and she was hungry. "They're not doing anything fun. They're looking for the Foundling. That's all. Nate's barely any better off than when we got him out of the prison, and for what? Why does it matter where the stupid Foundling is? It doesn't matter to me. Does it to you? Does it to anyone?"

Firo put a hand on Will's shoulder, and whatever nonsense had been happening under the table stopped. "Excellent question, Belinda. I'm curious, myself."

"You'd better stay here for the night, I think, Bin," Will said. "It's getting late and it's going to get a lot nastier out there before it gets safer."

With a start, Bindy realized that it had to be halfway to the fourth shift bell by now. "Oh! I have to go. My ma—"

Firo waved a hand. "Don't be ridiculous. You're not a child anymore, Belinda. You can't slip unnoticed through the shadows. And I'm not going to be responsible for what happens to you out there. You'll stay here. I'll go see your mother as soon as we're done eating. Nobody will bother me on the streets."

There was finality in his voice and a canny gleam in his

eye. Bindy found herself not quite brave enough to argue. She looked to Will for help, but he only shrugged. "He's right, Bin. Now, both of you need to tell me how good my hotpot is, or you'll make my mother cry."

"Your mother is too mean to cry," Firo said, and Will grinned and said, "You think she's bad, you should meet my grandmother."

Bindy knew Will's mother, and she wasn't mean at all, but her hotpot recipe was delicious. After the pot was empty, the table cleared, and the dishes washed, Firo said goodbye and went out, as promised, to see Bindy's mother. Will dragged a padded armchair out of their bedroom for Bindy to sleep on, and gave her a blanket.

But as she wrapped the blanket around herself, the sadness that had been dogging her all evening descended again. From the open window they could hear, faintly, the sounds of drunken singing. Vitriol Street was quiet, but the rest of Marketside still celebrated. She was in an unfamiliar place. Everything felt wrong.

"Bindy," Will said, and she looked up at him, standing over her. Very tall and broad, was Will Ember, but his face was soft and sympathetic. "You know Nate's a grown man. You're, what, thirteen? Whatever's going on with him and Saba, it's his doing and his choice. And it's not your responsibility."

She tried to smile. "I know that."

"Does he have some hold over you? Has he made you some—promise?"

Bindy blushed. It wasn't uncommon for girls her age to be promised to men Nate's age, or even married to them. That was what Will meant. "It's nothing like that. It's never been like that. He always did his best to look after me, that's all. From the moment I met him, when I was nothing to him but

327

a Marketside street rat with a sick brother. And he's all alone, Will. He's got nobody to look after him, does he?"

"No," Will said, gently, "but that doesn't mean you have to do it."

And Bindy said nothing to that, but pulled the blanket tighter around herself, and chewed her lip. Will waited a moment. When she still didn't speak, he turned, went into the bedroom, and left her alone.

Across the city in Fountain Hill—not too far from the fountain that gave the district its name—Nate Clare sat, exhausted, in a chair very like the one where Bindy slept in Marketside. Instead of a blanket, his hands gripped the carved arms of his chair, and instead of being full of Bess Ember's hotpot, his stomach was empty. Newly empty, as it happened. The room was nicer than Firo and William's room. The walls were covered in blue silk with a print of white forget-me-nots, and the glass in the windows was clear, flat, and hidden behind clean white curtains.

The curtains, alas, were the only part of the room still clean. Weeks of occupation by Saba Petrie had left a veil of filth over every available surface, empty liquor bottles and oily food wrappers and dishes full of tobacco ash. Nate could even see a few of his own drop vials in the layers, although he'd never seen Saba indulge. Just as he'd never seen Saba indulge in the women whose perfume he sometimes smelled in the air. Or maybe he was hallucinating that. Maybe his cracked brain was generating the sweet smells as one last favor, to counteract the nasty ones.

Right now, he was concentrating on breathing, no matter what the air smelled like. Long even breaths in. Long even breaths out. Saba, sitting in the room's other armchair, watched, stroking the rim of his wineglass with one finger.

Quiet, now, but Nate could still feel the barbed chain that ran from those dark reptilian eyes straight through the center of him. It was mercifully still for the moment.

Once, talking about compellers, his old teacher Derie had hoisted her cane in the air and said, *This kind of stick works well enough, most of the time. But some people have wills so strong they need to be beaten inside their heads.* Nate didn't think he possessed one of those wills. Any will he had at all was broken long ago, in no small part by Derie's cane. Something in him seemed to have been irreparably harmed by the surge of power that swept through him when Judah jumped. He could barely Work anymore—trying made him feel like a clockwork with a mistimed gear—and with every night he spent in the blue-walled room, it became more difficult. Still, every night, into the Work and his own fragmented, fragile memories Nate went, dragged by the chain Saba had through him. He heard Theron say, *No, I don't think it will hurt* before Nate drove his switchknife into his throat. He bent over Judah to stitch the purple thread of bound power through her, so she wouldn't die when they drained the blood from Elban's heir. He was beaten by Derie and saw John Slonim's apparition in the street and Charles died, endlessly.

Saba cared only about those last few moments in the tower. So it was those moments Nate had to relive, over and over again. Elban's heir kneeling on the floor, paralyzed by the Work Nate had done with his dead brother's blood. Judah leaning down to kiss him. Over and over, he watched her turn toward the yawning gap in the tower. Over and over, she stepped to the edge—one step, two—and Nate felt his hold over the heir break like a twig as he realized what she was going to do. Over and over, he panicked, as she stepped out into the open air—

And there Saba would take hold, Judah's second foot a bare

inch above the tower floor, the heir in an unsteady half-crouch with arms outstretched to grab her before she fell. And then the barbed chain in Nate's mind would begin to twist and buck and the pain would become agony, driving him deeper into the Work. Saba wanted him to go *into* Judah, to use her past to find her present. That would have been more than Nate could do at his best, but it was impossible now. So, over and over, with excruciating slowness, he jumped with her and fell and the weeds at the bottom of the light well beneath the tower zoomed closer and closer, spinning and twisting, Saba's mind spurring his like a cruel horseman. Over and over, he relived Judah's last moments, her last thoughts. There were two of them. The first, in words: *Oh, no.* The second, wordless: an overwhelming sense of relief.

And then the surge of power, blinding and tearing. There, in that horrible, interrupted moment, Saba would hold them again, and that wasn't even the worst part. The worst part was that in that moment, he could feel his mother. Her self coursing through him, as familiar as his own. And as Saba's chain twisted and pulled cruelly through his memory, Nate had to feel that precious self fracture, and dwindle, and vanish, and with it his connection to the rest of the Slonimi, and everything he'd known, and his entire world.

Over and over again.

"Well, then, Nathaniel," Saba said, in the blue room. "Shall we try again? Has your poor little head had enough rest?"

Never, Nate wanted to say. But he'd found it didn't do to say too much around Saba. Into the Work they went; into the tower; into Judah. She leans over. Kisses Elban's heir. *Tell Elly I'm sorry*, she says, and leaps, and midleap comes the nearly audible crack of Nate's control over the heir breaking, and then the fall and dizzying swirling weeds and Caterina and Derie, draining through him like water, taking Judah—where?

That was the question. That was the moment. That was where Saba held him. It was like having a limb pulled against the joint. Feeling things begin to tear, to give.

And what did all of this get him? Fragments. Wisps. A glimpse of firelight, some unintelligible words. Enough to know Judah was still alive, somewhere. Nothing that would tell them where she was. *Failure. Failure. Failure.* The word was a drumbeat inside him. Part of him desperately wanted to remedy that failure, to do what he'd trained all his life to do and complete the Unbinding. Part of him knew it didn't matter. The Slonimi would trample continents to find her. They would burn cities and tear down civilization. He was afraid for her and he was afraid for himself and still Saba pushed, and pushed, and pushed. The limb twisted farther and farther until something

snapped.

and Nate found himself lying on the floor of the blue-walled room, heaving and gasping for breath. Saba sat over him, glaring down in contempt. "You have to do better," the compeller said, and the barbed chain that ran through Nate flexed and shivered and *he* flexed and agony rippled through him, but he did not scream. Saba would not let him scream.

Somebody knocked. Saba frowned.

Nate lay where he was on the ground while Saba stood and crossed to the door, opening it wide enough so that he could see out but the person on the other side—probably the land-lady—couldn't see in. "Oh," Nate heard Saba say, surprise in his voice. "Come in."

And the someone who'd knocked came in, tall in a dark coat and a low brimmed hat. Nate's vision was still blurry. "Good gods, what's happened here?" the someone said, in a cool, cultured tone, and the voice belonged to Firo.

"I'm afraid the room is a bit of a mess," Saba said.

"The room is absolutely squalid," Firo said, "but I meant Nate." A firm hand gripped Nate, an arm slid under his shoulder, and he found himself lifted back into the armchair.

"He's drunk," Saba said. "He'll be fine when he sobers up."

"Drunk, eh?" Nate felt his bloody arm lifted, turned over, and placed back down again. The touch was gentle but Firo sounded faintly amused.

"Some men have trouble putting themselves back together again after prison. I'm afraid Nate is one of them." Nate could hear the shrug in Saba's voice.

"Poor fellow. Maybe he'd have an easier time if you quit making him look for the Foundling," Firo said.

Should not have said. Should not have known to say. Nate blinked his eyes to clear them, rubbed them with numb fingers. The only place to sit other than the two armchairs was the unmade, stale-smelling bed, and Firo had chosen to stand. The first time Nate had met him, he'd been dressed in his courtier's finest. Now he wore ordinary Marketside working clothes. The difference would have been stark, if not for the smug, slightly amused look on the courtier's face, which was exactly the same.

"What do you know about the Foundling?" Saba said.

"I know she seemed to live an unusually complicated life." Firo gave Saba a kind smile. A vicious smile. A *House* smile. "Why? What do you know about her?"

Snake on one side, spider on the other. Nate wondered who would win. When Saba spoke again, it was with the same casual interest that Firo used. "Only rumors. The usual stories. Who told you we were looking for her?"

It must have been Bindy. Nate still couldn't speak.

"You're not from the city, are you, Petrie?" Firo said. "Perhaps you don't know about courtiers. Courtiers are interested in money, and beautiful things, but most of all, they're interested in power. Some people who don't know any better think the power comes from the money, like the beautiful things, but those people are wrong. The power comes from information." Firo brushed something off his shoulder that looked for all the world like confetti. "The other interesting thing about being a courtier is that you keep being one, even when there's no court. It seems to leave a permanent mark on the way a person sees the world, whether they want it to or not." Firo's eyes drifted to Nate and over him, as if there was nothing there to catch his gaze. "Now, as for the Foundling—I knew the Foundling, back before the coup. You might even say we were something along the lines of friends, as far as either of us was dispositionally inclined toward that sort of thing. So when I hear that you're looking for her, naturally the courtier in me is intrigued. Tell me, are you investigating young Lord Gavin's whereabouts, as well? Because if Nate here is spending his night searching drop dens, that would explain why he always looks so ragged after he visits you."

The barbed chain twitched and thrummed with excitement, but Saba only said, as if he didn't particularly care, "Is that where Gavin is? Haven't heard that theory before. High-fall Prison, yes. Dead, sure. Drunkenly licking drops off some pretty girl's bosom? That's new."

Firo laughed. "I'm sure that's where he'd prefer to be." And then, as if unconcerned, "I did hear one rumor, which seemed to come from a credible source."

"What was the source?" Saba said. He, too, sounded unconcerned, but every muscle in his body was tense.

"Your patron and mine," Firo said. "Our good friend Vertus. I've never known him to be wrong yet."

"And what does Vertus think?"

Firo smiled. "And now we're back at the beginning of the conversation, where I explain that information is currency.

Perhaps in Old Highfall, I might be inclined to trade my information against a future favor. But the old world is dead, and I'm afraid I don't trust you."

Saba sighed, his impatience showing through. He was used, like all compellers, to being given what he wanted, instantly. Nate's spine rippled up and down with chills and the barbed chain thrummed. "Firo, what do you want?"

"A small country manor, with a manageably sized garden and a sunny room where my William can paint. A cook, perhaps a housemaid or two." Firo considered. "A dog. Yes, I'd rather like a dog."

"Nathaniel," Saba said. "Give Firo the scrip from your pocket."

With numb, fumbling fingers, Nate reached behind him to where his coat hung on the back of his chair. Looking for the purse Bindy had dropped off for him earlier that day, after she'd taken the vials to the Seneschal. But Firo was already waving a hand in denial.

"No, no. Not that scrip nonsense. I have all the scrip I need. And it's much less than I'd always assumed, isn't that interesting?"

"What, then?" Saba said, icily.

Firo lifted one eyebrow. "If you're looking for Judah, Gavin is as good a place to start as any, but if I'm going to give you the information I have about the one, I would very much like to know the source of your interest in the other."

"Perhaps the two have nothing to do with each other," Saba said.

"Impossible," Firo said. "Nobody's interested in Gavin for his own sake. Oh, in another fifteen or twenty years, he might turn into a worthwhile person. But right now he's—oh, like most boys his age. Bit callow, if you know what I mean. Frankly, Judah's the interesting one."

The barbed chain cracked like a whip. Nate wanted to scream but Saba still wouldn't let him. All that came out was a thin, broken moan. "This is a maddening way to communicate," Saba said, as if to himself. Then he said, "I represent interests outside Highfall."

Firo lifted an eyebrow. "Courtier interests? Because I wouldn't recommend trusting the former courtiers. They may claim to want Lord Gavin back in power, but what they really want is the power itself."

"I do not represent the courtiers," Saba said.

"Intriguing," Firo said. His eyes moved over Nate again. "I wasn't aware that there was a third player in this game. I'm glad to hear it. I don't particularly like the Seneschal, but neither am I interested in rejoining the courtiers' viper pit. I don't suppose you'll tell me any more about this third player?"

"It would mean nothing to you if I did," Saba said.

Firo's lips pursed. "Fair enough. Knowing there are additional interests is worth something, I suppose. According to Vertus, both Lord Gavin and Lady Eleanor are in Tiernan."

Saba, Nate saw, was barely breathing. "And the Foundling?"

"Reasonable to suggest she and the younger lord are there as well, isn't it?" Firo said, with a shrug. "They're not in the House, from everything I've heard."

"Tiernan." Saba's brow furrowed. The barbed chain trembled and Nate shuddered. Then, decisively, Saba stood up. "We'll leave in the morning. You, Nate—go back to Vitriol Street. We've promised Vertus another dozen vials and I don't think they're done yet, are they?" He turned to Firo and added, a bit grandly, "You and Vertus can have this batch for free. A going-away present, of sorts."

"Leave in the morning?" Nate said, befuddled.

"For Tiernan," Saba said, with little patience. "Now, come on, get up."

He ushered Nate and Firo downstairs and out. Nate's head was spinning, both with the movement and the prospect of leaving Highfall. How long had it been since he'd left Highfall? And Tiernan—he wasn't even sure he could find Tiernan on a map. Outside, the night air was clammy and smelled of the Brake and it reminded him of his first nights in Highfall, a year ago. In the distance he could hear crowd noises, singing and drums, but here in Fountain Hill the street was quiet. He turned to Firo. "Is it true? Is Judah in Tiernan?"

"I have no idea," Firo said. "But Gavin and Eleanor are. As is Lady Amie, apparently, which should make for interesting dinner party conversation." Firo was fussing with his coat, making sure it hung just so. The coat was plain Marketside broadcloth, but the man inside it was still a courtier. "You know, magus, if you don't want to go with Saba in the morning, you shouldn't."

"I have no choice. And I'm not a magus," Nate said.

Firo cocked his head and gave Nate a long, evaluating look. "What hold does he have over you? Do you owe him money? William and I thought it was sex, at first, but the closer he gets to you, the more nauseated you look. Do you love him?"

Even the idea of shaking Saba's hand made Nate feel ill, let alone embracing him. "No. Gods, no."

"I'm glad to hear it, because he treats you horribly. If you'd ever like to be rid of him, I'm sure William would be more than happy to pay him a friendly unfriendly visit. He doesn't care much for those who abuse their power over others." There was always music in Firo's voice when he discussed William. Now there was admiration, as well. Nate remembered the first time he'd met William, standing with Firo in the back garden of the old manor in Limley Square. He'd thought him a token, a big dull ox that Firo kept around for his amusement. Hearing them speak of each other, now, made him feel keenly lonely.

He also remembered, in the House, Firo saying, *Loving somebody who loves you back isn't such a terrible thing, magus.*

"You and William have been very kind to take me in," Nate said.

"We have, haven't we?" Firo said, pleasantly.

"I don't think I've ever thanked you."

"Ah, well," Firo said, "niceties," and they walked the rest of the way to Vitriol Street in silence.

Bindy woke to a sore neck, soft clinking noises, and the smell of fruit pastry. She opened her eyes. The small room was flooded with sun, but there was no sign of Will and Firo. The pastry she smelled waited on a plate next to her chair. In the corner, the magus stood at his small worktable with his back to her. He was doing something. She couldn't see what.

She sat up, rubbed her eyes, and picked up the pastry, which tasted as good as it smelled. As she chewed, she considered the magus's back, and the sunny room, and their knotted, difficult friendship. Except it wasn't that difficult, really, was it? She liked the magus. He was kind, and he had done good for the world. Maybe not with the drops, now, but back when he'd been the gate magus. He had helped the people of Marketside and Brakeside, had stitched their wounds and cured their fevers, when nobody else would. And he'd never asked for payment. Not once.

Help's not help if it comes with a price.

She was going to say good morning, but then he stepped away for a moment and she saw that he was wrapping all of his laboratory equipment in rags, and packing each piece into a wooden crate. The soft clinking she'd heard had been the sound of glass on glass. Packing?

Leaving.

He was leaving her.

A spear of rage stabbed through her, so forceful she shot to her feet. "What are you doing?"

He turned and started, guiltily. He looked tired, the fearful, querulous look still in his eyes. "Bindy. You're awake."

"You're packing your things." Prickly with anger, her fists went to her waist as if on their own accord. "You're leaving."

Nate looked at the crate as if he hadn't seen it before, and then looked back at her. "I don't—I—this is for storage."

"You're leaving," Bindy said, accusingly. "You're leaving and you weren't even going to wake me up to say goodbye."

"No." But he said the word too quickly. As soon as it was out of his mouth he blinked, and looked abashed. "It was just the timing."

"Timing, my backside. You knew I'd be mad. And you were right, I'm furious. Where are you going?" A faint hope bloomed in her. "Are you leaving Saba?"

Nate deflated. "He's leaving Highfall. I'm going with him. We're going to Tiernan. Lord Gavin is said to be there."

"Only you and Saba?"

Nate nodded.

The anger drained out of her. Leaving in its place—nothing. Nothing but flatness and blankness. Nothing but nothing. She looked down at her hands, no longer clenched but hanging as limp and lifeless as the rest of her felt. Her fingernails were dirty. "So that's it, then."

He was quiet for a moment. There was a stale, awkward feeling in the room that clogged things, took up too much of the air. She felt heavy and was half inclined to curl up again in the chair and go back to sleep. Wake up when things were—what? Better. Not so terrible. Different.

Nate cleared his throat. "I realized last night that I never thanked Firo," he said. "Did I ever thank you? For taking care of me in prison, and breaking me out, and—gods, everything."

"I'm not sure I did you any favors." She sounded as dull and heavy as she felt.

"The world is complicated."

"I know." And gods, she hated this hopeless, solid feeling. Like she was packed head to toe with mud. She looked up. A rim of tears trembled at the bottom of each of his eyes. "Don't go," she said. "Let Saba go to Tiernan alone, if he wants to."

Nate closed his eyes. When he opened them, the water was gone. "It's not that easy."

"The world is complicated," she said, bitterly.

He managed a sad smile, and for a moment she saw her old magus in him. "What are you going to do?"

"If I had half a brain, I'd go ask my sister to get me a factory job."

He cringed, visibly. "There must be some other work."

"Well," she said, and now her eyes were the ones that filled with tears, "I used to be apprentice to a magus. I liked that job a lot."

"Oh, Bin," the magus said, and his sadness was heartbreaking, and the tears spilled out of her. She pressed her hands to her face, smelling the dirt on them, smelling everything she'd touched for gods knew how long. When was the last time she'd washed them? All at once she couldn't stand herself. Her sore neck, her slept-in clothes. The thin slick of grease and misery and factory soot that coated every bit of her, that was all through her hair, all over her body. All of this. Everything that had happened since the coup. She wanted to wash it all off, to be the same person she'd been when she'd been happily running messages across Brakeside and it had all seemed normal, it had all seemed like life.

All right. She would take a bath later. Bindy dropped her hands and looked back up. "Tiernan, huh? How are you going to get there?"

He shook his head. "I don't know."

"Are you bringing any food?"

"I don't know," he said, again.

The anger surged back up in her. She said a very bad word, possibly the worst word she'd ever said. "Wait here," she said.

"Saba will be—"

"I said *wait*," she said, sternly. Like he was a child, like he was Canty.

When she was Mairead's age, she'd run races with the other Marketside children. The Brake to the city wall, Harteswell Gate to Beggar's Market. The farther, the more convoluted, the more people to dodge, the better. She hadn't raced anyone in years, since long before she'd gone to work for the magus, but now she ran as fast as she could. She dodged merchants with handcarts and pigmongers driving pigs and people. People, wandering through their lives. Her chest burned and the muscles in her thighs did, too. She scolded those muscles as she ran. *You can do this. Quit complaining.* And she scolded Saba. *Evil, evil, evil.* And Nate. *What is wrong with you? Why would you simply head into the wilderness with somebody you loathe and no preparation? You're going to die. After everything I've done for you. You.*

Are going to.

Die.

She reached the house on Winder's Alley. Nobody was there. Canty and Kate were at the factory crèche, Mairead was off with the other lampers, and Ma was at work. Quickly, she gathered up some things Nate might need in the wilderness, like a belt knife and an extra pair of her socks. They'd stretch to fit him. She took food from Ma's larder, although she hated to do it, wrapping up the less-fresh loaf of bread and some cheese so dry it would have to be warmed before it could be eaten. The prison had paid her in city scrip, good at any factory store, and she still had some left over; it wouldn't help when Ma came home to find the larder half-empty, but at least she'd be able to fill it again. Bindy left half of the money in an obvious place on the kitchen table and took the rest.

Then it was back out into the streets, running again. Back to Vitriol Street and the magus. First shift was about to ring. Nate would be meeting the loathsome Saba. They would be leaving. The closer she came, the more her chest pounded.

Evil. Evil. Evil.

You. Are going to. Die.

She was still a few blocks away when she heard the huge tuneless factory bell chiming first shift. Her stomach lurched. She'd been taking back alleys and side streets, so she could travel faster, but now she veered onto the main avenue. She could meet them, maybe. She could catch them on their way out of the city.

And she did, on the corner of Vitriol Street. The magus had a bag slung over one shoulder, a single rolled blanket hanging over the other by a strap. Saba, leading him through the crowd, carried a sturdy, comfortable-looking pack on his back, with a thick bedroll tied to the bottom of it. Naturally, *he* was prepared. "Wait!" she cried, and saw Nate's eyes find her. He stopped, looking confused. Saba glanced back at him, and the contempt in the foreigner's expression made the edges of her vision go red and her spine go prickly.

She planted herself in front of Saba. "Why?" she spat at him, through a clenched chest and clenched teeth. Not even thinking. "You don't even like him. Why don't you leave him here?"

"Go away," Saba said, coldly. "This is none of your business."

"I will *not* go away." Looked at the magus, standing with his mouth hanging open. Saw something in his eyes, some tiny little flicker of something. Life. Hope. It kindled something in her, too. Without giving herself time to think, without considering, she said, "I'm going with you."

"Bindy!" Nate said.

"You are not," Saba said.

She hated him so much. And that little flicker of something, life or hope or even surprise, drove her forward until she was toe to toe with the evil Saba, like they were two street rats about to come to blows over an apple or a loaf of bread or a picked pocket. She was shorter than he was, but she was shorter than a lot of people and she had never let it matter. She drew herself up. Didn't even flinch.

"Stop me," she said.

His jaw clenched. For a moment she thought they really were going to come to blows. Around them, a few people had stopped, curious to see what came of this odd pairing between the handsome man with the pack on his back, and the scrawny Marketside girl. But they were *her* people. They would take her side. He would probably kill her. She wouldn't make it easy.

Then Saba laughed. "Fine. Come along, then. If you die of starvation in the wilderness, it's not on me." Then he stepped around her, and walked away.

She turned to the magus. "Give me a piece of paper."

He reached into his pocket and tore a small sheet from the notebook he always carried. He gave her his pencil, too. "What are you doing?" he said.

"Sending a note to my mother," she said. Quickly, before she could lose her nerve, she scrawled a few lines, grabbed the first lamper she saw—they were everywhere, this time of day—and told her to take the note to Mairead Dovetail.

"Bindy," the magus said. The flicker of hope and life was gone, replaced by fear and sorrow. "Don't do this."

She was too used to seeing fear and sorrow there. The emotions didn't affect her the way they once would have. The near-fight still thrummed in her limbs, making her knees ache, her hands tremble.

"It's done," she said, and stormed after Saba.

SEVENTEEN

THE SLONIMI CAME FOR CLERIC AS THE FIRST GRAY
tendrils of light reached through the cracks in the wagon walls:
Daniel, Kendzi, and two others Judah didn't know. Merrit
trailed along behind. Judah had tried all night to break the
chains, begging and cajoling the iron to separate. Now she
was so exhausted she could barely stand, but the chains were
as sturdy as ever.

Cleric had hardly moved since they'd been imprisoned,
but the moment Daniel unlocked the cuff from his ankle he
launched himself toward the open door like water from a burst
dam. Kendzi and the two strangers were ready. They tackled
him and threw him against the wall. Kendzi locked his wrists
behind him with a new set of iron cuffs. "I hope they make
you watch me die," Cleric hissed at them, words muffled by
the pressure of his face on the wall. "I hope they make you
watch every bloody, screaming second."

None of the men said anything. As they dragged him out,

Lukash fixed his copper eyes on Merrit and growled, "His death is on your hands."

"I know," she said, and left.

The wagon seemed terribly empty without Cleric in it. Onya let her head fall to her knees. Lukash turned his back on the others. The expanse of his shoulders hurt Judah to see. She stared down at the chains—the damned, intractable chains—and said, "I tried."

"You did," Lukash said, but he didn't turn around.

The day passed in stiff, horrible silence. The tendrils of light turned to bright knives and moved across the floor until they were stabbing through the other side of the wagon. Then the door opened, and a small figure ran in with a basket. "Hi, Onya! I'm bringing the food today!" he cried.

"Inek!" the girl said, and the basket fell to the floor with a thump as she caught him up in a huge hug. It was difficult to see their pleasure at being together again, to hear their happy chatter once the boy was perched on his sister's lap. Onya grabbed for Inek's nose and he giggled and the sound was a spear through Judah's unhappy heart, so she did as Lukash had done and turned her back on them. Inek launched into what was apparently a minute-by-minute account of what he'd done since he'd last seen his sister, every bug he'd seen on the prairie and every game he'd played with the Slonimi children and every treat he'd eaten. Judah didn't know anything about children. She knew they were supposed to bring joy everywhere they went, and Onya certainly seemed delighted to see her brother again, but Cleric was somewhere out there in chains, being taken toward an extremely unpleasant future, and Judah hadn't helped him. Just like she hadn't helped Theron after Arkady poisoned him, when she'd held the antidote in her hand and had been too scared to give it to him. When she closed her eyes she saw Theron, bloody-nosed, writhing on the faded parlor carpet, so she kept her eyes open and stared at the boards that made up the wagon, at each knot and line of grain. At the motes of dust that drifted through the blades of light. At anything but Inek, or Theron.

Eventually the door opened again and a woman said, "Time to come out, Inek." Judah could not avoid watching as Inek threw his arms around Onya's neck and she wrapped hers around him.

"I love you, Onya," he said into his sister's chest.

Onya didn't answer, because she was crying. When he was gone, her sobs continued. Slowly they turned to snuffles, until finally she wiped her face on her dirty skirt and, surprisingly, held out a hand to Judah. "Here," she said. "Inek stuck this in my pocket, said to give it to you."

For a moment, Judah thought she'd gone mad. Because in Onya's hand was a small glass vial, exactly like the one that had held Theron's antidote. "What is it?"

Crossly, Onya said, "I don't know. Inek said the man-lady gave it to him."

Man-lady? Judah took the vial, which turned out to not be like the antidote vial at all. That had been brown glass; this was blue, with something dark and thick inside it. She opened and sniffed, cautiously. Salt, metal.

Lukash had turned around, and was watching. "Well?"

She capped the vial with one finger, tilted it over and righted it. The circle of liquid left on her finger was dark red, and thick, with a gelatinous blob in the middle. An uncomfortable mixture of hope, fear, and disgust sprouted within her. "Give me something sharp," she said, but even as she spoke she knew there was nothing sharp to be had, so she pulled up her shackled leg and raked the scabbed cut from her Work with Merrit over and over the rough edge of the iron cuff until the scab ripped and the cut began to ooze. In the tower she hadn't needed the blood but maybe here, chained to the wall in this wooden box—maybe she did. She touched the dark red liquid on her finger to the ooze on her arm. She remembered the sigil Pavla had drawn—the sturdy boundaries, the sweeping center—drew it as well as she could, and waited for the world to unfold.

It didn't. She held her breath, tried to will herself into the Work as fiercely as she'd tried to split the chains, the night before. Her effort hadn't made a difference then and for a long, bleak moment she was afraid it wouldn't make a difference now, either, and that would mean there truly was no hope.

Then—faintly, as if from a dream she'd mostly forgotten—she heard a faint crunching, like footfalls on gravel, and smelled something sweet and pungent and familiar. A smell so friendly and warm it made the hopelessness worse: horse. She had an impression of curtains of dark hair hanging down around her face. A stiffness on the back of her left hand. Despair, terrible purple despair.

When she opened her eyes, she felt like somebody had taken her hand and was tugging at her, a gentle pressure in a very specific direction. She pointed a finger at the back wall, behind Onya. "That way. That's the way they took Cleric."

"How do you know?" Lukash sounded dubious.

"Because this is his blood." Lukash's gaze, suddenly horrified, flicked down to the vial. On impulse she reached out, touched his shoulder. "No. I can find him with this. If we can get out of here, we can save him."

"We can't get out of here," he said, and turned away from her again.

But for the first time since they'd been locked up, Judah felt a prickle of something, some life or energy that had been missing. She could still feel Cleric's despair—dark and unbearable at its core—and she could feel the other presences, the unseen multitude. But, as in the Work with Merrit, they weren't watching. They didn't care. And there was something here, something her mind wanted her to find. Like digging through a box of keys, knowing the right one was there somewhere. She kept thinking of that hint of purple in Cleric's despair. Purple, like the Work with Merrit, like seeing out of Gavin's eyes. Making the knife, purifying the water, trying to break the chains—that had been the white. But when she'd pulled Pavla into the tower, that had been purple, too—

We are all like this mushroom, Pavla said in her head. *All connected, down deep where it can't be seen.*

And Daniel: *To save you from death, the tower needed a great deal of strength. So it pulled that strength from all of them.*

One Work purple, the other white. Both hers.

"Right," she said, decisively. She stood up and tried to cross to the door, but her chain wasn't long enough so she pounded on the wall instead. "Hey!" she screamed. "Hey, somebody!"

Almost immediately, an unfamiliar voice said, "What's the ruckus?"

"I want to see Daniel," she said. "Go get him."

There was a moment of hesitation, and then the voice said, "Daughter of Maia, are you ready to cooperate?"

"Oh, absolutely," Judah said. "Without a doubt, I am."

Daniel came alone, and wary. His sleeves were rolled up, his springknife on display. "The others are afraid of you, after what you did to Pavla," he said. "What do you want, Daughter of Maia?"

"When you were talking by the bonfire," she said, "you were disposing of my future children, weren't you?"

She saw Lukash stiffen, his mouth turning steely and tense. "You make it sound too harsh," Daniel said. "It's not like they'll be torn from your arms. They'll stay with you when they're small, and even after they go to their home caravans, you'll still see them. The mother-child relationship is very important to us."

Onya huffed. Judah ignored her. "What about the father-child relationship? Does that matter?"

"Most women choose to keep their children with them, so father and child tend to see each other less frequently."

"Like Nate and his father?"

Daniel gave her a sad smile. "Nate always belonged to Caterina, in every way, but Jasper has a claim, certainly. Why did you send for me, Daughter of Maia?"

"So the question now is whose caravan will get a baby, right? Not the actual—parentage." *Father*, she almost said, but the word felt wrong. *Father* was a word for Gavin and Theron, not her.

Daniel nodded. "The fathers will be decided later. Those choices are made very carefully. Don't be concerned. We've been doing this for many generations, and have found ways to make the experience as pleasant as possible for all involved."

Onya made an affronted noise. "Pleasant," she said. Across the wagon, Lukash watched suspiciously.

Do not say a word, Judah pleaded, silently, with all the force of her being. Do not say a single word. She took a careful breath in, looked back at Daniel, and was surprised at how even she sounded when she said, "Would you like the first one to be yours?"

His brow furrowed. "What?"

"I'll give you a child."

Daniel's head turned. His eyes dashed furtively to the locked door. Much more quietly, he said, "Willingly?"

"Conditionally."

Daniel relaxed, visibly. This was probably more what he was used to. "Condition being?"

"Condition being, you let these two go." She nodded toward the others. "My friend will help Onya back to her own village. And her brother, too."

"I'd have to strip them of their power first. People rarely live through that, or want to," Daniel said.

Onya's face had fallen from hope to fear. "Fine," Judah said, as if she didn't care. "Keep them, then. A life for a life. You get a baby. Lukash goes free."

Daniel gave her a gentle, admonishing grin. "So he can go after his abominator companion and slit the throats of my people?"

"He won't," Judah said, not looking at Lukash. "He has a strong sense of self-preservation. He'll go in the other direction."

"I'm not sure I believe you. Unless I miss my guess, your friend is a former Morgeni soldier. They do not forgive a wrong easily."

Judah looked at Lukash, who said nothing. She held her arm out to Daniel. She was surprised to see that the arm didn't shake. "Test me in the Work," she said, the way Merrit had that morning.

Daniel shook his head. "You nearly destroyed Pavla."

"Pavla tried to do things to my mind," she said.

Daniel rubbed at the back of his neck. "She was trying to make things easier for you. None of us want to keep you in chains." He sounded disgusted: by her or by himself, she didn't know.

"Let my friend go, and you won't have to," Judah said. "And you'll have the baby."

"I'd face censure," Daniel said. "The people would say I stole a child that was rightfully someone else's. The caravan might even elect a new leader." His eyes fell on Judah. She didn't think he was seeing her. "It might be worth it. Particularly after the Unbinding, when the power is free again." He shook his head. "I wish I trusted you."

Judah still held her arm out to him. It was beginning to get tired. Daniel stared at it for a long moment, and she could see thoughts clicking through his head like one of poor dead Theron's machines. Finally he nodded. "All right. In the Work, neither of us can lie." He took a small folding knife out of his pocket, and opened it.

"You're all insane," Lukash said.

Daniel and Judah both ignored him. Daniel cut Judah and drew the sigils.

He wasn't powerless. But compared to Pavla, he might as well have been. And the inside of Merrit's head had been so much—brighter, somehow. The place Daniel brought Judah to looked exactly like the same dusty caravan they'd just left, with the same chains on the walls. But now the chains were empty and the door stood open. Through it, Judah could see an ocean of gray-green grass. The tall fronds whispered against each other in the breeze.

In the Work, Daniel was slightly more handsome than he was in reality, broader in shoulder and flatter in stomach. *I swear,* he started to say, but stopped. The caravan was melting around them, the wooden slats of the walls shrinking to shelves and sprouting crumbling books like mushrooms along their top edges. The breeze that had played so gently in the grass fronds grew chilly, and the whisper of air thinned to a wavering whistle as it carved its way over the edge where a huge piece of the tower—roof, walls, floor—had been sheared away by some force that was able to cut stone like butter. The smoky smell of the grasslands deepened to the dry-corpse smell of dead leaves.

Daniel stared at all of it, eyes wide. She could feel his power, warm and dark and liquid as a samovar of hot coffee, flowing from Daniel to everyone in the caravan, to everyone he had ever Worked with, and back again. Daniel had led the caravan for many years, and Worked with the same people over and over, and the repetition had made the flow healthy and strong. All those multitudes, waiting and watching and Working. Judah opened her eyes and opened them again, like she'd once done in the tower, and now she could see the purplish web the Slonimi had woven together, through all those years of Work. It was less deliberately woven than the purple rope that bound her to Gavin—and unlike the rope, the strands of webbing were strong and distinct, and didn't fade away.

Daniel, meanwhile, stared around the tower, mouth agape. *What is this place? Is this...is this the tower of binding?*

That sounds awfully fancy, she said. Then she reached inside him, and drew.

Power coursed into her like, yes, hot coffee on a winter's day, warming her from the inside out. But this cup didn't empty. She saw his eyes go wide with shock and still she drew. She drew from him and through him, from everyone he'd ever Worked with, and she could even sense the flow reaching out to everyone *those* people had ever Worked with. Like Pavla had said: all connected, deep inside.

And at the same time, she reached into the shackle around her ankle. Into that reluctant iron, that wanted only to take the shape into which it had been formed, that refused to be anything else. The power was liquid and warm and the shackle was heavy and cold. She pushed a little of the warmth into it, and then a little more, and just as she had imagined the feel of a knife under her hand outside Black Lake, just as she had imagined her ball gown in the white, she imagined the iron cuff growing

softer.

airier.

what were you made of, iron?

before you were put to heat and formed to another's will, what were you?

The metal was a sponge, absorbing all of the power she could pour into it. So she gave it more, and more, and still more. Distantly, she heard screaming. It meant nothing. She was the power now, carrying all of that heat and force—

A great iridescent flash, her power and the Slonimi power joined together.

The flash was a lovely lavender, with hints of silver and blue and pink coursing through it. If it could be made into cloth and if there were still courtiers in Highfall, every last one of them would have been clamoring for it. Then she was back on her knees, on the floor of the wagon. Daniel lay crumpled in front of her, blood leaking from his nose and ears. Lukash crouched against the back of the caravan, shielding Onya with his body, staring at her—at Judah—as if she were something terrifying and unknown.

"What—did you do—" he said, hoarse with shock.

"The chains," Onya said, sounding dazed, and Judah looked down to see a small pile of black powder where her ankle cuff had been. And then the wagon collapsed.

It was a gentle collapse, if such a thing were possible. The walls fell outward, the shingles sliding from the roof in great heaps like mud and the roof panels giving way afterward, almost as if the collapse had been choreographed. There was a jarring thud as the floorboards hit the ground, and the four inhabitants of the wagon with it. Judah felt a little as if she'd been punched in the stomach by a giant fist. The air was full of dust. But through the haze she could see Lukash shaking himself off, too, staring down at the wooden planks that had been their prison. Tiny blisters of the same black powder dotted the wood, and a thin film of it coated almost everything. Judah crouched next to Daniel, laid a hand on his throat, and was relieved to find that he was still breathing.

"You dissolved all of the iron in the wagon," Lukash said, awestruck.

The dust was settling, now. Judah saw that what Lukash had said was true. Or at least mostly true. She had not dissolved all of the iron in the wagon; she had dissolved all of the iron in the camp. Instead of the ten wagons that had been circled around the clearing, there were ten piles of wood and black powder. Slumped figures were everywhere. She heard a child crying. Dismay filled her, oozing into the empty places where the hot liquid power had so recently been. "What have I done?" she said, numbly.

Lukash stared at her. It was Onya who responded, not with words but with a long, exultant howl that echoed in the stillness. "You freed us," she said. "You freed us, that was what you did."

"Onya!" A small figure dashed out of the settling dust, and Inek threw his arms around his sister. "Onya, did you see what happened? All the wagons fell down! Boom! And all the grown-ups did, too!"

Judah stumbled toward the nearest collapsed body. It was a woman. Judah didn't know her. Like Daniel, she was bleeding from her nose and ears. Like Daniel, she was breathing. Judah glanced back at the others. Lukash was rummaging in a pile of wood, Onya crouched next to her brother. Quickly, Judah touched her finger to the unconscious woman's blood, and then to the still-open cut on her own arm. The woman's sigil flashed into her mind but she didn't bother to draw it. She wanted to make sure the woman would be okay, and she only needed a little bit of the Work for that. Little enough that she could still see the real world around her. The woman was dazed and bewildered, drained and weak—but intact. Already drifting toward the surface.

Judah stood. "They'll wake up soon. We should leave."

"All of the iron is crumbled to nothing. Steel's fine." Lukash held up a long steel knife, and then slid it into his belt. "Can you ride?"

Judah shook her head. She liked horses. She didn't want to be responsible for caring for one. Onya said, "Oh, no, you don't." She was holding Inek now, his arms tight around her neck. "You're not leaving me here with these people. Not Inek, neither. We're coming with you."

"Onya," Judah said, "where we're going, there might be trouble."

"There will definitely be trouble," Lukash said.

Onya glared. "And what do you think will happen to me if I stay here? After what you've done?"

Lukash, at Judah's shoulder, said, quietly, "A blind woman and a child."

Judah looked at the set of Onya's jaw, her squinting eyes and the protective grip of her arms around Inek, and then looked back at Lukash. "How do you suggest we stop them?"

Lukash shook his head. "Find knives," he said. "And food. Maybe a map. I don't know this country."

"We don't need a map," Judah said, and gestured toward the south, where she still felt the pull of Cleric's blood. "We go that way."

They headed south along a ridge of solid rock that broke through the soil in a long seam, so they wouldn't leave tracks. Lukash said he'd noticed it that first day and remembered it in case they managed to escape. Then he hesitated, and said, "I'm sorry I was angry at you."

"You were worried about your friend. And I did get you into this."

"It doesn't sound like you had much choice in the matter."

"I chose to travel with you," she said. "I chose not to tell you the Slonimi were looking for me."

"Did you know they were looking for you?"

Judah stared down at the ridge, placing the dead boy's boots one after another on the narrow strip of mottled gray rock. Carefully, so they didn't touch the soil on either side. "I think I did," she finally said. "Or I would have, if I'd been willing to think about it at all." She gave Lukash a smile that felt rather wan. "I was worried about my friend, too. I still am."

"Because he's being tortured," Lukash said, and Judah said, "So is Cleric. And we know how to find him."

"You don't think you can find your friend the same way you're finding mine?" Lukash said.

"I don't know," she said, but it was a lie. She could absolutely find Gavin the way she was finding Cleric. She was afraid to do it.

The rock vein led into the foothills. The Barriers towered above them to the east, formidable blue peaks topped with snow. Looking at them, Judah could hardly imagine the world she'd known on the other side. They made slower progress than Lukash or Judah would have liked, but Onya was weak from inactivity after so long in the wagon and Inek's legs were small. He said almost nothing, and didn't whine, but his lower lip stuck farther and farther out until Onya finally stopped, bent over, and let him scramble up her body like a squirrel, wrap his arms around her neck and his legs around her stomach. An hour later, Lukash stopped. "I'll take him," he said to Onya, who immediately halted, and let Inek slide down.

"They fed him well, at least," she said, straightening up again, with one hand at the small of her back.

Lukash gave her a half smile. When Inek hesitated, he picked the boy up with one arm and slung him around to his back. As Inek grabbed hold, Judah saw his eyes widen with delight. The vial of Cleric's blood in her pocket pulled at her. How far away was the Elenesian stronghold? How long would be too long?

The sun was already gone and the light turning hazy when Lukash stopped and said, "Let's eat something." Inek had fallen asleep on his back. In the camp, Onya had stuffed a bag with thin flatbread, cheese, and dried meat. She'd also grabbed a bundle of grayish-brown leaves, thick and glossy, which she said would be good for energy while they traveled. As they ate, the sky grew dark. They made no fire.

After Judah ate, she asked Lukash for the knife he'd taken.

"It's a good one," he said, handing it over. "I grabbed one of the ones with the wrist cuffs, too, but I think I like this one better."

"The wrist ones are called switchknives." Judah had taken Daniel's Work kit, for the sake of the bandages and disinfectant in it, but she'd left his knife. Now she wiped the blade of Lukash's knife down with a moistened bit of her shirt. "Is this one as good as the one you lost in Black Lake?"

"The one I lost in Black Lake was the best knife I've ever owned," he said, slightly mournfully. "That's a bit disgusting, you know."

Because Judah was opening the cut in her arm again. "I know. I'm sorry," she said. Cleric's blood was thick, mostly solid, but she was still able to feel a faint tug. She drew his sigil on her arm, and was rewarded with an impression of a head resting on hard ground, looking up at a field of stars. The thick smell of wood smoke.

Then she blinked, and it was gone. "He's still alive," she told Lukash.

Lukash looked relieved. "Good. Let's sleep a bit. Can that Slonimi man find you as easily as you can find Cleric?"

"Daniel? Not anytime soon. He'll still be lying in his own

puke, unless I miss my guess." She heard her own satisfaction, remembered the disassembled wagons and the huddled bodies on the ground, and was faintly horrified all over again.

"You hate them," Lukash said, and Onya, holding the sleeping Inek against her body, said, "Of course she hates them. Did you hear him trading her children like horses?"

"I heard," Lukash said. "It was repulsive."

"To be clear, I would have stabbed myself repeatedly in the throat rather than have anything to do with that man." Judah sighed. "But they won't give up. You and Inek shouldn't stay with us, Onya. And, Lukash, when we find Cleric, you should leave, too. This kind of thing will keep happening."

"Thank you for saying *when* and not *if*," Lukash said. "Who was that man you all kept talking about? Nate?"

"He was a magus, in Highfall. A healer," she added, in case that wasn't clear. "And he was my friend. I thought he was my friend. I don't know, maybe he was. But he was Slonimi first." She remembered him at the end, weeping, sick. "I guess they're like the Elenesians. They don't let their people go without a fight."

Lukash gestured at her arm. "He taught you to do that mind trick?" She nodded, and he said, "You were better at it than he was, I'm guessing."

"Why do you think that?"

"Because you seem to be better at it than anyone else. Good enough to make them think your children are worth trading."

"They think all children are worth trading," Onya said. "All that matters is that Work of theirs, if they can do it or not. But I don't want it." She was defiant. "I don't want to make anyone do what they don't want to do."

Judah thought of all of the wonders Nate had shown her in the Work, oceans and mountains and plains and people; and of the horrid purple stitches he'd made in her flesh, when he'd sewn the Work-stuff through her. She didn't know if the wonders were enough to justify the horror. "It's not all like that," she said.

"Judah is right," Lukash said to Onya. "You shouldn't stay with us. There will be fighting."

"What, you don't think a three-quarters blind village girl will be much help to you?" Onya said, with a quick smile that faded as quickly into a frown. She looked down at her brother, who slept with his head pillowed on her thigh. "I wouldn't be. I'd probably walk off a cliff without Inek to stop me. Some choice: war against witches or led through the wilderness by a child."

She didn't say anything else, and neither did Judah or Lukash. There seemed to be nothing to say. Eventually Onya lay down, cradling Inek against her body. And, as she always had in the prison wagon, she fell asleep almost instantly. Judah envied her that skill, the ability to simply shut off her consciousness.

"This power," Lukash said, quietly. "The things you can do, with the metal—is that something all the Slonimi can do?"

Judah shook her head. "Not as far as I know, but I don't know much. I asked Nate once why I couldn't use it to light a fire and all he'd say was that it wasn't that kind of thing."

"So it will be regular fighting, this war against the witches. No magic."

"There are also the Elenesians. Cleric didn't make them sound particularly gentle." Judah hesitated. "Were you really a soldier?"

He nodded. "The Lapidistrians came for the gems in our mountains. The stories say we welcomed them. Maybe we did, but they treated us like beasts. Our bondage lasted a hundred years. The war to end it lasted seven. By the end, all the grown men with the will to fight were dead. So the young people took over. I was only a few years older than Inek." He took the knife back from Judah, who had cleaned it on her trouser leg, and began running a whetstone along the blade. She'd seen him do the same thing many times in the Ghostwood, but he would have lost that whetstone in Black Lake. He must have picked up another at the Slonimi camp. It seemed like such a natural thing, Lukash honing a knife. "The guildsmen killed many of us. We killed all of them. Now the Morgeni are free."

"And due to remain that way, I'd think," she said.

He didn't answer. For a while, they were quiet. Then she said, "I'm sorry that I got you into all of this." She stared down at the vial of Cleric's clotted blood in her hand. "Do you know his real name? It can't be Cleric."

"Many guilds take your name away on entering. You're nothing but your rank, until you achieve a high enough level. When we met, he told me to call him Cleric, so that's what I call him. You told me to call you Judah. Would you rather I called you Daughter of Maia?"

"Gods, please, no," Judah said, and they said nothing else, until they both slept.

Late in the afternoon, they came to a river, flowing west out of the Barriers. At such a close distance, the mountains were almost incomprehensibly enormous, rising to blue peaks so high that they had the same hazy look as the moon. Judah could almost understand why the Slonimi were willing to trade away a man's life for easy passage through them. Almost.

Cleric felt no farther away than he'd been the night before. It seemed safe to stop and rest a bit. On the riverbank, they ate more bread and the last of the cheese. The river was wide, lethargic, and clean. Growing on either side of the bank were clusters of short, stubby trees that exuded the same smoky smell as the grass. The remains of a campfire were clearly visible on the bank, and the ground was littered with scraps of roasted desert birds.

While Onya soaked her feet and Inek splashed in the shallows, Lukash took a branch from one of the trees and carved a spear from it. He took off his shirt and pants and swam in his braies to the far side of the river. There, he stood very still and, in what seemed like a remarkably short amount of time, speared four fish. One for each of them. "Hand some of those over," Onya said when he returned, taking out the knife she'd picked up at the Slonimi camp. "I'll help clean 'em."

But when Lukash handed her a fish, she held it for a long time. It looked to Judah like an ordinary fish, silvery on the underside and greenish along the top, except for a bright white ring around its eye and a double-lobed tail. But Onya brought it right up to her face, as if to smell it. "Well," she said, sounding like she was talking to the fish. Then, again, "Well," with finality this time. She picked up her knife and slit the fish along its belly, and that was when Judah looked away.

They made a second fire where the remains of the first had been. The smoky flavor of the burning wood flavored the fish. "I wish we had salt," Judah said.

"Me and Inek are leaving in the morning," Onya said. "These are the same kind of fish as the ones from the river that goes through our village. It's nowhere special, but my ma is there, and my other brothers and sisters."

"I want to see Ma!" Inek said, excited.

Onya grinned and ruffled his hair. "I do, too."

"Don't all fish look alike?" Judah said.

Lukash shook his head. "These fish are distinctive. The eyes and the tail."

Onya nodded. "Even a blind girl can follow a river. And there'll be villages where we can stop on the way."

The day before, Judah had told Onya to leave them. Now

she found herself reluctant to see the girl and her brother go. "What about bandits? Or the Slonimi?"

"Nothing to be done about bandits," Onya said, stoic. "And the Slonimi'll be busy looking for you. Even if they do ever come back to our village, I'll know not to go walking with any of them, won't I? Besides, you've got enough on your plate, rescuing your friend. Like you said, a blind girl and a child won't be much help. Even if the child is uncommonly strong and brave." Inek grinned broadly at the praise. Lukash nodded. Judah felt strangely empty.

In the morning, they divided up the travel bread and dried meat, then said their goodbyes. Lukash and Judah continued on to the north. "You gave them your share of the food," Judah said, when they were out of earshot, and Lukash said, "I can hunt. Onya can't."

Traveling without them was quiet. Inek had not been a particularly loud child, but his movement through the world had brought with it a constant level of ambient noise, and Onya's careful warnings, admonitions, and questions—are you tired, don't wander off, do you want water?—had added another layer. Traveling without Cleric, who had a penchant for muttering curses under his breath, was also quiet. The silence was lonely, but companionable. Judah and Lukash traveled faster, now, the land they traveled through growing rockier, the foothills turning to genuine hills. As the sun set, an icy breeze blew down from the Barriers to their east.

Judah was tired. Her legs and eyelids felt like lead. She was about to suggest they stop for a rest, when a flash of bright painful light exploded on one side of her vision. Then came another blow—that was what the flash had been—in her stomach, and one in her left thigh. She wasn't ready for it. Whoever was hurting Gavin had left him alone for several days. She heard herself cry out.

When the pain faded, she found herself curled on her side with Lukash crouched next to her, saying her name. "I'm all right," she said.

He passed her his water skin. "We never asked the Slonimi to help you with your pains."

"It seemed less important once they started talking about sending Cleric to be murdered." She sat up, carefully. "It's only pain. I'll be all right."

"How can you know that if you don't know where it comes from?" he said.

"I do know where it comes from," she said, wearily. "Help me up, and I'll tell you about it."

So he did, and she did, spilling it all in one complicated glut. After the knife and the chains and the Slonimi, she didn't think the rest of her story would seem all that strange. She told him about her parentage, as Nate had described it. Her birth, as Darid had described it. Her life, as she described it: feeling Gavin's every bruise and every ecstasy, drunk when he drank and sore when he ached. Her caning, which they'd both suffered. Elly and Theron and Elban and the Seneschal, the courtiers and the coup and the tower. The tower. The Work. The Unbinding. The moment when she'd realized that there was no way out of the tower. The moment when she'd jumped.

As she told the story—her story—he listened in silence, his face betraying nothing. She found herself watching her feet, stepping around rocks or over them as if the world hung on each footstep. Finally she ran out of things to say and he still said nothing. She felt weak and exhausted, as if she'd just been sick, but inside the exhaustion was a bubble of nervousness and tension. "Well?" she said, when she could stand it no longer.

"Your Lord Elban sounds evil," he said. "What the Slonimi did to you sounds evil, too. What they did to Cleric was evil, and Onya, and themselves. I don't know if they did it for an evil reason. It sounds like whatever they are trying to undo with their Unbinding was evil, too. I see why you wanted to extricate yourself from it."

"Which only led to more evil. Cleric, and whatever's happening to Gavin, and Elly—" Judah's throat grew tight, and she found herself unable to speak. Lukash did her the favor of looking away.

After a while, he said, "We Morgeni are not travelers by nature. My mother used to say there was more to learn and know on our mountain than a person could master in three lifetimes. But I travel. Most of those I fought with—those who survived—travel, too. That's how everybody we meet knows I was a soldier." Now, she saw, it was Lukash who watched his feet. "The war was necessary, but people who didn't fight are uncomfortable around me. It's hard to welcome a man into your home when you've seen him gut another man like a fish. Hard, even for me, to walk every day by the place where I gutted a man like a fish, if I'm not to be left dead inside by it. I don't want to be dead inside. I don't want to stop being horrified by the things I've done." He was silent for a moment, then said, "I still do horrible things sometimes, but the horror never fades. Those clothes you're wearing—"

He stopped, then. Judah waited a moment, and then, as gently as she could, she said, "You killed him, didn't you? The boy you took them from?" He opened his mouth to respond, but she cut him off. "No, I know you did. I can feel him. I can see him. I don't know why. Maybe he had some Work in him, too. But every time I put these clothes on, it's like he's walking into the room again. This angry dead boy."

Lukash stared at her, his copper eyes deep and hard to read. "You could have taken other clothes from the winemaker. Or the Slonimi. Why didn't you?"

Because it would have been like killing him all over again. "Who was he?" she said.

"The son of the sheriff of Harkerstown," Lukash said. "Very young. Very stupid. The sheriff hired us to steal the payroll. He thought he could cheat us, and he and his son could keep the money for themselves. It was a day before we found you. Close enough for me to go back and take his clothes. Obviously, I didn't know the boy would haunt you. I'm sorry for that. I'm sorry I had to kill him. We didn't even find the money. They hid it somewhere." From the slump of his shoulders and the unfocused look in his eyes, Judah believed that Lukash truly was sorry. "All we can control are the choices we make. You didn't choose to be found by us in the Ghostwood, and you didn't choose for all of us to be found by the Slonimi in the desert. But you chose to get us out of that wagon and you chose to go after Cleric. Some choices go bad. Others don't. We do the best we can."

Judah felt oddly reassured. "I wouldn't call it being haunted. I can feel him, that's all. Like an echo. And I don't mind, really. Who will hear him if I don't?"

Another silence. This was the kind of conversation that seemed to require a lot of those. Then, finally, Lukash said, "You're a bit frightening, sometimes."

"Why? Because I can see people's memories, and find them with their blood, and render entire camps full of people unconscious with the power of my mind? Is it better or worse than gutting a man like a fish?"

"About the same," he said, with a shrug.

They kept going.

The hours became a haze of bare ground and sharp rock and changing light. Judah began feeling a sense of increasing despair in Cleric's blood so they didn't stop to hunt or fish.

Sometimes as they hiked they listed things they would like to eat. "Roast potatoes with soured cream," Lukash would say, and Judah would counter with, "Chocolate-covered caramels. Soft ones." The game had no score and no points and no rules. Sometimes one of them would list a food the other had never had, and so they would try to describe it. They did not mention Cleric, but as afternoon became evening, the game withered away. The farther south they traveled, the more certain Judah was of their destination. When the sun set and darkness fell around them they kept going. She didn't need light to see where she was going.

The moon had just risen in the sky when she began to feel—strange. It was almost like being hot, but the night air was brisk. She had always loved nothing more than a warm blanket and a slightly cold nose and the combination was making her increasingly drowsy. Her brain drifted away, and she heard a satisfied voice say, *Why, I would know him anywhere.*

She snapped back to herself with a jerk. She had slipped into the white without realizing it. She touched the vial in her pocket and said, "We're close."

"Yes. I smell wood smoke," Lukash said, barely above a whisper.

So did she. The smell grew stronger, and the sensation of almost-heat intensified. *We're close.* One foot touched the ground, then the other. *We're close. I would know him anywhere. We're close.* Deeper and deeper into the words she fell, until her conscious mind had drifted away again. She was in a damp, smoky cell. Her hands were thin and dirty with a rippled burn on the back of the left one.

We're close.

A hand—an actual hand—grabbed her arm, and another clapped over her mouth. She jerked awake, ready to fight. But it was only Lukash. "You were sleepwalking," he whispered in her ear. "Look."

Judah looked.

They stood at the edge of a tall shard of rock that rose up out of the ground as if it had been pushed through from underneath. The ground sloped dramatically and Judah realized she was lucky that she hadn't fallen. The valley below them was less a valley than a torn place in the ground. In the moonlight she could see, some distance ahead, a massive building that Judah could only pick out by the straight lines and even spacing of the torches along its top. At its bottom nestled a cluster of flickering lights. Torches, a few campfires. She could see the shapes of tents and horses.

"The Slonimi," Lukash said. "Is he still with them?"

Judah realized that the cluster of tents was the source of the heat she'd been feeling, and that it wasn't exactly heat. The hair on her arms was standing on end. "No. He's in the fortress."

Judah heard Lukash release a breath, murderous and controlled. "We'll have to wait until daybreak to find a safe way down," he said.

Even then, as dawn bloomed behind the mountains, there were places where Judah had to cling to bare rock, her heart in her mouth. She'd never been afraid of heights before, but she'd also never clung to the side of a rocky cliff, her boots bound around her neck by their buckles so that her bare toes could dig into the slim crack that was the only thing supporting her weight. By the time they made it safely down her fingers and toes were raw everywhere and bleeding in places, and she'd lost a fingernail. Jamming her swollen feet back into her boots was painful, but she was grateful to have the tough soles between her feet and the ground again. The Slonimi camp lay ahead of them: two small tents and a handful of bedrolls, seemingly deserted.

"Where are they?" Judah said.

"Inside," someone said, behind them.

They both wheeled around. Lukash's knife was already out. But it was only Merrit, wearing the same floppy hat she had in the desert. "You sneak up on people," Lukash said, pointedly not sheathing his knife.

"I'm a scout. It's my job." Merrit looked at Judah. "I felt you coming."

"You sent me the vial," Judah said.

"I told you I'd help your friend in any way I could."

"You didn't bother trying to help him escape," Lukash said.

Merrit said, "I couldn't have done that. But I know where to find him in the stronghold. There's not much time. Last night, when we arrived, the guildmaster remembered your friend instantly. 'Welcome home,' he said."

"I'd know him anywhere," Judah said, without realizing she was going to.

But Merrit only nodded. "Yes. Kendzi and the others are still sleeping. There was a very large banquet."

"Why aren't you with them?" Lukash said.

"I told you. I felt you coming. I have been able to feel you behind us, all the way." Merrit paused. "You did something to the camp. What was it?"

"Convinced Daniel to let us go," Judah said. "They're all right?"

"They're weak. They'll live. Whatever you did to them weakened us, too. Kendzi isn't a strong Worker, but he's strong enough that he could have sensed you, had he not been drained. It cost us a day, or we would have been here sooner. But listen." Her brow furrowed with trouble. "There is a square pit in the courtyard. Stone-lined. Maybe five feet wide. On either side there are posts with holes bored through them. This morning there were two—they call them initiates, they are maybe eight years old—filling the pit with wood. I asked them what it was for. They said it was for the purification. So I asked what was being purified, and they said, the apostate."

"They're going to burn him alive," Lukash said. Judah felt sick.

Merrit nodded. "The initiates told me it was a mercy. If your friend's sins are burned away, then he'll return to the good graces of Eleni. They said his penance had already begun."

"So while you enjoyed your banquet, Cleric was being tortured," Judah said.

Merrit's thin lips pressed together. "There are bad people among the Slonimi, as there are anywhere. But there are more good people that feel their duty very strongly. Kendzi Baglia is one of those. He's also my friend." Judah remembered the weary-looking man with the springknife she'd seen in Merrit's memories. *I don't like it, either,* he'd said, *but there's no other way.* "The Elenesian pass is the fastest, safest way through the Barriers. I told him we could find another route. I told him, it is one thing to be executed, another to be tortured to death. He said, what do you want me to do, Merrit, break him out of his cell? And I said, yes, Kendzi, that is exactly what I want you to do." Her mouth grew tight and bitter. "And then he called your friend an abominator and I grew angry. I hate that word. The only abomination is causing more harm in this terrible nightmare world. So I told Kendzi to be sure to tell himself that, as he watched your friend be burned alive. Then I came here, to find you." She gave Judah a sad smile. "I don't think he'll be sending me on any more scouting missions."

"You said you know where Cleric is being held?" Lukash said.

"I do. I can get him out of his cell. But I can't get him

out of the stronghold without help. They won't simply let us walk out."

The stronghold gate loomed above them, made of immense slabs of wood that must have come from either very far away or very long ago. Judah hadn't seen any trees that massive since they'd left the Ghostwood. The slabs were bound with dark metal and huge rivets that looked larger than Judah's head. She stared up at it, remembering the feel of the shackles lightening, growing airy and soft.

"Then we'll have to help you," she said.

EIGHTEEN

THE LADIES OF TIERNAN HAD FINALLY FINISHED the winter panel, and plans were being sketched for the summer panel. Angen wanted the traditional cornflower replaced with glory plants. Since none of the women had ever stitched a glory plant, Elly volunteered to draw a pattern. "That's a fine idea," Peg said, eagerly. "In your day, ladies were taught to draw, weren't they, Elly?"

Yana, wrapping the winter panel in white paper, shot a narrow, bitter glance at Elly. Wonderful. "Times were different then," Elly said, mildly.

"Times were idle and wasteful," Yana snapped. She tied off the package holding the panel, turned on her heel—as well as she could in her current ungainly state—and walked out of the room.

A glory plant was brought up from the fields. Elly begged to be allowed to draw in Yana's room, where the light was better. Yana obviously didn't like the idea, but the house waiting for the panels was very wealthy, and the glory was a new motif which must not be fumbled. Finally, she gave Elly an hour, and strict instructions to touch nothing. So Elly took the sprig of glory into the room that had once been her mother's, opened the windows wide, and sat down at the desk. The glory was an odd, spindly thing, with jagged needles that would be difficult to stitch. This particular plant had one pod, swollen and bluish with seed, and two flowers still in bloom. The three papery petals of each blossom were fading to white around the edges as if already dying. It was an ugly plant. The patterns Elly drew—one with the stems curling to left, one to the right, and one of the full plant—would swap in for the traditional cornflowers, but it wouldn't be an improvement.

Leaving the drawings to dry, she knelt next to the writing desk and ran her fingers over every inch of it, looking for the latch that controlled the secret panel in the side. The wood was silky with age and polishing. She closed her eyes, so she could focus more clearly on the sensation from the tips of her fingers. Smoothness, woodgrain—then, finally, the smallest ripple. Pressing on the ripple did nothing. Neither did pressing to the side of it.

Then she tried a sliding motion and heard a deep, wooden click. She opened her eyes. A section of wood on the side of the desk had disappeared, and in the revealed space was the slim brown book she'd seen Yana put there. Maybe the ledger; maybe a diary, or a list of people Yana wanted to have killed. Elly reached in to touch the book—the cover was rough, oiled wool over paper—and then stopped. The Lady of Highfall traditionally had good reason to be paranoid, and so Elly's courtcraft lessons had included a section on securing one's belongings. Yana, loathed by nearly everyone and married to the equally loathsome Angen, had good reason to be paranoid, too. One could lay a hair across a book, or tuck it in between the pages; one could use a secret mark to know exactly where a book had been placed, measuring by exactly the length of a finger or some piece of jewelry that one carried on their person. There were hundreds of ways. Theron would have known them all, but Elly wasn't Theron. And even if she took the journal, she didn't have a plan for getting it to Eduard, or anywhere to hide it in her tiny nook of a room—by design, she suspected. She knew where the ledger was. It would keep.

Moira found her later that day in the salon, where Elly and the others were sketching the motif onto the summer panel's fine linen. "These are beautiful," Moira said with wonder, looking at Elly's sketches. "You really drew them?"

"I did my best," Elly said. "It's not a pretty plant. Do you draw?"

"Who has time? But, Elly—" her eyes, filled with concern, reminded Elly so much of her own mother's eyes that it was uncanny "—Lord Angen wants you. He's in his throne room. You're to go down immediately."

"All right," Elly said. Hopefully with more confidence than she felt. "Don't worry, Moira. Angen doesn't scare me."

"He should," Moira said.

Angen's throne room was the same one her father had used. The guard outside nodded a greeting when she approached and pushed the door open. It scraped loudly against the floor, the same way it had in her father's time. Only a single step into the room, Elly stopped short, her jaw falling open.

Say what one would about her father, but when he'd governed Tiernan, his throne room had been functional. There had been a desk, a few chairs; not too many, as he preferred people to stand awkwardly around while awaiting his attention. The windows had always been opened wide to clear the air of the stench of his visitors. He'd kept a samovar of coffee in the corner, and a bowl of nuts that he cracked with the blade of his knife. The only decoration had been—unsurprisingly— a piece of Tiernan blackwork, made by his own grandmother, with a pattern of crowns and swords. It hadn't been a pleasant room, but it had been a useful one, where even as a child, Elly had sensed that work was done. Had the room even held a throne? She couldn't remember one.

There was one there now. It was huge and ludicrous, painted gold and carved with lizards and lions. There were no lizards in Tiernan. There were no lions, either. The dais where the throne sat, which also hadn't existed in Elly's father's day, was covered with a thick rug. Where the petitioners would stand, the floor was bare. Elly's great-grandmother's blackwork was gone, replaced by red cloth hangings worked with gold. The plain samovar of coffee in the corner had been replaced by a gold one, as well as a crystal decanter of wine and a bowl of gloryseed pods. The windows were closed and the air in the room was thick with the smell of incense and heat from the brazier that burned against the wall. And upon the ridiculous throne sat her brother, his knees spread wide and one leg stretched in front of him. Seeming to mistake her shock for admiration, his voice was smug as he said, "What do you think of my throne room, sister? Far grander than our father's, isn't it?"

"I suppose so," she said, which wasn't a lie.

He waved a hand in the air, the light glinting on his gold ring. "The glory has brought us this. We are not humble shepherds anymore."

The cadence of his speech was stilted and forced. He was speaking the way he thought courtiers in Highfall spoke, and missing the mark. Elly said nothing.

Angen's eyes narrowed. "But perhaps you're not impressed

by my throne room, after your years in Highfall. I'm sure Lord Elban's throne room was far grander than this one."

Elban's throne room had been huge and empty, to make a person feel as small and insignificant as possible. His power hadn't lain in gold paint and wall hangings. But Elly still didn't know why Angen had sent for her, and so she was careful. "It was older," she said.

He threw his head back and laughed. She saw that he was missing several teeth. "Clever little kitten," he said, and prickly heat surged up from her stomach. "Lady Amie thinks your former betrothed has gone insane."

The prickly heat froze, became fear. "Has he?" Elly said, mildly.

"You don't seem terribly bothered by the idea."

"Does it matter what bothers me and what doesn't?"

"Not in the least." He waved a hand again, and this time his own eyes were on his glinting jewelry, as well. "Still, Amie thinks you can help."

"Amie seems to think a lot of things." Elly spoke as inoffensively as possible. "What do you think, Lord Angen?"

He smiled the lazy, curling smile she remembered all too well from her childhood. "I think it will be easier to take Highfall if he marches with us, but it's not strictly necessary. We can march in the names of the courtiers and the old families."

And Elban's lost heir, who no doubt would have died of an unexpected illness long before the army reached the Highfall gates. "You would need a bigger army, I think," she said.

The horrid smile vanished. "Our numbers match those of the Seneschal's guard."

"If you march in the name of the courtiers and old families, you won't just be fighting the Seneschal's guard. The people of Highfall aren't very enthusiastic about courtiers and old families."

"Peasants throwing rocks," Angen said, dismissively.

"By the thousands," Elly said.

Angen said nothing. He merely gazed at her. In anyone else, Elly might have characterized his expression as thoughtful, but she knew Angen. Thoughtful wasn't in his vocabulary. He pulled in his stretched leg, stood up, and, taking his time, stepped down from the dais and crossed to stand in front of her. "Well, then, it sounds like we'll need Lord Gavin's cooperation, won't we? What will make him cooperate, do you think?"

She felt her shoulders wanting to stiffen, her fists to clench. But Angen was an animal and animals sensed fear. "How can I say, if he's gone insane?" she said, as if the words were nothing.

Angen touched the scar on Elly's cheek. The tips of his fingers felt hot and repugnant. Somehow, she didn't flinch away. "Yana says you're a terrible maid. Obstinate. Slow." His words were drawn out and silky. His hand moved to cup her cheek. She wanted to scream. "You were always such an obedient little kitten, before you went to Highfall. Perhaps she needs to alter her methods of instruction."

Against the damp heat of his palm on her face, she thought cooling thoughts. Icicles, long and sharp and lethal. Deep drifts of snow. "She can't very well force me up a tree, in her condition," she managed to say.

He only smiled. The cupped hand began to caress, the hot fingers running along her scar. "You were such a pretty little kitten, back then. Our father never should have sold you away. Look at you now."

His hand slid around to the side of Elly's head, to the back. Then she was down on her knees with a searing pain in her scalp. Angen had her braid in his fist and was pulling her head almost down to the floor, and this was why this hairstyle was called a handle, this was why it must be tight enough to hang by, so that it didn't come loose when he dragged her across the smooth floor, her soft useless shoes scrabbling for purchase and her scalp in agony. When he yanked her head up, she found her face inches from the burning brazier.

"You are old and used up but you are still mine to do with as I please. Shall I make you even uglier?" he hissed in her ear, droplets of moisture from his breath hitting her skin like acid.

Elban had burned Judah's arm with a poker in Highfall. Distantly Elly was aware of her skin growing hot, and the beginnings of pain. She was somewhere high above. Somewhere between Tiernan and Highfall, watching as one man burned a wild-haired girl with a poker in a room surrounded by books and another pressed a scarred girl to the coals in a room hung with too much scarlet. Elban said, *Nothing belongs to you. Not even your life.* And why was it always thus, why always fire, why always *you are mine?* Women are furniture, Elly's grandmother had told her, years ago. If they were furniture, why were all the problems theirs to fix? Why were they not allowed to sit, like tables and chairs and wardrobes, and simply be?

She could smell her hair beginning to burn. Angen held her there a moment longer and said, "You will tell Lord Gavin to cooperate, or I will put you in the cell next to his, and have you torn apart piece by piece." Then, in one swift motion, he pulled her away from the brazier by her braid and kicked her aside. She scrabbled away from him. "Guard!"

Elly heard the screech of the door scraping against the floor. All his improvements, and Angen hadn't bothered to fix that. She tried to get to her feet but there was a blaze of pain in her hip where Angen had kicked her, and her legs wouldn't cooperate. The guard came in, looked at her with horror as she crawled like an animal on the ground—crying? yes, crying—and Elly was ashamed.

"Take her to the dungeon." Angen paused. The guard looked from him, to Elly, and back again. Now Elly's legs were working. She put a hand on the tapestry-covered wall to steady herself.

"My lord?" the guard said, and was that a slight note of incredulity Elly heard? Elly herself wasn't sure if Angen meant her to be imprisoned or escorted, and the guard didn't seem to be, either. The horrible possibility hung in the air like smoke from the brazier.

Then: "To see Elban's son," Angen said. "Then take her back to the women's salon."

Outside the throne room, the guard took Elly's arm. Not in an off-to-the-dungeon way, but in a please-don't-fall-down way. She found herself absurdly grateful for the help. They weren't in Highfall, after all. These weren't Elban's guards, plucked from prison cells and loyal to the end. Angen's guards were shepherds' sons, farm boys, apprentice weavers. This one had freckles, and the concern on his face wasn't feigned or even conscious. He handed her a handkerchief. It was roughspun, harsh on Elly's cheeks as she wiped away the tears, but clean. "Thank you," she said, handing it back.

The man with freckles folded it carefully. Too carefully, as if he was thinking about something. He hesitated, and then said, "I'll take you to the dungeon, Lady Eleanor, but Elban's son—he isn't well. He has a broken rib, and a broken finger. He won't leave them alone to heal, is what I hear." The guard's eyes were wide, with a lot of green in them. And a lot of concern, still. She remembered that note of incredulity in his voice, and wondered if he would have imprisoned her, if that was what Angen had meant.

Not that he would have had a choice. A great weariness slid

onto Elly. "What do you mean, he won't leave them alone to heal?"

"I mean he's reinjuring himself, Lady. Over and over."

Oh, Gavin. "Take me to him," she said.

Back through the dark corridors that should have smelled of lavender but didn't, back down the stairs to the dungeon. The chill of the air down there felt good on her face. And there was the same line of cells, with a single guard sitting on the same stool. A different guard, this time. He had his legs propped up against one side of the corridor, his back against the other. He must have been incredibly tall. He was also asleep. "Finch!" the guard barked.

The sleeping man started. He saw the guard and relaxed visibly. "Hey, Halwyn," he said, sleepily, and then saw Elly and sat bolt upright.

"Unlock Gavin's cell, please, Finch," Elly said.

Finch looked at Halwyn, who said, "Lord's orders. I'll wait, my lady," he added, to Elly.

Elly nodded. If Gavin's guard let himself sleep, maybe he'd let Gavin sleep, as well. It had bothered her, the way the other guard's metal baton had slammed against the cage bars every time Gavin nodded off. Such a petty, cruel thing to do. But inside the cell, Gavin was awake. He sat against the wall, hands propped up on his knees. Even from here, Elly could see that one of the fingers on his left hand was bent backward. Not that a broken finger was such a serious injury, but it would certainly hurt. His face was bruised, but the bruises were old. When he looked at her, his split lower lip curled in half a smile.

"Hi, El," he said.

"Look at you," she said, and then she was crouched next to him on the dirty cell floor. "Look at your hand." He smelled terrible, like sweat and blood and dirt. "Deep breath," she ordered. Then, as he inhaled, she grabbed the bent finger and pulled it straight. It moved more or less into place with a moist snap. Gavin gasped and—was gone. His body was still there, hair dirty and matted, but his eyes were glassy and faraway. He didn't respond when she said his name so she grabbed his shoulder, and shook him.

"Don't worry, Lady," the guard named Finch said. "He goes funny like that." The two guards were watching from the open doorway.

"Leave us alone, please," she said.

Finch shrugged and stepped back out of sight. Halwyn straightened his shoulders manfully, just as if he weren't an overgrown child wearing too much leather, and said, "I don't think—" but she gave him the same stern look she'd used to give Gavin when he was being irresponsible and annoying, and he quailed under the force of it. A much more satisfying reaction than she'd ever had from Gavin.

Who, when she turned back to him, was still—wherever he was, uncountable miles away. She didn't think he could see her, so she let her spine slump and her face sink into her hands. Her skin smelled like black embroidery dye and the perfumed smoke from Angen's brazier. She was angry. She was humiliated. All of these years later, and there she'd been, back at Angen's mercy. Halwyn had been kind, afterward, and she was grateful to him for that, but gratitude implied that the way Angen treated her was normal, and the way Halwyn treated her was some kind of heroic act. She didn't believe that. She refused to believe that.

Now, if Angen had meant her to be imprisoned, and Halwyn had refused—that would have been a heroic act.

"Elly," Gavin said, and she looked up to find Gavin looking at her out of those long-lashed blue eyes, exactly the color of the cornflowers that used to grow on the Tiernan moors before they were plowed under and turned into glory fields. If she only looked at his eyes and not the rest of him—not his matted hair or patchy beard—she could almost see those few happy weeks between their betrothal and the coup, when Amie was vanquished and Elban gone on his last campaign. Those weeks felt lived by entirely different people. Happy. Carefree. In love, or at least infatuated. The memory was a curl of steam from a bath, dissipating as soon as she reached for it. Gods, how she missed the bathing rooms in the House.

"Hello, love," she said, and tried to smile.

"Are you all right? You look unhappy." Gavin reached out with his good hand to touch her face. It would have been a nice gesture if Angen hadn't done exactly the same thing not twenty minutes before. She caught his hand and held it, before he could touch her.

But then he saw the bruises across her knuckles from Yana's riding crop, and frowned. Quickly, she made her voice stern and said, "Am I all right? What about you? The guard says you're hurting yourself."

He looked embarrassed. Ran the thumb of his broken hand over her bruises, so gently she could barely feel it. "Oh. Well."

"Gavin, you idiot," she said. "Don't hurt yourself."

He smiled. "You sound like Jude," he said, and then the smile faded. He leaned in close to Elly, close enough that she could smell his breath—which was not pleasant—and said, "I found her, El. Pain brings her closer."

Elly's breath caught. "Judah?"

He nodded. The weak smile came back. "Only when I'm hurting."

Pain and Judah, Judah and pain. And Gavin. All three, woven together in ways Elly still didn't understand but had come to accept. "You're absolutely sure it's her?"

"Who else would it be?" Then he saw her face and managed

381

a small, wheezy laugh. "I'm not crazy. At least, I don't think I am. I can—see things. Smell things. Not clearly. But it's her."

Elly's heart was beating fast. She gripped his good hand, hard. "Where is she? Can you tell?"

"There's a wall. Or maybe a building. Very high. I don't know, the details are blurry. It's like being very, very drunk." The smile came back. "But you've never been very, very drunk, have you, El?"

There had been a wall around the House, tall and white and unassailable. What other wall could there be? A savage hope welled up inside her. "Gavin," she said, "is it the Wall? Is she still in the House?"

But he would only shake his head. He didn't know.

She stayed a while longer. Halwyn brought warm water and she cleaned away some of Gavin's most obvious dirt. She was very tired, and so eventually she kissed his slightly-less-filthy cheek and left him. Halwyn took her up to the women's salon, and by the time they reached the locked door she'd had enough time to regain her composure. The guards liked her, Eduard had said. They called her Eleanor the Brave. "Thank you for your kindness earlier, Halwyn. I appreciate it." She hesitated, then said, "Before, in the throne room—did you think my brother was ordering me thrown in prison?"

He turned red. "I am glad he did not, Lady Eleanor," he said. Almost in a whisper. And she knew that she had been right, and Halwyn might not have obeyed that order, if it was really what Angen had wanted.

She went to Yana's room. Elly didn't know where her brother's wife was, and she didn't care. Judah was in Highfall. Judah was alive. If she could get the ledger to Eduard, she and Gavin could get away from Angen. They could go to Highfall, and find Judah. Maybe Theron, too, and who cared what happened after that? The four of them would be together. That was all that mattered.

Elly went to Yana's desk. She pressed, and pushed, and pulled, and slid, and finally the panel in the side of the desk opened. There was no dust on the ledger's cover. Inside were long columns of numbers and names.

5 chests, purchased from Ennis n. farm for 10 silver ea. Sold to Burim Sault for 100 gold ea.

Elly parsed it out. Ennis from the north farm (maybe there was another Ennis who farmed to the east, or something) had been paid 10 silvers each for chests that Angen had sold for 100 golds. Ten silver pieces bought a lot of bread, but not if the prices were inflated the way Eduard had said. And nowhere near as much as even a single gold piece would.

Eduard was right. Angen was growing rich, but Tiernan wasn't sharing in the profit.

She wrapped the book in a pillowcase, tucked it between her arm and her body, and went looking for Eduard. He wasn't in any of the places she checked, but when she glanced into the kitchen, she saw Moira sitting in a corner, polishing what little silver the House of Tiernan possessed. The kitchen was a big cavernous room full of steam and shouting and clanging pots. There was more activity than usual. Nobody noticed Elly slip around the edges of the room. "Moira," she said.

The girl looked up, puzzled. Elly was supposed to be up-stairs with Lady Yana. "What are you doing here?"

"Have you seen Eduard?" Elly said.

"He's out looking at the fields with Lord Angen and Burim, I think. He'll be back for dinner." Moira's fingers were gray with silver polish. There was a smudge of it on her cheek. "Do you want me to give him a message?"

Elly hesitated. If the broker was in Tiernan, Eduard might be busy all night. Moira would see Eduard long before Elly did. She held out the wrapped ledger. "Actually, will you give him this? He'll know it's from me. But Moira—" she added quickly, "—don't get caught with it."

Moira looked dubiously at the book. "What is it?"

"A book he loaned me. And listen, if you do get caught with it, tell them I gave it to you. Say I made you take it, that I threatened you. Whatever you have to do. All right?" Moira's brow was furrowed, her mouth drawn down. "Please. Eduard really needs it. He'll be so grateful," Elly said, and hated herself, because Moira thought the world of Eduard, and would do anything to make him happy.

Sure enough, Moira glanced around. Quickly, she took the parcel and slid it underneath her on the stool, so she was sitting on it. "Thank you," Elly said. She leaned over to kiss the girl's slightly sweaty head, and then slipped away again, before anybody noticed her.

Yana was angry that Elly had been gone so long, but Elly barely even flinched when Yana struck her outstretched palm with the crop. Her mind was with Gavin in the dungeon; it was with Judah and Theron—please, Theron, too—in Highfall. It was with the ledger, which might already be in Eduard's possession.

Yana kept Elly with her, putting her to work mending holes in chemises and stockings instead of working on the summer panel in the women's salon. Elly, distracted, kept making mistakes, which both infuriated and delighted Yana. Too many long hours passed before the bell for the evening meal rang. Yana said, "You're useless," and sent Elly to the kitchen for her tray.

Elly's knuckles ached from the crop, her cheeks felt sunburned from the brazier, and her scalp was still sore from Angen pulling her hair earlier, but as she entered the shabby dining hall, she felt light, almost giddy. The women lined up at the food table for mutton stew and oat bread moved aside for Elly, because Lady Yana's meal took precedence, but none of them said hello and several of them looked as if they might have been crying.

Elly glanced around for Moira, and didn't see her. Slowly, her giddiness disappeared, and a heavy sick feeling filled her stomach. "Have you seen Moira, Peg?" she asked, when she found the older woman sitting in a corner.

Peg's eyes filled with tears.

No. Dear gods, no.

Moira had been caught.

They were going to hang Moira the next day, at the last bell after the broker left. Angen wouldn't want his business associates to see him hang a child, even if that child had been doing an adult's work since she was six years old. Halwyn told Elly that everyone was being kind to Moira. "Don't worry, Lady, she's safe enough downstairs," he said, and didn't say that *downstairs* was the dungeon, and also didn't say that it didn't matter how safe Moira was right now because she would still be hanged as a thief the next day.

The house was silent and tense. The few guards Elly saw were scowling and mumbling, the women tearful and angry. Everyone knew Moira. Everyone liked Moira. More than once, Elly tried to slip away to search for Eduard—surely he must be fighting for his daughter's life, surely there must be something he and Elly could do, together—but the more Elly wanted to go, the more triumphantly Yana refused her.

"She's a little thief, your friend," Yana said, over and over again. "But she won't grow to be a big one."

Elly didn't sleep that night. (Because she was safe in bed and Moira was in one of the cells next to Gavin, and it was all her fault. Why hadn't Moira done as Elly told her, and blamed Elly? Or had she, and it hadn't made a difference?) Her stomach was sick. Yana berated her for her red eyes, berated her for not eating, and Elly trembled with rage. Finally, the next-last bell rang. Sitting in Yana's darkening bedroom—mending more of the woman's infernal underwear, stuff that by the looks of it hadn't fit her swelling body in months—Elly heard the shuffle of women from the salon, moving toward the courtyard. She put aside the slip she was hemming, and stuck her needle into a pincushion.

Yana's head jerked up. "What are you doing? I didn't say you could stop."

"I'm going to the courtyard," Elly said.

"You most certainly are not." Yana picked up the riding crop. "You're going to stay here and work."

"Lord Angen wants everyone there."

"You're not everyone," Yana said, with a sneer. "And you'll do as I say."

"I'm sorry for you," Elly said to her.

Yana started, as if Elly had slapped her. "What?"

"I'm sorry for you," she said. "I imagine you weren't much older than Moira when he married you, were you? You and I are the same age, you know. My mother sent me away to keep what happened to you from happening to me, and I'm sorry there was nobody to do the same for you."

Yana's eyes were wide, her cheeks scarlet. "You speak out of turn," she said, in the barest whisper. She raised the crop.

Elly snatched the crop out of her hand and broke it over her knee. The leather wrapping held the two pieces together and it dropped, limp and broken, to the floor. "I don't hate you," she said. "I hope the birth goes well. One way or another, I don't intend to be there."

Then she turned and walked away. She could hear Yana

screaming at her, calling her foul names, names Elly had never called anyone or been called herself. She didn't care. The corridors were empty and she took off her useless shoes and ran, barefoot, to the courtyard.

A cold fury rose inside her.

The courtyard was silent. It seemed as if all of Tiernan was assembled there, eyes on the hastily erected gallows where Moira stood, tearstained, with her hair bound on top of her head and the noose already around her neck. She wore a plain chemise that had once been white, but a night in the dungeon had left it dingy. Elly's fury only grew. They couldn't even allow the girl the dignity of a decent dress. Couldn't risk good clothes being ruined, after all. Not when some other serving girl could wear Moira's dresses after her. Eduard stood on the gallows, too, between his brother and his daughter, his expression stony but his eyes haunted. Amie stood on Angen's other side, her hair in a perfect handle and her face in perfect courtier impassivity. The mood was silent, sullen. Fearful.

Angen was reading Moira's sentence aloud. "This servant did steal from the family that has cared for her and provided for her, for all of her twelve years, and for this, will now be—"

Elly's fingers tingled. They wanted to twitch and shake. Her fury swelled to impossible levels and erupted out of her mouth. Her words rang out over the courtyard, echoing off the walls. "What did she steal?" she said.

A silent ripple moved through the crowd. The people spread apart, turning to look at her. From the gallows, Angen and Eduard did, too.

Angen kept his composure. "It doesn't matter. If it were a pin, the outcome is the same. A theft from the House of Tiernan is a theft from all of Tiernan."

The sun was near the top wall. Elly stepped into the clear space in front of her. "I know what she stole. It was a ledger," she said, loudly and clearly, as she walked all the way up to the scaffold, ignoring the bits of rock and straw and filth that stabbed her bare feet. The words did not seem to come from her as much as they came through her. "And she didn't steal it. I did. If you're going to hang someone, hang me."

The murmurs grew louder, more dissatisfied. Amie's eyes found hers. "What ledger?" a man called out.

Angen's face stayed impassive, his jaw rock-hard. "Lord's business."

Elly was making her way to the steps at the side of the gallows. One of the guards moved to block her, but the guard next to him put out an arm and kept her way clear. Halwyn. "Be careful, Lady," he whispered, as she passed, and then she was climbing the stairs, then she was on the gallows itself, standing on the rough-hewn wood, faintly sticky with sap.

"I'll tell you what was in it," she said, as loudly as she could without shouting. "Glory was in it. What was paid to the brokers and what was paid to the farmers."

Angen glared at her. His nostrils were flaring, his eyes darting. "Shut her up," he said to the nearest guard, and then, to another, who stood next to the trapdoor through which Moira's slight body was supposed to drop, "Hang the girl."

But the nearest guard was Halwyn, who had followed Elly onto the gallows. Elly's heart surged. The guard at the trapdoor looked uncertain. Eduard stepped up. "I think we would all hear more about this, Lord Angen."

"It is the lord's business," Angen insisted.

"Is the lord's business not the people's business?" Elly said. "What is a lord, without the people he protects?"

Dissatisfied assent moved through the crowd. It sounded like water, rushing through pipes. Angen's jaw was clenched. "Sister," he said, the word sinister and threatening, "you are clearly ill. Go inside and rest."

Moira was sobbing softly. Elly pushed in front of Eduard, pulled the noose away from the girl's neck and put an arm around her shoulder. Something else went through the crowd: a breath, a sigh. Moira's feet were bare, too, her toes tiny and pale as cotton. She was shivering. "I'm sorry," Elly whispered to her, and then, aloud, "I will not."

"Produce the ledger!" someone called from the crowd.

"Lord's business!" Angen shouted, and the crowd rumbled.

Amie tossed her head. "Oh, bother. I have it right here." And from the depths of her voluminous Highfall-style cloak, she pulled a slim, small book with a plain brown cover. Angen's eyes widened, and she gave him a look. "Well, it was sitting on your desk, after all. And it seemed to me that if it was important enough to hang a child over, it was worth bringing along." She spoke carelessly, as if it were all of little importance, but her eyes held on Elly for a moment. In that moment, as the horrid woman passed the ledger to Eduard, Elly could have kissed her.

Eduard opened it greedily. Quietly, so that only those on the dais could hear, Angen said, "Don't do this, Eduard. I'll spare the girl."

The crowd seemed to be holding its breath, waiting and watching. Elly watched, too, and saw the change in Eduard, when it happened. Eduard's spine drew a little straighter. The set of his mouth grew firm. He looked down at the ledger, flipped through a few pages. "Ennis," he called out. "Ennis, of the north farm. Are you here?" A man pushed through to the front of the crowd. He had red hair, and was terribly thin. Eduard pointed at him. "You sold your sheep to farm glory, didn't you?"

"I did," said Ennis of the north farm. "Lord Angen pays me ten silvers a chest for glory. Wool only gets fifty coppers."

Murmured agreement. Eduard waited for it to subside.

"Would you like to know what Burim Sault paid Lord Angen for that same chest?" Ennis nodded, and Eduard said, "One hundred gold."

The crowd erupted into shouts, Ennis of the north farm among them. "The risk is mine!" Angen said, loudly. "The responsibility is mine!"

"The profit is yours," Elly said.

Angen wheeled on her. "They don't need the money! What will they spend it on? Oats?"

"Whatever they like," Elly said. "It's theirs."

Loud, angry cheers exploded from the crowd at this. Angen turned to his guards. "Clear the courtyard," he hissed.

The guards didn't move. A rock hit Angen over his left eye, and he cried out. Amie watched, her lovely face mildly interested. The dissonant shouts from the crowd coalesced like smoke, forming words, finding rhythm.

Eleanor.

Eleanor.

"Shall we take him, Lady Eleanor?" one of the guards said, and Elly realized it was Halwyn, and he was talking to her.

"Angen?" she said. "Yes, I think so. Don't you?" And, without sparing her brother a glance, she led Moira down from the gallows.

Gavin awoke—was it waking? had he been asleep? *came aware*, then—when the door to his cell creaked open, and the tiny cramped space filled with life. He opened his eyes. Two people. No, three. Four. Dim in the light from the corridor outside the cell. "Bring a torch," Elly's voice said, and somebody did, and he blinked and could see her. She leaned over him. Her hair burned gold in the torchlight.

But who were the others? Two were Angen's guards. The other was a woman: Amie, her hands clasped in front of her and a worried crease on her forehead. For some reason, Elly was barefoot.

"Gavin," Elly said, gently. "Are you awake?"

"Mostly." Gavin couldn't figure out why Amie and Elly were in the same place. "What's happening?"

"Wouldn't it be easier to carry him upstairs?" Amie said.

Elly cast a glare over her shoulder at the Porterfield woman, who immediately shut up. That was interesting. He woke up a little more.

"Gavin," Elly said, "it's time to leave. You need to stand up now."

"Where are we going?" he said.

"Upstairs, first, to get you cleaned up, and let a magus take a look at you," Elly said. "Then we're going to go to Highfall."

He felt his eyes narrow. "Who's *we*?"

"You and me," Elly said. "And Amie. And as many soldiers as Eduard can spare."

"Eduard," he said. "Not Angen?"

Elly smiled, and it was a smile he'd never seen her wear before: satisfied, ruthless. "Angen is in the cell next to you. Come on, now, Gavin, love." Her hand took his—the uninjured one, and gently—and in that grip he could feel all the years he'd known her, and everything that had passed between them, the warm nights after their betrothal ball and cold ones after his father's death. "We're going to find Judah," she said, *and Theron*, she did not say, and maybe the crazy magus was lying about that, too. Maybe his brother was still alive somewhere.

But Judah—Judah was definitely still alive.

Slowly, he gathered himself. Found steel for his spine and strength for his legs. Stood up. Shook off the torpor that had fallen over him, all these long months.

Reached farther inside. Found his old grin. Put it on, like a dress coat unworn for too many seasons.

"All right," he said, and saw hope and joy flare in Elly's face. "Let's go."

NINETEEN

DARID FOUND THE COTTAGE ON WINDER'S ALLEY empty and dark, as he expected. Bindy would still be at work, Ma at the factory, and Kate and Canty at the factory crèche. Rina wouldn't come tonight, anyway, because it was his night, and Mairead was probably still either lamping or carousing with her fellow lampers. He'd brought lard with him from the abattoir, part of his unofficial wages. Ma had flour and salt in the pantry and milk keeping fresh in the cellar, so he set to making biscuits. He'd discovered that he enjoyed cooking. Simple dishes, satisfying and made with his own hand. There was no temptation to add sawdust or chalk powder to the biscuits, no overseer standing at his shoulder forcing him to skimp on the milk. Good food: he'd seen the lard rendered and knew it was pure, and no merchant in Marketside would dare cut Ma's flour.

He was putting the pan into the oven when Mairead tore into the room like a wild animal. He wasn't surprised by that, because that was what she always did, but he was very surprised by the look of her. Mairead was a rugged, cheerful girl, with a gap-toothed grin that nearly split her face in two, but now that face was red and tearstained. She vanished into the one small bedroom, slamming the door behind her before Darid could so much as say her name.

And then his other sister—the one he hadn't expected to see, the one he never expected to see—crashed into the room after her, waving a scrap of paper in one clenched fist. When Rina saw him she wheeled on him. "Your fault!" she screeched. Her face was red, too, but her eyes were dry. She still wore her factory apron, with the committee sash over it. "This is your doing, Darid Dovetail!"

"Take a breath, Rina," he said.

But Rina barely noticed. "Letting her run after that magus all the time. Encouraging her, even! And now look what you've done." She waved the paper again.

The magus. Bindy. Darid snatched the scrap away from Rina and read: *Ma & Littles, I am going out of the city with magus. I will be back soon. Please do not worry. I will be fine. Love, your daughter Belinda.*

The handwriting was horribly familiar. Bindy had written him letters inside the Wall from the moment she could write. He had known her through her words long before he'd ever met her. "Mairead was given it by some lamper out in the street," Rina spat at him. "And where could she go for help? Me, that's where. Not you, not in whatever dank warehouse you're squatting in these days."

"When did Mairead get this?" Darid said.

But Rina wasn't done. "If not for you Bindy would have a decent job at the factory. She'd be home safe where she belongs."

Heat began to rise in Darid. "Bindy knows her own mind

and she knows what she wants. And it's not to work in that bloody factory, spending her whole life running a pulper."

"I work in that bloody factory. Ma works in that bloody factory." Rina planted her hands on her hips and stared up at him. "Something wrong with our lives?"

"Not if it's the life you want. It's not the life Bindy wants."

"Bindy's not old enough to know what she wants. And even if she did—" she snatched the note back from him "—what kind of life is this? Wandering through the wilderness with some foreign man, doing who even knows what? Ma might have bought his goody-goody act, but I know better."

"The magus won't do her any harm." Darid wasn't so sure about Saba.

Rina shook her head. "You're a bad influence, Darid Dovetail. I'm sorry our dad died and Ma had to send you inside and you feel like your life's been ruined, but you don't have the right to ruin everyone else's life, too."

Darid had never said that. He'd never even thought it. But before he could respond, three loud footsteps came from the bedroom, and then Mairead, who had clearly been listening—not that she would have had to listen very closely, the way Rina had been yelling—burst back into the kitchen. "You shut your mouth, Rina!" she cried. "Darid's not ruining nothing."

Rina gave her younger sister a scathing look. "You talk like a street urchin."

"Better than being a factory stooge," Mairead shot back.

Rina gasped. "You wait until I tell Ma about this," she said. "You just wait." She threw the note on the table, turned around, and walked out.

He picked the note up. "When did you get this, Mairead?"

"Right before third shift. Jethro got it from Tapley who got it after first shift and I guess forgot about it—and then it took me ages to find Rina." Mairead turned her tearstained face to her brother. "What do we do, Darid?"

He looked down at the note again, which was grubby and crumpled. First shift was hours ago. Whatever Bindy was doing, it was too late to stop it. "Well," he said, as kindly and calmly as he could, "this note is for Ma. We'll wait, and give it to her, and see what she says."

"But Bin's going to be okay?" she said, anxiously.

With more conviction than he felt, Darid said, "I have no doubt whatsoever that Bindy will be fine."

Nora couldn't read the note. Darid had to read it to her. Her lips grew tight as she listened. Then she fished in her pocket, pulled out some scrip, and said, "Mairead, take the littles. Go over to Ember's and see what they have in the way of a cake or something for after dinner tonight."

Mairead scowled. "I'm not stupid. I know when I'm being got rid of."

"Get rid, then," Nora said. "And take your brother and sister with you."

When the children were gone, Nora turned to Darid. For the first time since he'd gone inside the Wall when he was ten years old, he saw tears in her eyes. "What does this mean, this note? Where could they have gone?"

He shook his head. "Maybe Firo and Will know something about it. I'll go over after dinner and have a word with them, shall I?"

"Please," she said, gratefully. "I don't think the magus would hurt her, but—"

"I know," he said.

She was silent for a long moment. "Darid, I asked a lot of you after your father died. I put our whole family's survival on you when I sent you inside, and you were just a little boy.

I can't take that back. And I don't feel it's right to ask anything else of you." She nodded at the biscuits cooling on the table. "I don't even like taking those from you. I should be feeding you, after all those years when someone else did it."

"Ma, it's all right." And it didn't matter. The House was in the past. What mattered, right now, was Bindy.

And sure enough, Ma's steely blue eyes fixed on him, and she said, "You'll find her. There's nobody else I can send. You'll bring her home."

"I'll do everything I can," he said.

Nora didn't feel like eating, which was all for the best. She'd brought some apples from the factory store but divided them up among the littles, after dinner, along with the three sugar cakes Mairead bought from Ember's. She noticed Darid pushing his food around his plate, too, slipping a bite to Canty or Kate when they were looking the other direction. She remembered doing the same with him when he was a little, himself. In his years away, he'd grown into a solid wall of a man, like the father he and Rina shared.

When the cakes were mostly gone she caught his eye and they shared a moment, mother and son. Nora could not have said, later, what the moment was. Only that there was one. "Well," he said. "I suppose I'd better—"

But at that moment there came a great pounding on the door, like a giant man with a giant hammer was determined to break it down. Mairead looked anxiously at Nora, who stood up. "I'll get it."

Outside, on the lamp-lit street, four men wearing the colors of the Seneschal's guard waited, long wicked knives drawn. Behind them was a boxcart, the kind they put wild dogs and drunks in, with one lone window in the one lone door and that set through with bars. "We've come for Darid Dovetail," the one with the white badge on his chest said. "Step aside."

She drew herself up to refuse but they were already pushing in toward Darid, who was clearly the only person named Darid in the room, and who stood up to meet them. "You are under arrest," the badged guard said.

"For what?" Darid said.

"Sedition and sabotage."

Kate began to cry. Mairead clapped a hand over her tiny mouth. Nora ignored them, for now, and said, "Who sent you here?"

"We have reliable reports," the guard said, stolid.

Reliable reports meant factory committee. There was only one factory committee member Nora could think of who knew about Darid. Even thinking of Rina made her sick with rage but she had no choice but to stand, her remaining children clinging to her skirts—even Mairead, who normally considered herself too big for such comforts—as they dragged her oldest son out into the street, and put him in the boxcart, and took him away. She didn't watch the cart drive away. She had seen him taken from her once, already, and she couldn't watch it happen again.

Three left. Only three, of the great brood she'd started with. Bindy gone, Darid gone, Rina as good as gone. All the others, the babies. The world had taken and taken from her, like her children were so many chicks in a hen yard, like they weren't anything at all.

But the small warm bodies that pressed close to her were very much real, and very much something. "Ma," Mairead whispered, at her shoulder. "What are we going to do?"

Nora pulled her closer. If that were even possible. "I'm not sure."

"But we're going to do something?" Mairead said.

Nora's mouth grew tight. Staring at the closed door as if the very heat of her gaze could bore through it, Nora stroked her daughter's dirty hair and said, "Oh, yes, my darling girl. We are most certainly going to do something."

Highfall Prison was exactly as Darid had thought it would be. The air was bad. The food was bad. The guards were people, some bad and some decent enough. He even knew one of them a little, from Alva's tavern. A man named Bruno Post, who grimaced when he saw Darid brought in and apologized the first time he pushed bread and water through the feeding slot. Bruno brought extra from home, after that, and so the dreary meals were at least punctuated by the occasional piece of decent bread with Mary Post's homemade pickle on it.

Lying there in his damp, dim cell, Darid thought of many things. He thought of all the masters he'd had inside the Wall, the horses he'd tended, the way he'd felt the first time a letter came from the little sister he didn't know existed. He'd read it so often he knew it by heart. *Dear Darid I am your sister Belinda we have never met but Ma talks of you all the time and said now that I could write I should and so here I am doing so. Hello!*

He thought of that strange day when he'd floated in a skiff in the Brake, waiting for the magus's shrouded body to slide down the prison trash chute, and of little Mairead asking him if he knew of any work she could do. He remembered Rina—Rina had been the one to turn him in, he had figured that out before the boxcart even reached the prison—weeping when he joined the line of children entering the House on that long-ago Staff Day, and Bindy weeping with joy when the magus had come back to himself, in Darid's tiny warehouse cubby.

And he thought of Judah. He thought of her more than he had dared, all the time he had lived in the city. How long ago that all seemed, those days when he had known what he was doing in the stables and the barracks and everywhere except with her, because when he was with her all his sense flew out the window. There had been a few women since her, because he'd thought he'd never see her again. But his weeks with her still glittered in his mind, the one bright reckless thing he'd done behind the Wall, and he wondered where she was. If she was okay. And he wondered where his sister was, and if she was okay. And he wished, many times, for that dinner he'd barely eaten, back at his mother's house on that last night.

He lost track of time. There was no natural light in his cell, and the faint purplish glow of the Wilmerian gaslight flickered day and night. He remembered when the Wilmerians had come to the House to install gaslights there, when he'd worked day and night trying to save their starving, mistreated horses. When Judah told him about the gaslights, then, how strange it had seemed to have light without fire. Now he wished to never see that weird purple light again. He had vivid dreams about being outside, in the wide pastures near the House or riding a barge down the Brake. Waking from those dreams into the dim purple light of his cell was backward. Waking should be bright. Sleeping dark. Everything was wrong.

It was a welcome surprise when, after an interminable time, he heard a key in the lock, and the door swung open. "Upstairs you go," the guard said, as he shackled Darid's hands together in front of him. If it had been Bruno, Darid would have asked why, but he didn't think this guard would answer him. And even if they were taking him to the gallows or the headsman's block, he would at least walk through open air to get there, wouldn't he?

But the guard didn't lead him outside. Instead, they went down the corridor, up the stairs, and into a room with a thick carpet and incense to cover up the damp smell. There were windows in this room, and chairs and sofas. It wasn't fancy like the courtier's room Darid had seen once in the House, but it was clearly intended for people without a guard's hand on their elbow and chains between their wrists.

On the softest chair, with the best view of the sky, sat the Seneschal.

Darid had to keep his back from straightening. This man had ordered Judah caned, and Darid himself put to death, for nothing more than knowing each other. He hated him for those orders, and for all the other orders he'd given that had condemned or mutilated countless House staff over the twenty-two years Darid had spent inside the Wall. Still, the Seneschal had been the most powerful person in Darid's world since he was ten years old. To the staff, Elban was like a storm that crashed through their lives, destroying without reason, but the Seneschal governed. He assigned and reassigned and punished and praised. For most of Darid's life, he had judged the gray man tough, but fair. Ever since the day Judah had collapsed and Darid had picked her up and run into the House with her in his arms, he had hated nobody more. He found himself savagely, unpleasantly glad to see the new scar on the Seneschal's neck. It would have seemed wrong if the man had escaped the past year unscathed.

For a few long minutes, the two men—one seated comfortably, with a cup of hot tea near to hand, and the other standing in chains—stared at each other. Finally, the Seneschal said, "Well. It *is* you, after all. I'm fairly sure I ordered you executed, Darid Dovetail."

Darid didn't respond to that. Instead, he reminded himself that the Seneschal was not in charge of him anymore, and mustered the courage to say, "How is Judah?"

Darid was glad to see the Seneschal's mouth tighten with displeasure. Instead of answering, the man said, "I suppose I should be angry that you're still alive. Oddly, I'm not. I'm a bit curious as to how you managed it, but it's not as if who-ever helped you is likely to be in a position to do it again. I would have been quite happy to let you go your way." He leaned forward and picked up a piece of paper from the table in front of him. "Unfortunately, there's this. Sedition. Sabo-tage. That, I can't allow."

"Your managers run this city as if the people who live here don't matter," Darid said. "Fuel for the fire, that's all we are to you. Like I was only a stableman, and Judah only—"

Darid stopped. A satisfied grin spread across the Seneschal's face. "Yes. You don't know what Judah was, do you? You have no idea how she was important, or why she was allowed to live as she did. Her role in New Highfall is bigger than you can comprehend, but all you know is that she was a girl and you liked her, so you treated her like any other girl."

It didn't escape Darid's notice, the way the Seneschal swung back and forth between past tense and present when talking about Judah.

The gray man held up the warrant. "It's much like this. You cannot possibly understand the reasoning behind the way this city is run, nor can you understand why your petty sabotage doesn't matter. And yet, I can't let you continue to do it. If I let you go, your fellow Warehousers—" the word dripped with contempt "—will think they can get away with mak-ing nuisances of themselves. Your sister and her compatriots on the committee will feel as if I don't take her seriously, and that her sacrifice doesn't matter, and the factory managers—if they hear of you at all—will be angry that I allowed a known saboteur to go free." He tossed the warrant back down on the table and sat back. "So you see, my personal opinion about you doesn't matter at all. If the machine is to continue run-ning, you must be reallocated."

A sick chill came over Darid. "Reallocated."

"Killing you would be a waste of resources." The Seneschal sat back in his armchair, looking pleased with himself. "You are going back behind the Wall, Darid Dovetail. And I don't think there's anyone there who can help you escape, now."

Then he stood up, and called the guards, and Darid was taken outside and put back in the boxcart. Before they shoved him into the tiny stale space, he looked up at the clear spring sky, and tried to fix it in his memory, so he could call it whenever he needed it.

TWENTY

"I WANT TO MAKE SURE IT'S CLEAR TO HER," KORSA said, with no small amount of frustration. "Do you think it's clear to her?"

Korsa, Liam, and Ida were in the tower room. They had brought chairs up from their old room, so there would be places to sit, but none of them were sitting now (although Ida stood on one of the chairs, to bring her eyes closer to level with Korsa's and Liam's). Korsa wasn't the only one who was frustrated. Ida's lips were pressed tight together and Liam's hands jammed tight in his pockets.

The focus of all of this frustration, Florence, knelt on the floor under a small colored-glass window, examining some circles of metal she'd found there. "She's not stupid, Chief," Ida said, angrily. "She's inward, that's all."

"You know Florence," Liam said. "Do you really think she would have come up here if she didn't want to?"

"It's not just coming up here. It's that." Korsa gestured at the table, where several small glass bottles of the liquid in question waited. "I don't even know exactly what it will do, so she can't possibly, and how can I ask her to take a risk she doesn't fully understand?"

Ida let out an inarticulate huff of rage. "Chief. You're being—what's that word, Li? The deliberate one?"

"Obtuse." Liam glowered at Korsa. "Deliberately not understanding."

"That." Ida nodded vigorously. "I've known Florence for years, all right? Years. If you explain something to her, she understands. She might not put on a big show like some people, but she understands."

Korsa shook his head. "Then I guess I need the big show. I can't give it to her if I'm not absolutely sure."

Ida let out another huff and moved on her strong arms over to where Florence knelt on the ground, turning a wide flat loop of brass over and over in her hands. "Florence," she said. "You listening?"

Florence's hands, and the brass circle in them, stilled and fell to her lap.

"There, see, Chief? Just because she doesn't look straight at you and say, 'Go ahead, I'm listening,' doesn't mean she isn't," Ida said, and Liam said, "You have to meet her where she is."

This was why the thirteen-fourteens were frustrated, Korsa knew. All of them moved through a world not made for them, adjusting in whatever ways they could. And it was a source of great vexation to them that the world never seemed to be able to do the same in return, even in the smallest of ways. Of all people, they bluntly told him, more than once, they expected Korsa to be more understanding. And generally he tried to be, but they seemed to have reached an impasse. He desperately needed to hear Florence say, "Why, yes, Chief, I understand the risks and am willing to drink the mind-herb anyway." And since they had never heard Florence utter a single word—"I've known her for years, Chief!" Ida had cried in frustration—the young people found this completely unreasonable.

Now, Ida was trying to bite back her irritation. "If Florence didn't want to be here, she wouldn't be. Look. Watch." She put a hand on Florence's shoulder. "Florence, Chief wants to make sure you want to take the mind-herb. If you don't, leave the room now."

As soon as they'd started talking again, Florence had resumed her examination of the brass loop, holding it in front of her eyes, turning it over and over. Now the loop stopped moving in midair. Florence was still. Korsa barely breathed.

Then the loop began to move again. Back and forth, side to side.

Korsa shook his head. "It's not good enough, Ida."

"Bloody hells," Ida said. "Then I'll do it, how's that? Test it out on me and then let Florence volunteer, like she wants."

Not even Ida expected the strength of Florence's reaction to that. She leapt to her feet and stomped her boot down, once, twice, three times. Florence was not a small person and she did not wear small boots. Korsa had no doubt that if the floors had been anything other than stone, they would have shaken under the blows. Her head was turned toward Korsa, her eyes fixed somewhere in the region of his lower ribs, and she was scowling. Her fist was clenched so tightly on the brass loop that Korsa could see the tendons stand out, furious and white.

"You see?" Ida cried. "You see? She wants to, Chief! She wants to!"

Korsa threw up his hands. "Then do it, Florence. Go over to the table and take the dose. It's right there on the table, waiting."

Korsa saw Florence's eyes dart toward the vials and then back toward his midsection. Liam muttered something about how this was what they should have done all along. The tension in Florence's fists relaxed. Her hands hung easy at her sides. Carefully, she put the brass loop down on the floor. Then, stepping gently and softly, she walked to the table, picked up the vial, uncorked it, and poured it down her throat.

"Oh, *kagirh*," Korsa said, and grabbed a vial, himself.

Theron didn't have to experience the passage of time between when Korsa had told him about his intention to bring the girl up to the tower and when he actually succeeded. He didn't understand exactly how it worked, but he knew that he could simply *not-be* until they arrived; that their presence in what Korsa called *kagirh*-space would call him there, too. But he found that he liked waiting, now that he had something to wait for. Also, the temptation to slide into that blank state of nonbeing was more than a little terrifying. What if nothing ever called him back?

He was in the old tower now, which looked as it had when Judah retreated there. He saw the yawning emptiness left by the missing chunk of wall, the dead leaves littering the floor under the odd stained-glass window, the ratty blanket Judah had used. He had created this version of the tower from memory, as surely as he'd built the parlor where he first brought Korsa, after sensing him flailing—where? Somewhere else. Somewhere he didn't create. This place, like the parlor, was a bubble, sealed away from the seething mass of purple. He could sense that mass without seeing it, the thick web of power that filled it. He could feel the multitudes of minds and lives that power touched, the vast distance it spanned. It made him feel the same way crowded rooms did, which is to say anxious and caged in—but it also felt necessary, somehow.

He wondered, now, if all of those minds and multitudes had been drained away, like Korsa's Anna. He had no idea how to keep it from doing the same to the new girl, and even if they succeeded, he didn't know if it would be any kind of favor to her.

It sounded like the Seneschal would hate it. So that made it worth doing.

He was thinking that Judah must have been incredibly uncomfortable, staying here, when Korsa and the girl appeared. The girl was tall and strong-looking, with hair the color of impure gold and quick blue eyes. She looked around curiously, wearing a faint proud smile. Then Theron realized that the girl's edges were growing a bit purple, and so were Korsa's. They were falling out of his bubble-tower and into the purple one. Quickly, before they drifted too far, he went after them.

Like leaping into cold water, a full-body shock and the sense of everything different all at once. And all those eyes, all those minds. The purple filled the room like cobwebs, great livid curtains of it in every direction. Theron knew to expect it but neither of the other two did. Korsa gasped.

"What is this?" he said.

"It's the power," Theron said, and grabbed the nearest fistful of it. It didn't like being grabbed, oh no. To continue his water metaphor, it was like grabbing a fistful of fish, squiggling and writhing and objecting most strenuously. And fistful was the right word, because the power was not simply one thing. It was a hundred things, a thousand, each separate and distinct and angry. When he pulled it toward the girl, it stretched in a sticky, unwholesome way.

"Hold this," he said, thrusting it into her hand. "It'll help."

The instant the girl touched the web, she snapped into solidity, and as soon as she did, Theron longed for his safe bubble, but couldn't risk the girl's solidity.

She blinked, and inhaled, and looked down at the fistful of purple she held and the spilled-over threads of it vanishing back down into the other place. Then she said, "That's much easier." The words came clear and distinct, as if made of cut glass.

Korsa let out a long breath. "Florence, you're speaking."

"Yes, it's very convenient," she said, absently.

Korsa was staring around himself, dazedly. "This is the purple you showed me downstairs, Theron. But—there's so much of it."

"It's all through the House, but it's strongest here." Theron held up his hand and opened his fingers slightly, to show them the faint sticky haze of purple he sometimes saw between them. "I think I'm made of it."

Korsa reached out to touch the purple rope that Florence held. As soon as his finger touched it, he jerked back, and shuddered. Before Theron could ask him what he'd felt, Florence did something terrible and incredible. She put the purple stuff between her teeth and bit down on it. "Dear gods," Theron said, at the same time that Korsa said, "Florence, no!"

Her eyes widened. Then the muscles in her jaw went tight and determined. She knelt below the small stained-glass window and began to dig in the leaf litter there. The wad of purple in her teeth came with her, the tendrils that reached out to the wall stretching but never breaking. In a moment Florence had unearthed a series of brass rings and discs, which she began to fit together.

Theron, fascinated, took a step closer. Korsa said, "Florence, what are you doing?"

She didn't answer. How could she with the purple stuff in her mouth? Theron watched as she connected one piece around another, attached a third to the end. Occasionally, she needed a tool, and when she reached a hand down without looking, it would just—be there. Soon, she'd made something that looked sort of like a clumsy musical instrument, wider at one end than the other.

Now she'd found something that looked like a bracket, with a ring on one end and two prongs on the other. The tube fit into the ring. Florence stood and examined the window. Sweat was beginning to bead on her forehead but in moments, she had the two prongs slotted neatly into two holes in the frame. Which wouldn't have been there, in the bubble he'd made, because Theron had never noticed them, but this was not his bubble. The wide end of the tube slotted into a brass fitting in the window that he'd also never noticed. The end result looked like a telescope pressed against the window, but it felt alive, somehow, and as if it were…probing.

Finally, Florence took the purple stuff out of her mouth, and shuddered. "So many people," she said.

Korsa looked puzzled, but Theron understood. "I know," he said.

She turned and looked at him. Theron saw something in her that he recognized: an efficiency, an apartness. He had spent most of his short life in his workshop, and had never seriously considered that he would ever be anything but alone. And he still didn't, because he was no longer exactly alive, and people who were no longer exactly alive did not have a choice in such matters. But if he'd had a choice, he would have liked to be friends with this girl. He thought he had a lot in common with her.

"Take me back down," Florence said. "I need to build the other side."

Before Florence and Korsa went back down, as she called it, Theron told her where his old, real tools were, or where they should be, and the first thing she did when she came back to herself was—well, the first thing she did was throw up neatly into a basin that Liam was smart enough to have waiting. Then she wiped her mouth and, with great determination, walked out of the tower. The other young people stared at Korsa in shock.

"Did it work?" Ida said.

"It must have. She's not dead, is she?" Liam said, and headed after her.

Korsa followed, too. Theron might have told her where he remembered his tools being, but this was not the world that Theron remembered, and he did not want the thirteen-four-teens out in it on their own. He'd had so little exercise in the past six months that by the time he caught up to Liam and Florence, at the entrance to the old wing, he was breathing heavily. Raghri and Giorsa, the physically strongest of his four *kagirhi*, would very much disapprove of his weakness.

Liam was young and strong and barely sweating at all. "Where is she going?" he said.

Too winded to speak, Korsa shook his head. With no hesitation, Florence marched down a dusty corridor, up some stairs, down another corridor. Recently swept, this time. The door where she stopped wasn't locked, and they followed her through it into a room with a bare floor. Four utilitarian cots—the same kind Korsa and the thirteen-fourteens used—were squeezed into the room, as well as a small table with a washstand. Crude hooks holding assorted unidentifiable garments hung from the walls.

But under the hooks, those walls were covered in faded silk. Across the room, a gracious glass door—chained shut—led onto a sunny terrace. Empty holes in each of the other two walls had clearly once held doors, now long gone, and through one of the openings, Korsa saw a grand carved bed. The bedcovers looked like the same coarse cloth as those on the cots.

"I've been here before," Korsa said.

But Florence was already moving toward the other room, so Korsa and Liam did, too. Inside was another ornate bed, but now Korsa could see two more cots squeezed in with it. Off to the side was a tiny room holding a third cot, and barely big enough for it.

"This must be where the women sleep," Liam said, softly. His eyes darted away and back as he tried not to look too closely at the garments that hung from hooks here, too.

Florence went straight to a narrow table jammed up against a window. There was a washstand here, too, as well as an assortment of hairbrushes and cosmetics. She stared down at the table as if it wasn't what she'd expected to see. Then, abruptly, she dropped onto her knees, and burrowed beneath the grand bed.

Liam's brow furrowed, but Korsa found himself drawn back into the main room, to those gracious glass doors. The handles were solid brass and the glass had a decorative bevel. Out the window, in the distance, he could see the Wall, and the ivy that covered it, and the dense thickets of shrubbery at its base. This room had not been built for a servant. Korsa realized that this was the place where he'd first met Theron, the place the Highfaller called the parlor. It had been stripped of everything of comfort or value that would fit through the doors, but this is where Theron had lived. It was too easy to think of the places he saw in the *kagirh*-space as places apart from the real, actual House, but they weren't. Theron wasn't. He had slept in that room, and stood on that terrace. He had been alive once. In Korsa's old *kagirh*, everything was as real as everything else. *Kagirh*, there, was merely another way of speaking and being. But whatever was happening here in the House was something different. Something sadder.

Florence emerged from the bedroom with dust in her hair, a burlap sack in her hands, and Liam a few steps behind. "She found what she was looking for," he said. "It was in that bag, under the bed." As he spoke, Florence marched back out of the room without so much as a glance back. As Korsa and Liam scrambled after her, Liam said, "What do you think's in that bag, Chief?"

"Tools," Korsa said. "Theron's tools."

Liam looked confused. "Who's Theron?" he said, but Florence was already gone, and Korsa followed her.

In the workshop, Florence picked up her box of scraps and dumped the bag holding the tools on top of it. Then she carried the whole dusty, clanking mess back up the stairs into the tower. Korsa sat on the settee, watching her pull knobs and gears out of the box and wiping them carefully with her not-particularly-clean skirt before fitting them into a device that looked exactly like the one she'd built in *kagirh*, as seamlessly as if she were referring to a diagram. The colored-glass window above her head shone. Korsa decided that he would close his eyes for a moment, and naturally fell asleep.

At some later point—not enough later, from the hot, gritty feeling of his eyeballs—Florence shook him awake. It took him a moment to see the fully assembled not-quite-a-telescope against the colored window, and a moment more to find his words. "You're finished," he said to her.

She held up a vial of the mind-herb. He could see that she held another in her own hand. Both were uncorked.

Korsa groaned. "I need more sleep."

She shook him again, more insistently.

"All right, all right," he said, and grudgingly sat up. Among his own people, he could slip into *kagirh* as easily as he'd slipped into sleep, but doing it here felt like pushing himself into a crowded room full of people who refused to move. He wondered if people in Highfall had ever heard of coffee. The elixir in the vial was a poor substitute, but in a moment they were back in the purple maelstrom, where Florence's outline only grew the slightest bit hazy before she grabbed a wad of purple. Just as she did, Theron appeared.

"Is it a telescope?" he said, puzzling over the device Florence had built against the window.

"Other direction," she said. "Not out, but in."

Gripping the thread of purple that kept her solid in one hand, Florence moved something in the tracery of the window with the other. A lever popped out. When she pulled it, a panel of glass sprang open, and she slid the device neatly through the open space, into whatever strange sort of *outside* existed beyond. Tracing a path down the device with her finger, she said, "Collects the power from out there, pulls it in, focuses it down and—" her small finger, grubby even here, moved along the lead between the panes of colored glass "—this way. Into the stone, I guess. But I made some alterations. We're going to use it backward. Tower is full of purple stuff, right? So this pulls the purple stuff out of the stone, and into us. So we can stay."

Theron, obviously intrigued, moved closer. "How?"

Florence turned a knob, then another knob, and then twisted the parts of the device gently. The tower trembled slightly under their feet, as if somebody were slamming a door in another room, but the slam lasted seconds instead of an instant. A power that could make solid stone tremble was a power to be wary of. Korsa couldn't help stepping back, toward the stairs. Theron didn't bother—he was already dead, after all—and, in fact, he nodded.

"The tower didn't like that," he said.

"The tower," Florence said, "is a tower."

As they watched, the tip of the device—where one would put one's eye, if it really was a telescope—began to shine, and expand, like a drop of water falling from a leaf. But instead of water-clear, the drop was the same sickly purple as the webbing that filled the other layer of the tower. It was also brilliant, like fire.

Florence put out her hand. The drop fell into her palm. For an instant it rested there, like a jewel. Then it sank in. She let go of the purple wad. Her outline stayed sharp and distinct. "There," she said. "Shall we bring the others up now?"

The thirteen-fourteens accepted the purple—and Theron—without question, and no little excitement. It wasn't quite the *kagirh* that Korsa had told them about, but even the ones who had trouble walking could now travel wherever they wanted in the House, simply by following the purple threads. The tower filled with a faint hum as they shouted excitedly to each other about the things they'd found. The gardens, the catacombs, the food. Ida raved about a room made entirely of glass, and Jesse kept them all up-to-date on what was cooking in the enormous kitchen. When Korsa touched the web, he still felt that jolt of too-many-too-much that he had before, but this time, the thirteen-fourteens were among the multitudes. It was like recognizing a specific voice in a crowd of singers.

"This isn't exactly what the Seneschal wanted," Korsa said to Theron. "You know him better than I do. Will this satisfy him?"

"Florence and the others are all linked to the purple," Theron said. "I don't know if it will work outside the tower, and eventually the Seneschal is going to want to test that. But in the meantime, they'll be able to communicate with each other, even if it's not exactly how Gavin and Judah did it."

"How did Gavin and Judah do it?"

Ida flashed into existence, grinned at them brilliantly, and vanished again. Korsa noticed that she had not created legs for herself. Theron smiled, bleakly. "Pain. When one of them was hurt, the other was. The Seneschal tested it extensively. Knives. Acid. Hot coals."

"That's horrible." Korsa shook his head. "It should not be this way. *Kagirh* should be easy, natural. And once you know, inescapably, that other people feel things just as strongly as you do—"

He stopped, unable to say any more. Everything that had happened since he'd met Theron had distracted him from the sadness, but now it slid back down onto him, suffocating and bleak. Raghri and Giorsa, Faolaru and Meita. Five fingers on a hand, five members of a *kagirh*. Together, a fist.

"You're missing your friends," Theron said. "I miss mine, too."

Korsa forced a smile and said, "If it helps at all, I think your brother has managed to escape. The Seneschal said he—how did he put it?—*lost access* to him."

Theron looked up sharply. "What does that mean? And what about Elly?"

"I don't know. A lot of what he has told me makes no sense. He said the other woman, Judah, jumped from a tower—this tower, I suppose—" Theron's eyes widened "—but he still seems to think she is alive. He is still looking for her. All of this, what I am doing with the thirteen-fourteens, is in case he doesn't find her."

Theron let out a low whistle. "Jumped from the tower, eh? That's impressive."

Confused, Korsa said, "You are not concerned about her?"

A wry smile twisted Theron's thin lips. "Always. Chaos follows Jude wherever she goes. But if you mean am I concerned that she's dead, no." He gestured around him. "This purple stuff is bound into her as much as it is me. She's very much alive. She's just not here."

"How do you know?"

"How do I know anything?" Theron lifted his hands and dropped them again. "None of this makes any logical sense. For instance, I'm dead. But I can feel her, that's all. And I would very much like to know how she pulled off that jumping trick." Theron chewed his lip, his brow furrowed, and Korsa had again that sense of unseen motion as the young man's mind considered. "I'll tell you one thing I do know," he finally said. "I don't think the Seneschal is the only one looking for her. And I don't think any of the people looking for her should find her, including him."

"I don't know what we can do about that," said Korsa, and Theron said, "Neither do I. But I'm thinking."

That night, back in the reality of the workshop, the young people picked at their food—even Jesse, who generally ate twice his share and anything the others didn't want, as well. The thirteen-fourteens always ate well. Korsa was concerned. "Do you still feel ill?" he said, to anyone who would answer. "Is it from the elixir?"

At first, nobody responded. Then Ida said, "No. It feels pretty terrible to come out, but my stomach's all right now." Liam and Jesse murmured unenthusiastic assent. But something hovered over the table, threatening and dour. Korsa waited for it to fall.

Sure enough, not more than a few breaths had passed before Liam threw down the crust of bread he was gradually tearing to pieces and said, "They barely feed the workers who live in the barracks. That's what I'm thinking about. This is a feast compared to what they get. They work so hard and they're so hungry."

"And scared," Jesse said. "The guards don't care if they get hurt or sick. At least in the orphan house, they let you stay in bed when you were sick."

"What about the boys and girls who work on the pleasure side?" Ida said. "You know what they go through? What happens to them, there? Some of them are sick, too. They get to see a magus, at least, but he's—" She shuddered.

"Some of them are our age," Liam said, barely audible.

Florence had brought a piece of metal to the table, and was carefully turning it over and over next to her untouched plate. But Korsa knew she was listening.

"Why is everything horrible?" Ida said, and Korsa was shocked to see that her eyes were filled with tears. "The orphan house was horrible. The streets are horrible. This entire place is horrible, except for us. What's the point of living? So we can experience more horribleness?"

"The point is," Korsa said, gently, "to try to make it less horrible."

"How? We're prisoners, too," Jesse said, and there was a murmur of agreement. All of those eyes turned to Korsa, waiting for him to answer. Korsa was not sure what to say. Theron was right: they could only fake the bond for so long, and when the Seneschal figured out that it was not the bond he wanted, it would not end well for any of them. He did not want the thirteen-fourteens to suffer—but the prisoners suffered, the pleasure-women and men suffered, the orphans still in the orphan house suffered. And what was there to do about any of it? What solution was there, to this unsolvable problem?

"Your minds are not prisoners," Korsa said. "The Seneschal is not a wise man. He thinks that *kagirh* is merely about communication. It's not about talking. It's not even about seeing. It's about knowing."

Ida snuffled. "I wish I didn't know about those girls. I knew about brothels. But I didn't—know."

"Who wants to know something so awful?" Liam said. Korsa could feel the unhappiness coming off him in sharp, dangerous spikes. "But now we do, don't we? So far as I can see, we either figure out how to live with the knowing or we do something about it."

"What can we do?" Jesse said, again. "Look at us. We can't even do the worst of the factory work, can we? Can't even crawl on the floor picking up scraps."

Ida wheeled on him. "Do you want to, Jesse? Do you want to crawl on the floor picking up scraps? Because that's what living with this will feel like to me."

"Yeah, well, what's your suggestion?" Jesse said.

"Burn this nasty place down to the ground," Ida said, and began to cry.

"It's stone," Liam said, morosely. "Stone doesn't burn."

Florence slammed her hand down on the table. The plates and bowls jumped with the force of it, and all of the thirteen-fourteens turned to stare at her, shocked into silence. Her lips were pressed tightly together and her eyes swept around the table—not stopping long enough on any one person to make anything like eye contact, but close enough.

Korsa waited.

Ida raised her head. Her face was still covered in tears, her nose dripping and her lip trembling. But her eyes were bright. "We can move through stone," she said, and Florence smiled triumphantly.

TWENTY-ONE

"DON'T TALK, AND DON'T LAG BEHIND," SABA TOLD Bindy before they left New Highfall, and then glared at the magus. "Her food comes out of your share, Nathaniel."

"I brought my own food," Bindy said, and Saba said, "I said, don't talk."

At the Harteswell Gate, Saba bought a map from a trader and three places on a paper bale wagon with real money, not scrip. He rode on the seat with the wagon driver, and in no time at all they were passing the driver's flask back and forth, and Saba was making the man laugh. Bindy was happy in the back, sitting next to the magus. The paper bales were solid as bricks and not very comfortable to sit on, but as far as she was concerned, the farther she was away from Saba, the better.

Despite the circumstances of her departure, Bindy couldn't help but feel a sizzle of excitement as they passed through the gate. She remembered the giant map on the warehouse warren roof, all of Highfall drawn out as big as the canvas. On Saba's map, that massive city, with its streets and alleys and factories and the House and a whole entire *river*, all fit inside one tiny dot. She'd never even seen the Steel District on the other side of Highfall, and now she was going all the way to Tiernan.

On the western side of the road, as the paper wagon left the city, Bindy saw a shantytown. People there lived in huts made of all sorts of thrown-away things: planks of splintered wood, patched-together pieces of burlap and canvas, even old bones. She knew these shantytowns existed—it was where you went when you were too poor for even Brakeside—but it was one thing to know about them and another to smell the cooking fires and latrines, to see the thin children staring with big, hollow eyes at the passing cart. Bindy thought she knew poverty, but what she knew was nothing like this. Then she remembered that more than one alley in Brakeside was filled with shacks like these, and that she didn't like to go there because it was depressing and scary. And that made her feel guilty, because there were probably children there, too, and not looking at them didn't keep them from existing.

Past the magus, the other side of the road was filled, as if by agreement, with sturdy, serviceable tents. The people lolling outside them had all sorts of colors of skin and hair and eyes. Some wore ordinary Highfall clothes, but some wore beautiful costumes that Bindy had never seen before. For that matter, some wore plain costumes she'd never seen before, and she found those just as wonderful. She was fascinated and terrified by all of the difference that apparently existed in the world, and all of the people who lived lives totally unlike hers, with completely different histories.

"They're traders," the magus said, as they swayed and rolled with the cart. "Nothing to be afraid of."

"I'm not," she said.

"You look a little afraid," he said, very gently.

421

Bindy shook her head. "The world is big, isn't it, magus?"

"The world is very big." He sighed. "It's also very small."

That didn't make much sense to Bindy. She pondered it, off and on, the whole of that first day, as they left the city behind. She kept expecting them to enter the wilderness, which she imagined as a dark place with trees and ferocious beasts waiting to eat her, but nothing like that appeared. They passed midden heaps, livestock markets, a very large blacksmithery, and the barracks where the standing army was stationed. They passed several wide empty patches in various states of weediness, which the magus said were mass graves. She'd known that poor people were taken outside the city to be buried, but she hadn't imagined those graves to be so barren, or so lonely, or so huge. There were no markers, no sign at all to indicate which people's bones rested there. In the city, the metalworkers sold grave tokens made of small bits of scrap. An expensive one might have the dead person's name engraved on it in fancy script, but the cheapest ones were made of lead, which was soft enough to scratch a name in on your own. Bindy's mother had lost four children in infancy. Some people waited a year to name their children, to make sure they'd live, and just called them *baby* before that, but Nora named all of her children. Bindy remembered watching quietly as her mother scratched a name on a token and tucked it into the clean wrapper around the tiny body. (That baby's name had been Asa. Bindy didn't even remember if Asa was a boy or a girl.) Bindy had thought the markers were simply a nice thing to do but now she understood. Even when the places where her lost brothers and sisters lay became so overgrown they were forgotten, deep under the grass and weeds, each of them would have their name. Hundreds and hundreds of years from now, if a great storm washed the grave open again, they would still have their names.

Eventually the outbuildings of Highfall were replaced by small farms that grew hops and grapes and sheep and cattle and geese. These, too, Bindy found fascinating, having never seen a lot of these foodstuffs in their natural state. This time of year, there were a few baby animals, too, tiny wobbly sheep and skinny baby cows, and she found these as delightful as she'd found the graves sobering. They made even the magus smile. Saba, up front, didn't notice. He was entertaining the driver, telling stories that probably weren't true, in which he always seemed to play the role of clever trickster. The two men passed the flask back and forth until it was empty. Sometimes one of them held the reins while the other stood up and pissed over the edge of the wagon. They never offered to stop so that Bindy could relieve herself. She stopped drinking from the water flask she'd brought, to be on the safe side, but by the time they stopped for lunch, she badly needed to go. So she went to the far side of the wagon. She would have liked a little more of a boundary between herself and the two drunk men, but they barely seemed to notice her. The farms had been replaced by flat rolling hills. She and the magus ate the bread Bindy had brought from Winder's Alley. He had dried meat and she had cheese and between the two of them they managed to make a decent lunch.

Then it was back on the wagon, the gentle sway, the sound of the horses' hooves against the dirt road. Saba and the driver eventually shut up, for which Bindy was eternally grateful. Once she glanced up at them and saw they were both asleep, the reins slack in the driver's hands. She was alarmed, but the magus said the horses knew the way and he must have been right, because they kept plodding along as if nothing had changed.

It was winding toward evening when they came to an inn. Saba told the innkeeper that his servants—Bindy and the magus—could sleep in the stable. Bindy didn't mind. The stable was quiet except for the warm snuffling of the horses, and the moment she sat down in the straw a barn cat jumped into her lap, purring.

"Friendly for a mouser," the magus said, observing.

"She's practically a baby," Bindy said. Because the cat had all of its grown-up teeth, but was still kitten-fluffy. "She hasn't learned to be afraid of people yet. Living out here with nobody to cuddle her or be nice to her, she'll be wild in another few months."

"Maybe not." The magus lay back in the straw. "Some cats are sweet-tempered."

Unexpectedly, Bindy felt her eyes well up with tears. "Well, I hope she's not sweet-tempered. I hope she learns to stay away from people, so they don't hurt her." She picked the cat up and pressed her nose into the soft fur, hoping to hide the tears from the magus.

But he knew better. "I'm sorry, Bindy," he said, quietly.

She sniffled, wiped her nose, and let the squirming cat go. "Why are we here, magus? Why do you do whatever that awful Saba tells you? He's not even nice."

He sighed, and sat up again. "He's what my people call a compeller, which is somebody who makes other people do their bidding. Forcing people to do things is his life's work."

There weren't a lot of kind compellers, Bindy guessed. "But you don't have to do what he says. There's nobody to *make* you."

The magus was silent for a long time. When the little cat crawled into his lap, he scratched it under the chin. Finally he said, "It's not only a figure of speech, Bindy. There used to be a power in the world that most people could use, a little bit—to make crops grow faster, or to make a child be healthier. Some people could do more. Enough so that the Lord of the City—one of Elban's ancestors—became afraid of it and gathered his scholars together to try to control it. And they succeeded."

He stopped, then. Perhaps to see how she'd react. And how would she react? It seemed preposterous, like the peasants who came to the city and burned colored candles for luck or prosperity. Nora had always scoffed at such people. If Bindy had heard her say it once, she'd heard it a hundred times: burning a candle won't make the world other than what it is.

But Bindy had heard other things, too. "My gran used to say, every time something bad happened, 'Life used to be easier,'" she said. "Every old person I've ever known has said it. I always thought it was just—sweet memory."

"Part of it, sure. The time I was talking about was so long ago that even your grandmother wasn't alive yet. But life really was easier, before the power was bound. Maybe the stories were passed down to her."

"But if it was that long ago, you weren't alive, either."

"My mother knew it from her mother, and she knew it from hers. All the people I grew up with knew it—the people I came from. Who were also the people Saba came from, and Charles. Do you remember Charles?"

Charles was the drop addict who'd killed himself at the magus's kitchen table. Bindy nodded. "So Saba wasn't lying about being a childhood friend?"

The magus smiled bleakly. "Oh, he was. I might have met him once—there aren't that many of us—but we weren't anything like friends. I'm not sure we would have been friends even if we had known each other. Most compellers show their talent early. They're trained young, and separately from other Workers."

"What's a Worker?" she said, trying the word out in her

mouth the way he said it. Not like a factory worker. Something different. The little cat was asleep, still purring faintly.

The magus hesitated for a moment. "Do you know about how Alva sells some of her pies for half price?"

She wished he hadn't mentioned the pies. All the innkeeper had sent was porridge without salt. Alva's pies were very delicious and very far away. "Sure. When the dough is too thin, they leak, so there's not as much filling. Magus, this conversation is hurting my stomach."

He smiled. "Exactly. The dough gets thin in places, and the filling is under pressure, and it breaks through. The same thing happened with the power that the scholars bound. I don't know why it landed in us, so far away. The first Worker was a man named John Slonim, and he could actually create things from the power, but nobody else has ever been able to. Maybe there was something special about him, and he broke through the crust enough for the rest of us to use the power. We call it the Work. I was always told that it's nothing compared to what the power used to be, but it seems strong enough to me. Some people use it to send messages, or share experiences. My mother used it to heal people with broken minds."

"That sounds useful," Bindy said. But cautiously.

The magus was still staring down at the kitten, drawing the little tail out gently through his fingers and letting it curl back. "It's like anything. It's a tool. After you pulled me out of the Brake, Saba cut my arm, didn't he? Drew a symbol in my blood, and then went sort of blank for a minute?" Bindy winced, not liking to remember, but nodded. "Well, that was Work. He used it to bring me back to myself." The soft tail twined through his fingers. The kitten purred. The magus's voice grew bitter. "He also used it to put a chain around my neck, and spurs to my sides. If I balk, or try to fight him, the pain is—bad. But the worst part is that he doesn't just make me obey him. He makes me want to obey him."

He picked up the kitten, handed it to Bindy with a sigh, and lay back down. She pressed the little animal to her chest, feeling faintly sick. "But you know it's only a trick. You don't really want to obey him."

"If I stuck my head under water, my lungs would want to breathe even though there was no air. Eventually I wouldn't be able to fight it. That's what being compelled is like. You know you'll die if you inhale, but you have no choice."

It all sounded absurd. It also made a terrible kind of sense. "If you're a Worker, too, can't you undo what he did?"

"It's not that simple," the magus said. "Every Worker maintains a connection to every other person they've Worked with. We pull strength from each other. Everyone I Worked most closely with is dead. I'm not strong enough to fight him. I'll be lucky if I survive."

The kitten squirmed in Bindy's arm. It smelled like dust and cat pee. She let it go. They watched it pad off into the darkness, and then the magus said, "I wish you'd go back to the city, Bindy. I never wanted you to be involved in this."

"Well, too late," Bindy said. "Is the Foundling in Tiernan?"

"I don't know." The magus's expression reminded her of Ma's on those rare occasions when she talked about Mairead's father, anger so intermingled with wounded love that the two emotions were one and the same. "But Elban's heir is. He can help us find her, maybe."

"Lord Gavin?" Although he wasn't lord of anything, anymore. "How?"

"Gavin and Judah are special." The magus managed a wan smile. "It's difficult to explain."

"Well, I think you're special," Bindy said.

His smile warmed a bit. "You've always had an outsized

opinion of me, Bindy. I'm not special at all. I just looked okay with my hair bleached, and I was a good enough healer to earn my keep."

"You are an excellent healer," Bindy said, surprised at the force of her own anger. "You saved Canty when he was sun-starved. You've saved lots of people."

"Not my mother, or Charles, or Derie." The magus leaned over, then, and turned the lantern down so that only a tiny flicker remained. "Please don't ask any more questions. I've probably already told you too much. You need to slip away at the first possible opportunity. You can still walk back to the city from here, even if it'll take a while."

In the hay-scented darkness, Bindy heard rustling. "I won't leave you," she said, doggedly.

"I'm sorry to hear that," he said.

In the morning, Saba was hungover, and mean. They were barely awake when he hurried them into the back of another wagon. As before, he sat up front. As before, he shared a flask with the driver. This wagon had recently held chickens and still held their feathers and droppings. It smelled terrible and by the end of the day, so did Bindy and the magus. The inn they stopped at that night was shabbier than the first, but it still had a stable. Bindy and the magus were shooed off to sleep there again. There were a few other servants sleeping in the hay that night, who gave them a little ribbing about their smell but also gave them fresh bread and cheese and apples. In the morning, Bindy and the two other women managed to sneak out to the pump for a wash before the rest of the inn was awake.

A week passed this way. Merchant wagons with varying degrees of comfort during the day, stables—or, once, a hay-stack—at night. One of the inns had an actual servant's room but it was full of drunken porters so the magus said they should sleep in the stables, anyway. Saba, Bindy was grateful to discover, had very little interest in the two of them now that they were out of the city. He barely spoke to them except to tell them to get into or out of whatever wagon he'd hired. Once, the daughter of one of the innkeepers came out to fetch water from the well and shook her head sympathetically when she heard who Bindy's supposed master was.

"I don't envy you a bit. He's nasty," she said. "If I were you, I'd run away as soon as I got the chance." She gave Bindy a look, then, eyeing Bindy's strong arms. "Come back here, if you want. We could use an extra pair of hands, and my ma and dad are good people."

"Thanks," Bindy said, "but I need to stay with my friend."

"The skinny one?" The girl made a face. "Must be a pretty good friend if he's worth putting up with that Saba for. My ma threatened to take a poker to him if he grabbed at me one more time. Want me to steal you a poker?"

It was a joke. Bindy laughed. It felt like the first time in ages. "I've got my belt knife, and I'm not afraid to use it. I might need to stay with my friend, but I don't owe Saba a damn thing."

But the magus seemed to feel that he owed Saba a great deal. Twice while they were traveling, the Slonimi man came out to the stables in the middle of the night and shook the magus awake, and the magus trailed obediently after him into the darkness without a word. He was sickly, the mornings after those visits, and didn't want to eat until Bindy forced him. She asked him, once, what Saba wanted from him. "The same thing," he said. "Always the same."

"To look for the Foundling?"

"Over and over." From the set of his jaw, she could tell that he didn't want to talk about it, so she didn't ask anything else.

The last place they stayed was less an inn than a waystation, only a small house with a single extra room where travelers could sleep. In the morning there was no wagon ride in the direction Saba wanted to go. Instead, they set off directly into a forest, which to Bindy's eyes—which had never seen a forest—was incredibly thick and dark, exactly like her imaginings of what a wilderness would be. Saba's map showed no roads through it, but he said as long as they traveled due west they'd be fine. Before they left, the magus showed Bindy how to make her things into a pack she could wear on her back, and Saba—his pack already made and strapped to his shoulders—stood by, impatiently criticizing. Bindy and the magus had spent the night in a lean-to where the house normally stored firewood. They were sore, and moved stiffly.

The man who owned the house stood by, as well, looking from Bindy and the magus to the forest and chewing his lip. Bindy could guess what he was thinking. She was thinking it herself. A frail man and a girl barely fourteen, in a forest without even a path? Not a great idea. "You know," the man said, his letters sounding blunted and dull to Bindy's ears, "there's a right good road to Tiernan. Only a week's travel. I'd go that way, if I were you."

"You're not me," Saba said. Bindy noticed he didn't say *us*. "And if we cut through the forest, we'll be there in two days."

"Cut might be the right word," the houseowner said. "There's no path through those woods big enough for anything larger than a deer."

"Good. That means there's nothing larger than a deer that will interfere with us." Saba cast his eyes at the magus and Bindy, who were finally strapped up and ready to travel, and Bindy thought, Nothing except you. You're larger than a deer.

The forest wasn't as bad as Bindy expected. The undergrowth was thickest at the edge, where the sun could reach. Under the trees, there was some growth—ferns and the like—

but it wasn't impassable. On the whole, Bindy would rather have been walking through the woods than riding in the back of a chicken wagon any day. She was fascinated by the curling tips of the ferns, the thick cushions of moss and colorful mats of lichen, and she loved the way the light filtered down through the leaves. The forest felt like a cool dark room in the middle of summer. They crossed several streams and those were lovely, too, the chasing of the current over the rocks and the tiny silver fish that darted through the bubbling water.

Still, her feet grew tired, and so did her back. Saba wasn't a huge believer in rest. At least here, Bindy was able to duck into a bush when she needed to, and still catch up. They ate as they walked, strips of unidentifiable dried meat or hard crackers. Saba had dried fruit but he didn't offer to share it. By the time the light began to dim, she was hungry and exhausted. At times she caught herself thinking of her comfortable bed in Ma's house on Winder's Alley, and wondering why in the world she'd come along on this trip, anyway. But some things that weren't entirely pleasant were worth doing anyway, and when she looked at the magus she knew that this was one of those.

They came to a relatively clear place with a gentle slope. "Right." Saba dropped down onto a thick patch of moss, and began to unlace his boots. "Go to it."

Bindy gave him a belligerent stare. "Go to what?"

Saba looked at her as if she were stupid. "Set up camp. Fire. Water. A hole to shit in."

She scowled at him, and almost argued—he wasn't going to help?—but then the magus touched her arm and said, "Don't worry about it, Bin. I'll show you."

He did. She knew how to make a fire in a stove with good seasoned firewood, but not in the woods with stray sticks. The magus knew how to do everything. He was good at explaining it, too. He showed her how to find the best place for the hole and how to dig it and how to find the driest kindling. He even found a patch of greens, which he said would be good to eat, either stewed or raw.

Back at camp, Saba lay still on the moss, his hat pulled low over his eyes. She and the magus cleared the ground where their fire would go and built a tiny pyramid of kindling. The sulfur matches they used in the city were easier than the magus's flint and steel, but she lit the tinder on her second try. The piece of kindling she lay atop it was too large, though, and the tiny smolder of flame went out.

She looked at the magus in frustration. "It's all right," he said. "Try again."

"By all means, let her try again," Saba said. Nate and Bindy jumped. They hadn't realized he was awake. "It's only twelve hours until the sun comes up. I'm sure we'll be perfectly comfortable sleeping in the cold."

"I'm trying," Bindy said.

"And failing. You're not much use."

A dozen quick retorts leapt to Bindy's mind, but Saba's eyes on her were cruel and contemptuous. She held her tongue.

When the fire was finally lit, Nate boiled water for tea. They dipped the travel bread into it, and that was dinner. The next morning—Bindy's feet still hurt when she woke up—Nate showed her how to strike camp. Cleaning up was something she understood, but she could still feel Saba watching her the entire time. The compeller consulted his compass, pointed their direction, and they were off.

As he had the day before, Saba walked ahead, leaving it to Bindy and the magus to keep up or fall behind. Close to midday, they stopped at a deadfall, where there were fallen trunks big enough to sit on. Nate passed Bindy a piece of dried meat.

She tore off a third of it and gave it back to him. "Bindy," he said, but she said, "I'm smaller. I need less food."

He glared at her, but took the meat. "At some point, we're going to have a conversation about putting yourself first occasionally."

"But not now," she said, with a smile.

"Not now," the magus agreed.

Bindy could feel Saba watching them. The way he was looking at her today made her shudder. "Why give up your own food to fill his stomach?" he said.

"Not that it's your business," she said, "but it was his food to start with."

"And you're eating it because you already gave him all the food you brought." Saba leaned forward. "Why are you so attached to him, Marketside girl?"

Bindy lifted her chin and said, "He's a good man."

Saba laughed. "Trust me, my dear. He's neither." He looked at the magus. "You were paired off before you crossed the Barriers, weren't you? Whatever came of that? I know you're not strong enough to stay in touch, but your old teacher was. Does your line continue or did it die with your mother?"

"It died with her," the magus said, quietly.

Saba grinned. "That must have been a comfort to her in her last moments," he said, and Bindy saw Nate wince.

Later, when they were moving again and Saba was a comfortable distance ahead, Bindy said, "What did he mean, paired off? Were you married, magus?"

He looked uncomfortable, and she felt bad for asking. She was about to say never mind, it was none of her business, but then he said, "My people don't really get married. Bloodlines are very important to us. There was a concern that I might die in Highfall, so they paired me off before I left." He hesitated. His cheeks were pink. "With a woman. I was supposed to leave her with a child. I didn't."

"Oh." Bindy remembered Canty and the other littles, how kind the magus had always been to them. She had little experience of fathers herself, but he would have made a good one. "What was her name?"

He blushed even more deeply, and gave her a weak grin. "I'm afraid I don't remember. It was my first official pairing, and the tradition is to get blind drunk. I'm not sure I'd recognize her if she walked up to me and punched me."

Bindy giggled, at first, because she couldn't imagine the careful, deliberate magus blind drunk. Then she stopped laughing, because even if his last words had sounded like a joke, he was staring at the ground, the corners of his mouth turned down. "It's not always so easy," she said, as gently as she could. "I mean, my ma has a million kids, but we've got three different fathers and I don't even know how many years between us. And Will's ma, Bess Ember, she and her man were together for ten years before she had Will, and he's their only. Sometimes it doesn't happen. Besides," she added, more brightly, "you're young. You have time."

"Except that no Slonimi woman would have him," Saba said. Bindy hadn't noticed him hanging back, or listening to their conversation. "Unless you're volunteering. Girls your age have babies in Highfall. I see it all the time."

The magus's lips grew tight, but Bindy gave Saba a baleful look and said, "Not me. I'm going to be a magus, like Nate."

Saba snorted. "No, you're not. At the very best, you're going to be a factory slave and have a million kids, like your 'ma.' At the worst, you're going to waste your life taking care of this piece of garbage. How much do you have to hold his hand while he makes those drops? You think he'll be able to keep it together enough to do that forever? What skills do you have, for the day when he wakes up drooling? What do you have to sell, Marketside girl?" Mocking her now. He let his eyes wander up and down the length of her. Showed what he knew, because they slid right over the place where she'd hidden her belt knife.

"Stop, Saba," the magus said, with the closest thing to anger she had ever heard from him. "She's a child."

Saba turned around and, before Bindy even knew what was happening, punched the magus in the nose. The magus cried out and fell backward, holding a hand to his nose, streams of blood already running down his chin.

"There," Saba said to Bindy. "Heal that, little magus."

That night, Bindy went to sleep with one hand on her belt knife. When the magus shook her gently awake, he was lucky she didn't stab him. He put his fingers to his lips and indicated that she should follow, so she shook out her boots and slid her aching feet back into them. He had taken Saba's lantern, she saw by moonlight, but he didn't light it until they were well away from camp, near the edge of the stream where she'd fetched water for their tea the evening before. Then he brushed the leaves away from the soft dirt next to the stream, and picked up a stick. In the soft mud, he drew a complicated sort of swirl, with three protrusions like leafless branches. "This is a sigil," he said, quietly. "This is how we connect with each other, in the Work. Everybody has their own. This one is mine. Can you draw it?"

He held the stick out to her. She took it—wary, because he was talking about Work-with-a-big-W—and, carefully, made a near-perfect copy of the mark in the mud next to the first.

The magus nodded. "Good. Practice that. Remember it." He rolled up his left sleeve, and held out his arm next to the lantern, showing her again the neat lines of scars (and some that were newer, and less neat). "The Work lives in the blood," he said. "One of the reasons we're so damned obsessed with bloodlines, I guess. You'll have to make a little cut, like these. You only need enough blood to draw my sigil. It's best done on a mirror, but I don't have one."

Bindy frowned. "Magus—"

He held up a hand. "I don't know if you can do it, Bindy. Derie said you didn't have any power. I can't tell. I've been in Highfall too long, and I'm too broken." He sighed. "I used to be able to feel people with power. We used to go village to village, seeking them out. I wish you'd known me when I was good, Bindy."

"You're still good," Bindy said, loyally. "But, magus—why, all of this?"

"Because I don't trust Saba," he said. "And if something happens—it's probably overly optimistic to believe that he'll leave enough of me to save, but I'd like someone around who can at least try. I don't even know if this will work. I have to admit, I'm making it up as I go, a bit."

She shook her head. "I don't know," she said. "I don't know if I can."

He smiled. It was the saddest smile she'd ever seen. "I understand. But will you draw the sigil again for me? Just once or twice."

In the morning she was tired, but she would have been tired anyway. Saba splashed water on his face, his sleeves rolled up, and she noticed that his arms bore the same scars that the magus's did. One time, Canty had fallen on a broken bottle and a piece of glass had stuck in his knee; Ma had been at work, working the long shift and not due home for two more days. So Mairead had held Canty tight, and Bindy had taken her knife, made a cut in that precious little knee she loved so much, and oh, how he'd screamed. But she'd done it anyway, because she loved her little brother, and wanted to help him.

But to cut the magus—to draw shapes in his blood—thinking about it made her shudder.

Late in the day, they came upon a bush thick with dark red berries. The magus said they were called thawberries, because they came after the thaw, and were safe to eat. They tasted like pine resin, but after so many days of stale bread and meat and cheese, they were delicious. Soon after, they made camp at a place where a jagged boulder jutted up through the soft ground, ancient broken-away pieces of it littering the clearing like crumbs. Saba said, "Marketside. Go find us more of those berries," and threw her his hat. It smelled like the oil he put in his hair.

She glanced at the magus, who nodded.

Suddenly Saba grabbed her arm and shook her, roughly enough to make her teeth click together. "When I tell you to do something, do it," he said. "Look at that waste for permission again and it'll be the last time you do, I promise."

Bindy glanced at his arm as if it were a dead frog and gave him her coldest glare. "Try it. I've held my own against bigger men than you."

But that only got her a sly, nasty smile. "Have you, now?"

Bindy felt her cheeks grow hot, and hated it. She jerked away from him, clenched his hat between her fists, and stomped back toward the berry bushes.

The heat in her face soon faded, but her temper didn't. She was tired of the woods, tired of pushing bracken out of the way and swatting at midges. The next thawberry bush she found was buzzing with bees, and once she'd put a few berries into the hat, the hat was, too. Her fingers were sticky and filthy and what she wouldn't give for a room with a door she could close to keep the bugs out. And a chair to sit on. And a table to eat at. And a pitcher of clean water to wash in.

At least Saba's hat would be sticky with berry juice, too. Served him right. She may or may not have squeezed the hat a bit as she returned to camp, to let more juices free. "Here are your stupid berries," she said, coming into the clearing, and then froze.

Saba and the magus sat cross-legged on the ground. Their backs were straight but their eyes stared, unseeing, at nothing. Bindy's first thought was the berries hadn't been safe after all, and this was some kind of poisoning, but then she stepped closer and saw that both men had one sleeve rolled up. Saba's slack fingers held a small silver knife and both of their forearms were smeared with blood.

And, indeed, there in the blood on the magus's arm, she saw a drawn symbol. It didn't look at first glance like the one he'd taught her the night before, but when she looked closer she saw the three leafless branches, just where she remembered them being. Another sigil had been drawn on top of it, that was all.

Saba's body was still, even peaceful. But the magus was trembling, his fists clenching and unclenching. Tears spilled out of his unseeing eyes and his lips were working, as if he were trying to speak. Abruptly his neck arced back, pain and grief written on his face. "Magus," Bindy said, reaching out— but as soon as the moment had come, it was gone. The magus's head fell forward again.

This must be the Work. It was frightening. Was it like sleepwalking, and she shouldn't wake him? Would it hurt him if she tried to shake him? The magus's neck arced again and she realized it was a pattern: the grimace of pain and grief twisted his face, his neck straightened, his head fell forward, the grimace faded. Something bad was happening to him, and it was happening over and over again.

I'd like someone around who can at least try.

Her hand was shaking as she reached for the magus's arm. Touching the damp, sticky blood made her flinch, she couldn't help it. But then she steeled herself, and quickly drew the sigil he'd taught her. Right on top of Saba's. Obliterating it like she wished she could obliterate Saba himself. Take that, you nasty man.

Nate gasped, a long painful tearing at the air. His staring eyes found her, and saw her, and he began to sob. "My mother," he said. Then he leaned over, and vomited next to the fire.

Blood made Bindy nervous, but vomit didn't bother her in the least. She grabbed the water skin and knelt next to him, on the other side from the puddle of sick, and pushed back his too-dark hair. "How can I help, magus?" she said, softly.

A grubby hand reached out and grabbed Nate's arm. Saba. He stared down at the sigil Bindy had drawn. "Very clever," he said, dark and—of course—nasty. "The waste has been teaching you tricks. But it doesn't matter. I can see inside you, you stupid girl. You have no power. None." He stood. "You know what we Slonimi call people with no power?"

Bindy was angry. She would not be intimidated. She would not be afraid. She stood up, planted her fists on her hips. "What?" she said, challenging.

Saba bared his teeth in a grin. "Nothing. We call them nothing, because they don't matter." With contempt, he added, "You think you can save him with a sigil? Poor sweet, dumb Marketside."

The magus cried out. He was hunched over, his fists clenched, sweat standing out in beads on his forehead. "Stop it," Bindy said. "Stop hurting him."

"Me? I'm just standing here," Saba said. "Watch your friend, nothing girl."

And Bindy did watch, horrified, as Nate reached out, first one hand and then the other, and began to crawl. It looked almost as if he were being dragged. Bindy rushed to his side, crouched down next to him, tried to pull him up. He brushed her off and kept crawling. All the way to the edge of the clearing, to a place where the ridge of rock jutted out of the ground. And then, before Bindy could stop him, he slammed his forehead against it. Bindy screamed.

"Again?" Saba said, conversationally. "All right."

The magus's head lifted, one whole side of it covered with blood. Then down it came, back on the jagged edge of the ridge, and Bindy cried out, "Stop it!"

"Stop what?" Saba said. "I'm not doing anything. If I were doing something, nothing girl, it would look like this." Bindy scrambled back, terrified, as Saba pulled back a leg and kicked the magus in the ribs. The impact was fierce enough to make the magus twist backward onto his back. "Or this." Saba grabbed the magus by the collar, lifted him up, and hit him with a closed fist.

"Stop," Bindy said. Her teeth were clenched.

But Saba didn't stop. He punched the magus again, laughed, then dropped him to the dirt and kicked him. The magus's head lolled.

Bindy had seen too many bad things happen to too many people she cared about. She'd stood by, powerless, as her father died of plague, as Kate and Mairead and Canty's father drank himself to death, as Ma grew wan and gray from long shifts and there was no question at all of the littles going to school because it was all they could do to put decent food in their stomachs. Rina was lost. Darid was consumed with anger. She could do nothing about any of this.

But she would not stand here and watch the magus be beaten to death. She would not.

Enough.

She bent down and picked up the biggest rock she saw. Big enough that when she held one side of it in each fist, there was space for another fist again in the middle. It was heavy but she could hold it. She was strong. She could carry it. She could lift it, raise it high over her head.

Saba's laughter slashed the air in the clearing, broke the natural calm of the place in a thousand ugly pieces.

Belinda Dovetail brought the rock down on the back of his head, as hard as she could. He collapsed and she hit him again. His hands twitched. His legs kicked.

Then he was still.

"I'm not nothing," she spat down at him, and only realized when her breath hitched that she was weeping. Her hands were splattered with blood. "You're nothing."

She heard a low, desperate gurgle, and looked up. The magus was writhing in the dirt, almost the same way Saba had. She dropped the rock and ran to his side—again! Again and again and again. Blood covered his face. Could she draw the sigil anywhere? Did it need to be his wrist? She took his head in the crook of her arm. Her poor magus. His cheek was swollen, one of his eyes nearly closed. The blood came from a nasty cut above one of his eyes. He had feared that there would be nothing left of him to save. He had wanted someone around who could try.

She wiped her hand on her skirt, trying to get the last traces of Saba's blood off so none of it mixed with the magus's. His body kept bucking and twisting but she managed to hold his head still enough that she could draw the sigil on his cheek. The complicated swirl. The three leafless branches.

He went limp in her arms. She stared down at him, vision blurred with tears. Was she too late? Was she nothing, after all?

Then his eyes opened—at least, the one that wasn't swollen shut did—and in them she saw a clarity that had been missing since long before the prison. He sat up, looked around the clearing. His eyes came to rest on Saba's crumpled body. Bindy couldn't speak. She couldn't breathe.

Then he stood and went to Saba. He moved slowly, in obvious pain. Bindy expected him to say something about the state of Saba's head, but the magus only leaned down and put a finger against Saba's throat. "Still alive," he said.

Bindy let out a long breath. She could probably have spoken again, too, but she didn't know what to say. The magus pulled up Saba's sleeve, the side the compeller hadn't cut open. On his wrist was a tooled leather cuff that fastened with buckles. The magus undid the buckles, and put the cuff around his own wrist. "What's that, magus?" she managed to say, finally.

"A springknife. Every Slonimi man wears one. I used to, as well. Long gone, now. I haven't seen it since before prison." He flexed his wrist, and a silver blade leapt out of the casing, next to his palm. Then he looked back at Saba.

"Leave him, magus," Bindy said. "Let's go before he wakes up. We still have a little light."

"One second," Nate said, in that flat voice she had never heard from him before, and buried the knife in Saba's throat.

Saba had yelled at Bindy more than once for making noise as she walked. Now she dropped her feet in each step as loudly as she could, because she would rather hear the crunch of her feet on dead leaves than remember the crunch of the rock against Saba's skull. She'd had no choice. She knew she'd had no choice. Her legs burned. The crunch of rock on skull reverberated inside her own brain. She was tired. She was so tired.

The light turned golden, then silver. The magus's hurt eye was swollen, his breathing labored. Still, they walked. They should stop, Bindy thought, more than once. Stop and make a fire and wrap the magus's chest, where he kept clutching it, and rest. She was beginning to feel faint with stress and fatigue. Blindly she followed the magus, who himself was half-blind, but she didn't care. She would crunch these leaves instead of crunching Saba's head and when somebody finally told her she could stop, she would be so exhausted she would drop right where she stood and she would not see him in her dreams. Perhaps this whole nightmarish trip was a dream. Perhaps she would wake in her small warm bed in her ma's house, grateful for her life, for her brothers and her sisters and Ma and Marketside and all the nice, ordinary work that had to be done. And she could forget all of this, nasty Saba who told her she was nothing and the sigils and the way the magus writhed on the forest floor and the crunch of rock on skull—

The magus put his arm out in front of her. She stopped, looking at him blearily. He seemed to be listening. She listened, too, but she heard nothing except the crunch of rock on skull and a few evening birds calling their own names into the silvering light.

No. Wait. She did hear something. Rocks falling against each other? Rocks being dumped out of a bucket? Rocks hitting skulls?

With no warning, Nate bolted forward. She was surprised he could run like that, hurt as he was. The brush was getting thick again, too. She remembered what he'd said, that the brush in forests only grew at the edges where the light could get through. But there was no light in the direction they went, after she gathered what little strength she had and ran after him. In fact, it seemed darker and darker. Still he ran, and the rocky sound grew louder, and then all at once he vanished. "Magus!" she cried, and found the strength, somehow, to run even more—

—and crashed through a thick curtain of ivy that hung at the forest's edge to find herself on a road. An actual road, wide and well paved and full of people on horses, and that was when she realized that the rock-on-rock sound had actually been steel-shod hoof on road. She saw flags and banners and the glint of weapons. She saw the magus, throwing himself down on his knees in front of the first riders.

And, as Bindy watched, one of those riders jumped down from his horse, sword already in hand before his boots touched the ground. In hand and drawn and raised. Face contorted in rage. About to strike.

She screamed and hurled herself forward, into the slim space between the magus and the shining blade, and all she was thinking was, not now, not after all this. She threw herself over the magus like a blanket, wrapped her arms around him. The swordsman stared at her out of hollow, burning eyes. She had never met him before in her life but he hated her and he hated the magus and they were about to die, here, on his sword.

Oh, Ma, she thought. I'm so sorry.

But another of the riders leapt down, too—a woman, incredibly, despite the trousers and coat she wore, a woman with long loose blond hair and a scar on her cheek, and she was gripping the swordsman's upraised arm. Holding him back. Stopping him. "Gavin," she was saying. "Gavin, no."

And Bindy realized that the man standing over her was the great Lord Gavin, and that meant the woman standing next to him was the Lady Eleanor, although nobody had ever told her that Eleanor's cheek was scarred and nobody had ever told her that Gavin was haggard and drawn, and horses stomped and blew and the sound was nothing like the sound of the rock on the skull, nothing.

The great Lord Gavin sheathed his sword, rage still burning in his eyes. "Nathaniel Magus," he said, coldly. "What an interesting surprise."

TWENTY-TWO

MERRIT HAD LITTLE TROUBLE FINDING CLERIC IN the cells beneath the Elenesian stronghold. There weren't many of them, and he was the only occupant. She could tell by the way he lay crumpled on the floor that he'd been badly beaten. But they'd spared his face, she saw. So that he would be recognizable when he died; so that there would be no doubt who he was.

For some reason, she found that particularly horrible.

The cells weren't guarded. There was nowhere to flee, in this desert stronghold, and one of the guildsmen had told her, proudly, that they trusted their locks. But locks weren't trustworthy. They didn't care who opened them or how, and Merrit had picks hidden in an inner pocket of her coat. She also had a flask of water and another of whiskey, just in case.

Inside the cell, she crouched next to the crumpled figure on the floor. His eyes were closed. "Cleric," she said. "It's Merrit Idris. Wake up."

In a voice rusted through with pain, he said, "Leave me alone."

It was more than he'd said during the entire trip to the stronghold. Merrit, who rarely cried, found that her throat was thick and sore. "I didn't intend this."

"I deserve it. I deserve everything they're going to do to me."

Merrit remembered the square pit outside, filling with wood even as they spoke. Fiercely, she said, "Bullshit. Now stand up. We're getting out of here."

"It hurts too much," he said.

"It will hurt more if I drag you." The urge to cry was gone. Merrit had no patience for self-pity. "And I will drag you, if I need to."

She opened her switchknife, drew a little blood from her arm, and did a very quick Work. She had no talent for Working inside a person's mind, but she was very skilled at sending messages, and she was particularly good at sending messages to Kendzi. It was a shallower kind of Work, but important. Especially to a scout.

Meet me in the courtyard.

Why? Even through the Work, she could sense his exhausted suspicions. *What have you done?*

The right thing.

She could feel the conflict in him, deep and authentic. *I'll think about it*, he finally said. *Be careful, Merrit.*

Instead of answering, she wiped out his sigil and retracted her switchknife. "Come on, now," she said, to Cleric. She put an arm around his chest, pulling him upright. "Am I dragging you, or are you walking?"

Cleric groaned but put his feet under him, and stood under his own power. Mostly. Merrit took his arm over her shoulder as they made their way out of the catacombs, and up the narrow stairs to the hall. It was late at night, and they found two acolytes scrubbing the floor who stared openmouthed at Cleric. They were both boys, without even the slightest hint of hair on their faces. Merrit ignored them.

As she helped Cleric limp out of the hall one of them stood and bolted. So much for a quiet exit, then. "If you can walk faster, that would be good," she said to Cleric. He didn't answer.

Outside, the sun was not yet up. The oil lamps that burned in the courtyard gave barely enough light to see by, and filled the air with a sour, nutty smell. In the center of the yard she was relieved to see Kendzi waiting with not quite all of the Slonimi contingent. "The rest are hungover, but they'll be here," he said, with slightly bared teeth. Kendzi had no patience for drunkenness.

The Elenesians kept gaslights burning all night and the weird purple light made Merrit feel as if she were drunk herself. "I thought the Elenesians were ascetics," she said.

"The people in charge are never ascetics." Then he looked at Cleric and sighed. "Well, Merry, what do we do with him now?"

"Get him out of here, unless you want to watch him be burned alive," she answered.

"It's nothing to me," Kendzi said, but his eyes slid to the burn pit, and Merrit knew she had him. It was one thing to discuss the Northerner's death by a Slonimi campfire, but it was entirely another to see the place where it would happen. "Here are the others."

The last two Slonimi, both rumpled and one a bit green around the gills, were trudging across the courtyard. "We must get the gate open," Merrit said.

"That will take at least two people," Kendzi said, and so Merrit knew he had already investigated the gearhouse next to the enormous gate, where the winches that worked the opening mechanism could be found. Had he investigated out of his natural caution, or had he known what would have to happen? Merrit chose to believe the latter. "Take Benoit and Anurak." Two of the less hungover-looking men stepped forward.

The door to the stronghold opened, and a swarm of Elenesian guards emerged. They might even have been the same ones who'd taken Cleric the night before—in their uniforms, with their identical shaven heads, it was impossible to tell—but all were armed with the many-tailed chain flails they carried in lieu of swords. Merrit had noticed these weapons the night before. Painful, but not lethal, she had decided, and mostly for show. Since there were three times as many guards as Slonimi, she hoped she was right.

The man she presumed to be in charge, who carried a shield emblazoned with an image of a blue flail, called out, "Stop. The apostate belongs to us."

Kendzi shot Merrit a dark look, then stepped forward. His hands hung empty at his sides but his sword hilt protruded over his shoulder and his springknife was strapped to his wrist. "So sorry," he called, cheerfully, to the guardsmen. "I'm afraid there's been a misunderstanding. We can't leave him with you, after all."

"What the hells is going on?" Merrit heard one of the Slonimi mutter. She didn't turn around to see who it was.

"The apostate stays," the guardsman in charge said, striding forward, flail in hand. Kendzi drew his sword. Despite their confusion, so did the other Slonimi. Six against—Merrit's eyes scanned the courtyard, which had continued to fill with Elenesian guards streaming out of the stronghold—two dozen, easily.

But the Slonimi had swords and switchknives, and they were used to uneven odds. "Go," Kendzi snapped at her. She grabbed Cleric and dragged him away as, behind them, the Slonimi fell into a tight knot, back to back, making of themselves one solid target too small for all of the Elenesians to attack at once. The small door that led to the gearhouse was right next to the massive closed gate. Benoit and Anurak had stayed with Kendzi. She and Cleric would have to open it themselves.

But they would have to get there first, and Cleric couldn't run. The best he could do was a halting stagger. Too slow. The Slonimi had disappeared behind a field of brown cloaks and shining flails and the air was full of the clangs and cries of combat. Every clang was a blocked blow, every cry a landed one. Merrit and Cleric wouldn't escape notice forever. Her eyes fell upon the enormous square pit, half full of wood. And halfway between the battle and the gearhouse.

"Come on," she said, and put an arm around Cleric.

He saw where she was leading him. "No," he said, with a strangled sob. "No." But he was weak and she was strong. She dragged him to the pit, kicking and fighting all the way. Down into the hole they went. The walls were blackened with soot and the air at the bottom was dense with ashes and the rich aroma of cut wood. She pulled a big log over them, then another, making a kind of shelter. Cleric clutched his head, moaning. His body was curled tight in on itself. "We have to go the rest of the way," she said, desperate. "Get ready."

But he didn't—or couldn't—move. Merrit scratched open the wound she'd used to reach Kendzi. This time, the sigil she drew was Judah's. Drawing it made her fingers tingle. *Help me. I've got Cleric. We're in the courtyard. But Kendzi and the others are fighting and outnumbered. We can't get to the gearhouse. Cleric can't move.*

The reply came through a sort of haze. Judah was not used to this sort of communication. *Do a Work on him?*

I can't. All I do is this.

Merrit heard a scream. She hoped it wasn't one of the Slonimi.

Help us, she begged. *Help us. He's got to move. We've got to open the gate.*

"Give me a knife," Judah said to Lukash.

The knife he gave her was one she'd made. Not that first terrible one, but one of her subsequent efforts. She hoped she'd put a decent edge on it. "What's wrong?"

"They have Cleric," she said. "But they can't get him to the gearhouse to open the gate."

Lukash's teeth clenched. He had wanted to go inside the stronghold to rescue his friend, but Merrit had said no. He would be too conspicuous among all the underfed Elenesian acolytes, she said: his ropes of hair, the sheer bulk of him. Judah guessed he hated this, waiting outside with her. She guessed he thought he would have been able to get Cleric to move, if he'd been inside, and she also guessed he was right. She took out the vial of clotted blood. Then she took off the dead boy's coat and pushed up her sleeve. "What are you doing?" Lukash said.

"I don't know yet, but don't let anyone kill me while I do it," she said, and cut.

In the pit, Cleric's back arched and his jaw clenched. Merrit could feel the Work coming off him like heat, and knew Judah was doing something. She didn't know what. She hoped it wouldn't leave Cleric in the same quivering heap that it had left Pavla. His eyes were squeezed shut and as she watched he curled into himself like a scared child. She hazarded a glance up over the edge of the pit. The sky was a shade lighter than it had been, but there still wasn't enough light to see much more from the battle than the knot of brown-cloaked Elenesians. The noise was waking the rest of the stronghold. Boys were beginning to creep outside to see what was happening. Some of them were so small. So young. Merrit hated guilds. She hated the whole guild system.

As she watched, one of the boys picked up a stick.

Judah burned.

The fire tore at her hair, licked into her nostrils. She opened her mouth to scream and the flames reached down her throat and she remembered that this was Cleric's mind. Gavin's mind had been a book, Nate's a hallway with many doors. Cleric's mind was a jumble, a terrible torn-apart mess, in flames. That woman, that Pavla. It was incredible that Cleric had survived at all, the way she'd scattered him. Judah didn't know where any-thing belonged. Meanwhile, she could hear the battle raging in the stronghold. Meanwhile, she knew Lukash was standing guard over her body. Meanwhile, their lives were all slipping through her fingers.

If there was a Work equivalent of pulling Cleric up by his collar, that was exactly what she did. *Get up*, she said. *Move. You have to help Merrit open the gate.*

She could feel his resistance as the flames surged. She pushed it down. *I'm going to put you back together whether you like it or not. Show me where to start.*

He refused. Fire. Screaming.

But she was stronger than he was. *No fire. Where do I start? Where?*

A long wail, tragic and broken.

He relented.

She starts in the snow. Deep snow, up over his knees—al-though this is small Cleric, back when his name had been something else, so perhaps the snow wasn't so deep. His boots are warm and the sky is dark and bright with stars, and it is silent and peaceful out here in the snow. She looks back over his shoulder and sees a sturdy stone house, windows lit and white smoke drifting up from the chimney. His house. Home. Too many people there, too much noise, too much chaos. Fourteen brothers and sisters, all older. His mother and father are talking about guilding him. His mother says it will be herbs and plants and healing and he thinks of it wistfully, herbs and plants and healing and quiet and snow, there is snow.

The Elenesian boy holding the stick crept toward the knot of fighting men. He barely came up to their chests, and Merrit felt sorry for him—until he looked up, and saw her. His eyes grew wide with surprise, and then a rapturous, terrifying delight.

Merrit ducked down again. Too late. The boy raised the stick overhead, screamed, and ran toward her.

Snow, Judah said. *Then what?*

The stronghold. Teaching rooms, the smells of herbs and dust. The garden. Damp soil, warm sun. Salves and oils and elixirs and he is good at this, his mind is suited to it. To the puzzles of it. What combination of ailments means which disease and which combination of plants would treat, would cure. Punishments, but where weren't there punishments? Pain, but where wasn't there pain?

The older boys find a long-legged rabbit eating the greens in the garden, put a box over it, go away to fetch a knife. He lifts the box. Chases it away. Hopes it will not come back.

The fierce running boy's thin legs poked out of his robes as he ran in a way that was almost funny, but it wouldn't be funny if he reached the pit and Merrit had to kill him. It wouldn't be funny if he managed to kill her instead—or Cleric, while Judah was Working in him. Merrit didn't know what would happen then but didn't think it would be anything good.

"I'll be back," she said to Cleric, who couldn't hear her anyway, and hoisted herself up out of the pit. She flexed her wrist and the switchknife popped out again, quick and deadly.

Please, boy, don't make me kill you, she thought, as he ran at her, wild-eyed, murderous.

Then what?

Older still. Long fingers, bony wrists. New rituals, every morning: the god Eleni finds us through suffering. His first flail, knotted leather now but it would be chains soon enough. Punishment and pain, but when has there not been punishment and pain? At least he holds the lash that strokes his back, this time. He knows when each blow is coming. Twenty boys, all the same age. Twenty bare chests, some sprouting the barest beginnings of hair. Twenty backs, some weeping beads of bright blood. The morning light gentle and gorgeous, catching the blood like rubies.

Hesitation. Judah pressed, gently. *Then?*

The library. Bitter, oaky smell of ink and dry parchment. Twenty boys, copying scroll after scroll. Twenty shaved heads, twenty spines bent in the same way, twenty hands curled just so around their pens. Twenty shoulders with the same underfed, overworked wiriness, thin ropes of muscle over bones. But one boy, across the room, glows as if lit from within. His hands—the left newly tattooed with the guild mark they all bear—are graceful, his eyelashes thick and dark. Judah can feel the boy who would be Cleric forcing his attention down to the scroll he's copying, only to feel it drawn up again. To the hands, to the eyelashes.

And once, to eyes as gray as storm clouds, as frank as truth. The instant the two gazes touch, they spring away from each other, as if terrified.

They have good reason to be terrified.

The boy held his stick like a lance, charging toward Merrit. But her arms were longer than his and she knocked the stick away. "Stop," she hissed at him. "Go back inside."

But he merely shrieked and threw himself toward her legs. More boys were running toward her now and absurdly, she almost laughed—all those years of training with Kendzi Baglia, and for what? For fighting off a half dozen children with murder in their eyes. They were not monsters. They were children, defending the only home they knew. The murder in their eyes would kill, just the same.

"Stop!" she yelled at them. "Go back inside!"

They didn't stop. Merrit readied herself to fight.

Stop! Go back inside! Judah hears. She thinks it's Merrit. She can't pay any attention. She has to find Cleric's next memory, to set it alongside the others, and when she does she finds

twenty boys sitting in silence, bent over plates of thin porridge. The boy who will be Cleric sits next to the dark-lashed boy on the uncomfortable refectory bench. The gruel is tepid and the dark-lashed boy's hip against his seems the only warmth in the world. Those scant inches of connection are everything. They are all that matters.

In the garden, clipping herbs, there is a moment. A blade-like leaf crushed between two fingers, an aroma released, the crushed leaf offered as a gift. From that moment on, the woody smell will remind him of this moment, of warm sun and a faint haze of sweat. Thick dark lashes surrounding eyes as gray as storms; eyes that touch the boy who will be Cleric's eyes. This time they don't move away.

We are put here on earth to serve Eleni, the guildmaster says. *All pain is his gift to us. How easy it is to sink into pleasure, to drown in it. But we must be strong. If there is ecstasy to be found, find it in your own self-deprivation.*

Merrit heard another yell. Out of the corner of her eye saw a figure break away from the knot of fighting men. Slither away, really, down under the blur of weapons: it was Anurak. Merrit knew him. He was scarcely a decade older than the boys attacking her, too young to even have been matched yet. Young enough to remember being a boy himself, maybe, and so he came at the boys with eyes comically wide and mouth distorted by bellowing, waving his sword in a ridiculous way that nobody who'd ever actually been in a swordfight would find at all threatening. He looked as if he was scattering birds off a cornfield. Into the flock of boys he went, and indeed, they scattered. The few he had to hit, he hit with the flat of his sword, enough to knock them back off their feet but not enough to do any serious damage.

And damned if it didn't work. Merrit had forgotten how easy it was to scare a child. The knocked-aside boys scuttled away, terrified, back to the doors and crates and whatever other hiding places they could find. The few boys that were still focused on her, she drove away with some showy but in-effectual stabs with the switchknife, drawing them away from the pit and away from Cleric.

She found herself standing by Anurak. "The gearhouse," she said to him. He nodded. They ran.

The dark-lashed boy's name is Alec, a word that quickly becomes, to the boy who will be Cleric, a song and a poem and a caress, even if he only thinks it to himself as he scrubs a floor. The trip of the tongue from the *l* to the quick, clipped *c*. Alec carries a sprig of rosemary inside his tunic, where it crushes and warms against his heart, and soon the boy who will be Cleric takes to doing the same thing, and the smell of it—the smell of Alec—permeates all of him, saturates even his blood, even all the years later when Judah will use a vial of it to find him.

They are together whenever they can be. Theirs is an affair conducted entirely in the dark, and Judah feels the pain and the bliss of it, the glittering sweetness of every moment. The sightless joy of each press of hand and lip, each furtive fumbling. Both boys had been guilded by the time they were eight. What they do not know, they have to discover, and the discovery is a joy. When they can't be together, the boy who will be Cleric thinks of Alec constantly. He makes mistakes in his copying and is beaten. He is caught touching himself in the small hours of the morning and is sent to bed with his hands bound. He doesn't care. Alec. Alec. Alec of the rosemary smell, the graceful hands, the warm heart.

When we are journeymen, Alec says, *let's travel together. Away from here, with no eyes to see us—*

Such bliss, at the very notion. It consumes the boy who will be Cleric, night and day. Finally he takes a small scrap of parchment from the burn heap in the library and, in the darkness, writes a verse. He has never done such a thing before.

The storm in your eyes breaks over me.

I am drowned in you. I am drowned.

Alec weeps when he reads it, and seizes the boy who would be Cleric, and they drown in each other.

Merrit and Anurak had almost reached the gearhouse when the boys—or at least some of the boys—recovered enough to attack again. The gearhouse door was locked. Anurak had a hand axe in his belt. "Hack through it," Merrit said, and pressed her back to his. She could feel his muscles work as he went after the wooden door, close enough that she could hear the grunts of effort and hear the thuds as the blade hit the too-solid wood. The boys grew bolder, swinging their sticks and flails uncomfortably close to her—realizing, maybe, that she had no intention of actually stabbing them with her switch-knife, which meant that she would probably have to.

"Hurry," she said, panting, to Anurak, who gritted his teeth and said, between hacks, "These people—are obsessed—with keeping—people—*in*."

Aren't we all, she almost said, but then one of the boys lunged at her with particular viciousness. Before she knew it, she'd put her knife through his tiny hand. All that training with Kendzi. Years of it. Too strong to overcome.

The boy screamed. In the center of the courtyard, a few of the Elenesians on the outside of the knot looked up at the sound, noticing the tiny ridiculous battle by the gearhouse for the first time. One of them almost smiled. They broke away from the real battle, flails held ready.

Merrit decided the weapons weren't mostly for show, after all.

You were in love, Judah says, as kindly as she can. *It's very sweet, but Cleric, you have to get up and help Merrit open the gate.*

But the love is not the point. Because one morning Alec is not at morning rituals. Not in the garden. Not at the mid-day meal, or the library for copy work. The boy who will be Cleric asks casually, the only way he can. *Is Alec ill?* As if he doesn't care. As if it doesn't matter.

The unimportant other boy blinks. *You didn't hear? They took him to the guildmaster. Self-indulgence.*

The boy who would be Cleric is astounded. He had only had his hands bound. *To the guildmaster? For that?*

The unimportant boy shrugs. *He must really have been going at it.*

Before dinner, they are called to the courtyard.

Anurak swore and whipped his body around, so he and Merrit are both facing the approaching Elenesians. "Metal-reinforced," he gasped. "Can't hack through it."

"That's a problem," she said, her switchknife glistening with the boy's blood.

"Fucked, aren't we?" Anurak said.

In the guards' eyes she sees excitement and frustration and bloodlust. "Seems so," she said, and they readied themselves.

No, Judah says. *Oh, no.*

In the courtyard, the same pit where Merrit and Cleric would crouch so many years later, is filled with wood. Chains are fastened to the poles on either side of the pit and fastened to the chains, naked, is—

Alec. Brutalized Alec. The storm-cloud eyes are swollen shut, the dark lashes buried in damaged tissue. The perfect skin is marred in every possible way. He has been cut. Beaten. Burned, cruelly, in the most sensitive places of his body.

The guildmaster steps up to the waiting podium. *Behold one of your brethren*, he says to the assembled acolytes. *Sunk deep beneath the weight of pleasure and transgression. As Eleni's own sun rose, it found him in a private room, indulging his basest instincts. And yet I fear I have even worse transgressions to reveal.*

The guildmaster reaches into the folds of his robe, pulled out a scrap of paper, and the boy who will be Cleric's knees give way beneath him. The boys are jammed together like stones in a wall and that is all that keeps him upright. His stomach is roiling, acid.

Our brother has not transgressed alone. He was found with this in his pocket, the guildmaster says, holding the scrap of parchment aloft. His pitiless eyes scanned the crowd. *Someone in this yard shares his transgression. Somebody owes us his pain.*

The boy who will be Cleric does not particularly care about Eleni but he prays silently, now, more earnestly than he has ever prayed before. *O holy Eleni, if you exist, prove that this isn't your will. May lightning strike the stronghold. May the ground swallow the pit. Please, save Alec. Please save him. He is the only person I love.*

The guildmaster continues. *So deeply misled is this boy that he will not reveal the name of the acolyte who led him astray. He would not be coerced by suffering or by righteousness. This boy owes half of his burden to another. If that other steps forward, we will divide his punishment between you.*

The courtyard is silent, except for the crackle of torches next to the unlit pyre. The boy who will be Cleric can't move. His mouth is dry. His vision is gray. All he can see is Alec. The guildmaster signals to a guard. The guard steps forward, pulls Alec's head up. And somebody must know, the boy who will be Cleric thinks. They were not that careful. Somebody will know. Somebody will call his name.

Please. Somebody. Call his name.

Who will step forward to receive his share of justice?

Nobody speaks. The boy who will be Cleric is paralyzed. His tongue will not move. His lungs will not draw. His mouth will not open. A trickle of urine runs down the inside of his leg.

Before it is over, the boy who will be Cleric will hope an ugly hope that he was not Alec's only lover, that there was some other, worthier boy who would be brave enough to stand forward. He loves Alec enough to hope he is untrue, but no other lover emerges. So he stands, and watches, and does not move as they take Alec's eyes, and his fingers, and everything, and when there is nothing left to take, he still does not move. He hates himself. He does not move.

Later, he will climb to the top of the stronghold ramparts, but he cannot jump. He ties a noose in the orchard, but can't put his neck through it. He steals poison from the apothecary, but can't bring himself to drink. As a last resort, he flees into the wilderness on a dark, cold night, unprepared in any way. If he can't end his life, he'll let Eleni end it for him. When he's tired, he lies down in the mud to die.

But instead he wakes up. Finds a spring. Thawberries. A place to steal a knife, better boots. This, then, is his share of Alec's punishment: to live, knowing he did nothing. He builds a fire. When the fire is hot, he heats the stolen knife in it until it glows red, then presses it against the guild mark on his hand. Over and over again, night after night, until the skin is as blackened and melted as Alec's was, at the end. Until the mark is obliterated. It is his prayer, his penance.

Alec, he says, through clenched teeth. *Alec*, as his own flesh hisses.

Alec. Alec. Alec.

By the gatehouse, the first flail landed across Anurak's face. He'd had a lovely face but Merrit had never realized it until the moment when it was suddenly marred by five deep bloody gashes, down to the bone. Merrit screamed and drove her switchknife through the soft place under the guard's chin. She thought of Cleric in the pit, who was probably going to die anyway now, and regretted nothing.

Judah found herself in her own body, outside the stronghold gate. Lukash crouched next to her with his knife drawn, looking worried. "Are you all right?" he said. "Where is Cleric?"

She stared up at him. But instead of his dark skin and copper eyes, she saw another face that had once leaned over her with concern. A broad face, plain, with curly hair. Darid. Who had loved her, and who had been ordered by the Seneschal to die much like Cleric's lost Alec. Months had passed before Judah had learned that Darid had escaped. A government had fallen, the House been plundered, her world changed utterly, all while she lived in a world where Darid had been tortured to death. When she had learned that at least that one awful thing hadn't happened, she'd been relieved, and she'd been furious.

And now she was furious again. Because what Darid escaped in Highfall had happened to others—in the House, in the stronghold. Everywhere, throughout history. Others who were loved, who knew songs and jokes and stories. They'd had favorite foods and quirks that annoyed their friends and some of them had ideas nobody else had or would have, before or since. Lost forever. All of it.

She stood up. Lukash stepped back, his eyes wary, as she turned to the hulking beast of the stronghold. Which had been built to protect the powerful people within it, and the powerful people only. Nobody protected acolytes like Alec and the boy who would be Cleric, who was so damaged by what he had seen and done—or not done—that he could no longer even think the name he had been given at birth. That boy no longer existed. The Elenesians had murdered him as surely as they had murdered Alec.

And now, on the other side of that wall, they wanted to do it again.

She walked to the gate and lay a hand flat on its surface. The cacophony of the battle on the other side was muffled by the thick wood. She couldn't even feel a vibration. It was as if the battle weren't even happening, and why should it be otherwise? What was human conflict to a gate, or a wall, or a building? What was human conflict to a slab of wood?

She closed her eyes. Found the white. All the years this gate had stood here, all the humans who had passed through it. All these years that the gate had been a gate. The wood felt solid beneath her hand but the deeper she went into the wood, into the white, the more space she found. Before the gate had been a gate, it had been wood, and that wood had been alive. It had pulled what it needed to survive from the soil, formed those necessities into bonds and structures that held it together. She could feel each discrete particle and each fragile bond.

In the white, she traced those bonds, like she'd traced the bonds between the Workers in the Slonimi camp. Like in the camp, she drew—except now she drew power from earth itself, and the earth, ancient and old and alive, gave as much as she could draw. She touched the bonds that held the gate together.

And then she released them. For a moment, nothing happened. Then, slowly, the wood at the bottom of the door began to wrinkle like paper. Then to fold. Then to collapse.

From far away, outside the white, she heard Lukash's drawing-in of breath, as the great and ancient door fell into itself with a soft, dry whisper. A stack of unbound pages falling to the floor. The breath of air stirred by its falling touched Judah's cheek, her upraised palm, her hair.

"Gods," she heard Lukash say.

She stepped into the courtyard.

All within was chaos. She was in the white but she could see everything. The Elenesians were clustered in the center of the courtyard, wielding flails and clubs and any other weapons they could find. She could feel the Slonimi fighting for their lives in the center of the cluster. Next to the gate Merrit stood over a bloody-faced body wearing Slonimi clothes. She was fighting off two guards whose flails swung in the air and a countless horde of children. Children whose home was being attacked. Children like Lukash had been. But they were trying to kill Merrit and she was trying not to die and the world was a terrible mess. Merrit's switchknife dripped with blood.

She could feel Cleric somewhere ahead of her. She expected she would always be able to feel him, the rosemary and burned flesh smell that was everywhere in his mind, his blood. And, yes, there was the pit where Alec had been slaughtered, full of wood waiting to burn. She knew wood, now. She understood it. She didn't need to stand next to it or touch it. She merely looked at it, and determined that it would not burn her friend, and it flattened into something like paper, and then something like dust: a golden haze that settled gently over the pit, and Cleric within it.

He stood up. She felt him stand up.

Those few Elenesians who had noticed the dissolution of the great wooden gate stared slack-jawed at the space where it had been, but most were too deep in the rage of battle to notice or care. In the white, Judah felt the stone beneath her feet and felt within it the smallest possible fragments that could still be called stone, fragments so tiny they might as well be grains of sand. And sand was malleable. Sand could be rearranged. Sand could creep up a man's legs as he fought. It could encircle his waist. It could even reach up and bind an arm that held a sword, and then it could become stone again.

The cries from the Elenesians changed.

Kendzi Baglia, knocked to his knees in the center of the scrum, looked up expecting to see his own death in the Elenesian guard standing over him. Expecting that the shining, barbed flail in the man's hand would be the last thing he ever saw, as it rippled down toward him. He was not a strong Worker, he could not heal, he had no talent for training horses.

Fighting was what he did. Eventually he would die doing it. He had hoped it would not be now, because this whole thing with Merrit and the Elenesian apostate and the Daughter of Maia was as tangled a clusterfuck as he'd ever tried to slash his way out of, but Slonim knew a person didn't always get what they hoped for. He would not have minded as much if the Elenesians had intended to kill the Northerner clean, and quick. But he didn't like torture.

He looked into the eyes of the Elenesian who was going to kill him, because by Kendzi's morality, they owed each other that much. So he saw when the blood-heat in the man's eyes turned to puzzlement, and then trepidation, and then terror. He watched as the stone crept up the man's legs, then his waist, and then his sword arm.

The guard screamed, eyes wide and terrified. Kendzi looked down at himself. His own legs were free. Looking around, he saw that all of the Slonimi were free. All of the Elenesians were immobilized, the granite as solid around their feet as if it had been there for millennia. Beyond them, he saw Cleric emerge from the firepit, covered in golden dust. By the gatehouse, Merrit stood over a body that he was terribly afraid was Anurak's, two immobilized Elenesians, and—gods—a massive horde of robed children, all screaming and wailing in front of her. The Morgeni stood in the empty gate, frozen in shock and horror, one hand holding a knife slack at his side. Past him was the world outside, away from all of this.

He turned back to call a retreat to his people, and saw the Daughter of Maia disappearing into the stronghold.

Still in the white, still burning with rage, stopping the Elenesian guards in the stronghold cost Judah no effort. Their flails dissolved and fell to the floor in glittering showers. Stone floors reached up to grab booted feet. Wooden wall panel-

ing grew around arms and shoulders. A tapestry of a ghoul-
ish figure she took to be the god Eleni wove itself around the
head of a guard who had pulled a knife to run her through.
The earth gave its power to her gladly and gladly, she took it.

None of this mattered. Judah knew the stronghold as well
as Cleric did. She knew where the guildmaster's office was.
She knew where the penitence chapel was. She knew where
the child acolytes were buried when they died. She could feel
them, their small yellowing bones surrounded by dirt. When
she passed living acolytes, if they were screaming and fleeing, she let them flee. Only if they tried to stop her did she
stop them.

She came to a locked door. The door was wood, the hinges
and bolts iron. At a touch, the wood dissolved. The iron crumbled to black dust. Inside stood a robed man, well-fed and
oily, with fearful, panicked eyes and white hair. Even from
the doorway she could tell that his robes were soft and rich
and warm, not the same stiff, uncomfortable stuff as that of
his guards and acolytes. Unlike every soldier in his stronghold,
he held a sword. The trembling blade was pointed at her. She
recognized him: it was the same man. The same guildmaster
who had stood by as Alec was carved to pieces, the same one
who ordered the pyre lit, the same one who had held up the
scrap of parchment with the poem on it.

I am drowned in you. I am drowned.

The floor in his office was marble. The heart of marble was
not sand. The heart of marble was crystal and it was crystal
that crawled up the guildmaster's legs, like ice forming on a
fern. Like his men, his eyes went wide and afraid. He looked
from the crystal shell enclosing him to her and back again.
"Witch!" he cried. The crystal grew up over his arm, took the
hand that held the sword. "Hell-bound witch!" he screamed,
high with panic and terror.

From deep in the white, Judah frowned. "I don't like that word," she said, and stepped forward to touch his forehead.

Cleric had told her that the godswill wasn't meant to cure, but to join body and mind, so the mind couldn't escape the suffering of the body. But this man was fleshy. This man was old. This man had escaped too much of the suffering that he'd caused. She dug in his head, found Alec. Found the smell of his flesh, the blaze of the coals. Found the faces of the acolytes forced to watch, the flames shining on their sweat-dewed foreheads. Found Cleric. Found all of the others: every boy, through all the years. Every boy beaten, every boy killed. Every punishment. Every death. She opened each of them, slipped in through the soft places. Brought out their pain so the guildmaster could see it, so he could *live* it. When he began to scream she filled his mouth with crystal but she left his nose, she left his lungs, so that he would stay alive. So that he would live their suffering, so that he would live their deaths. Every scream. Every breath.

And then she left him there.

As Judah left the stronghold, all she saw was suffering. All she could feel, with every footfall, was suffering. The building was made of wood and stone and iron and clay but the glue that bound it was suffering, the agony of the children who had become men here—men who went out into the world and bound sick people to their suffering with godswill, men who stayed within the stronghold walls and taught a new generation how to suffer. The stronghold was a terrible place. The suffering had infused it to its very core and there was no way to make anything good of it.

And so, the moment she stepped out of it, she took it down. Every stone of it. Every brick. Every bloodstain and every lash. Down to the smallest possible bits, down to powder. The building shuddered and trembled, seemed almost to shimmer—and then it was gone, and there was nothing but a cloud of dust. Which she couldn't see through, and urged gently toward the ground. The air cleared and she saw that the stronghold itself was gone but the walls that surrounded it remained, so she focused there, next. Every stone of it. Every brick.

But someone was gripping her shoulders. Someone who clearly wanted to shake her—she knew what that felt like, that tightening of the fingers—but who did not quite dare. The someone said her name over and over and at first it was merely a word but as she came down out of the white, into the thin eddies of dust that still swirled in the empty courtyard, she began to truly hear it.

Judah. Judah.

Something else.

Judah, stop now. Please. Judah—

"—stop." It was Lukash. His eyes were dry but huge with some strong emotion. After a split second she realized that it was shock. He must have seen her come back into herself, because his hands on her arms relaxed and he let out a great sigh. "You can stop now," he said. "It's over. It's all done."

Then she heard something else. Weeping. The last of the dust cleared, and Judah looked around her.

The Elenesians were fixed in solid rock where she'd left them. They were the source of the weeping. Horrified and afraid, their eyes rolled skyward and tears cut channels through the dust and muck on their cheeks as they begged for their freedom, begged for their lives. Two of the Slonimi were pulling on the arms of one man, trying to pull his body from his stone prison. Another was bashing against the stone circling a second man's upraised arm. Still another was using the hilt of his own sword as a chisel.

Kendzi, Merrit, and Cleric were crouched over the outstretched body by the gearhouse. All three turned when Lukash said Judah's name and what she saw in their eyes was bleak horror, but it wasn't the battle they were afraid of. It was her.

"What have I done?" she whispered.

Lukash, hand still on her arm, said, more gently, "Judah."

But she was already gone. Fled. As far into the white as she could go.

She wanted to be somewhere safe. And comfortable—it had been so long since she was comfortable. She wanted a chair to sit on; when was the last time she'd sat on a chair? She wanted a hot cup of coffee to drink, a caramel to soften against the roof of her mouth. She pushed all of the dust and the stronghold and the stonebound Elenesians out of her mind. Soft chair. Coffee. Caramels. Warm. Clean. Safe.

The chair formed under her in the white. Her clenched fists eased, spread open to hold a chipped mug, the ceramic warm under her fingers. Her mouth filled with milky sweetness. Around her, walls came out of the white, covered in patterned silk and faded with time. To her left were two glass doors onto a wide terrace. There was a settee and a table and then—

She was in the parlor. Home and prison all in one. From where she sat she could see the room she'd shared with Elly on one side, and Gavin and Theron's room on the other. There was Theron's coat, slung lazily over the back of a chair, and his old boots that she'd long since appropriated. Elly's sketchbook lay on the sofa. The terrace doors were open and it was spring, the fields were blooming. All that was missing were the others. Elly wouldn't be on the terrace, not with her fear of heights. Perhaps in one of the bedrooms, but which one? Elly had slept in Gavin's room after the betrothal, and how ridiculous and happy she'd been then. Did Judah want her ridiculous and happy, or younger, when she and Elly would share the bed in the other room, and Elly would press her shins against Judah's back and it was so warm, so comfortable? She didn't know. And Theron. Theron would be in his workshop. Not dead, no matter what the magus had said. Building something. Fixing something.

But Gavin—Gavin might be here. Tall and confident, as he'd been before the coup and before Amie of Porterfield and before everything. Wearing his blue waistcoat, maybe. The one with the embroidery that was nearly too much, but tell him that. His hair trimmed in the back but long on top, so his golden curls shone in the sun from the terrace—

And then he was there, just as she'd imagined him. *Jude!* he said merrily.

But something was wrong. Even as he spoke and smiled, the nearly-too-much waistcoat dulled, and the white sleeves of the shirt beneath it darkened, until he wore a dun-colored travel coat that was a bit short in the arms and dust-stained trousers. His hair grew longer, a short beard sprouting from his cheeks and chin. Beneath it his face thinned, hollows deepening under his eyes as the flesh drained away from his frame. The smile vanished. *Jude*, he said again, but this time there was no merriment in it. Only weariness and wonder and a terrible grief.

He reached out to her and she saw that his fingernails had been pulled out. The raw flesh where they should have been was healing and she could see that they were barely starting to grow in again. She had felt that, she realized. She remembered dousing her hands in the bad-smelling turquoise pool to quench the burning in her fingers. He took a few steps closer. *It's you*, he said, in that grief-filled, un-Gavin-like voice. *It's really you.*

She shook her head. She couldn't look away from him. *No. I'm—this isn't real. I'm not here.*

That got a smile. A faint one. *I'm not here, either.*

Where are you? She stood up. She wanted to reach out to him, but she didn't dare. Remembering the swirling maelstrom that had always engulfed her when they touched. *What happened to you?*

Quite a bit, he said, gravely. *We're in—I don't know, some inn between Tiernan and Highfall.* His eyes flickered upward. *Hey, you cut off your hair.*

I—

But before she could finish the sentence, the parlor door flew open and Theron burst in. Not a wraith or a ghost or a revenant but Theron, flush-cheeked and healthy, the eyes behind his glasses full of wonderful quick intelligence. *Judah!* he cried. *What are you doing? Stop it. It can see you. They can all see you!*

Around her, the walls of the parlor melted away, turned to gray stone. Dead leaves sprouted over the faded rug, and the tower grew up around them like the rock had grown up around the Elenesians. And with it, Judah sensed a creeping familiarity. That sense of being watched, the sense of observing multitudes—it was here, surrounding her on every side, circling her like a closing fist. It wasn't only the Slonimi who had been watching her. It was the tower. It was this place.

Go, Theron said, urgent. And, like that, she was gone.

TWENTY-THREE

KORSA SAT BOLT UPRIGHT IN HIS NARROW COT IN the tower room, feeling as if his breath had been snatched out of his lungs. His eyes slid across the room, over the device Florence had built and the distiller and the empty shelves, until they landed on Theron. As he'd somehow known they would. "The girl I met in Elban's room," Korsa said.

Theron nodded. "Judah."

"She's more powerful than I thought," Korsa said, awestruck.

"She's coming here."

Korsa frowned. "I didn't hear her say that. The man said he was coming here. He was your brother?"

And at that, Theron smiled. The smile was a bit sad, as it always was when Theron talked about his family. "If Gavin is coming, Judah is coming. That's the way it's always been."

But Korsa's mind was spinning. "The Seneschal only wants my children because he cannot have her." He had never spoken about them that way—*my children*—and they were not children, really, but the words felt right and sound and real. "What will he do to them, if he gets her?"

"You don't know Judah. She won't be so easy to get. Also, I very much doubt Judah and Gavin are coming back to see the sights. The Seneschal will have other things on his mind."

"You think there will be trouble?"

"Not only from them. That web I told you about—all of those people linked into whatever's in this tower. Whether she meant it to be or not, what Judah did was basically the equivalent of grabbing it with both hands and shaking as hard as she could. Anyone with any sort of power heard it." Theron shook his head. "The tower heard it."

"What do you mean?" Korsa said.

"The force in this tower," Theron said. "Whatever it is. Couldn't you feel it pulling at her?"

But before Korsa could answer, they heard quick footsteps on the tower stairs, and Liam came through the door. "Who were they?" he said, breathless. "We all saw them. Ida thinks they were Lord Gavin and the Foundling. Were they?"

He didn't seem to notice Theron's presence. Wonderful. Korsa couldn't tell the difference between *kagirh*-space and reality anymore. That wasn't a great sign. "I think so."

"He said they're coming here," Liam said. "Are they going to try to overthrow the Seneschal?"

Korsa looked at Theron, who said, "Try to, maybe." And again, Liam didn't react, but the long-sleeping part of Korsa's brain that had once planned battles began to shake off sleep, and plan.

"If the Seneschal is under attack from outside," he said, "he will be paying less attention to the inside."

Theron said nothing. But Liam's eyes lit up. "A distraction," Liam said.

"A distraction," Korsa agreed. He swung his legs over the edge of his cot and began to put on his boots. "I think we had better get ready."

TWENTY-FOUR

IN THE DARK GARRET OF AN INN, SOMEWHERE BE-tween Tiernan and Highfall, Nathaniel Clare, too, jerked awake, his heart pounding and his mind full of certainty.

There were no beds in the garret, but the floor was crowded with bedrolls. The soft sound of breathing and the assorted smells of bodies filled the air in the small space. Most of the Tiernan soldiers were sleeping outside, in the inn yard, but the Tiernan magus—Ambrose something, Nate tried his best to avoid him —and a few others rated indoor accommodations. Bindy was downstairs, sleeping in her own bedroll on the floor of Eleanor's room. She had insisted Nate be given a place inside. He had promised to return the favor.

"When we get back to Highfall, you can teach me to be a magus, for real," she said. As if they weren't just going back to Highfall but going back in time, to those retrospectively glorious days when he'd still had possession of Arkady's beautiful lab on Limley Square. Everything had seemed so possible then, so clear and easy. Thinking of it made his heart hurt.

Or maybe it was thinking of Bindy that did that.

Three days had passed since they'd joined the force that Eleanor and Gavin were leading to Highfall, and Nate had spent much of it riding in the supply cart and contemplating his future. The Slonimi would not forgive him for failing so spectacularly, and they would definitely not forgive him for killing Saba. That path led to ruin and death. He could not go back to them, which wasn't necessarily a bad thing. He knew he would find a kind of satisfaction in life as a working magus in Highfall, probably in one of its poorer neighborhoods, but it would be a hardscrabble existence. Bindy would insist on staying to be trained in it and he wasn't sure he wanted to damn her to that life. She was determined and clever and might be able to do better for herself without him.

The previous night, before falling asleep, Nate had considered the life he'd spent devoted to the Unbinding. There had been no forks in that path, no deviation. Staring up through the darkness to the underside of the inn's shingled roof, he wasn't sure he'd wanted to go back to Highfall at all. His mind felt more his than it had since he'd arrived there with Derie and Charles a year ago. Maybe more than it had since he was eight years old, actually. As he'd fallen asleep—what couldn't have been more than a few hours before—it had occurred to him that, for the first time since he'd been apprenticed to Derie, he actually did have a choice in what he did next.

Now, after what he'd seen in the Work, he was no longer sure that was true.

Gingerly, he sat up. Careful not to wake any of the others, he rolled up his bedding and slung his satchel over his shoulder, wincing a little. He carried his boots to the narrow garret stair and went down.

Unexpectedly, a light burned in the kitchen. Gavin stood at the stove, wearing his traveling coat and making tea. He looked up when Nate entered and for a moment the two men stared at each other in silence. Nate had been avoiding the young lord for days, ever since Eleanor had held back Gavin's sword arm and kept Nate from being slaughtered in the road. The past year had left its mark on Elban's son. Not in his face, but in the way he carried himself, in the set of his mouth and the tension around his eyes. His left hand was bandaged. "You saw her, too," Gavin said.

It was a question that didn't need an answer. Nate pulled up a stool and sat down to put his boots on.

Gavin poured the tea into a clay flask. "Can you find her?"

Nate nodded. "South."

"You killed my brother."

"I did," Nate said. "I'm sorry. I wasn't in my right mind."

"I loved my brother," Gavin said, tuneless and flat.

Experimentally, Nate prodded the place where Saba had broken his rib. It hurt, but not too much. "The tower wants her back."

"The tower is a pile of stone."

"It is and it isn't."

Gavin tucked the flask into his pocket. "Are you in your right mind now?"

"I am," Nate said simply.

The young lord buttoned his coat and nodded toward the kitchen door, where his own travel pack waited, ready. "You and I will go south. We'll find Jude."

"And then," Nate said, and Gavin said, "Yes. And then."

TWENTY-FIVE

JUDAH, LUKASH, CLERIC, AND MERRIT FLED TO THE southeast, into the Barriers. Kendzi Baglia did not go with them. Most of the Elenesians who had survived the collapse of the stronghold were free now, although one would probably lose a foot where the stone had cut off the circulation. When they left, Kendzi's soldiers were working to free the last few, and Kendzi had his own reasons for wanting to linger.

"After last night—" his eyes flickered to Judah "—every Slonimi who can will be headed toward Highfall. They'll come through the Elenesian pass. I don't know what they'll do, but I want to be there when they decide to do it."

"I think we don't want to be there," Lukash said.

"Then you should continue south, toward the Southern Kingdom," Kendzi said. "Will you stay or go, Merry?"

"Go," the scout said.

"When they catch you, they'll strip you of your power."

"They have to catch me first," Merrit said, and smiled.

Kendzi's answering smile was tired. "If they do, call me, and I'll come. Not everything we do is right simply because we're the ones doing it." He turned to Judah. "It was an honor to know you, Daughter of Maia."

Judah said nothing. She had said nothing at all since coming back to herself. She was horrified by what she'd done to the Elenesians in the throes of rage. What they'd done to Alec and Cleric and so many others was evil, but was what she had done any different? If horror begat horror, on and on forever, would there be anything left of the world?

But then she would think of Alec's long, dark eyelashes.

The storm in your eyes breaks over me.

I am drowned in you.

The destruction she'd wrought in the stronghold writhed in her mind, a thrashing, unhappy thing. The destruction she'd seen in Cleric's memory writhed with it.

Kendzi and Merrit said that they had felt the tower closing in around them, the night before. They had felt its presence in the parlor like another person. Judah could feel it still. She asked Kendzi and Merrit if they could, and they nodded.

"Feels like when a cramp eases, but you can still feel the place it was," Merrit said, and Kendzi said, "Like armor that doesn't fit right. It rubs at you."

Neither of those comparisons sounded quite right to Judah. For her, it felt as if some part of her was still caught there, the same incessant tug she'd felt from the vial of Cleric's blood. But stronger. Fiercer. It burned through her like a beacon. She desperately wanted to reach out to Gavin, but she was afraid of what their contact would do. *It can see you*, Theron had said, in the parlor. *They can all see you.*

The southern foothills of the Barriers trailed away into a vast, dry plain, where a constant dull wind blew. Nothing grew there except for some small, yellowed shrubs, barely ankle high.

Merrit pointed to the far horizon, where the others could see nothing but where—she swore—were the rainforests of the Southern Kingdom. In the meantime, she said, water would be scarce. There was a river. They would need to find it.

At night they made camp and slept. Merrit brought out her ocarina but the way the thin, mournful music mixed with the constant sweep of the wind unnerved them all, and she soon put it away again. Kendzi had given them travel bread and pemmican. None of them ate much, and all of them slept long past dawn the next morning.

That afternoon, they came to a place where rocks as tall as buildings stood above the hard dirt, their surfaces pitted and worn by eons of wind and sand. They camped this time in the lee of a house-sized rock with a sheer face that seemed to have been blasted away by force. As the sun went down, Cleric came to Judah. He'd been quiet since they'd left the stronghold. The Elenesian storerooms had survived the collapse and he'd spent some time there alone, returning with a satchel and herb box like the one he'd had when Judah first met him. He didn't complain about the pain of his injuries. Several times she thought she'd detected the smell of godswill around him.

Now, as he crouched next to her, there was no doubt. The reek of spoiled milk and mint came off him like sweat. His eyes were red, his lip trembling. "Thorn Bush," he said, and tried to smile. Judah started to smile back, but then he said, "Go into my head. Take him away," and her smile faded.

"No," she said, quietly.

Cleric shook his head. Twitchy and convulsive, like a dog with a burr in its ear. "I had it under control. Until that— that woman—went into my mind and she dragged him back out. And I can't live like this." He held out his arm. "Please. Fix what she did. Take him away." Then, barely audible, "I'm in agony."

Lukash and Merrit, Judah knew, were watching closely. She'd told them the barest version of the story that afternoon. Cleric had loved someone, and that someone had been killed. Merrit had only nodded but there'd been a flicker of recognition in Lukash's face, as if years' worth of fragments had fallen into place, and made a picture. "His death wasn't your fault," she said to Cleric, now.

"I let him die."

"You couldn't have saved him. You could only have suffered with him."

"His suffering is over," Cleric said, harshly. "Mine endures. I saved you in the Ghostwood; now, you save me. Fix this. Take him away."

She thought of Darid, of standing in the Work with the magus, knowing something had been taken away from her. Keenly feeling the loss. The magus had taken her love for Darid and left in its place a blankness that nagged at her, like a numb limb. The empty place had shrunk a bit; she could remember Darid dressing her burned arms, how grateful she'd been for his friendship when he'd taught her to mend tack and muck out stables. She remembered lying next to him in the pasture and feeling happy.

And yet she felt almost as if she were seeing those things through gauze. She didn't know if that was the result of the magus's Work or of time, all of the people and places that had piled up in her life since then. The fingers that had mended tack with him didn't feel like her own. The scars from the burns he'd dressed had vanished. The empty place was a loss.

"You don't want that," she said, softly, to Cleric.

His jaw clenched and she saw in him again the Cleric who could kill a human being as easily as he could heal one. But his red eyes glistened with tears. "Cleric," Merrit said, but he stalked away without answering.

When he was gone, Lukash said to Judah, "What happened at the stronghold wasn't your fault, either."

"Then whose fault was it?" she said. "Who brought down the stronghold and killed everyone in it? Some of them weren't even grown men. Some of them were boys."

"Some of those boys tried to kill me," Merrit said.

"When I was a boy, I killed a dozen grown men," Lukash said.

"For a noble cause. I killed a bunch of healers." Judah shook her head. "Who were also monsters. Why is everything so confusing?"

"Because the only reliable thing is change," Merrit said. "Even mountains change, with enough time and air and water."

"You can only be the person you are in any given moment," Lukash said, "and you can only make the choices you see open to you. Perhaps next time, you'll see different choices. Personally, I haven't gutted a man like a fish in years."

"Your bad choices can't destroy buildings," Judah said, but she felt a smile tugging at the corners of her mouth.

"You've already done that once," Lukash said. "I don't really see you doing it again."

Cleric came back as the sun was setting. "I found the river," he said, surly, and took them to a place not far from camp where the world fell away in a high steep slope that was almost, but not quite, a cliff. At the bottom—half a mile down, maybe more—jagged rocks landed like grains of salt among unexpectedly green foliage, and a silver thread traced its way through the valley. In the distance, low clouds clung to a mat of thicker, deeper green.

"What is that?" Judah said.

"Rainforest. And the Southern Kingdom, eventually," Merrit said, and shrugged. "At least, I think so. I've never been."

Lukash, Judah noticed, was watching Cleric, whose gaze was somewhere up in the sky. Pointedly up in the sky, she realized; very determinedly, away from the rocks. He had been alone when he found this place, after she told him that she wouldn't take Alec away for him. She wondered if he had considered jumping. She was glad he hadn't. She'd jumped, back in the tower; it had seemed like the only solution, the only way to change anything. And many things had changed, but nothing had been solved, had it? All she had managed to do was wrap all of these people—and others, Onya and Daniel and Pavla and all the rest—in the chaotic web of her existence. A web that still held Gavin and Elly and maybe even Theron. No, nothing had been solved at all.

Back at camp, when the food was gone, Judah looked at the other three around the fire. "I'm going back to Highfall," she said.

Merrit cocked her head and said, "Is that wise?"

"Probably not. But if I don't, things like this—" she waved a hand in the air, meaning not only their camp in the wasteland but also the winemaker's vineyard and the killing field at Black Lake and the swamp; Merrit and Daniel and Caterina and Nate, Cleric's injuries and the dead Elenesians and the Slonimi wagons dissolved in piles of black dust "—are going to keep happening. Maybe it's like a bad tooth, and it won't stop hurting until I yank it."

"How would you know, Lady Perfect Teeth?" Cleric said. The dry twist in his voice reminded her of the Ghostwood, when he'd told her she must be rich because of her teeth. But it was her new body that had perfect teeth, not her old one. It was so good to hear him sounding even a little like himself again that she couldn't help grinning. Just for a moment.

"I know," she said, before the grin fell away and a great sigh leaked out of her. "Besides, I think my friends are going there. I don't know what's going to happen when they get there, but—"

"You suspect nothing good," Lukash said.

Grimly, Judah nodded. "I suspect nothing good." Unaccountably shy, she looked at her hands. "None of you have to come."

"Debatable, that," Merrit said. "A person could say I had a fair hand in what happened to you. A person might say I had an obligation to see it all through." She shrugged. "Besides, I'd like to see Highfall."

There was a long pause. Judah suspected that Lukash and Cleric were having one of their silent conversations. Finally, Cleric said, sounding almost normal, "I don't think we're wanted in the south yet, are we?"

"Might as well fix that," Lukash said, and Judah let go a breath she hadn't known she was holding in.

"In the morning, then," she said. "When the sun rises."

EPILOGUE

DARID DOVETAIL FOUND IT EXCEEDINGLY DISCON-
certing to be back inside the Wall, sleeping in the same
barracks where he had lived for so many years. The accommodations had been spartan then and they were doubly so
now, with only a narrow wooden cot and single blanket for
every worker. Instead of merely plain, the food was now ined-
ible. A gallows now stood in the corral where the horses had
grazed. There were no horses anymore, only oxen for plow-
ing. Darid didn't know much about oxen but it didn't matter,
because he didn't rate highly enough to be able to drive the
plow anyway. He was a sower. Once, when one of the other
men sprained an ankle, he was taken to the Promenade and
given a pair of dull shears, to trim hedges and clear away dead
leaves. A guard stood behind him the entire time with a hand
on the hilt of his sword. The Promenade didn't look the same.
It looked like somebody had heard it described, and tried to
re-create it. And the gardeners who had kept it beautiful for

so long were all Returned, now. Out in the city, and probably using all their finely developed horticultural skills to pump a handle on a factory machine.

The last time Darid had lived here, he had been resigned, if not happy. Now anger burned inside him all day and all night. It fueled his labor and heated his dreams. Somewhere out there in the world, Bindy was wandering at the addled magus's side, and she might be injured or dead or who even knew what, and he couldn't help her because he was here. And he understood how Rina, who had put him here, had become the person she was, but he was angry at her nonetheless, and angry at the people who had made her that way, and angry at the people who had allowed her to continue on.

He could barely control the anger. Sometimes he trembled with it.

Work was over for the day. He was in the barn, putting away the hoes they used to chop weeds out of the oat field when he heard a very deliberate throat-clearing behind him. He turned and saw what at first looked like an imp sitting on top of what had once been the feed bin. Then he realized that the figure was a girl, and that she only looked short because she had no legs. She grinned merrily. "Hello," she said. "Are you Darid?"

His throat felt paralyzed with fear—a child? here?—but years of subservience had taught him to answer a question when asked, even when the asker was utterly mysterious. "I am."

"I'm Ida. You have no idea how long I've been waiting for you." Her Highfall accent was broad and cheerful. "Theron said you'd be here eventually but I didn't know that would mean hours. It's really filthy in here, isn't it?"

Darid blinked at her. "Lord Theron?"

"I guess so. Yeah. It's sort of complicated." She gave him

another friendly grin. "Anyway, he said you used to work inside. Have you ever been to the tower in the old wing?"

Darid shook his head, numbly. "No. I've barely been in the House at all."

Her grin grew even broader and brighter, if that were possible. "Oh, you should really see it," she said. "Come with me. I'll show you."

★ ★ ★ ★ ★

PEOPLE OF BARRIER LANDS

OLD HIGHFALL

Judah the Foundling, mystery
Gavin, former heir of Highfall
Eleanor of Tiernan (Elly), formerly betrothed to Gavin
Theron of Highfall, former second son of Highfall (deceased)
Elban, Lord of the City (deceased)
Arkady Magus, former House Magus (deceased)

THE WEST

Lukash, Morgeni, former soldier and current bandit
Cleric, former guildsman and current bandit
Sevedra, winemaker
Merrit Idris, traveler, ocarina-player
Onya, prisoner, very nearsighted
Inek, child

THE SLONIMI

Daniel, caravan leader
Pavla, Daniel's best Worker
Kendzi Baglia, in charge of guards and scouts
Caterina Clare, healer and Nathaniel's mother (deceased)
Jasper Arasgain, Nathaniel's father
Gerda, leader of Nate and Caterina's caravan
Anurak, guard
Benoit, guard

NEW HIGHFALL

The Seneschal, Elban's former factotum and current ruler of New
  Highfall

IN THE CITY

Firo, former courtier
William Ember, dye worker and Firo's beloved
Bess Ember, William's mother and baker
Alva, friendly tavernkeeper and chicken pie purveyor
Clem, prison cook
Bruno Post, prison guard
Jethro, medium-sized child, lamper

THE SLONIMI

Nathaniel Clare (Nate), prisoner and former House Magus of
  Highfall
Saba Petrie, agent
Derie Kulash, Nate's former teacher (deceased)
Charles Whelan, Nate's childhood friend and former faux cour-
  tier (deceased)

THE DOVETAILS

Nora, mother and Paper Factory
Darid, Nora's oldest son, former House head stableman, current
  saboteur
Rina, member of the Paper Factory committee
Belinda, former apprentice to Nathaniel Magus, current cleaner
Mairead, medium-sized child and lamper
Kate, small child
Canty, very small child

IN THE HOUSE

Korsa, Nali prisoner and current researcher

THE THIRTEEN-FOURTEENS

Liam, orphan and prospective *kaghiri*
Jesse, orphan and prospective *kaghiri*
Ida, orphan and prospective *kaghiri*
Anna, orphan and prospective *kaghiri*
Florence, orphan and prospective *kaghiri*

KORSA'S *KAGHIRI* (ABSENT)

Raghri, the pragmatist
Giorsa, the pacifist
Faolaru, the charming
Meita, the kind

TIERNAN

Lady Yana, Angen's wife
Amie of Porterfield, deposed courtier and Gavin's former lover
Moira, housemaid
Margaret (Peg), woman of Tiernan, somehow related to Elly
Halwyn, guard
Burim Sault, glory broker
Ambrose, Tiernan magus
Finch, guard

ELEANOR'S BROTHERS

Angen, eldest surviving and current Lord of Tiernan
Eduard, next eldest and Angen's second-in-command
Raymond and Lorens, the remaining younger brothers
Millar, eldest (deceased)

ACKNOWLEDGMENTS

UNENDING GRATITUDE TO JULIE BARER FOR HER unflappable and enthusiastic support for this series; to Kathy Sagan for her smart, careful suggestions; and to everyone at Mira—but especially Justine Sha—for cheering behind the scenes. Thanks to Nicole Cunningham for always answering my emails, even when they're ridiculous. Thanks to Erin Morgenstern, Anthony Breznican, Gwenda Bond, Alex Segura, Ellen Datlow, Kelly Link, Kat Howard, Liberty Hardy, and Christa Carmen for early support. Thanks to the McTiernan family, the Baglia family, and the Goudy family for loaning me your beautiful names, and to Tabba—as always—for being my best reader. Thanks also to the booksellers, deities among humans, without which none of this would work and all of it would be less interesting: Elisabeth Jewell and Ryan Elizabeth Clark at Gibson's Bookstore in Concord, NH; Suzanna Hermans, Jennifer Laughran, and Nicole Brinkley at Oblong Books and Music in Rhinebeck, NY; Jesse Post at Postmark Books in

Rosendale, NY; and everyone at the Savoy Bookshop and Cafe in Westerley, RI. And thanks, also, to everyone—and literally, I mean everyone—who read The Unwilling, or blogged about it, including all of those people who made the gorgeous flat lays of the cover. If there's anything better than a smart, thoughtful reader out there, I haven't found it.

Personally speaking, thanks to all of the beasts for being very delightfully nonhuman; all of the extended family for love and support; to Z for putting up with this ridiculous thing we do for a living; and to Owen for being there, always, despite everything.